Penguin Books
Children at the Gate

Lynne Reid Banks, the daughter of a Scots doctor and an Irish actress, was born in London and was evacuated to the Canadian prairies during the war. On her return to England she studied for the stage at RADA and then had several years' experience with repertory companies all over the country. The first play she wrote was produced by a number of rep companies and later performed on BBC television. She wrote and had published several other plays; one was put on in a London 'little theatre', and others have been performed on radio and television. She was one of the first two women reporters on British television. She worked for ITN for seven years – from its inception until 1962 – initially as a reporter and later as a scriptwriter. After leaving ITN she emigrated to Israel, where she married a sculptor. They lived on a kibbutz for nine years and have three sons. She now lives in Dorset and writes full-time.

Lynne Reid Banks's first novel, *The L-Shaped Room*, appeared in 1960, was made into a successful film and has been in print ever since. It was followed by *An End to Running* (1962), *Children at the Gate* (1968), the second and third books in *The L-Shaped Room* trilogy – *The Backward Shadow* (1970) and *Two is Lonely* (1974) – *Defy the Wilderness* (1981), *The Warning Bell* (1984) and *Casualties* (1987), all published by Penguin.

Dark Quartet: The Story of the Brontës (1976) won the Yorkshire Arts Association Award in 1977. *Path to the Silent Country: Charlotte Brontë's Years of Fame* is the sequel to it and was first published in 1977. Both are now reissued by Penguin.

Lynne Reid Banks has also written several books for children and young adults. Her children's books include *The Adventures of King Midas*, *The Farthest-Away Mountain*, *Maura's Angel*, *The Indian in the Cupboard*, *Return of the Indian* and *The Fairy Rebel*. Her books for teenagers include *One More River*, *Sarah and After*, *My Darling Villain* and *The Writing on the Wall*. In addition, she has written two historical books about Israel, *Letters to My Israeli Sons* and *Torn Country*.

Lynne Reid Banks

Children at the Gate

Penguin Books
in association with Chatto & Windus

PENGUIN BOOKS

Published by the Penguin Group
27 Wrights Lane, London W8 5TZ, England
Viking Penguin Inc., 40 West 23rd Street, New York, New York 10010, USA
Penguin Books Australia Ltd, Ringwood, Victoria, Australia
Penguin Books Canada Ltd, 2801 John Street, Markham, Ontario, Canada L3R 1B4
Penguin Books (NZ) Ltd, 182–190 Wairau Road, Auckland 10, New Zealand

Penguin Books Ltd, Registered Offices: Harmondsworth, Middlesex, England

First published by Chatto & Windus 1968
Published in Penguin Books 1971

Copyright © Lynne Reid Banks, 1968
All rights reserved

Set, printed and bound in Great Britain by
Cox & Wyman Ltd, Reading
Set in Linotype Times

Except in the United States of America, this book is sold subject
to the condition that it shall not, by way of trade or otherwise, be lent,
re-sold, hired out, or otherwise circulated without the
publisher's prior consent in any form of binding or cover other than
that in which it is published and without a similar condition
including this condition being imposed on the subsequent purchaser

For all half-and-halfs,
especially Adiel and Gillon

All the characters in this novel are fictitious. The kibbutz is not based even loosely on any actual kibbutz. Only the two towns are real.

Contents

Part One: Acre

Chapter 1

My name is Gerda Shaffer.

My name is Mrs Alec Shaffer, née Osborn.

Giddy Osborn. Giddy Gerda, sister of Judy the Prudy. (I am not sure any longer what I am called. Those names belong to someone who existed before I was born.)

My father was a German Canadian. His name was Gunther which became Gordon. My mother was a third-generation English Jewish Canadian. She talked about England as 'the Old Country' and thought she had a cousin in Leeds. Her name was Wilma and she hated it.

What else can I write? Oh yes. I am thirty-nine. I look at least forty-five. More? I am divorced. My husband has gone back to Canada. I shall never see him again. I don't want to and I don't care, except for the business of having no one to comfort me when I wake from a nightmare. That is the only good thing I can remember about marriage now. And that only happened a few times. When I was having bad nightmares, the same one every night, Alec was having his own and I was the one who had to do the comforting.

And that's all.

Except that if I had a way, and more courage, I'd like to finish myself off now, before another night comes.

Funny. It worked. ... Writing something, anything, nonsense, facts – it worked. A little bit anyway. It staved off the demons for another night. I drank less and slept better. ... Now another night is due and I shall try again.

But the facts are written. What more is there? Describe something. The pencil in my hand, the wobbly table ... the room. ... Too big. Too far outside myself. (I'm like a baby who must begin by learning itself. I have to relearn the world, since I don't seem able to leave it.) Something small, then – not too far outside the confines of my body – the brandy bottle. Empty. Like me. Hey – Gerda – you made a joke! Pretty thin, but it shows the old Giddy isn't quite a thing of the past. Oh God, if I could recover that – the laugh-at-myself weapon which once kept all the bogies at bay – but it's long gone. Long, long gone. Caught in the weeds at the bottom of a –

No. Too close. Too damn close.

Don't be frightened. Stop shaking. Cigarette.

Something else ... a fly. A fly! Bastard things. I'll kill it! Damn – missed. It's buzzing round my head. The flies here don't learn. You flick them away and they come back and back and back. You have to kill them to get rid of them. Kofi says they're Jewish flies, that's why they never learn when they're not wanted.

Three days. I think it's three.

The days when I write are better – I admit it. Usually inertia is too strong – I can't get myself to the table, open the note-book, pick up the pencil – there's no more *reason* to do that than to do anything else. Yet when I can do it, it helps. It's an activity. But then so is crapping ...

I am not womanly. (Put that in quotes.) 'You are not womanly.' What does that mean, Alec? What do you call womanly? 'Women are soft. Women don't drink and swear. Women are gentle and sweet-spoken.' And don't they have back passages? 'You disgust me sometimes.' Alec, don't worry. I disgust me all the time. I like disgusting myself. It reminds me that I'm still alive.

And why, pray, should I wish to be reminded of that, when I've just finished saying I wish I were dead? As Len would say, 'Life's just a dichotomous old crapheap.'

I haven't given the facts about Len. Len is my brother-in-law. He is married to my sister Judith and they have a million kids. I like Len better than I like my sister Judith. Come to think of it, Kofi excepted, Len is the only person I can think of that I wouldn't spit at, and might even be glad to see if he walked through that door, spouting his mixture of homely and obscene epigrams. But he's three thousand miles away making money to keep those teeming millions in cornflakes and loafers, so why think about it?

There *is* something I want to write. I want to write it so I can read it. I want to read it so – maybe – I will be able to look at it. Look at your fears, that's what it says in my Pocketbook of Common Phobias, spelt Fobias. Most fears are phobias, i.e. irrational. So write it down, Gerda, write it and read it and look at it.

I'm afraid of

Can't do it, isn't that odd. Can't write the words.

Len would write them for me in big Gothic letters and read them to me in a funny accent. He'd say, 'So what? I always said you wuz buggy. I always wanted a buggy sister-in-law.' And he'd flip his lower lip and cross his eyes . . .

Now – quick. I'm afraid of going crazy.

No good. Crazy's a funny word. Write the proper word.

Mad? Mad. Mad.

But that's funny too. You can only laugh at the very idea. Like when the undertaker came to ask what hymns we wanted for the funeral. He was all in black with a long face like a Dickens illustration and nothing, *nothing* about him was tragic. I wanted to kick him out of the house because he dared to make me want to laugh.

I wrote for half an hour yesterday. Two pages in this exercise book. It wasn't half an hour's worth of writing, of course. I used to rough out an article in that time. Yesterday there were long pauses, long stares out of the window, long drags on butt-ends, long-lasting sips of that filthy Vermouth. (I wonder why I kid myself Vermouth's cheaper or less vicious than brandy just because you get more for the same price? You don't get more effect.)

I'll describe the exercise book.

It's brown. It has – no, better not start counting the pages. 'Counting things can be part of a psychotic syndrome.' Well, it has lots of pages. The lines are arranged in threes, two close

13

together and one further away, two and then one, all down the page. They're like that to guide the child's writing. To make sure the tail-letters, and the loop-letters, don't extend too far up or down. This book should be filled with rows of p's and h's and q's and carefully-drawn sentences like 'My name is Rami Lavy'. It's an English copybook, but the people who put on the cover didn't notice and fitted it back to front as if it were for Hebrew. I can't go on with this. It is a stupid game and I am bored with it, so bored I could scream.

Kofi came last night. He knocked on the door. I was drunk and crying and I kept quiet. He kept knocking till I wanted to kill him. If I had had a gun I'd have shot him through the door. He knocks in series of four, mechanically, like a trip-hammer, getting louder and louder. At last I screamed out if you don't get out I'll throw myself off the balcony. Then he went away. I went out on to the balcony and watched him come out of the door under it and down the outside stairway. He crossed the square without looking back *once*. If he'd looked back even once I'd have called him. How could the bastard go like that, knowing the state I was in?

The room is full of flies. Most of them are those hateful blue and green ones from the meat-shops in the market. They buzz and blunder and fly against my face. They are attracted by my sweat. They are the worst thing in the world with their filthy filthy feet. One exploded against my mouth in the night and I struck myself so hard trying to kill it that I cut my lip.

I am sick and mad. If one keeps on knowing it, perhaps it isn't true.

The room. The ceiling is very high and has faded patterns painted on it, between the beams, like in Italy only the patterns are Arab patterns, stencilled and crude. There are more of them round the lower part of the walls. I quite like looking at them because they have a repetitive symmetry which is soothing. I lie on my back and look at them.

> I've got tears in my ears
> From lying on my back
> In my bed while I cry
> Over you-oo . . .

(It does help to write. Even nonsense.)

Alec, the Alec of afterwards who had lost his sense of silence, used to sing that when I lay in bed with him crying. Trying to jolly me out of it. Trying to make me laugh. Trying to make light of his hurt.

> And those tears in my ears
> Are off the beaten track,
> Since you said it's goodbye
> We are through.

How *could* anything have been less appropriate, less–seemly? Once, he would have had too much taste and sense. No wonder I went cold with him.

The room. One light-bulb hangs on a cord, so high I couldn't reach it to fix the copper shade, which is really a fretted dish on chains, that Kofi bought me in the market. They're costly and I told him (instead of thank you) that it wasn't worth it. I suppose I'll never put it up. I don't use the light much anyway. At night I go to bed early or else I sit out on the balcony looking down over the square; or sometimes I go out and walk about Acco. I don't turn the light on much except when he comes. When he comes and I let him in. Which is only on good nights, and they don't come often.

He went past today when I was sitting on the balcony. I thought at first he was going to walk by without looking up. I had a plastic glass in my hand full of the revolting local wine and I thought, if he doesn't look up I'll let him have it right on his bloody bald head. He was carrying his shopping-basket, a hideous thing made of bright yellow plastic. (Two plastic objects in one paragraph. Typical of this lousy town.) The basket, I could see, was full of things only Kofi would buy. A roll of sheet-copper for his mobiles. A huge house-painter's brush, which means he has a new job in the offing. A bundle of rubber straps for his Japanese sandals which are always break-ing because he is never out of them – the soles are already as thin as paper and new ones would cost only two lira, but he goes on buying the replacement straps and spending hours soaping the ends and forcing them through the holes with a gimlet. An egg-plant, gleaming purple like some obscene bird's egg, lay on top, sunk in a nest of that feathery parsley the old women sell. ... They sit cross-legged in their black satin skirts and sell nothing but parsley, spread on the slippery cobbles, collecting the tinny grushim they get for it in hidden pockets. I could even see a trail of bloody drops from what must have been a parcel of meat at the bottom; that certainly meant a job, or how would he afford even the fly-blown cheap cuts from the stinking butch-ers deep in the souk? (The alternative is kosher meat, which costs a lot more; I haven't tasted meat for months.) And he'd been to the spice-shop, too, for the inevitable fresh-ground coffee. One of the things I find hard to bear about him is that he always seems to have a package of it in his pocket and he reeks of it as some men do of whisky. That smell is so unspeakably warm, nostalgic and affirmative that I find it unendurable now.

He walked past with all these symbols of a home-life dangling from one arm; in the curve of the other was his daugh-ter. They were talking animatedly together. The sight sickened me and I tried to slip in through the tall windows out of sight. But he glanced up at the last minute, glanced, knowing I was there, and grinned and waved as if last night had never been.

I've read this over from the beginning. Funny how I keep using swear-words, like a child. They look awful written down. Perhaps they sounded to Alec's ears as awful as they look to my eyes. Once I called him a prig and I suppose he thought I said prick, which happens not to be one of my words, anyway it was then he said I wasn't womanly. That's what we need women for, he said, to soften and shame our crudities, not add to them. Smoking, drinking, swearing ... the masculine delinquencies.

I can't help it.

It's only 9 p.m. but already I want to go to bed. I slept till eleven this morning. I hate waking. The heat by then is so intense that I wake up in damp sheets with a splitting head. Kofi says the early morning is the only time. For what? For work, for love, he answers with his toothy smile, cocking his head at me. He doesn't look simian (his name means monkey in Hebrew) but more like a big parrot in splendid but clashing colours.

Alas, poor Kofi! No crest of hair, though. He hates being bald.

I didn't go to bed last night. (A small victory?) At least not then. I went out instead. I didn't change. I wore the same crumpled *halook* I'd had on all day. The buttons strain at the front and show my underwear and it is dirty but I have nothing else. (I lie, I was too lazy to change, I was too indifferent. At least until I was outside. Then one of the local children came close and stared at me and I wanted to flee back up the stairway but it became a point of honour to walk through the night-streets in my grubby house-coat outfacing the stares. ... What is the matter with me ... why is it not rather a point of honour to keep myself clean? How deep am I sunk in this self-sickness that even that has been lost?)

Old Acco is two towns. By day squalid, crumbling, foetid. The beauty the buildings once had – an Oriental suitability to their site by the sea, to the white glare of summer sunlight – stumbles as you approach it and then seems to fall at your feet when you draw near. The arches connecting the ruined squares, like the one below me here, are rotten underneath, their linings falling away on to the greasy cobbles, showing rough decaying plaster all scratched and smeared with the modern defilement of names and dates, and patched with old posters. Dirt is everywhere; I used to be afraid to touch things, and the children in their impenetrable layers of grime appalled me, but now I find my hands going out towards their scabrous heads or bare bony shoulders sticking through rags. As I grow less fastidious about myself so their filth seems less of a barrier. ... But my heart is not touched, nothing moves inside as my hand stretches out towards some sharp-eyed creature that will flash away, laughing or shouting Arab street-curses, before my fingers get within reach ..

Acco is two towns.

How this writing wanders, disordered and disorganized, obsessed with dirt, avoiding recollection. I keep thinking, as the pencil whispers on between the pale blue lines, that I can't after all be quite empty if I can produce all this. It is useless, it is rather disgusting, but *it is an activity*. And while I write I drink less and do not feel the heat. And when I stop and flex my hands it is coffee I want, twice I have even bothered to make it, just for myself. The stuff in the tin had none of that disturbing odour left, it was weeks old, it had very little taste either and as I drank it I suddenly thought that real coffee, fresh and fragrant, might be endurable if drunk at such a moment when I had just finished writing something in this absurd children's book.

Acco is two towns . . .

Tonight I'll go out and look at its other self and remember what I see so that tomorrow I'll have something to describe.

Kofi is here.

He came just as I was going out. I heard him on the stairs outside and I went to look, for I could hear him talking to someone. He had brought his daughter with him. It was ten o'clock at night and he was leading this tiny girl up my stairs. It was hard to believe. Hard to believe he would have the temerity to bring her at all after I have told him a hundred times I didn't want her here. I suppose he knew, the cunning bastard, that at that hour I couldn't shut my door in a child's face.

Nevertheless I did not welcome them. I merely let them in and gave the child some leben and olives (she is so thin) – nothing at all did I offer *him* – and then told them I had letters to write. I hope he knows it is a lie, that I am just waiting for them to go. But the child, having eaten only a little, is lying on my unswept floor making complex patterns on the uneven tiles with some things she has found – a dead pine-branch with a cone on it, brought long ago by Kofi after one of his trips to the kibbutz where he does occasional house-painting jobs; a broken sandal and some hairpins from the dust and rubbish in the corner under my bed; a yellowing page from the *Jerusalem Post*

18

(how long is it since I read a newspaper?), but principally stones from my jar. Kofi, uninvited, has gone to the corner where my makeshift 'kitchen' is to make himself coffee (out of his pocket). I would like to stop him – What right has he to treat this room as if he lived here? – but somehow I can't abuse him in front of the child.

Now she asks 'Where did the stones come from?' and grudgingly I tell her I collected them. She appears interested (can she sense I don't want her here and is she trying to win me?). She holds up the stones one by one and asks where I found each of them. I answer mechanically: that from the beach at Ashkelon, that from a tel in the North, the salt-crystal formation from the shores of the Dead Sea, the green one from Eilat. She examines and appraises each one carefully before adding it to her pattern. My God, children are subtle operators! She has just brought me a small, smooth pebble with a rough eruption of turquoise glass embedded in it and announced that this is her favourite. Why? She likes the smoothness with the roughness, she says, and also one doesn't expect the glass to be there so it is like a surprise. But, she adds, it would look better wet – all the stones would; water brings out their colours. May she fill the jar with water? I shrug ungraciously. An older child would take it for a refusal but this is Kofi's daughter; like him she must be hit on the head with a no before it registers. Joyfully she runs to the stained and slimy sink standing in the corner on its stiff intestinal pipes and carries the water back, painstakingly, leben-jar by leben-jar. Kofi gives her soft glances. You would think he would offer to carry the heavy jar to the sink for her, but he leaves her to it. The jar is before my eyes, filling up slowly, but already all the stones are wet and gleaming, their colours restored like a newly-cleaned painting. And at last something is beginning to move in me, as this thin child in her unpressed dress and her bare feet (for she has kicked off her sandals) leaves a thickening trail of water turning the dust on my tiles to mud. Children all do the same things. She is a little undernourished Arab waif with rusty curls and light green eyes like grapes; her legs and arms are like ropes with knots in the middle and Kofi's evident attempts to clean her for this visit missed her ears and her finger-nails. She *could not* look less like fat-fisted blond Jake who never even reached her age and yet I remember a day when he tracked mud through my spotless gleaming immaculate kitchen with its pine and its stainless steel and its easy-wash linoleum which I had just easily washed and I shouted at him and he looked up at me frightened because I had slapped him once or twice for no worse naughtiness – oh Christ why did that filthy bastard have to bring her here I knew what would happen if she ever came

That was ugly. I must try to stop this. To frighten another child does nothing to help my regrets for having frightened mine.

I crawled on to the bed after they'd gone and cried myself into a stupor. Usually I have to be drunk before the relieving tears will come; last night my sudden furious outburst released emotion like a plug of dynamite bursting in a dam wall.

I am sick and mad and I must keep away from people. I am not to be trusted.

I saw him in the market. The child was with him. They were standing beside a huge blackened barrel in which scarred olives swam like some single-cell life form in their brine. The child was dipping her hands into a big sack of rice, letting it run through her fingers. By day Kofi dresses her like a kibbutz child, in coloured bloomers and a blouse which is the top part of an old dress with the skirt and sleeves chopped off. She is almost the only Arab girl who shows her legs in shorts and the others mock her for it but for some reason Kofi does not notice. He admires the kibbutz children and despises the method of his own people. For instance he does not let the child play in the streets, but takes her with him everywhere on his random ill-paid jobs, chiefly on the fringes of the building trade. She is entirely self-contained and will play absorbedly by herself wherever she is. He loves her like ten mothers and can scarcely bear her out of his sight but his desire to educate her is stronger than his need to be near her, and he has already begun to send her to school. What she suffers there for her irregular dress and precocious ability to read and to speak Hebrew (both of which

Kofi has taught her) I do not know, but Kofi says he has told her there is a price for everything and that everyone who is better or cleverer than others has to pay for it. A child who can already manage money and do the shopping for her father doesn't find such an abstraction impossible to grasp, apparently.

When I saw them standing there together I dodged down one of the sullen refuse-filled side-alleys and hid myself in a hole in the wall which was also a bake-shop. There were round trays of cakes made of honey and sum-sum seeds cut into parallelograms. They were smothered in flies and wasps, but I bought one for a few *grush* and ate it standing in the low doorway. A sharp young Arab passed looking me up and down (he must be new here. The residents all know me). 'Tourist?' he asked me. I was surprised, for no tourist looks like me in my faded dress, my dusty feet thrust into *kafkafim*, my hair tied back with a shoe-lace and my face not only unmade-up but unwashed. But foreign residents don't normally eat these particular cakes because of the insects that have crawled all over them, so perhaps it was a natural question. Anyway I answered no. Nevertheless (perhaps he thought I was a rich eccentric, living in Acco in retreat – there are some like that) he invited me to his 'gift'-shop and gave me a card. 'I've just taken over,' he said in good English. 'You are American?' The man in the shop across the alley, where once, many months ago, I had my shoes repaired, called out that I am not American, I am Canadian, and that they are not the same except to the ignorant. At once I remembered having said the same thing to him sharply on my one meeting with him. He had borne no grudge for my rudeness and in fact was proud that he remembered me and could supply the information.

But his voice attracted Kofi who came to find me, the little girl holding his hand and chewing a carob-pod. She regarded me calmly as if nothing had happened. Kofi said, 'We are going to the kibbutz tomorrow to paint a new house. Come with us.' I refused, saying how would I get there? Kofi makes his journeys on a bicycle, with his brushes and paints in a huge unwieldy box behind him and the child perched on the crossbar; he has twice been stopped by the police for carrying her like this but he has no alternative except leaving her behind so he continues to do it. But he said that for tomorrow the kibbutz is sending a jeep for him because he has to take a lot of paint – 'It is a big job – four room-and-a-halfs, porches, bathrooms . . .' The job will take a week and he will need an assistant. He is willing to employ me! I couldn't help it – I laughed. I laughed! What would the kibbutz say to such an arrangement? 'Women in the kibbutz are the equal of men. What they will say depends upon the quality of the work in the first room that we do.' I looked down at the child, who smiled up at me, the carob embedded between her teeth like a cutlass. I simply did not know how to answer. I wanted to say the idea was ridiculous, which it is, but I couldn't say it in the face of the child whom only two nights ago I reduced to tears by ordering her out of my room. And here she was grinning at me and saying, 'It's nice in the kibbutz, I play on the swings.' Kofi, sternly: 'Tomorrow you will not play on the swings. You will lay down newspapers and carry water and clean the brushes and wipe off the splashes before they get hard.' She nodded at him lovingly as if this were a beautiful new game he had just invented for her. I said I must think about it and he said he would come round later and hear what I have thought.

Back in my room I know it's a fantastic idea. As it happens I know how to paint walls because Alec and I did our Montreal house up together and we learned from our mistakes until by the time we reached the attic, which didn't matter, we were experts. But Kofi doesn't know that. He is sorry for me. He wants to help me. For ten months he has tried to help me against all the odds of my determination not to be helped. He knows nothing about me or why I am here or what happened to Jake or why I am not married any longer. He does not demand personal information from me in exchange for all he has told me about himself. I have sat in this room for hours listening to his broken Hebrew (at first only half understanding it until my own improved), gleaning his story in snatches. The lighthouse flashes its turning beam through my long balcony window in much the same way – a moving band of light shows me the patterned walls, the sagging table, the sink, the tall door with its moorish moulding, the ominous looming wardrobe, the tousled bed – a remorseless semi-circle of revelation of my poverty and sluttishness before it withdraws again for exactly eight seconds to travel over the quiet sea. Thus – and in fact by the same light – Kofi told his story. Peasant-born, no education, primitive farm labour into young manhood. Then some more or less idiot political involvements, resulting in months of squalor and fear in Acco Jail, under the British, freedom of a sort with the end of the Mandate, but then the '48 war. His relatives left early and in droves (they are now in a refugee camp in Lebanon); he, lonely and frightened, attempted to follow, but failed, due to a silly accident in which he twisted his ankle and had to crawl ignominiously to a Jewish patrol and be driven back to Acco by an exasperated young soldier.

Then the slow struggle, begun only in his late twenties, to learn something, to be something; a struggle which has ended, according to him, in 'half-failure'. At forty-six he is semi-skilled, semi employed, semi-literate and semi-alone. (Of the last, he says this: 'My daughter is more to me than a hundred mothers and sisters, but less, on occasions, than one common prostitute whom I pay to lie with me for quarter of an hour.') Of the child's mother, he will say little; but I've heard from others, who find Kofi a natural subject for gossip, that she was a neurotic French Jewess – 'very educated, very crazy' – who married him for reasons unknown (but which I can understand), took him back to France for a time to try to civilize him (this was his own phrase) but eventually found her situation intolerable in either country and left him with the child. What has become of her, whether he ever sees her, I don't know, though I gather she still lives in Israel. But somehow I've guessed that I remind him of her. Perhaps only my Westernness, the tattered paperbacks littering my room which give an entirely false impression of 'culture', my foreign accent, my alien relationship to Acco. I can think of no other reason why he should ever have bothered about me, and still less why, in the face of my unpredictable moods and insults, he has persisted in 'being my friend' for so long.

What does he get out of it? Not the sexual companionship he needs so sadly. The only time he tried – most diffidently, most gently, one could almost think it hadn't happened – to touch me, I flung his hand away and actually tried to hit him in the face. He prevented me, for which I'm grateful, as I'm always grateful to be prevented from inflicting my egoistic savageries. I can't explain this reaction of mine except as fear, fear of any kind of involvement which might, even might lead to a repetition of my failure with Alec. ... Anyhow I threshed out wildly, and Kofi held my hands to my sides (he is immensely powerful physically, with shoulders and arms like a blacksmith) murmuring 'Softly, softly ...' as one quiets a child or an animal. ... Afterwards I begged his pardon and he mine, with almost stylized politeness, and since then there has been nothing but 'being my friend'.

It is a very bulky nothing in a life where nothing else of any sort exists.

I know I am neurotic (is that worse than being mad? Or is it the same? Sometimes it is at least a preferable image). Once he asked me to go to dinner with him – 'a formal dinner at my house, with candles as in Europe'. I was shrunk almost to invisibility at the time – it was the end of the week when I did not get out of bed at all except to go to the lavatory, and that seldom for I was losing most of my liquid intake (from an increasingly stagnant jug of water) in tears and sweat and I was not eating anything. I think I really hoped I would die, and that as slowly and miserably as possible. And Kofi came, and came back, and came again, and at last he contrived to lean a painters' ladder against my balcony from the top of the stairway and so got in. Seeing me lying tangled in the grey bed he threw up his great paws in an almost feminine gesture of disapproval and dismay and rushed at me, a wave of coffee odour buffering my face at his approach. 'You mustn't do such things, Gerda! You mustn't frighten your friend this way!' He dashed away and returned shortly with an assortment of 'invalid food' – milk, eggs, brandy – together with some other, indescribable items which his old Arab neighbour had told him I should eat. To forestall these I took some milk. What a thin-souled traitor the body is! The poor thing wanted its life, and as a gesture of defiance it relished the milk, thrilled to it as it ran down my throat; my stomach seemed to convulse with an almost indecent joy at receiving it. With its ingress my will to die dissolved and I ate the rest, drank the brandy, and was soon sitting up in my malodorous bed smoking a cigarette and feeling like a small child rescued from drowning.

(Strange how a phrase like that will slip in by itself, without conscious relationship to the past. I stopped in mid-sentence and stared at it with mouth dry with a sort of *embarrassed* shock – the monumental gaffe, almost compulsive, like the meaningless phrases about madness or dying that pop out in the presence of someone who has been in a mental home or who is suffering from cancer. Who could guess that it's possible to receive a pang from *one's own* tactlessness?)

It was then that Kofi, perching his rather squat parrot-frame on the end of my bed, invited me for this 'formal' meal. 'I will entertain you in the hospitable Arab tradition. We will cook for you, my daughter and I, all the finest local delicacies. I will paint a new mural on the big wall in your honour, and perhaps even sweep the floor. After the meal you will recline on a couch (it is really my bed of course, but I will disguise it with some mats) and I will teach you to play shashbesh. I do not know myself, but I will go to the café today and learn from the old men who play there all the hours of their days. Then we will perhaps walk by the sea and watch the fishing-boats go out, and drink coffee as thick as honey, and you will smoke one of your little cigars.' He smacked his knees with pleasure; the twin blows sent tiny puffs of white paint-dust out of his trousers.

I stared at him throughout this. What is the difference between the sane and the mad, the neurotic and the well-adjusted? Can it be simply that sane, normal people more or less understand their feelings and can respond to them logically, whereas the insane feel one thing, fail to comprehend its meaning, and behave in some unrelated way at a tangent to their feelings? If this is so, then I am certainly mad. For I felt – I can remember it – a whole pattern of simple emotions, gratitude, warmth, even a sluggish stirring of pleasure and anticipation.

But something – something – (guilt? Can it be that simple?) blocked them and twisted them until I was hating him for punishing me with his solicitude and affection. It was like being paid for a job done badly or praised for dishonesty. The words with which I dismissed his invitation sent him out of the room with feet so dragging that he stumbled on one of the broken tiles. They have sunk into the black bog of memory where so many other evils are swarming beneath the slime, but I know they contained not one word of thanks, not a hint of decent kindness, but only rejection and resentment more savage than the blow I once aimed at his eyes as retribution for his desiring my empty useless body.

Chapter 2

I wrote this morning until nearly 2 a.m. I told myself I was waiting up for Kofi, who had promised to come, but long after it was too late for him to turn up I kept writing and writing. I stopped at last only because I came to the end of the exercise book. I wrote the final half-paragraph on the inside of the back-to-front cover, and then threw the book across the vast gloomy expanse of the room because I wanted to go on writing and there was no more space. (I bought a new one first thing this morning.)

I didn't want to go to sleep even then. My brain seems to have broken through its alcoholic torpor lately. I sat and looked round the room. I saw that for all its heavy ugly furniture the general effect is of empty spaces – it is so huge. It must be about thirty metres square. All the rooms in the house are like that. The main hall downstairs, with the gallery running round it and the rooms opening off it – typical Arab family arrangement – is as vast as a baronial ballroom. Some very rich family must have owned it once. Now it is slowly crumbling to pieces, the walls cracking like dry riverbeds, the floors sinking unevenly, giving the once-coloured tiles the appearance of flat cobbles, the stone stairs worn until the edges droop like flaccid underlips, the elaborate mouldings falling away with occasional sharp cracks or dusty patterings. No one seems to be responsible for the common parts of the house but there is cne house-proud tenant, a little old woman of a male artist who has one of the ground-floor rooms. His painting is terrible but he would make an excellent janitor: he comes out daily to sweep a passage for himself across the abandoned wastes of the hall. At one time he swept the whole hall once a week, but seeing that nobody else cared he became embittered and now sweeps only for himself –

one can see his 'path' clearly, for it is not only clean but marked on both sides along its length by a growing hedge of dust and debris. I have never spoken a single word to him or any of the other ill-assorted people who live under this roof with me. It is a strange house, full of a feeling of sad history, and its inhabitants must also be strange and to some extent sad or why would we be here?

Anyway, last night. ... I found the room depressing once I had stopped writing, and for once I didn't want to be depressed. I had a headache too, from writing by that terrible overhead bulb which is about the same as writing by moonlight, almost as faint and far away. So I went out. The house was silent except for a cat which was yowling somewhere to be let out and a very faint but definite ticking sound which you can hear if you listen carefully and which is presumably hordes of destructive insects eating away at the walls, or perhaps just the sound of slow decay.

The square outside was pitch dark except for a paraffin lamp hissing high up in one of the arched galleries opposite. Our house has iron balconies but the rest of the square was built much earlier and has a kind of cloister with beautiful arches at first-floor level which goes round three sides of the square. I say 'beautiful' because at night they are – this is Acco's second self, her night-self, when all the day-smells are lifted from her and replaced by cool sea-winds drifting through her narrow alleys and flooding softly into the open squares; when darkness covers the dirt and squalor like snow, leaving only the shapes, the smooth outlines of domes and minarets against the stars, the perfectly balanced archways, the mysterious broken flights of stairs and half-open doorways, the cold but not unkind flare of a paraffin lamp showing a brief interior, its walls painted in grotto shades of blue and green and hung with prints whose cheap tastelessness a passing glimpse does not show.

I have noticed all this many times, the dichotomy between the day- and night-towns, but until last night I have never consciously realized that it might be possible actively to love a town by night which one loathed and shrank from by day. Even the people one passed during a midnight walk are more bearable.

When I have to go out in the heat of the day I try to avoid even looking at them, for the Arabs seemed to me an ugly race, ugly not from any physical defect but because their faces are dull with stupidity, crafty from years of subservience, first to their own kind and now, alas, to us. Their worlds are like cages from which they glance out with dull indifferent eyes, unaware (certainly in the case of the women) that they are behind bars. But at night one does not see this. The bodies of night walkers either stride along strongly, full of whatever purpose keeps them from bed, or slip by like graceful shadows; the unknowingness does not show in eyes which merely flash as they catch a gleam from some chance light in a coal-dark street.

Last night as usual I gravitated towards the tiny harbour. On the way I passed the café where Kofi sometimes goes for his evening meal. I have never sat there because women hardly ever do, and as it is, the men (a villainous-looking lot, mostly smugglers, according to Kofi) stare at me hostilely as I pass – they seem to think the whole square belongs to them and resent intruders. There is a television set perched high on a shelf under the ceiling of vine, which relays comedies and dramas (both equally turgid and funny) from Cairo and Beirut; the raucous noises from the set compete with the clack of shashbesh pieces and the spitting of the kebab grilling over a shallow tin of charcoal. The men do not talk much, but sit and stare at the set or attack their food or play their endless games; only the proprietor, who is either a large dwarf or very stunted, is cheerful and garrulous. He alone always smiles and beckons when I pass, sometimes even pulling one of the kitchen chairs (painted a blistered blue) out from under a beer-puddled table and pretending to flick the dust off it for me.

Through the next arch, unexpectedly, is the sea. It is such a quiet sea there that until you enter the archway and see it stretching away, glinting like black patent-leather, you wouldn't guess it was anywhere near. Last night I decided to sit on the jetty and just watch the water until I grew sleepy, but there were a couple of tourist-lovers necking rather self-consciously among the tarry ropes. I was about to go away when I saw Kofi sitting at another café by the harbour wall, a rather primmer, cleaner

29

and more Formica'd one, talking to a fisherman. They seemed to be very involved. I drifted nearer, hoping he would notice me, but his back was half-turned and he was deep in conversation. The other man – a queer-looking guy with high, egg-shaped cheeks, flicked his eyes at me, as if to assess whether I understood enough Arabic to eavesdrop, plainly decided I didn't, and returned his oddly-shaped eyes to his bottle of beer.

I walked home through the maze of cobbled alleys and archways and squares. My loneliness was, for once, simple and uncomplicated. It was a relief to feel anything so clean and normal. I knew Kofi would not come now – it was already nearly dawn. I filled the sink, after cleaning some of the slime and coffee-stains off with an old bit of wire-wool, and standing on the dirty tiles I washed myself all over, including my hair. I suddenly wanted to clean the whole room but I was much too tired. I lay down on top of the bedclothes and slept deeply and well.

And now it's 9 a.m. and I suppose Kofi and the child have gone to the kibbutz without me. I feel unaccountably angry about it, even though I had decided not to go. I have not been to a kibbutz for more than two years, and then my visit was a brief, formal one with Alec when we first came. Alec had some idea – quite absurd of course – that that might be a solution for us. The truth was he was out of his depth here, felt as lost and vulnerable as a snail without its shell, away from the whole carefully-built-up protective framework of his life in Montreal, which we had left not because of any flaw in it but because within it our lives had been flawed. Strange (and rather contemptible) how Jews like us only run away from our comfortable ticky-tacky boxes when we are driven out – idealism seldom enters into it really, though Alec let himself pretend and if I'd been kind I would have encouraged him to believe it instead of tearing down the fabric of his illusions at every chance I got.

I remember how I used to listen to him talking about it, while he was deciding to come. I was still in a kind of stupor, rather like being unhappily drunk (though I knew nothing then about drunkenness except the repulsiveness that one sees at parties full

30

of successful Canadians where anyone who arrives late is handed a full tumbler of Bourbon and told 'Drink up quick, we're three ahead of you'). I was moving through the saving routines of life slowly and carefully, almost apprehensively, like a man with a fatal wound whose only remaining, half-numb, half-frenzied hope is to die before the agony begins. Alec reacted oddly to grief. Before, he had been quiet, even to a fault, mentally composing every small sentence before ponderously taking his pipe from his mouth and giving voice to it, planning every action meticulously in advance, the exact antithesis of myself, and for that very reason good for me, an enforced but unforced control, a brake on my impulsiveness and my explosiveness. Living for eight years with so placid a man had made of me a calmer, less frenetic personality, for he would not answer my rages nor involve himself in my fluctuations of mood, waiting as it were just outside the door for the fever to go down and for the woman he loved to come out again. But afterwards, quite suddenly, this stable, patient man lost weight, his nerves stood out like veins in a tense wrist, jumping and quivering at every touch. His movements lost their directed quality and became darting, purposeless, often incompleted. Worst of all for me, he turned into a compulsive talker. While I shut my once garrulous tongue in my mouth and could hardly say a word, he chattered like some mindless bird, fluttering noisily from topic to topic, skidding across their surfaces and jabbering his way on to the next. Alec, who hated shallow wit, now became a nervous giggler, a nudging punster. An intolerable, a pitiable transformation. It was as if he could not allow himself a single moment's silence, as if the constant patter was the last defence thrown up against his thoughts – or perhaps against mine.

In any case he brought up Israel among many other possibilities for us when it became obvious to us both that to continue our lives in the place where Jake had been part of them was beyond our joint power. Which had once been considerable: 'Together we are greater than the sum of our parts' ... a better joke than it sounds now because at the moment he said it our 'parts' were in fact conjoined. ... How terrible that the intimacy of our laughter is easier, and sadder, to remember now than the physical rapture. Even the memory of that mutual delight is ruined now by the wretched realization that if we had never had it, we would never so have resented its loss as to part later for the lack of it, when perhaps – *perhaps* plain, daily-bread companionship basically matters more.

And then when we got here and found a country much like any other, full of fallible people rather like ourselves, neither a great deal better or worse; when we ran headlong into enveloping nets of red tape; when people were curt to us in shops, when we couldn't get the food we were used to, when we fully realized what it meant to live as strangers amid an entrenched and fiercely chauvinistic population who didn't speak our language in any sense of the words . . . when all this came home to us, we began to hate it and to wish we'd never come. I remember Alec even got mad because everything wasn't kosher! Alec, for whom breakfast wasn't breakfast without a slice of grilled ham under his egg. 'In a Jewish country we should live like the goyim?' he asked me once. I was infuriated by what I thought of as his hypocrisy, his unreasonableness about the country; yet I myself was wretched and disappointed, having expected it to work some individual miracle for me. I wonder just what I did expect? What converts expect from their new religion, I guess. I thought a sense of identification with a nation would give me a sense of personal identity. Whereas of course, until one has developed that *for oneself*, one simply has nothing to bring to any outside relationship, even the delicate one that a person should have with his country. And so I have no country now, any more than I have a husband or a child or any damn thing in this world that matters. . . . Oh shut up with your stinking self-pity. Whose fault is it, all of it, but your own, you worthless bitch!

I was writing so clearly before, yet when I began to remember, to write about Alec, I got entangled and couldn't seem to finish my thoughts. It is better not to think about the past at all, much less write about it. There is no doubt now that this diary or whatever it is is having exactly the therapeutic effect I dimly hoped for when, two weeks ago, I started it so pathetically and bittily. . . . But I must stick with *now*, and write dispassionately, which should be easy for there is nothing left to get passionate about, *provided* I keep my eye on the ground just ahead of my feet and don't look either forward or back.

Several days have gone by. I have not been nearly so unhappy, though Kofi has not turned up and I have missed him. I have stopped being annoyed about his not coming that night; the notion of my painting houses in a kibbutz now only makes me smile, though I must admit that at the time some part of me wanted to do it. It is the healthy part that gulped down the milk that time, that made me begin this private writing, that now, having for the time being at least gained the upper hand, obliges me to keep some sort of order in my room and some sort of curb on my drinking. (On my smoking it has so far had no effect!)

. . . I find it more difficult than I had thought, to write without reference to the past. It is like pretending to have lost one's memory. Yet when I let my mind venture backwards my hand begins to shake and my eyes dart towards the clutter of half-empty bottles which stand in a basket beside my bed. I have not been really high for nearly a week and obviously I feel better for it; though it's not easy to keep off it. Drinking heavily is not really my style, any more than living – squatting, existing – in this gaunt, foetid room is my style. That is my whole trouble, perhaps – I have lost touch with my own reality, the sense of living within my own legend. When I hear myself speaking Hebrew in the market, or look down at my unwashed feet, or catch sight of myself in a shop window – face grey, uncared-for, rather bloated, figure lumpy in its creased shift, and hair schizoid with the last of its futile peroxide disguise – at these moments I have to stamp down a panicky feeling that I am separating from myself like curds, drawing away from my original nature into some no-man's-wilderness from which I can never get back.

At the onset of this feeling I inevitably succumb to an urge to flee back to this room from wherever I am – even if it's only out on the balcony, for even there I can feel exposed, as if every

33

lorry-driver or shop-keeper or casual passer-by below who happened to glance up could see my whole truth far clearer than I can see it myself. I come in and shut the long windows, though this means airlessness; there are no curtains so the sun sreams in and I go and lie in the shadow of the wall on the aged mat of split bamboo which allows some of the coolth from the tiles to relieve my skin. The best thing of course would be to do as Kofi does at home, so he tells me – lie naked on the tiles themselves. But I cannot quite bring myself to put my skin against the tiles in their present state, nor can I rouse myself to wash them. Yet I so want them to be clean – I so want to be clean myself. At home people said I was too fussy – Alec had to stop me going round all the time wiping out ashtrays and picking threads off the carpet – 'an over-rigid personality breaks soonest and most completely' – it was a joke-warning. Oh Alec! If you could see how I have reversed myself since you went away! sliding down into some kind of swamp of indifference and indolence . . . it is bad enough to be like this, but to see it clearly, to *know* it, is the ultimate cruelty, for I was not born to be a slut. In more senses than one I've fallen on hard times. Not only am I really poor financially but my character is also on its uppers. That is far more degrading, since the money-poverty I am not ashamed of – I could have taken Alec's settlement and been very comfortable – but I'm glad I didn't.

Sometimes I have a nightmare in which he finds me here, in these circumstances, and shouts at me as he never once in our lives really shouted at me: 'Liar! Liar!' – because I told him that I still had my mother's money when actually I had given it away. Given it away! Of course I see now that I must have been mad even then. To give away nearly twelve thousand dollars to an orphanage! The quixotry of that! The folly! As if that paid for anything, as if such a sickly sentimental, hysterical gesture could 'wash out a line' of the past! And yet, being still under the influence of a defensive madness, I don't regret it. Because it's suitable for me to live like this. But in dirt? In squalor? This pertains to self-respect. In which case, yes, the dirt is suitable too, which must be why I cannot wash the floor.

Chapter 3

Well, life takes hold of one sometimes with surprise-grips, a judo expert throwing one from behind. Kofi turned up at last, looking somehow as if he'd been on a not-very-satisfactory binge, sat himself down on the least rocky of the chairs without a word of apology for his mysterious absence and announced that we would be going to the kibbutz to start work next morning.

Of course I asked him where he'd been for a week but he simply said he'd been busy with another job but was now free. I was glad to see him again. It's necessary to write that down because it was, inevitably, only part of my reaction. In a way his absence had been a relief. I've always felt I didn't deserve Kofi, not merely because total loneliness fits my idea of what life should give me but for the more personal reason that I have nothing to give him in exchange for his persistent, and often maddening, kindness to me. But when I saw him sitting there, his broad, squat figure parked so four-squarely on the feeble frame of the chair, his intelligent eyes peering out of that rough-cut face, I suddenly wanted to go and sit at his feet and hold his hand and feel safe. For whatever his shortcomings, Kofi is a natural protector. Perhaps this was what attracted his Jewish wife to him in the face of all the taboos on both sides – the certainty of a stable emotional flow embalming her life under his care.

He is like Alec in this. Why did I never realize that till now? I wonder if, like Alec, he has a weak place inside, which life can break into and expose . . .

I refused to entertain the kibbutz idea, and he smiled quietly and went away. He returned at 5 o'clock next morning with the child. The jeep-horn honked beneath my window till I woke up,

35

and Kofi hammered on my door until at last to restore quiet I let him in. He was full of beans, ignored my anger and insisted on making me coffee while I dressed; the child was directed to hold a sheet up between us as a screen. The horn below sounded at regular intervals of one minute. I gulped the coffee, still arguing but too newly-awakened to do it effectively, and almost without knowing how, I found myself on a hard bench seat in the back of the jeep with a collapsing cardboard box of paint-tins at my feet and Kofi grinning like a zany and holding his battered bicycle which had been brought into the jeep. The little girl sat in front next to the driver, who was elderly and short-tempered, probably because we had kept him waiting so long.

It wasn't until we'd arrived at the kibbutz, a matter of fifteen minutes' journey, and were unloading the bicycle, that I realized its significance. Kofi glibly explained that as he could leave the paints there overnight there had been no arrangement to drive him back in the evening. 'But what about me?' I asked. 'Do you plan to sit *me* on your crossbar, too?' 'Of course,' he said cheerfully. 'The girl can sit on the shelf at the back.' I told him he was insane and he looked surprised. 'But why? – Oh well, if you don't want to, you can go by bus.' 'But I didn't bring any money.' 'I'll give you some. You are my assistant after all. You can have an advance on your wages.' He slapped his knee and bent over to laugh. The child looked up from her squatting position on the floor, sorting brushes wider than her own hips, and her mouth fell open in a total smile. She looked at me and said delightedly, 'My daddy's laughing!' – as if it was the first time it had happened.

I've been trying to work out how many years it is since I did any physical work. When I was about fifteen I got a job as a haymaker one scorching prairie summer. It was, on the face of it, an odd thing to do, when all my high-school contemporaries in Toronto were getting genteel little jobs in down-town shoe-shops or behind soda fountains. Only the older boys went travelling north to earn good money as lumberjacks or on the railway. I used to look at them when they came back to school each fall, noticing their apparent (or perhaps actual) increase in height and shoulder-width, swaggering about with a new confidence quite lacking in those who had earned their holiday-money at tame jobs near home. The idea came to me that I might gain the same inner cachet (I was not so interested in improving my social status – I knew in advance that among my 'crowd' one could only lose, not gain, prestige from doing anything wildly unusual) by going north in the wake of the boys and getting work on a farm. My mother's horrified refusal to allow it merely intensified my intention. My father, I felt, would have understood; but he was dead and I had no ally, for my sister was seventeen and a-hunting and had no time for me. When the time came I simply took a train north, leaving a long letter for my mother, knowing that she would merely read it, weep immoderately, and eventually send me parcels of food all the summer; which is precisely what she did. (I still remember the condition of the cheese-puffs after they'd been brought the last seventy miles by truck from the nearest one-grain-elevator, one-train-a-day whistle stop.) But it was a good summer – the best of my life, between the death of Dad and meeting Alec; I returned home in September sun-blackened and horny-handed and bursting with self-satisfaction, and promptly lost all my friends by openly despising them for their piddling little summers in drug-store and swimming-pool.

Remembering that feeling as we stood, the three of us, in the blistering sun (not so very much worse, though, than the one that ripens two wheat-crops a year in Alberta) I joined in the laughter and together we carried the sagging carton along the dusty path to the new building. A little boy, in shining white underwear, raced to meet us. 'Have you come to paint our new house?' he cried. 'Hurry up!' – as if he and his family were waiting outside with all their possessions to move in. He was five, which is the worst age from my point of view, but he was dark and there was no other resemblance beyond the inevitable small-boy shrillness of excitement in the voice, the eagerness to take part which resulted shortly in Kofi shooing him away from the box of paints. He then stood off a little way, one bare foot set on its side on the hot rubbly ground, and watched while we carried the things on to the porch. Then he suddenly burst into a run and disappeared.

'You frightened him,' I said.

Kofi grunted. 'He knows me,' he said. 'He'll be back soon, with all his gang. He knows me. He gave me this name you laugh at, this Kofi. I was not Kofi until a year ago when I first started to do jobs here. That little satan would stand near me while I worked and whisper "Monkey, Monkey" until I was nearly mad with anger. Each time I turned round he would run like a lizard. Sometimes others would come and hear that he called me *kofi*, a monkey, and once a grown-up heard him and told him that to say such things was impolite. (They meant that he should not speak so to an Arab. They are very careful, these kibbutz Jews, to speak ill of us only when we cannot hear it, because it is in their principles that we are equals with them.) But what did he say in reply? That Kofi was my name, an Arab name. I could not give him away! So I became Kofi. My daughter grew very angry and when anyone would say it she would cry, but in the end I began to like the name myself and laugh when anyone spoke it and when she saw that, she too began to like it. She always laughs when I do, don't you, *habuba*?' He bent to her, putting his nose against hers.

Suddenly I asked, 'Is that her name – Habuba?' For it occurred to me amazingly that, although some reference to his child was always in his mouth, I had never heard him call her anything but 'the child' or 'my daughter' or 'my little girl'. Now she looked up at me with what was almost a look of appeal, and Kofi, straightening slowly, said: 'It is not her name.' Then, to forestall my obvious next question, he said with reluctance, 'Her name is Hanna but we don't use it. You understand why?' 'Because it's a Jewish name?' He didn't answer. 'But,' I asked, 'why don't you decide on another name to use, if the Jewish name is not – suitable?' His face became dark and quiet, like a shuttered house. 'It is her given name. To invent another would be like covering her with a lie. We do not use her name; that's all.' 'And yet,' I couldn't help saying, 'you dress her differently from other children in Acco – as a Jewish child, in fact.' He looked at me, it seemed in disappointment. 'You haven't understood,' he said patiently. 'I do not avoid her name so as to save her from trouble with her playmates. She is different in her blood, and I hope in her life too she will be different – and better. For that they will punish her anyway, and she may as well get used to it. No. The reason I do not use her name is because – it was not my choice. The name speaks to us both of the giver of the name.'

He said all this in a low voice so that the child, who was spreading sheets of newspaper over the tiles, moving with crab-like rapidity about the floor, shouldn't hear us.

The work began. I let Kofi show me how to do the simplest, least 'showy' portions of the walls and then, dipping my brush and delicately purling off just the right amount of overspill on the tin's edge, I imitated him expertly. He stood a moment and watched me drawing the brush back and forth, scarcely spilling a drop, and I waited for him to express surprise and delight, but instead he said casually, 'Yes, that's not bad. You'll improve as you go along.' I was no better and no worse than he had expected and I experienced a childish sense of disappointment that I had failed to impress him with my prowess, but almost at once the situation struck me as comic and unimportant. I dipped my brush again and began to work in earnest.

The kibbutz dwellers, I'm told 'believe in' manual work, as the devout believe in God – not merely in its existence but in its mystic powers. When one *first* begins to apply one's body, plus some small acquired skill perhaps but minus one's intelligence, to work of that kind, one understands this odd devotion better than at any time later. By breakfast time I had painted a whole, if small, wall, which was now as a consequence pale yellow instead of dirty grey, and I was filled with an immense and altogether disproportionate satisfaction. I stood back from it and gazed as if I had successfully completed a masterpiece. (I painted pictures once, for a hobby – one of my many demi-talents.) It was partly the sense of purpose, however un-ambitious, which suffused me with this feeling of rampant pleasure. And then, for two hours my mind had hung idle, subordinate to the careful motions of my right arm, and it was as if the flesh-eating jungle-growths swarming in there had grown weak and lain down limply for lack of the stimulus of my constant attention.

We downed tools and left the house. There were now six children outside, sitting astride red tricycles with an air of patient expectancy. 'Look at them,' said Kofi. 'They are waiting for us to go to eat so that they can go in and explore and play with the paint.' He turned to his daughter – to Hanna, for so I think of her now, such is the power of a name to attach itself to its owner. 'You must wait here and guard our things,' he told her. 'But her breakfast!' I protested. He drew me past the waiting semi-circle of children, leaving Hanna behind sitting on the steps of the porch. 'She can wait,' he said. 'I'll bring her something.' 'How will she manage six of them?' he laughed. 'You forget she is accustomed to "managing" the ruffians in the streets of Acco,' he said with pride. 'Last week, when she was alone – ' He stopped, but I had heard enough.

'You were away last week? She was alone in your house?'

He frowned, angry with himself. 'I was away for a day or two,' he muttered. 'She knows what to do. I have a neighbour who looks after her, as much as is needed. But she has plenty to occupy her now she can read, and the shopping she can do for herself. I left her enough money.'

'I thought you took her with you everywhere.'

He seemed irritated – something I had never seen, despite the indescribable provocations I've given him over the months. 'I cannot take her everywhere,' he said shortly.

We ate in the communal dining-hall, a splendid new building lined with teak panelling and fitted with every possible gadget, including a three-pump soda-fountain. Kofi noticed my attention to it and guessed my thought. 'Don't worry,' he said. 'She's seen it before, and she will see it again at lunchtime. Perhaps we'll send her mid-morning to bring us soda to drink – that is her chief delight.'

For someone who has not eaten properly since a time beyond memory, I enjoyed my breakfast very much. The woman who served me from a mobile heated trolley eyed me with open interest. She was plump and small, around my age or a bit younger, with a type of face which keeps its youth – snub, freckled, rather round brown eyes – a pussy-cat face – and reddish hair. It was familiar somehow, as a type, and out of place here.

Kofi introduced us: 'Gerda, my assistant. This is Raya.'

Raya spoke to me in Hebrew, but with an accent I instantly recognized. 'You're Canadian!' It was the first English I have spoken for a long time, other than to myself. She looked incredulously at me, and I became, for the first time, hideously aware of myself as I must look in the eyes of a woman, and a fellow country-woman at that. My hand rose automatically to my hair, and drifted hopelessly down the side of my face to my dirty shirt. Her eyes followed the hand and then snapped up to my eyes; I knew my finger-nails were broken and dirty.

'You're living in Acco?' she asked. The incredulity was in her voice, too. She forced me to resent her, if only because her pained surprise was entirely justified. I answered her tersely and cut short further questions by asking for a soft egg. She gave it to me silently and pushed the trolley on.

Kofi told me that she is one of his 'half-friends' in the kibbutz. 'I have no real friends here. For all their beliefs they are snobs, not work-snobs perhaps but mind-snobs, and what is worse they don't even inquire whether a poor Arab who comes on his bicycle to paint their houses, when their regular contractors fail them, might perhaps have read a book in his life or have an interest in the flesh on this world's dry bones.' He often used this expression – the bones of the world were, so to speak, the absolute essentials – making a living, sex and children. The flesh stood roughly for the important non-essentials, culture, education, independence of mind.

Raya, he told me, was the mother of the small 'satan' and two other children, a girl of eleven and another boy of sixteen. 'That is how they have children here – according to plan.' Hard to tell if he admired or despised it. 'It's said that in the early days, when the settlements were poor, couples were allowed only one child each. If a woman conceived a second time, she had to – ' He made a gesture of throwing something aside. 'Such matters are easily arranged here, you know.' Unthinkingly, I said quite right too. He raised his eyes, which are enormous and lustrous and black as great polished damsons, and stared at me, his spoon arrested. 'Don't say that,' he said quietly. 'I don't like to hear you speak like that – cynically, like a man.' He went on eating, but clearly what I'd said troubled him. As we walked to the counter with our dirty dishes, he suddenly said, 'You would not have such a thing done to yourself, surely?'

Some protective mechanism clicked in my mind like a well-oiled door, keeping off excessive pain at this innocent remark. Instead of feeling hurt, I let myself wonder briefly – objectively – what went through his mind on the occasion of that one self-defeating advance he made to me; for where the creation of children is concerned, prevention is obviously as far outside his sense of propriety as cure. Perhaps in the mind of such a man – some essentials of whose primitivity remain unspoilt, for all his contact with our more sophisticated mores – no great split exists between the act and its natural outcome. What, then? Would he have welcomed a child from me? The idea was startling but not unpleasant, until it ended sickeningly against the pain-barrier.

We left the dining-hall carrying on a plate a hard-boiled egg, a tomato, cheese and leben. I almost burst out laughing as we came into sight of our work-place, for the tableau was exactly as we had left it – the six children across their tricycles, but now with an air of being at bay, with Hanna unmoving on the steps, chin in hands, gazing at them in silence as if she had them mesmerized. Kofi handed her her breakfast and she ate it where she was, under the eyes of the others, as unselfconsciously as if she were alone. When she'd finished, she came in and wiped up our paint splashes without being told, and then her father told her she might go and play in the playground. She flashed away, and two minutes later we heard her outside chattering like a jaybird to the others. I went to the porch to look, and saw her, perched on the bar behind one of the tricyclists, being pedalled furiously away at the head of the convoy. 'What happened?' I asked. Kofi shrugged. 'Nothing. She is off-duty now. The others do not know what to make of her, for none of them have responsibilities as she has. They like her but they are a little afraid of her. That is how I like it to be.'

We worked until lunchtime, a matter of nearly four more hours, by which time the two main rooms – one small and one

42

very small – had been completed and we had started on the tiny passage inside the front door. That left only the shower-room, which was mainly tiled, and the porch and shutters to do; the doors and window-frames are to be done separately later. Kofi was now openly satisfied with me and had even praised me, saying I learned *dai mahair* – fast enough. The little flat was cool and quiet after the continual commercial racket of the square I was accustomed to. I was becoming aware of a slow inflow of contentment, creeping in on my tired spirit like an incoming tide over a baked, refuse-strewn beach. I struggled against it, but then gave in, as if to some physical temptation.

We walked back to the dining-hall in the heat of noon, the child dancing at our side. It was the first time I had ever seen her behaving as one expects a child of seven to behave – with abandon. She even nagged a little for us to hurry and tugged her father's hand, singing 'So-da, so-da, we're going to have some so-da.'

Everywhere I looked were children. The sight of these hit me (as the street-children of Acco don't), for their very cleanness and health reminded me, and there were several who looked like him – in Canada a blond and blue-eyed Jewish child was looked on as unusual, but here just such little boys seemed to be riding down every path towards me, peering from trees, playing in sandpits, running across shaded lawns, as green as our lawn at home and watered with the same sort of revolving spray as we had. . . . One child, less shy than the rest who merely stared, stood in our way and asked 'Whose are you?' – because in the kibbutz, everyone belongs to someone, it is the law of life. I answered without thinking: 'Ani lo shel af ehad' – 'I'm not anybody's.' He at once stopped smiling and said simply, 'You poor thing!' I was somehow touched, but to Hanna the words clearly carried overtones of a pity she found intolerable. 'She's not a poor thing!' she countered swiftly. 'She belongs to us,' and pulled us past without looking back. I slammed shut the inner door before the looming onrush as her hand gripped mine. It didn't feel like a child's hand – too bony and decisive – but still it was like touching something blisteringly hot and I snatched mine away in a second. How I wish I hadn't! But I couldn't control it.

Raya served us again, this time with some passable pizza and spaghetti. Again I was hungry, and again I enjoyed being hungry as if I had no more guilt than Hanna, who was so happy she could scarcely keep still on her chair. Raya said to me in English, 'Perhaps you'd like to come and have tea with us before you go back to Acco.' I was speechless with surprise. I stared at her. 'Like this?' I asked. 'If you feel hot and want a shower, you can have one at our place,' she said, with commendable tact. I couldn't answer; I felt suddenly so confused I couldn't either accept or refuse. She nodded as if I had spoken and said, 'About four if that's all right. You can still catch the 5.30 bus.' And she wheeled the trolley away.

Hanna had been watching my lips during all this. 'That was English!' she announced. 'The tourists speak English in the copper-shops, I've heard them. I can speak English too. How-much-is-that-god-save-the-queen,' she demonstrated all in a rush.

'Very good,' I said. 'Now say "My name is Hanna. What is your name?"'

'My-name-is –' She stopped short, guiltily. Kofi was looking at me. 'I shouldn't have told you,' he said quietly. I felt ashamed and said no more.

The afternoon was no good. I was not concentrating; I was thinking about going to Raya's and what it would be like to have tea with a family. The women in the kibbutz are plain-faced but clean and self-respecting, they hold themselves well and their clothes are pretty and well-kept. And there would be the boy –

When we stopped work at three I sent Hanna with a message that I couldn't come. I stood at the bus-stop for half an hour after Kofi had reeled away on his bicycle, the child's little brown stick-legs waving for balance. It was still very hot. I arrived back here in a mood of black despondency which pushed me towards my bedside basket; but after two glasses I began this writing (objective, dispassionate) and now I have patched my hurt for tonight. It's very late and Kofi is coming for me at five to put me on the bus (he doesn't trust me to come otherwise). I don't want to go but he's never asked anything of me before.

This Raya is persistent. What does she want? She won't leave me alone. Again yesterday and today she asked me to tea; I've had to say definitely I'll go tomorrow. I've run out of excuses. Besides, I've begun to think it's cowardly not to go. I can't run from children all my life, or even hide myself from the sight of the other things I've lost.

I'm half looking forward to going. I've actually washed a dress to change into after work. I can't iron it but it's Dacron (five years old, bought in Montreal) so it won't look too bad. I am clean all over, I've even done my nails. . . . Yet I dread it, I'm physically afraid. Is the half-wish to go in itself a perverse form of self-punishment?

The work is going quickly, we will easily finish by Friday including the doors. I have actually begun to think what I will do with the little money I am earning. How odd to have something of my own in my pocket again!

Chapter 4

Well, it's over. It wasn't too bad after all.

She's an attractive person, this Raya. She is the only Canadian in the kibbutz, which is principally composed of people from Germany and middle Europe. According to her own laughing description, she got stuck here, like fly to fly-paper, during a casual holiday seventeen years ago. I don't entirely believe her claim to have not a jot or tittle of Zionism in her make-up; seventeen years ago, Canadian girls didn't come to Israel for casual holidays.

She had made an excellent tea (specially? No way of knowing) – cake, salads nicely arranged for helping oneself, plenty of bread and margarine, home-made cookies. It was disarming to hear them called 'cookies' again. I took advantage of her offer of a shower and even put a bit of lipstick on for the first time in many months.

Raya's room – one room until they move to the new 'house' – showed distinct touches of individuality and taste. Her husband works in the metal-shop of the kibbutz and his hobby is metal-sculpture; he also seems to be good at wrought-iron, and there were several little tables and a couple of very nice figures of welded metal, one large enough to occupy a whole corner. I noticed too that the curtains and covers were of materials which didn't look particularly 'local'.

'I blush to tell you, I asked my father to bring them when he came for a visit,' Raya said when I admired them. 'I'm not a model kibbutznik, I'm afraid.' She showed me a small fridge. 'See this? This nearly brought about the end of my career here. My father gave it to me while he was here, and the kibbutz told me I must refuse it. Well, do you know, I couldn't? I wanted to – I meant to – but when it came, I just looked at it – that little

46

white box representing so much *more* that just ice-cream for the kids and cold melon and ... Well, in short, I stood it on the porch and plugged it in and said anyone who liked could come and put things in it, but I wasn't giving it up.' I asked what happened. 'I was cut dead for three weeks,' she said. 'Oh, I can laugh about it now. But when you're as gregarious as I am. ... Not that I blamed them, it wasn't just jealousy of course, it was a matter of principle – a principle I even agree with. Oh, it was awful! The kids begged me to give it up, I wanted to, yet somehow I couldn't. I felt crazy – not like myself. A mad streak of stubbornness, I suppose, combined with the longest *hamsin* on record.' And in the end? 'Oh well, in the end we all got fridges. I mean, the kibbutz decided to buy every family a fridge.' And has anyone ever thanked her? She looked at me uncomprehendingly. 'What the hell for? I still feel guilty about it, if you want to know.' All this was before the kids came, mostly while I was in the shower and she was making tea. 'Would you prefer coffee? I've got a bit of Maxwell House left that Mom sent me – gee, don't you miss coffee with cream? And marshmallow sundaes? Do you know, once I got one of my terrible fits of homesickness and I suddenly thought how my kids'd never tasted a marshmallow sundae or barbecue'd spare-ribs or waffles with maple-syrup and all of a sudden I burst out crying. And I haven't cried for *years*.'

She seems to be a misfit in the kibbutz, for all her apparent good cheer – these were just a few of the ways it came out. She's as adjusted as she can get, but she's still got a lot of jagged corners sticking out. I felt for her, because there's something about the whole idea of that life that makes my flesh creep, the more so because at the same time it has a definite appeal to me. The security! I've been so worried about money this last year that the mere idea of never having to handle it any more is like contemplating a soft bed when you're dizzy with exhaustion. But it's a form of surrender – no doubt of that. I speak as an expert on the subject.

When I emerged in my dress and with my face and hair done she did a spontaneous double-take. 'Hey!' she said. 'That's better.' I laughed uneasily. 'Is it?' 'Hell, yes! You're a downright credit to your country now. You don't mind my asking, but why on earth did you bleach your hair?'

'To make myself look different.'

'Oho! In hiding, eh?'

'In a way.' Trying to make me unrecognizable to myself – instead I had only succeeded in further corrupting my own identity.

'I dyed my hair once. Do sit down, the kids'll be here in a minute and where Dan is I can't imagine, working late on a statue maybe. It was after an unsuccessful love affair when I hated the sight of my face because some monumental HE had managed to resist it. . . . You won't mind my asking, but have you ever been on the stage?'

'Not really.'

'Oh, neither have I, if you mean professionally, though I wanted to. I meant have you ever acted?' I said yes. Her bland, freckled face brightened another 50 watts. 'I knew it! The minute I saw you, I knew you were a fellow actress. One can always tell!'

Recording her chatter now, as well as I can remember it, I'm rather bemused. Why did she make such a pleasant impression on me when quite clearly she is rather silly? She is a typical campus girl who has never really grown out of it. And yet she warmed me. By the time the children came drifting or bursting in, according to their temperaments, I was relaxed and ready for them, the breathless stifled feeling only coming back for a minute as each one was introduced. Their names are Amir, Shula and (the satan) Dubi. The latter is a love-name for David and means, roughly, Teddy-bear, a most unsuitable name for this child who is all spikes and angles and sharp, suspicious turns of the head – a most uncuddlesome child, for which I was grateful.

The husband, Dan, arrived half-way through the meal. ('Here comes the fly-paper I got stuck to!' Raya cried gaily as he came in.) He's a striking fellow, in his way – about forty-five I should think, though with prematurely white hair it's hard to tell, typically 'kibbutz' in his healthy appearance and deliberate, confident movements – rather taciturn, perhaps because Raya seldom lets him get a word in edgeways. He speaks good English – 'He didn't, but he just had to learn or he couldn't understand my long monologues.' 'My knowledge is chiefly passive,' Dan said with a quiet humour which I liked.

They pumped me discreetly. Dan didn't ask very much, but once when he put in a diffident question of his own Raya exclaimed gleefully: 'You see? He pretends to be detached and disinterested, but he's just as curious as I am really.' She then began to expatiate on the subject of kibbutz men. 'Of course on the whole they're much more fulfilled than the women, but even they're affected by the narrowness of the life – I mean, the physical narrowness; whether it's spiritually narrow depends on oneself. The trouble after a while between married couples is that there's seldom anything to talk about, except gossip. Hardly anything *new* ever happens, one almost never meets new people – that's partly why I pounced on you, as no doubt you guessed.' I said I hadn't guessed, and what was the other part? She slid over this and went on: 'So even the most intelligent kibbutzunikim, like my old man here, I mean men who *read* and have *resources*, they're all as gossipy as a pack of old women. If you listened to Dan talking to me in private about some of our fellow members, you'd think he was the most awful misanthropist, I mean he doesn't seem to have a good word to say for anybody – the real truth is, he knows them all so well that he's bored with them. That's something terribly sad one learns in a small community like this – that when you get to know someone inside out, nine times out of ten it's their negative qualities that come out on top in the end. And of course, they must feel the same about you. After seventeen years, believe me, one has no intimate friends left. You've been through everybody about four times, had rows, "not spoken", made it up out of desperation, etc. etc., and after a while you're all just like played-out chewing-gum to each other. Not a bit of flavour left.' She bit glumly into a large crumbly slice of cake.

They asked me where I was living and I told them I had a room in Acco. The older children, who had more or less ignored me until then, perked up when they heard this and the girl, Shula, asked me whether it wasn't awful, living with all those smelly Arabs. This provoked Dan to a quiet anger I wouldn't have expected from him. He told her off roundly, and almost reduced her to tears. All she said at the end, in a rebellious mutter, was, 'Well, when we went on that picnic with the kids from the village, they smelt dirty, that's all I know.' Surprisingly after his outburst, Dan let her have the last word and there was an uncomfortable few minutes' silence. Dubi broke it to announce that Kofi did not smell. 'Kofi's different,' mumbled Shula. 'He's not like a real Arab.'

'Do tell us about Kofi,' Raya jumped in. 'He's something of a mystery to us. He *is* different from the others. Well, he is, honey,' she said soothingly as Dan flicked her a warning look. 'Not just because he washes.' 'Raya.' 'Sorry, honey.' Then to me again: 'Dubi found out from his daughter that they used to live somewhere near Tel Aviv. Not many Arabs live in the new *shikkunim* – it's very mysterious. And the little girl is so odd! Did you know she can read? Dubi and his *gan* get her to read them stories. They're quite agog about her. He must be a pretty cultured sort of fellow, for an – I mean, for a house-painter.' I told them he paints murals, too, and suggested they go to see the one he did in a new night-club that's just opened in one of the old Crusader crypts in the Old City. 'Oh, how I wish we could! But we can't afford night-clubs.' 'Maybe Kofi would invite you one night.' 'Why should he?' 'Aren't you a friend of his?' I saw Dan and Raya exchange looks. 'Well . . . sort of, I suppose.'

'Half-friends?' I suggested.

'If you put it like that – yes. He doesn't seem to expect anything closer.' I gave Kofi a silent mark for perspicacity.

After tea, the children dashed off to the swimming-pool. Raya, who was obviously dying to join them, suggested lending me a costume. The warmth generated by the unaccustomed tea and chatter, fled from my mind and body; I found my hands icy and trembling as I said I'd rather not. She looked so disappointed that I eventually had to agree to go with her, but only to watch.

The pool is scooped out of the highest ground near the kibbutz, so that it overlooks the settlement and the surrounding countryside, a flat patchwork sweep to the sea on one side and

an amphitheatre of purple hills round the others. The hillscapes
are broken up by Arab villages, large and small, looking from
that distance like blocks of natural stone tumbled at random
into the hammocks between the hills. The kibbutz itself is a
pretty sight from above, with its white and red houses and
pointilliste gardens, all gathered together by a trellis-work of
trees.

The pool is a snail-shaped jewel. Lawns spread up and away
from it, massed flower-beds form the setting and some young
trees are just beginning to give shade. The swollen heat of the
day had just started to deflate; the hills were bathed in pink light
like the reflection of a huge bubble of molten glass just beginning to cool. The whole thing was beautiful beyond words;
the icy trembling went away and I was able to enjoy the sight of
the children shrieking and foaming through the aquamarine
glitter without too great a pang; I sat beside Raya on a welter of
coloured towels. She began eating again; she eats without cease
(compensation?) and was now nibbling sunflower seeds.

'It's a shame you have to catch that bus,' she said. 'We've got
a film tonight.'

'I don't like films much.'

She gave me a mock-incredulous look. '*Don't like* films! Oh,
you'd never make a kibbutznik!' She cracked another seed between her teeth and spat out the shell like a child. 'What I did
think was, it seems silly you making that journey twice a day
when you're working here all the week. . . . There must be some
spare rooms. . . . Why don't you stay over till you've finished
your work?' 'But it's Wednesday now – there are only two more
nights.' 'All the same. . . . Wouldn't you like to?' I shook my
head. 'It's kind of you, but . . .' She looked disappointed (politeness? loneliness?) but dropped the matter at once. 'Okay – I
just wondered. Still, maybe you could come to tea again
tomorrow?' What *is* she up to? I got out of it by saying I had a
'date' (a word from our common past). Her inquisitive soul rose
to the windows of her eyes and looked out unblushingly at this.
'Oh! Have you a – of course I shouldn't ask – '

Mercifully Shula arrived at that moment and interrupted.

I just caught the 5.30 bus. I felt somehow refreshed; my brain

51

reacted with pleasure and relief – for the time of the short bus-ride, there seemed nothing to be unhappy about. But when I walked up the sloping stairs and pushed open this door, I smelt the musty interior of this room as if for the first time – dust and dirt, stale brandy, sour milk, sweat, the stench of my own misery and my own weakness. The bed was unmade, the sink piled with dishes; the bucket of slops under it, the heap of soiled clothes on the floor, the rug, unshaken since time began for me here in this room ten endless months ago. . . . I looked around, feeling a shame having no connection with the guilt which is the shallow bottom of all my actions. About the guilt, nothing can be done, but the shame, poor, petty disease, could at least be cured.

Cleaning the room, when I had once embarked on it, was an indescribable, almost sensual pleasure. The accumulation of dirt and junk was sickening, but floors and cupboards, wood and metal, are not harbourers of grudges, and when restored to order and their surfaces cleaned, they respond without rancour by appearing never to have been neglected.

So now I sit at a tidy table with a clean bed awaiting me. My body is healthily and not sickly tired for once, and perhaps the same could be said for my mind, for tonight I can think of Jake without anguish and of Alec with. . . . I can't analyse this feeling. What an irony if by any chance it was – too late – simple hunger?

Chapter 5

It is Saturday morning. The work is finished. I have some money of my own in my wallet, which accepted the grubby notes like a starved little animal gulping down its first meal for months and looking all the better for it, its worn leather sides bulging unaccustomedly.

I'm sitting writing on the balcony, with my coffee beside me, relishing the pleasures of a day of rest earned by six that were not. The square below, by daylight, is fascinatingly awful. Much of it is covered by derelict cars, other areas by crates of miserable white chickens crammed together, their beaks gaping with thirst. Right under the balcony, where a vegetable cart stood early this morning, is a reeking pile of refuse which may, possibly, be perfunctorily swept away this evening. But the place seethes with life from dawn till nightfall, and, once one is used to the ugliness and smells, one can sit above it and stare down for hours without boredom.

I am writing these not-very-good descriptions to postpone a port-mortem on last night. But the habit of writing is ingrained now. It has helped me so much, I am superstitiously afraid to abandon it or even to cheat by leaving unpleasant things out.

Last night after we'd returned from work and I, having fattened my wallet and had a wash, was sitting out here having a nightcap (nothing dangerous, it was really instead of eating) I saw Kofi's child climbing the steps alone. She entered through the ever-open front door at the top of them, and I could hear her sandals clapping at the tiles as she ran up the inside flight to my door. She opened it without knocking and stood in the doorway.

'Daddy says to come to supper.'

I looked at her . . . there was no light in the room except what came in from the twilight outside; she looked like a small phantom in her faded dress, until she mundanely began scratching a mosquito-bite on her calf. (Alec never wanted girls, but I did. I always wanted a girl.)

'Not tonight, Hanna.'

'Don't call me that.'

'What shall I call you, then?'

She thought for a moment. 'Yakiri (my dear one)' she suggested. 'That's the Hebrew for what my Daddy calls me.'

'That's a family name,' I said. 'I want to call you Hanna. It's a good Jewish name.'

'I'm not Jewish,' she said out of the darkness.

'You are half and half.'

'That means you aren't really anything.'

After a moment I said, 'Nonsense' – though it wasn't. 'I'm half and half, too.'

She came in, leaving the door open, and came slowly towards me. 'Half and half? You?' she said in a low voice, her sandals whispering closer. 'Half what?'

'Half Jewish and half – not Jewish.'

'Was your Daddy an Arab?'

'No, he was a Canadian. His family came from Germany a long time ago.'

But clearly in her world, there were only Jews and Arabs. 'If he wasn't a Jew, he must have been an Arab,' she said reasonably, explaining it to me. 'Perhaps he didn't want you to know. My Daddy didn't want people to know about him, either.'

She was standing almost against me now, wedged between my chair and the balcony railing. I put my hand along the railing, not quite touching her, in case it gave way – it's very rusty.

'How was that?' I asked curiously.

She rubbed her mosquito bite against the roughness of the iron and stared over into the square. 'We lived in a *shikkun*, near Tel Aviv,' she said, as if that explained everything. In a way, it did. The *shikkunim* are like stacks of egg-boxes, piled cheek by jowl, the inhabitants almost as intimately connected with each other as if the thin walls didn't exist.

'When was this?'

'Until Mummy went away.'

Her voice took on a floating quality which I recognized with a crippling pang as the nearness of tears. I touched her back; then my hand moved away again and gripped the rail.

'Go and tell Daddy I'll come to supper,' I said. Anything to get rid of her before her tears fell and scalded me. She ran out without looking at me.

Nevertheless, I didn't want to dine alone with him at his place, and I was glad when, crossing the square a little later on my reluctant way there, I met him slip-slapping across the cobbles towards me.

'I have not been shopping today,' he said, 'so we're going to the smugglers' café. I know you Americans like local colour.' He was teasing me, and I smiled, and we walked through the lumpy, still-rank streets together to the café in the square, with its outdoor tables and its vine and its false well full of chilling beer and its television. There were few people there at that hour – some young men playing cards in a corner, the dwarfish proprietor setting out his bits of charcoal in their battered tin-like chess-pieces. A starveling cat leapt off one of the tables, and fled before our approach like a ferret. The video was mercifully dark.

'There is no menu here,' Kofi said. 'You take what they bring. It's always the same and it's always good. There is comfort in such an arrangement. Where did you learn to paint walls?'

The devil! He'd known all the time. I told him my husband and I had taught ourselves, in order to redecorate a large house we'd bought. He watched me curiously out of his dark, brimming eyes, with their lustrous long lashes like a woman's – an inconsistency in that rugged face. He hadn't heard me speak of my husband before, though of course he must have known I'd been married.

'This husband. May a friend ask questions?'

I said yes, he might ask. I was testing myself. After all, a year is, or should be, long enough to gain some sense of perspective, even if only a false one.

Something in the reserve of my permission seemed to give him the impression that I would only tolerate a limited ration of questions, and a longish pause followed while he worked out the ones most calculated to elicit the information for which his naturally inquisitive soul must have hungered. (He can't know that my whole mind, my whole past, is like a gaping ulcer, only just beginning – am I being too hopeful? – to be overspread by a thin membrane of healing.) He signalled for beer and it was brought in wet, label-less bottles from the well's watery belly. Our kebab had been threaded on to skewers and laid across the glowing charcoal.

'This husband,' he asked at last. 'In what ways was he different from you?'

It was a clever question, for there is no short answer to it. I said he was different in many ways, yet at the same moment my mind was fingering only our ironic similarities. Similarities of level, of need, of talents for self-deceit. ... We were, of course, different in looks, he being a tall, thick-built man, ruddy and fair, while I am dark and small. Though only half Jewish, I am far more the conventional Semitic type physically than he. Then our interests were very unalike. He was an 'outdoor man', obsessed by physical health and the exercise needed to keep it; he played endless squash and golf, went swimming and skiing, watched his diet against a tendency to paunchiness, and took a boyish, prideful interest in his body. All sports other than swimming bored me, though a passable game of tennis was something I learned from (and for) him and I would sometimes allow myself to be taken to his club (one of those exclusive Jewish clubs on the outskirts of the city, pervaded by a slight air of defensiveness); there he and I would pair up with another rich, dull young couple like ourselves for doubles followed by Tom Collinses beside the echoing indoor pool.

'We had a comfortable little life,' I said.

Kofi pressed me gently with a subsidiary question – if I did not share my husband's sporting interests, did I understand his work? I smiled. Who understands accountancy, or can take the smallest interest in it, other than accountants? What else are accountants for, but to make it unnecessary for people to take an intelligent interest in the figures that support their lives? No, his work was a closed book to me. But, Kofi asked, did I have no work of my own? For Western women (as he understood it) were always trained for careers, even if they didn't have them. I explained about having studied physiotherapy, for lack of a better idea, leaving college on a stupid impulse before taking the exams because I'd been offered a job with the local radio-station which lasted exactly two months. . . . I never did anything with my training beyond massaging the aching back of my brother-in-law after his infrequent gardening bouts, because I'd taken it into my head that I ought to be an 'artist'. Besides, my mother kept insisting I had no need of a career. My sister had married at eighteen, and according to my mother I was the prettier of the two and could have my pick of the rich young bachelors who seemed to abound in our vicinity. True, she had spent the years of our childhoods anxiously wondering whether our mixed blood would hamper our marriageability, but only the most rigidly orthodox on either side actually tried to keep their sons away from us, for we were both good-looking, presentable and rich, at least rich enough.

I, too, had taken it for granted that I would marry young and settle immediately to the raising of a family. But it didn't happen. The matter simply was that I couldn't fall in love. After I had been to Europe on the essential 'Grand Tour' after college – I can still blush at the picture of backwoods naïveté I must have presented in my shirtwaist dresses and shoulder bags and page-boy bob, my Bermuda shorts and my eager-beaver attitudes – none of the young men at home seemed other than hopelessly boring, unsophisticated, and provincial. Even, oddly enough, the very ones who had been all over Europe themselves. And I was their exact female counterpart, which only made things worse.

The truth, I suppose, was that none of us had done any living, though we had travelled and studied and 'been around' as the euphemism had it then. I personally had had three affairs by the time I was twenty-four, not one of them untrivial enough to be worth recalling now, all with smooth, well-mannered, sexually insecure Canadian simpletons. Why, I wonder, are we such a *doughy* nation? We try so hard to acquire the depth of the Old World passions or the fine glittering surface panache of the States; we fail in both, and end up smiling through our beautiful milk-fed teeth and contact-lenses out of colour snaps taken with our families in front of white clapboard houses, or perhaps on toboggans wearing rugged plaid lumberjackets. And the Jews are worse because they have an added split-level inferior-superiority complex to cope with. It's no wonder that I made the mistake of agreeing with Alec that Israel might have something to offer us. The air in Canada smells just a little too strongly of fresh bread, bourbon and new-mown hay. But Israel, too, has a smell of its own. The smell of gunpowder and bad blood, the smell of war hanging over us all the time. Of course one doesn't dwell on it, one can forget it for days together ... but I sometimes think it is a symptom of the emptiness of my life that I am not afraid. I have nothing to fear losing.

I knew I shouldn't begin writing – far less talking – about the past. So far I have scarcely touched on Alec or any of the untouchable things, but already I am filled with all sorts of unnatural, filial spleens ... soon it will be time to begin attacking my poor mother again, making snide remarks and blaming her for my mistakes. ... Was marrying Alec a mistake? In the long run, it evidently was, but how dare I abuse my mother or even myself in my thoughts when for five years I enjoyed such total, irrational happiness with him that I began for the first time looking round for a God to thank.

Well, dispassionately then, since I've begun, for the beginning is not too dangerous to think about. Until I was twenty-nine I simply hung around Toronto. That is what it amounts to, though my time was well-filled somehow. .... I had a little so-called studio where I painted my little so-called canvasses, and sometimes sold one to a friend; I took part in amateur dramatics (oh God!) and even did some odd broadcasts for the C.B.C. I tried for a time to write, and succeeded in getting an article or two and some short stories published. Each miniscule success in any of my 'fields' would fill me with a totally spurious ambition to develop this particular 'gift' and scale the heights with it; but nothing could have been more futile. My 'gifts' were too puny and diffuse. I'd have done better to graduate and settle down to professional back-rubbing like a real person.

At first my mother participated in my life, living as it were squeezed into my inconsiderable shadow. When I think of our shopping expeditions together, for instance, to buy me a new bathing-suit or dress for a party with 'the gang', a little verse of Alec's comes to mind (he was not all brawn, Alec, by any means):

> Toronto is very genteel –
> *Not* the sort of place where you'd streel
> Downtown minus gloves, or have illicit loves,
> Or murder your father, or steal . . .

She would trot along beside me, a smart, well-corsetted little Jewish lady, mildly frivolous hat tee'd on her mildly blue coiffeur, handbag and shoes immaculate and matching, short silk gloves over manicured hands showing the proud ridges of rather too many rings . . .

I lived with her, and she would wait up for me at night, with milk and cookies and my nightgown warming on the radiator. . . . How I contrived to have affairs under those circumstances, even such piffling ones, is hard to imagine now, except that she only pried very timidly because, after that summer when I had defied her, she was always a little afraid – not of me, exactly, but of some dim realization she must have had of her negative power over me – the power to provoke me into doing the exact opposite of what she wanted.

My single state began, as the years rolled by, to hurt her (as my brother-in-law used to say) 'right where she lived'. That a daughter of hers, endowed with her now-faded prettiness, embellished with education, travel and modest (very modest) success in a wide range of media, should pass her middle-twenties unmarried, was unbearable to her. I need not recount the increasingly unblushing attacks she made on my spinsterhood; enough to say they caused me acute embarrassment and several times threatened to open a permanent breach between us. I told her there was nothing she or I could do about it

– I had nothing against marriage, on the contrary; but I could find no one I wanted. 'But you're surrounded by desirable men!' I recall her wailing. 'Surrounded!' That was rather how it felt, in the pejorative sense of being trapped. 'Aren't they good enough for you?' 'No.' 'What's wrong with them?' 'They're dull.' 'And are you so interesting?' 'No, I'm dull too. But to marry another drip won't improve me, and I want to be improved.'

And after all, to marry Alec!

My mother organized the whole thing. She wouldn't have pulled it off, I'm sure, for I was wise to her tricks by then and very tired of them, if I hadn't been fed up and more than a little scared, if the truth must be told. One does get scared, at twenty-nine; surely it must be *the* age for compromise marriages, for settling for second best. As soon as my mother set eyes on Alec, she determined to get him for me. I think it must have had something to do with a certain physical likeness to my father – the same (oddly enough) rather Teutonic heaviness of build, the same phlegmatism which had stood my parents' marriage in good stead through all my mother's Semitic storms. In her eyes, Alec had everything; he was the right age for me, he had 'position', character, good looks. . . . She didn't actually say, 'And he's a good Jewish boy as well!' but I could see her thinking it.

She pushed and she pushed and I resisted with all my perverse fed-up strength, and suddenly I gave way and went over the edge and Alec caught me.

Although Jewish, Alec was the very quintessential Canadian male – rather hearty, kind, naïve, a little pompous. . . . How to answer Kofi's simple, sincere, question: 'But what had he, for you?'

My inclination was to answer, 'the other side of my plain penny, just as loneliness was wearing it thin.' But how could two commonplace provincials, joined in nothing more transmogrifying than everyday marriage, have managed to give each other such uncommon treasure? Or was our happiness Jake's doing? Would we have bored ourselves and each other without Jake, and was that the reason – part of it, the other part is obvious – why his death changed us back to our pre-marriage selves and washed us up, like two empty coconut shells, on to the dry sands of our own limitations?

Of course I didn't say all this to Kofi. He wasn't interested in the fine details of my history, only in the rough bold outlines. I thought, as I sketched them in for him, that I was merely satisfying his curiosity. It wasn't until later that I realized, what I should have known, that as always he had a purpose.

Our dinner was brought to us – a big bowl of chips mixed with highly-seasoned felafel balls, a pile of hot pita bread, the kebab shucked off its skewers by a grubby asbestos thumb, a salad of sharp, bruised olives, fresh tomatoes and chunks of picked lemon and chili. Kofi asked for a bowl of tchina, a thick cream made of sesame seeds, into which we dipped the chips and meat-chunks like a fondu. There were no forks; the meat scorched our fingers and the hot chili made my eyes water. But it was a superb meal, washed down with more beer, more talk ... beer is a talk-maker after the sullenness of brandy.

'You loved him, this husband?'

'Once – very much.'

'And I also – my wife,' he volunteered suddenly, and added, with a wealth of bitter meaning, 'Once.'

We ate silently. The television was turned on now. Two women in straight, floor-length black shifts, glittering with sequins, concealing everything but hands and faces, were doing a dance which would have been banned for indecency in Canada. The café was filling up.

'Where is he now?' He had to speak loudly, over the nasal music.

'Back in Montreal.'

'In the house you painted together?'

'No, that was sold.'

'That must be a relief for you, that he doesn't live there.'

He had enormous insight sometimes. 'He wouldn't have wanted to live there, either,' I said.

'Because you were happy there – or the opposite?'

'Because something bad happened to us there.'

61

'Your child,' he said softly.

I stopped eating. I asked him how he had known.

'By watching you,' he said. 'No woman avoids children as you do who has never had one.' He took a drink from his glass, his eyes fastened to mine like buttons in button-holes. 'How old are you? You forgive this question from your friend.'

'I am thirty-nine.'

'You must have another child.'

'Kofi –'

'You must. It is the thing you *must* do.'

'I don't want to discuss this.'

'You are ill from not discussing it.'

'Shut up, Kofi. Friend or no friend. I'm warning you.'

'And I am warning you. Another few years and it will be too late.'

'It's too late now.'

Our voices were rising over the din of the television, which was now blaring out some kind of bizarre musical comedy. I had stopped eating and was staring at my plate (which was enamelled, like a dog's dish) as if watching some plot unfolding in it. Let him stop, I thought, in some cold, despairing recess. Let him stop right now, before I have to say the words and hear them in my own ears.

'What does that mean too late?' he went on. 'Our women have children until they are nearly fifty sometimes. The only difficulty is finding a worthy –'

'Yes, that is a slight problem always, isn't it?' I almost shouted. 'Perhaps you would care to volunteer?'

'I would be honoured,' he said with quiet, shaming sincerity. There was a long silence, and attention around us went back to other things. Then he continued as if without a pause. 'But I realize I am not suitable. However, there are other men – Jewish men. In the kibbutz, for instance –'

Some sudden insight prickled down my spine. 'The kibbutz?'

'There are, I believe, some nine or ten bachelors and two widowers in the kibbutz.'

Well, naturally, I saw at once what had been going on this

week. I saw it instantly. I also saw my thick-wittedness at not having seen it before.

'You,' I said, deadly quiet. 'You took me to the kibbutz – for that. You arranged for Raya to adopt me for that.'

'I only suggested to her – '

'I can imagine the conversation perfectly.' *There is this woman living in Acco, she is from your country. She's in great trouble. Perhaps if I brought her here you could. . . .* Could what? Take her in hand? Reorganize her shabby broken life, put her back into some nice, tidy little box, find her a husband, start the pain-train chugging along again with her firmly locked in the caboose? And Raya, alias Rhoda, ex-belle of the sophomore ball, Raya, the unwitting fly in the kibbutz web, making the best of it but plagued with residual bourgeois longings, how readily and unthinkingly she would pounce upon such a project, a real small-town match-making scheme to occupy her mind and, incidentally, give her the hope of a friend who would not, for a while anyway, have the taste of stale chewing-gum in her mouth.

I was so angry (let me at least attempt honesty – so humiliated) that I got up and tried to leave. But Kofi caught my wrist and pulled me back quite roughly. 'Don't be stupid,' he said brusquely. He has never spoken to me in that tone before. 'Your time for that kind of pride has gone past you.' Holding me firmly he beckoned the proprietor, paid the account, and then led me slowly away from the racket, through the archway to the harbour. We stood facing the glinting black water, watching the long boats dip and scrape on the slippery sea-walls, smelling the strong clean odour of wet weed and brine and fresh scales. My chest was heaving and I wanted to go on being angry, but Kofi's hand was hard round my wrist and I felt my rage suddenly for the childish, inverted thing it was. I pulled my hand up into his and said, 'I'm sorry. You wanted to help me. But it's useless.'

'You still love your husband?'

'Not because of that.' I couldn't say any more for the moment. He tugged my hand gently and we began to walk, turning through another tunnel-like archway into another maze of little streets, with high walls either side which revealed the starry sky like another pattern of alleys reversed over our heads. We were alone but for the ever hungry cats which flattened themselves into low doorways or fled from beneath our feet on their unprofitable night-hunts among the grimy cobbles and lintels.

After a long time of walking and feeling him waiting patiently for me to speak, I got the tired words out, the words which had exhausted themselves without ever being actually formed into a manageable sentence in my head.

'You see, when I had my son, something went wrong, and now I can't have any more.'

There was a measure of relief in saying it. It is a greater one to write it. Perhaps only because in this I am not to blame, I am the victim.

'Ah,' said Kofi. 'Now I understand.'

We walked on, and at last, by a roundabout route, arrived back at my square. We stood at the foot of the staircase. He was still holding my hand. He continued as if there had been no pause: 'If that is how things are, there is only one thing for you to do. You must adopt a child.' The words hit me like a blast of ice-water.

Adopt a child! Go through that again for a child not even my own! I touched the stained wall to draw myself back to reality, for the thought had lifted me like a scrap of paper and tossed me into a whirlwind of confusion.

'I could never do that,' I said, feeling oddly dismayed.

'You must take responsibility for some other life,' he persisted out of the dark silhouette of his head.

'I could never do that,' I repeated numbly.

Now as I write the words, I can hear the echo of my own voice saying them – faintly, weakly, dazed beyond conviction. No wonder I sensed Kofi smile as he said: 'What we think we could never do are just the things we do at last, because life drives us to them. Tomorrow I will make inquiries.' He pressed my hand and left me standing there in the darkness, listening to his sandals clapping away from me across the uneven stones.

Chapter 6

An indeterminate number of days – perhaps it's weeks already – have passed since I wrote the above. I have been back where I began – in a black pit of drink and sleep and anger and nothingness.

The first rain fell in the night and now the cobbles and rusty car-chassies in the square are steaming in the early sun, and the air smells clean. I touched bottom in the night. Perhaps my 'dank humours' have lifted a little this morning, too, and that is why I was able to pull myself together sufficiently to go out early, replenish my supplies and to buy, as an act of hope, a new notebook in which to begin the therapy again. Towards what? Have I made some decision without knowing it? So many of my decisions seem to be reached so deep down that I can never trace the source of them, I simply find myself acting them out like an automaton.

It was that damned idea of Kofi's that plunged me back again. A way out when I'd resigned myself to there being no way out, a hope when I'd begun to draw comfort from the total absence of hope. I thought I'd killed the desire within myself for a child, in these three dreadful years, but of course it was there all the time, or why should I behave in such a way that Kofi recognized my whole situation? (Well, no, not all of it. He doesn't know the worst, the thing which makes it completely impossible for me to undertake the upbringing of another child, especially somebody else's.) If nature were kinder, she would pull maternalism out of barren women like a dead tooth, as she removes desire from eunuchs. As it is, the uselessness of one's longing multiplies the pain.

I mustn't think about it or dwell on it any more. An idea like that could permanently undermine my feeble will to remake my life somehow. In the hollow black trenches I've been travelling the last days, I have played the hostess to all sorts of contemptibly adolescent dreams. ... Kofi has been here every day, and every day the door has been locked against him. I have spoken through it rationally and calmly so that he would not try to break in. My 'solitary' moods he has reluctantly come to accept, though not without anxiety. His daily calls, his footsteps, his knock, his anxious voice, have, unknown to him, held me together, given the black days and nights some shape.

And last night I did let him in.

The rain had started to fall, and I had pulled myself round sufficiently to notice it needling in through the open french windows, splashing in huge drops on the tiles ... it is such an unfamiliar sound after the long rainless summer. I was lying on the mat and I lifted myself on my elbows and watched a trickle of water breaking away from the pool inside the windows. I could barely see it in the dark, it was just a lustrous black rivulet creeping near. ... I lit my torch and watched its approach, bearing particles of dust and a tiny chicken's feather that must have blown in from the fowl-market. I lifted it out – it was minute and perfect, a little white quill. I remembered the symbolism; I have been living with symbols, mostly nightmare ones, for the past days, and it somehow restored some sense of proportion to hold in my fingers this neat gift from fate; ruefully I thought, 'I'm not even a fair-sized coward, I'm just a footling little one, all but invisible to the naked eye.' With a long relieving sigh I stood up and went outside and let the wind blow the thick, heavy drops against my face until the pressure marks of the split bamboo and the endless, useless tears, and the residue of brandy on my chin, had been washed away.

When I felt better (and was also soaked to the skin) I was just going in when I saw a moving smudge in the wet gloom of the square. Kofi and Hanna came clattering up the steps with some kind of canvas spread over their heads to keep out the rain. Kofi was carrying something heavy and they came noisily across the hall and up the inner stairs calling 'Gerda! Gerda! Let us in, quick!'

I had no wish left to keep them out. They burst in together, laughing and drenched. Hanna's hair and dress were sticking to her, her bare legs were splashed up the backs with mud. Kofi's shirt was one wet stain. They both, by common consent, sank on to the floor, where they lay back-to-back against each other, as if they had run and laughed themselves to helplessness.

'What are you doing out with her at this hour? In this weather?' I asked Kofi severely.

'He's brought me to stay with you,' Hanna answered.

I looked at Kofi. He could not quite meet my eye.

'What new trick is this?' I asked him. 'You know your last attempts at rehabilitation weren't exactly an unqualified success.' He was looking round. He nodded.

'This is not for you, but for me – really for me,' he said seriously. He scrambled to his feet, pulling Hanna with him. 'Get up, you will dirty your dress. Now go and play with the stones while I talk to Gerda.' She obediently took the jar into a far corner. I followed her and put a blanket over her shoulders, but she shook it off. Her mood of elation seemed to have passed and she was suddenly quiet and withdrawn. I returned to Kofi and we sat down near the table. He offered me a cigarette and lit it, looking at me keenly.

'Why have you brought her?' I asked him.

'Now I see you, I am not sure if. . . . You are ill again.' I didn't deny it. To Kofi, anything but normality and a perfect ability to adjust oneself to life counts as illness. He stared at me for a moment and then said: 'I have never asked you a favour, I mean, a real favour, as one friend to another.'

I didn't answer. I glanced at the piece of canvas, which had been left on the floor. It had been draped over something which looked like a holdall. A feeling close to fear had begun to take hold of me.

'I have to go away for a few days. A painting job a long distance away. I can't take her with me this time. School has started and she mustn't miss it.'

'But why can't you leave her at your house? Before, you've always—'

'I was going to,' he said. 'But the rains have begun early.'

'What has that got to do with it?'

67

He stared at the window, against which the drops were battering. The downpour had begun to turn into a storm. One heard a rumble in the distance, and there was a dull, faraway flash which lit up the exquisite skyline with its running design of curves and rectangles and the jutting spires of the minarets. I gazed, struck by the sudden beauty, so swiftly wiped away again; but then I became aware of a little movement in the corner and the next moment Hanna was cowering in Kofi's arms, shivering like a dog.

'Just this,' he said simply. 'This is her fear. I mustn't leave her to sleep alone.'

I looked at them. I searched my mind – ransacked it, rather – for some excuse, some 'out'. But ten months of one-sided devotion makes debts.

'How long will you be gone?'

'Not long. Two days – three at most.'

'When are you leaving?' (although I knew already).

'Tonight.' He sounded apologetic. 'Gerda, I am sorry. It's not what you think. I'm not trying in my clumsy way to force a child on you. I – I – to tell you the truth, now I see you – and *those* – ' he indicated the basket of bottles with his eyes over Hanna's shivering back – 'I could wish there were someone else. I don't feel easy to leave her with you – I must tell you honestly. But there's no one, only you. Anyway, she wouldn't go to anyone else.'

Could that have been true? I wonder again as I write, looking at the child still fast asleep in my bed. I'm afraid – deadly afraid. The fear is quite irrational – what can happen to her? But having let my own child slip through my hands, simply to have charge of this one frightens me beyond reason. I would like to lock her in this room and sit over her until Kofi returns, to avoid the least risk . . .

I look at her, trustfully asleep in the first sunlight dazzling off the steaming roofs across the square. Her arms are flung upward. They fell that way as I tucked in the sheet last night; she reached for me and I backed away, and she dropped into the sudden, defensive sleep of childhood. I try to calm my racing fearful pulse by thinking of comparisons: the precious vase smashed, the fall from the horse, the car crash, the electric shock – all the accidents which can physically and mentally disable one for years from trying again, from touching . . .

An accident. 'It could have happened to anyone' . . . so they said, and said, and said. Even the Coroner said it. They tried to make the word 'accident' sound like an act of God, instead of something brought about by human carelessness. (Carelessness! What a word to match with death! What a petty, trivial, untragic word to load to sinking-point with guilt.)

But in the end, I find there are no comparisons that measure up to this. There was my dead child on the stones with a pint of lake-water in each lung and no more strength in my arms to keep trying to pump it out of him, and now when I look at other children I see the wet stones again and hear the sounds of my own despair. I guess that learning to live with that inevitability is, after all, only the smallest part of the punishment.

Chapter 7

There was no time to write during the three days I had Hanna with me. Now Kofi is back and she has gone home with him; I am alone again and my decision has risen to the surface as swiftly as a bubble released from the ooze. I must find a child, I have already begun to look.

From the moment she woke on that first morning until Kofi lifted her, kicking and screaming with joy, and squeezed out her breath against his heart, all fear, all guilt and in fact every self-directed thought left me and I was wholly – well, happy isn't really the word. I was wholly occupied. Perhaps it's the same thing in my case, for it left no time to be anything else.

The child is a wonder! Dare I hope to find anything like her in the exciting search that's begun? I didn't know how much I admired Kofi till I saw him reflected in her. She might have been just a commonplace street child, her intelligence mere sharp cunning, her humour slyness, her independence twisted into defiance. But he has held her close to him and shaped her; he has even cushioned her to some extent from the dreadful blow of her mother's abandonment. How this came about is inconceivable to me, now more than before I knew something of the reason behind it. For this child is too valuable, by any standards, to forego, if one had the smallest right or title to her.

These three days have swept my past life up in a small heap of dust and thrust it out of sight as if under a rug. Where it is presumably still waiting for me to deal with, but meantime. . . . Each morning I got up early, with amazing ease, to get her breakfast and make lunch sandwiches. She would then set off to school alone, with her books in a rush-basket. Then I would make the room spotless, after my old fashion, and afterwards go out shopping – not only for food, but for other small things which I thought might amuse her; I walked the alleys of the *souk* as a magpie flies, slowly, eye cocked for any bright gleam. I soon had nothing left of the money Kofi gave me for her, nor for that matter of what he paid me for my work. What raw, unbridled, selfish pleasure it was to buy things for her! I was like a lover, trying in vain to check myself. We spent the evenings cooking. (I haven't cooked properly since Alec went.) I only have an oil stove to do it on, and one ancient frying-pan, but I managed quite creditably. I showed Hanna how to make omelettes and she showed me how to make *humous*, a disproportionately complicated business. She tasted pancakes for the first time. Thinking of Raya, I tried to make marshmallow by mixing egg-white and sugar and gelatine in a frying-pan ... a culinary disaster which we turned into a triumph by dipping grapes into the sticky mess and later seeing who could spit the pips the furthest over the balcony rail. After supper we would play cards with the beautiful pack some forgotten girl-friend gave me at my wedding 'shower', and which was never used until the last two years of our marriage, when we used to sit, Alec and I, on the balcony of our Haifa apartment, playing endless, endless hands of gin-rummy and whist and demon solitaire to pass the hours before we had to face the growing horror of going to bed together. ... The cards were a small, sneering ghost which Hanna unwittingly helped me to lay.

I want to record one conversation I had with her on the second day as we sat on the beach, she in a new bathing-suit I had bought her out of my earnings. She had been flashing in and out of the clear shallows, cautious at first – incredibly she had never been swimming before – and then with sudden wild freedom as if the innocent touch of the waves on her legs had awoken something ungovernable in her – shrieking and flinging herself full-length, rolling and threshing half in sea, half in sand. ... It had taken all my courage to bring her near the water – it was the need to grasp the nettle, all or nothing, and as I watched her the fear and even the grief slipped away. I even felt near to swimming myself. But I couldn't quite do it. I sat on the dark, wet sand near the water's edge and soaked up the sight of

Hanna's pleasure. The lifeguard's stand threw its afternoon shadow over us like a safety-net; in any case, she didn't venture beyond knee-depth.

When she had exhausted herself she came and sat by me, our feet stretched out to meet the beginnings of the sea. (That was how she put it – 'The sea begins here and grows to America.') I had brought a picnic and we ate it there, my behind growing wetter and colder but she refusing to go further up the beach, away from the magic new element. We began to talk about our lives.

First she asked my age, and when I told it, remarked after some calculation that I was seven years younger than her father and nine years older than her mother. This was immediately interesting, throwing a new element of imbalance into the relationship of Kofi and his wife. She must have been no more than twenty-two when they married, and he thirty-eight or so. Then Hanna volunteered the information that her mummy was now living in Rehovot. She has a new husband. (Did she leave Kofi for him? Very probably. Few women leave their husbands and children out of mere unhappiness if they have no one else to run to.) I ventured to ask Hanna, then, a question about her life in the *kirya* – the new suburb on the outskirts of Tel Aviv – where the family had lived. She began to draw with her fingers on the crisp sand between her knees, letting the thin waves wipe it away every few seconds.

'It wasn't so nice there,' she said.

'Did you live alone – the three of you?'

'No. We lived with Grandmother.'

'Your mother's mother?'

'Yes, her.' Something in the 'her' told me Hanna had not liked her. 'She wasn't nice to Daddy.'

'Oh?'

'No. She said things to him. And she told me I mustn't tell anyone.'

'Tell them what? About the things she said?'

'No. About me being half and half.'

'Why not?'

'She said if people knew, they wouldn't let us live there.'

'But could that really be so?'

'Oh yes, it was. Because in the end, someone found out, and there was – business. People came to our flat and said things to Daddy. And when I went shopping with Mummy, nobody would speak to her. And the children I played with, who lived in our block, they wouldn't play with me after that. They would just shout things and run away.' She was making angry zig-zag patterns with all her fingers digging deep into the sand.

'So did you move away?'

'Yes. We went to another *shikkun*, a long way away, on the other side of the city. We couldn't move away from the city because Daddy had a job. He said we wouldn't move again, no matter what. He promised us.'

'And was it better there?'

'Not better – the same as before at the other flat. But almost right away, it all happened again. This time people did things, not just talked. Somebody cut the rope with all Mummy's clean washing on it. They threw things on to our balcony. Then one night we smelled burning and we started to run out of the flat, and outside in the passage we found our dustbin. Someone had brought it up and set fire to all the dirty rubbish in it. Mummy started screaming. And Grandmother screamed too, and she began saying things to Daddy just like those others. She even said things to me.'

'What things?'

'She said, "Because of you, because of you." I didn't understand.'

'And do you now?'

'Oh yes, *now* I do.'

'Why did she say that?'

'Because Daddy's an Arab and she and Mummy are *Yehudiot*.'

'Rinse your fingers now and have another sandwich.'

She ate readily enough. Clearly she has come to terms with some of it. Another thing on the credit side for Kofi.

'And is Acco a good place to live, do you think?'

She stared, munching, out to sea.

'Our house is not so nice as the flats. It's big and dark. At night it's *very* dark. There's no electricity. Look, there's a big ship! It's going into the harbour at Haifa. I like ships. Once Daddy took me out in a fishing-boat. That was dark too, but I didn't mind that.'

'Did they turn on the big light to bring the fish?'

'Oh no. The boat was just travelling, not fishing.'

'Travelling where?'

'I don't know – a long way. I fell asleep. The ropes in the bottom all smelt of old fish.'

(I begin to be slightly uneasy about these journeys of Kofi's. Where does he go? Are they really the innocent painting jobs he says they are? I accepted it at first, but suddenly too many little things are adding up. Still, it's none of my business.)

When Kofi came to get her he asked me if she had been a good girl, and I, equally formal, answered yes, very good. Then he turned solemnly to her and said, 'And has Gerda been good, too?' She looked at me with those grape-green eyes and a look of complicity passed between us because of the fun we'd shared, and she said, 'Very good.' And then she added, in the casual way of children so that one never quite knows if they know what they are saying: 'She pretended to be my mummy.' There was an awkward moment's silence. Kofi looked at me sharply, and I half shook my head, hoping he would understand that this had been in the child's mind only. Then he asked Hanna, 'And did you believe her?' and she answered lightly, 'No, I knew all the time it was only Gerda.'

And that brought me down to earth, very firmly.

But the bubble, mysteriously formed below the crust of my conscious will, had risen, and all day today I have thought of nothing but of how, when, where, who. ... *If* is the question-word I should be concentrating on, *if* it's possible at all, *if* there are children available, *if* a single woman, a divorced woman, a foreigner, can adopt. ... But the desire is so strong it rules out doubts; the impossible has turned itself inside out into necessity. 'Responsibility for another life,' Kofi said. Yes, as usual he is right. That's my solution and my cure.

Chapter 8

So Kofi is always right, is he? Let me remember that, in my present furious exasperation with him for pricking my latest bubble of unrealism.

I really went to a lot of trouble. I first took stock of my possessions – which didn't, God save the mark, take long. I have been living more or less on air – a token allowance from Alec which he insisted on 'for his own peace of mind', plus a bit I had left, dating from before my marriage. . . . The only current earnings were some pennies-from-heaven in the form of foreign rights for an old magazine story and a cheque from Len, the timeliness of which I hope he never knows, 'to buy myself a birthday present' (it bought me a bottle of brandy and kept me in cigarettes for a month). Once when I ran really short and the rent was overdue, I sold a piece of jewellery. No doubt it's been melted down and is now dangling from the wrist of some Arab lady in the form of a serpent. That one hurt, but only because it was the first. . . . Gold is a status-symbol among the Arabs, and has a high market value here. So, the need arising, I burrowed like a mole in my old suitcase, and came up from under my badly-packed winter skirts with a chunky necklace, three and a half pairs of earrings and an all-gold charm-bracelet. Only for the last had I any regrets . . . it dated back to my 21st birthday and included a lot of my comparatively pleasant and innocent past in the sentimental disguise of boots and sailing-ships and buckets of ice. . . . Oh, what the hell! It went in the scale with the rest.

With the proceeds I bought myself a totally spurious air of respectability which included a hat in which I look alarmingly like my mother; in this store-bought armour I was preparing to head for the big city tomorrow to make my first proper inquiries. But then who should come barging in but my very good friend the milkman, or rather the bubble-buster. How pleased he was to hear my decision – how overjoyed – until he saw my new disguise and heard my simple straightforward plans. Then he stopped dead in his rejoicings and looked at me, it seemed, in frank despair.

'For a middle-aged woman,' he said brutally, 'you are unbelievably childish. You waste months of your life, months you cannot afford at your age' (I do wish he would *stop* about my age) – 'and then suddenly – BOOM! – over-night you are reborn. New hat, new dress, new resolves, new life! And what? You want the moon before you have made even a ladder! Listen. Did you ever hear of a woman getting a child before she got a man? It cannot be done, not even by you. First, you must find a husband. Then he must help to make a proper home. Look at this room! No kitchen – no bathroom – '

Stung to the quick by his hateful practicality, I all but shouted: 'Have you a kitchen? Have you a bathroom?'

'Certainly,' he said promptly, damn him. 'But even if I lived in an overturned boat, it would be no one's business because the child is mine. Now Gerda – ' (as I turned away, furious, burning with rage) 'I am hurting you to save you from worse pain from people who don't care about you. Do you know what those people will say, sitting there in those city offices behind their big desks when you go to beg them to give you a little something to love? They will say, Madame, where is your husband? From where comes your money? From where will come security for the child?'

'I can offer emotional security! And as for money, Alec might – '

'Ah! Now you will run to your husband for help – your not-husband, I should say. But how if he will not do what you ask? How if these people you go to beg from are not idiots (and they are not idiots, Gerda) and they make checks, and ask questions, and. . . . There now, don't cry. Don't you see? It's *you* who need what you call "emotional security". You cannot give it till you have it. Don't expect to get the love you need from some poor little thrown-out piece of human-kind who – *if* you get him –

76

will only want to seize you and sink his teeth into you and suck the blood of your heart to feed his need for love, giving nothing back for months and months if ever ... that is how these children are, Gerda; I've seen it, even with my own girl when her mother left us. She sucked me dry for months, she wouldn't let me from her sight, and at the same time she fought me and defied me and tested me in every way she could ... punishing me for her pain, demanding love with every cruel hurt she gave me. ... Are you prepared for that, Gerda?'

I was curled up on the bed by this time, crying my stupid head off, wishing he would drop dead only to stop these dreadful – truths, I nearly said, but I don't believe it. The business of having to have money and a home – that's all true, I suppose, and I should have thought it out more clearly; there is no sense in having them reject me on practical grounds and then trying to go back later. But nobody can tell me that some unhappy, abandoned child would not respond to love and security. It was contemptible of him, anyway, to imply that I am planning this for what *I* will get out of it emotionally. Of course he doesn't know that I have a debt to pay, that I have to *prove* my ability to look after a child properly and not allow anything to happen to it ... he couldn't have been so cruel if he'd known.

Also how maddening these glib men are when they talk about women like me 'finding husbands', as if one just saved up one's pennies prudently and then trotted off and chose one in the supermarket. I am thirty-nine years old and the last three years have all but wrecked my looks. It's true that in the few months in Haifa, after Alec left, I had offers of various kinds, at least one reasonably 'honourable'. ... Yosef 'Hairy Joe'. I wonder what the hell happened to him? He was a nice fellow, but oh God! He was quite definitely *not* the one to restore my confidence in my bedworthiness, crippled as it was by those unspeakable last years with Alec. ... I'm so afraid of sex now! Perhaps my appetite for it has just passed, perhaps it was not simply that I couldn't want it with Alec any more because of what had happened. How terrible it was, each half-hating the other, each so changed that it was (for us both, I know, not only me) like going to bed with someone you scarcely know and

77

don't much like ... yet at the same time the technique grimly familiar, the opening moves, the special caress that never used to fail, the desperately rubbing fingers meeting an unyielding dryness – oh, poor Alec! It was so sad. Just when we needed it most! And I, stiffly striving, filling my mind deliberately with erotic images which left me colder than before. ... Am I permanently frigid now? That is what I'm afraid to find out. That, not virtue, not even snobbery, was why I hit out at Kofi. ... Once I would have found him all too attractive, I always secretly wanted someone like that, rather ugly, rather primitive – God forgive me, Kofi is not primitive, but something about his body *is*, he has the hands of a labourer and thick, strong shoulders and neck ... even the bald head is somehow virile. ... One feels he has it in him to rape women but controls it. There! How self-revelatory can one get? I had better stop before my whole libido is exposed between these innocuous pale-blue lines.

Anyway, I am not going to Tel Aviv tomorrow in my new hat after all. I am going to write, under a false name, and ask for one of their forms, and from that I'll learn what is necessary. And what is necessary, I will do. Because I must find a child now – the need is burning me up – the doubts are all gone. That very feeling of clarity, of positive wanting, is what obsesses me and drives me forward. But Kofi is right. I must curb my impulsiveness and go about this sensibly or I will spoil my chances.

I should date these bits of writing. I don't know how long it is since I wrote, but it is now the end of October. Rain has been pouring down without pause for nearly three days; the square is like an aerial view of Ontario, a gleaming mass of water with the more irregular cobbles and bits of junk rising through it like scores of little islands. This room is far from waterproof and the floor is dotted with pans and jar which are in constant need of emptying. My bed stands out from the wall, at an unnatural angle, in the only drip-free area. The whole town is sodden and depressed and the same goes for me.

In short, then – Kofi was right. To his credit he didn't crow over me. He has been very good as always, and as always I resent it. I won't go into details about all the letters I have written, journeys made and people seen in the last few weeks. I shall just write, in order, the *basic necessities* in this country before one can even apply to adopt a child:

1. A husband. (Of the same race, creed and colour as oneself.)
2. A ticky-tacky box to live in, i.e., nothing bohemian, or even unusual, is permitted – it must be a nice little house or a nice little flat in a nice, ordinary district equipped with all the nice, civilized urban amenities.
3. A stable and sufficient income.
4. An appearance of sobriety, placidity and normality. Correction: Not merely an appearance. These sterling qualities must be genuine, because they – They – check and double-check to make sure.
5. An unblemished record of worthy endeavour and clean living.

In other words, practically nobody really *needing* to adopt a child can do so. Certainly I am ruled out on all counts.

Hence the depression. But why, I ask myself, am I not back in my slough of total despond? I have exhausted every area of possibility that I know about, yet still I am *sure,* and I am burning up with the frustration of it, that somewhere near at hand there is a child waiting for me. Is this a typical neurotic delusion? Kofi, for one, does not think so; but his plans for me are in no way akin to mine. He wants me to secure Points 1–3 in the list – the rest, he says, will take care of itself.

Although even he was somewhat dismayed to learn from me how astonishingly few children are available for adoption in this country. Of course, it's A Good Thing; illegitimates, the chief source of adoptable babies at home, are seldom parted with here, and children of broken homes, orphans and so on, are nearly always gathered in by *somebody* close at hand – relative or neighbour – and the authorities don't get to hear about them.

Of course there are the usual number of defective children, but it's no use – famished as I am, I don't want that. I couldn't, not after Jake, not after Hanna. On the other hand, about its racial origins I don't give a damn. It can be a positive knicker-bocker-glory for all I care; who am I to be fussy? They come in

79

all shapes and colours in the market, and my hands stray towards the frizzy heads just the same as to the blond ones whose grandpas flew back to Glasgow and Stockport twenty-odd years ago with their units, well out of the mess they left . . .

God almighty, it's cold in here! My feet and legs are like ice. A drink is called for . . .

All right, then. I can't go shopping for a husband, but at least I can try and get a job and a proper home. It must obviously be in that order, since I am broke. It shouldn't be hard to find a job as a physiotherapist, even though I never actually qualified . . . or practised . . . wonder if I still remember any of it? I'd better. But on the other hand – round the tread-mill once again – if I have a job, how could I look after a child?

A single dim hope sustains me. It's based imprudently on a letter I wrote two weeks ago to my sister Judy. This unwonted appeal (I can't pretend it was anything but that) followed, on a crazy impulse, a series of letters, abortively begun and destroyed, to Alec, one night when I as feeling so alone that I didn't give a monkey's foreskin any more. It was this inelegant expression, as a matter of fact, popping into my mind half-way through my fifth drink, that reminded me of Len who in turn inevitably brought Jude into my head. We were never what you'd call close, but we are sisters, and surely that counts for something when one of you has everything and the other is on her beam-ends. . . . I see I am already forging tranquillizers for my pride, which is still sour and jumpy from the stunning blow I had to give it before it would allow me to write that letter. That begging letter. . . . Every time I think about it, I feel slightly sick, slightly defiant. . . . My God, though, what a difference a nice little borrowed lump sum would make! Mother used to say Jude was jealous of me. Well, if so, she has had her revenge, the last ten years or so; maybe that'll have a softening effect on any sour recollections she may be harbouring of gay, sparkling (Christ!) free-as-air Gerda waltzing through the shallows of half-a-dozen careers and affairs and delicious impulsive holidays, while she was struggling through her first few pregnancies in a clapped-out leaky bungalow on the wrong side of town. .... Perhaps she'll remember that I did try to help, baby-sitting and so on: baby-sitting is fun when you're still enjoying your freedom and have no sneaking terrors that those infant nephews and nieces may one day be the source of the most agonizing envy. I wonder how many of them there are, round about now? There were five, last I heard, and Len was talking about rounding out the half-dozen in a not entirely joking way, despite Judy being late on in her thirties then. ... Of course the days of the broken-down bungalow were long gone, it was a four-bedroom, two-garage stucco duplex by then, standing in its own ground, with trikes and bikes littering up the curving drive and a summer cottage by the lake. .... Good old Len. He worked hard and deserved it. I *would* love to see him. Not Judy; Len. He always liked me, even when she didn't. If it were up to him, maybe he'd even give me one of the kids to keep, never mind the money. They're all alike anyway, with their shiny brown 'bangs' and doe's-eye specs and big, crookedy teeth. ... Every time Judy got in pod, she'd say, 'Ah well, the first one took all the time I had, so how can another take up any more?' Hey, sis ... give us a baby. Aw gwan, you can spare one ... just that li'l one with the piggy eyes and the braces that make her lisp, you don't want that one! You know what you are, you're mean. You got five and I haven't even got one. You got a husband who works hard and thinks the sun goes in every night the same place he does, you got enough money, you got 'a lovely home' (oh Mother, your words! You should see mine!) And you got kids, Jude. It all looked damn dull to me once, but right now I'd change places with you like a shot if I could. There. .... If I'd said that in the letter, you'd have been so pleased to have won and licked me so completely that you'd have sent me a whole year's housekeeping as freely as you once emptied a jug of fresh coffee over my new dress.

I got my reply. I got it all right. I got just what was coming to me by this morning's mail – my first letter for a thousand years, and if that's a sample I hope it's the last.

'Hiya, G., honey! Great, great, GREAT to hear from you AT LAST! Gee, I almost forgot I HAD a sister, for heaven's sake!

If Chuckie hadn't recognized the writing on the envelope (I guess he never forgot you gave him his very first cheque) I swear I'd have thought your letter was some Zionist circular and slung it in the trash-basket! Seriously though, it sure has been an age – but no more reproaches. Honey, I'm so glad you turned to me for once in your life. It meant more to me than you could ever guess. You were always so darned independent, and you were always the giver, the generous benefactor, all of those gorgeous presents you used to give the kids when we could scarcely afford to keep them in clothes – they thought you were Santa Claus without his beard! Of COURSE Len and I want to help you now you seem to be in such an untypically tight spot. (Never knew you to get into anything you couldn't get out of, but I guess it comes to us all!) As I say, we'd love to help, BUT! And it's a big BUT, because guess what? Steiner Mark Six arrived two months ago. Am I blushing? Me at forty years young, what'll the neighbours say? But it's great to have a new baby around again. The old house was just about big enough for the seven of us, but with Donny's arrival (it's Daniel really, but Donny's cuter) we just had to look around for something bigger, and thank God we've found it – six-bed, TWO-BATHROOM – a perfect palace by comparison, on 85th, way out by the terminus which is still pretty countryfied and an up-and-up district we hear, so it's a good investment, but oh boy! What a capital outlay, mortgage and all!

'On top of that we have to start thinking about Louis' college money, not to mention Mary-Sue who still has three years of nursing to get through. PLUS the endless extras, teeth-straightening, dancing lessons for Carla (you just should have been there to see her solo at the parent-teachers' evening, she even got a notice in the local paper) . . .'

And so on. And so on. A plethora of parenthesis – clearly a family weakness – and capitalization, and needless to say, no money forthcoming at the end of it all, not a plugged nickel.

Judy, baby, you sure know all the wrinkles. You must have revelled in every word of that letter, knowing how cleverly you were making me squirm. You always were a stickler for the book of rules. . . . Judy the Prudy they called her, but they laughed the other sides of their faces when they saw how you took that little old book full of mothers' advices and proved the whole lot were true. Don't smoke or drink, it's not becoming; don't show off your intelligence in front of men, its scares them; dress nicely but not conspicuously; take Domestic Science in college, don't neck on first dates, don't pet below the waist, they only lose respect. ... Choose a sober citizen with a clean collar and prospects and don't go to bed with him first; marry young, keep your home clean and give him plenty of good meals, wear a pretty negligee at breakfast and wear your curlers when he's at work ... and be sure to give him lots of kids. Well, you filled the bill, honey, and I muffed it. As for those kids you had, you knew better than to let any of *them* fall out of a boat; and I bet you'd have known better than to believe your upright husband if he told you on his scouts' honour that your five-year-old could swim like a fish. You're the one who understands men. *You'd* have known – wouldn't you? – that a man who's sport-crazy, a man who only wanted sons, a man who went the colour of old rust and started choking at the mere suggestion that homosexuals are not criminals. ... You'd have guessed that such a fellow might be tempted to exaggerate his little son's athletic achievements – especially to his mother who was against him being plunged into the cold lake early every morning, who had the idea maybe the boy was scared of water, scared of boats, scared of climbing rocks and ski-ing and riding horse-back, even a little bit scared of his big, tall, hearty daddy. So with you, Judy, the situation with the boat and the child and the lake would never have arisen, but if it had, I'll just bet you'd have jumped in like a streak of lightning to pull that baby out, even though he wasn't crying ... you'd have known his daddy had told him it wasn't manly to bawl, even when you're drowning. *You* wouldn't have stood on the shore with one hand shading your eyes, watching him bobbing around out there, merely calling out 'Jakie, are you okay?' and not knowing, not *knowing* the numb, dumb terror in that little head until it went under. But then, Judy, you couldn't, even you couldn't have swum out there faster than I did, you couldn't have dived and dived in that thick black water until you felt his shirt among the sharp reeds. You couldn't have pulled him up and out with any more desperate strength than I used, or dragged him to the shore, or pumped at him for longer than I did. ... And when you realized he was dead, would you have walked out into the lake again by yourself and put your head under and breathed in the water, gratefully, the way a fish might breathe after being stranded on the shore? I don't think you would because you had the others, and besides you're not a coward like I am. But if you had tried to kill yourself that way, Judy, you might have succeeded because you know all the rules and you know you have to tie a weight round your neck to drown yourself because the body's will to live is stronger than the mind's will to die.

So I wrote it down at last. How oddly it came out – quite unexpected, the way those mediums write, their hands moved by something outside themselves ... so it felt, as if suddenly my hand was possessed. It must have been time for it to tell itself. ... But how very terrible that it all came out as accusations against Alec, hidden bitterness against Judy.... I was in charge of him, and I let him die. If only once Alec had said it was partly his fault – then I could have accepted that it was mainly mine – I could have shouldered the blame, instead of constantly, inwardly trying to put it on to him. ... Oh God, what a mess I made. What a mess I'm in. There is really no basis for this mad hope, I am only using it like a life-line to keep afloat ... anyway I don't want any other child ... how could I love another child after Jake? What right have I? ... Suddenly the writing is turning against me, it's working in reverse, bringing me from hope to despair. The rain goes on and on and the floor is covered with little pools, little lakes. I would like to die but I don't know how. There must be a hundred ways out of this life and I can't find one, because in every one you have to take the step of tying a stone round your neck.

Chapter 9

Whining, snivelling, miserable weakling that I am. The reason I have no right to a child is *not* that I lost my own, but that I have all too little to offer to another. Kofi is right, he is right, he is always so god-damned *right*. What if I got a child, and then sank into one of those despicable troughs and started reaching for the bottle? Or even merely bursting into tears? What would this do to a normal child, let alone to the sort of disturbed, life-wounded creature Kofi describes as the sort I might possibly get?

I have been hunting for the sort of job I could do mornings only. Of course I could find more openings if I moved away from Acco into a city; but the strange thing is, that though I will leave if I have to, something makes me want to hang on here if possible. ... Not in this room necessarily, but in this town. In the new section, dozens of identical blocks are going up almost while you watch, to house new immigrants. I shall soon be in a category to get one, since I have decided to abandon my long-extended tourist visa and apply for citizenship. (That must surely be Point Six of the Adopters' charter.)

Kofi asked me the other day why I don't go back to Canada. It was the first time the thought had crossed my mind! My first answer was, 'What for?' and that's the kernel of it. There is nothing there for me. Pain, old history, doughiness – nothing. I have no mother, no father, no husband there – only a sister with a large family, whom I hate with all the considerable venom of my nature right about now.

No, Canada's not home any more. Nor is Israel, really. I will not have a home again until I have a child to put in it. If I thought I could get one easier in Canada. ... But I couldn't. ... My child is here somewhere. I am sure of it. Everything in

Canada is so snug – so tied up tight and sealed. Here nothing is snug, everything is still in flux; immigrants pour in every week from God knows what countries and conditions; and they breed like moles. The other day I walked past the National Health Clinic and I saw them by the score, women with three or four children hanging on to them, many of them bulging with the next – there were dozens of kids running around who didn't seem to belong to anyone – and in the streets below me here, they teem, they swarm. The country is bursting with fecundity, and it is not properly organized yet, that is my great hope – to find a child somewhere, not through an official agency (I recognize the hopelessness of that now) but under the counter, so to speak – some child that nobody wants. There must be hundreds! Sometimes I feel I could snatch any one of fifty that I brush past every day in the market, and nobody would even notice he'd gone ... yet Kofi assures me they all belong to someone; though they look so dirty and uncared for, they are loved and wanted just as I loved and wanted Jake.

It's December now. I am broke again, and nothing accomplished. It's a fantastic winter for here, there's even been a sprinkling of snow, and a lot of frost. I have had to get myself an old stove to supplement my cooking one; this room is hell to heat – even with both stoves going full blast (which I only allow myself for a few hours at night, to warm myself up before going to bed) the knife-edge is hardly taken off the cold and perpetual damp. It sinks into your bones. ... I seem to be constantly blue, in both senses. ... I just haven't enough warm clothes and am always shivery and miserable, like a wet dog that can't dry itself out. Come and bask through the winter in Sunny Israel!

Nothing is happening about my child – *nothing*. I have exhausted every possibility. I have even been to the local convent to see if I could foster (already I'm reduced to that!) a foundling. They asked if I were a Catholic (what a question, with my profile!) – I said no, I was a Jewess, but I did happen to be a woman, if that counted for anything. Apparently it doesn't. ... There was a child there while I had this abortive interview,

which wasn't really even that, just a stand-up chat in the courtyard with one of the sisters. He was obviously not quite all
there; he held the sister's robe in both little fists and stared up at
me unseeingly. He had the face of an old monkey, and wore a
perpetual cynical half-smile. And I wanted even him, I'd have
picked him up and carried him off then and there if that woman
had only said 'Here, take this one, nobody else wants him. . . .'
But evidently she wanted him, because when I turned away I
saw her lift him up in her arms and as she walked off with him
he was patting her crisp cowl with strange uncertain hands and
she was talking to him as one talks to a friend.

. . . I've been re-reading all these notebooks. Something
strikes me forcibly – the utter lack of humour. It's horrifying. I
had a sense of humour once, a very reliable one that was equal
to nearly everything. I guess I lost it when Jake died. I suppose I
won't really have recovered until I recover that. Actually it's
hard to imagine how I failed to appreciate the comic side
of Gerda the Great Coper, the original Laughing Girl, sitting
sozzled and tear-stained sobbing out her maudlin woes into a
child's copybook. . . . Yes, I begin to see the funny side! Oh boy,
as Judy would say – daylight! So now I must try and keep my
renaissant sense of humour alive with frequent shots of keen
self-appraisal. But with a light touch, Gerda – lightly does it, or
you'll find the shot going straight through your head.

January. Mother used to say once Christmas was over she
always felt spring was on the way, although God knows in
Canada winter's only just getting started. Christmas. . . . We
were lucky at home, we had *all* the festivals. Father was a great
one for Christmas. It always made Mother a bit uncomfortable, but she put up with it as long as Dad was alive. Then she
let it lapse. . . . But I still remember the big fir on the lawn fixed
up with fairy-lights glowing in the lumps of snow. We always
used to go sledding on Christmas Eve with the gang, and come
back afterwards for hot chocolate and turkey. . . . We would
peel off our snow-suits, thick with ice where we'd rolled each
other in snow banks or been hit by snowballs, and leave them
steaming in bright heaps on the radiators and dripping on

mother's parquet floor. She used to wax it in the living-room so when we started jiving in our thick indoor socks we polished it for her at the same time. And later Judy would come in with her latest 'slave' and look in tolerantly, perhaps even joining in the dancing for a few minutes or filling a plate with turkey and potato crisps and pumpernikl, before retiring to the relative peace of the kitchen to eat and neck discreetly until Mother came down at last to chase everyone home. . . . Why did things go so wrong between Judy and me, and Mother and me, as I grew older? *Answer:* Because it's unnatural to stay single till you're thirty and it changes all your relationships, I suppose. But it's sad to remember the good times now because of what came after.

. . . I haven't really eaten much for the last week and I'm feeling a trifle light-headed, which may be why I'm getting sentimental about the past (and specially about the food it contained). I have a bit of drink left but I'm afraid to take it on such a very empty stomach. I don't quite know where I go from here, as a matter of fact, because I have nothing else to sell and I'm two months behind on the rent. It was quite funny yesterday, I went out in the torrential rain with my ex-new Tel Aviv hat wrapped up in polythene and took it to one of the second-hand (tenth-hand) clothes-booths in the *souk* to see what they'd give me for it – the old Arab man there laughed when he saw it and tried it on himself over his *kefia*. He looked ridiculous and I laughed as loud as anyone, but my laughter faded somewhat when he told me what it was worth to him. A few grush, enough to buy some rolls and a hundred grams of coffee. They tasted wonderful but they were soon gone. My allowance from Alec isn't due for a fortnight, if I haven't lost complete track of the date . . .

I wonder where Kofi is.

Thank God I didn't find a child. I must have been mad, irresponsible and mad. Since it's only myself it doesn't matter so much, although I must say being hungry is awful; but if one had to watch. . . . Surely there must be jobs. . . . I was on the way to one or two back in November but I felt sure I could do better and let them go. Now I can't seem to muster the energy even to go and look, and besides, I've nothing to wear – nothing but an old pair of plaid slacks and a couple of sweaters. One of them was Alec's – I often wore his clothes. Putting it on now gives me a minute moment of specious comfort, as if his arms were going round me. Do I imagine it, or does it still faintly smell of his tobacco? . . . I must be going off my head a bit. I'd better get into bed.

Chapter 10

Kofi's mission in life seems to be to save me from starving.

Poor fellow! He got such a shock when he got back from wherever-it-is (and I'm more and more convinced it's not where he says it is) and found me . . . well, let's not go into details. The annoying thing is that of course he thinks I was doing it on purpose again, and after he had propped me up and poured into my gawping mouth some foul concoction which miraculously revived me, he suddenly lost his temper and without warning started striking my hands . . . such an odd thing to do . . . obviously he was overcome by a desire to hit some part of me, couldn't quite bring himself to slap my face or box my ears or turn me over his knee, so he stood there, heaping abuse on me in what sounded like real gutter Arabic, and swiping away at my hands as if swatting flies. He was really dancing and gibbering with rage. At last he broke into stuttering Hebrew – 'Every time I go away for five minutes – can't you be trusted by yourself? – you're nothing but a silly child, angry with life – trying to punish it by dying – ' and so on. The more I told him it had been all a mistake and an accident, the more infuriated he became, until at last the sting from my hands and my general weak state made me burst into tears. . . . A wise move, always, with Kofi, especially if he's angry. He immediately gathered my hands together like spilt flowers, petting them and arranging the fingers, muttering apologies and even going so far as to put his mouth against the sore backs. 'Poor little things, I didn't mean it – '

And finally he sat down, wiped his face with a big grubby *kefia* that he had tied round his neck, and said, 'You don't deserve the good news I'm bringing you. I don't think I ought to tell you at all.'

'Tell me. Please. Oh Kofi! I need good news!'

'I have found a child for you.'

I sat quite still in the stale bed and heard the words buzz round in my head like bees.

'Don't get too excited. There are drawbacks. There are difficulties.'

'I don't care!'

'*Many* difficulties.'

'Later. Tell me about the child. Tell me about the child!'

He told me it was a girl, three years old. Her parents are dead. She and her brother, who is six, were sent by their old grandmother to be looked after by an uncle in one of the local villages ... at this point I interrupted.

'She's an Arab?'

'Yes. Do you mind?'

For one second, I hesitated. He watched me steadily. Then I thought: If I do mind, I can't face myself. I'll deal with that separately. I answered: 'No. Go on.'

The uncle has a large family already, and was none too pleased at being saddled with two more. He was particularly unenthusiastic about the girl, though he was persuaded to accept the boy, who was healthy and strong.

'The girl isn't healthy?'

'Not very. She comes from very poor people, very primitive people. They hadn't enough food at times, and when that happened they favoured the boy. But there is nothing wrong with her – I think nothing – that good food will not cure.' He hesitated, as if about to tell me something else, and then went on: 'She is a very silent child.'

'You've seen her?'

'Yes. It was I who brought her to her uncle.'

'From where?'

'Another village – a long way from here.'

'Where you go to work?'

'Nearby.'

'Where *do* you go, Kofi?'

'A small town – a long way off – '

'Where is it near?'

91

'What does it matter?'

'I want to know where she comes from.'

He sat silently looking at me. His great eyes seemed to veil themselves. At last he stirred himself and said, 'Listen, Gerda. I could tell you a lie, but it would lead to other lies – like those I have told you already. I am your friend and so I don't ask you what you don't wish to answer. Believe me, it is not your business.'

'But I must know where the child comes from! I must go and see the grandmother.'

'No, that would not be – wise.'

'Why not?'

'She is old and a little mad. She would not – agree to the child going to a Jewess.'

'And the uncle?'

'That's something else. The uncle is by no means mad. He wants to be rid of the girl, and he does not care where she goes. But if you go to see *him*, he will ask you for money.'

'*He* will ask *me* for money?'

'Yes – the more he sees you want the child, the more money he will ask.'

Now I was silent. At last I said, 'In that case, I'd better not go to see him either.'

'That would be much better. There is no point anyway, since he disowns her.' He seemed relieved. Is he being honest with me? I am shutting my eyes to every sign that he isn't. The child is real; she has dropped from God knows where into my life. It's better not to inquire too closely into the source of manna.

'When can I see her?'

He hesitated. 'Whenever you like.'

For a moment the room drew away from me and I thought I was going to faint. It was so sudden, almost a physical shock. ... 'What do you mean?' I asked faintly. 'Where is she?'

'She is at my house. Her uncle wouldn't keep her for even a day – he wouldn't let me leave her there for fear he never saw me again.'

I leaned back and closed my eyes. 'Kofi. I'm afraid! Without warning like this – what shall I do with her? Where shall I put her?'

'She can stay with me until you are ready.'

'Oh my dear. . . . Thank you.'

'It's nothing. You are my friend. Anyway, it's I who should be grateful. Now get up and come to my house for some food.'

I got slowly out of bed. He helped me like a doctor helps a patient, or as he might help Hanna, to wash and dress – I felt very weak. I was trembling all over from weakness and from – fear, I suppose. I kept saying, 'She is real, isn't she? You're not just inventing her?' But suddenly I thought of a more pertinent question.

'What language does she speak?'

'I haven't heard her speak a word, but it must be Arabic, of course.'

'Not a word! Kofi, is she dumb?'

'No. Just – silent.'

'But – '

'Her mother died four days ago.'

'How?'

He paused. 'Of a heart-attack, it seems. She died in her sleep. The girl woke up one morning and found her like that. They slept in the same bed.'

I pulled Alec's sweater slowly over my head and stared at the wall. The fear deepened. What was I getting into? This was no ordinary child. But still, at three – one gets over anything . . .

'What's her name?'

Kofi drew a deep slow breath and went to the long windows, his kafkafim dragging. 'Gerda, I don't want to give you too much all at once. You are weak and you have had enough for today. But tomorrow, when you have seen the child and decided whether you want her or not, then we must talk some more.'

'I only asked her name!'

'Her name is Fatma. But I think it would be better if – right from the beginning, from tonight – you called her by some other name.'

My brain was not working well. I couldn't understand. 'But why?'

He turned to face me. 'Because Gerda, she is a little Arab child and you are a Jewess. If you are going to adopt her, you must pretend she is Jewish too.' He sighed again at my blank face. 'I do not want to give you too much to think of tonight.'

'It's so – complicated.'

'Yes. As I told you, there are difficulties.'

We walked slowly through the dark wet streets. Kofi held my arm firmly against his side to steady me over the slippery cobbles.

'I suppose you don't know if she is intelligent.'

'The grandmother said she was. The grandmother ... it seemed to me she was more reluctant to part with the girl than the boy.'

'Did the children cry when you took them?'

'No, but the old woman did. She held them in her arms. . . . The little girl's head was quite wet afterwards.'

'Couldn't she have kept them?'

'She can hardly walk, and she has spells of foolishness. She knew herself she must give them up. But it was hard for her, one could see that.'

'I could take the girl to visit her sometimes . . .'

'Gerda, don't think of that. It is not wise. If you are thinking of the old woman, she has parted with them now; it would only make things worse.'

'But if she has no one – '

'Gerda! Stop. You must stop that. You are not stealing the child. If her future is to be with you, there must be no looking back. It would be far better if she forgets her origins altogether.'

I stopped walking. 'You don't mean you want *her* to think she's Jewish?'

'It might be better. We can discuss that later.'

We arrived at his house – where in all these months I have never been. It was part of a long, one-storey street, punctuated with low doorways – a slum alley. We went through an arch and down three steep steps into a minute courtyard, off which a number of doors opened. Outside one of the doors he stopped and took my other arm in his big hand.

'Gerda, there is one other small thing. She. . . .' He hesitated and then went on in a very casual voice, 'for the moment, she has no hair.' I gasped, but he went straight on, 'well, almost none. But don't worry, because I have seen such things before, and it is only the result of not having enough to eat, not enough – vitamins, you understand? The hair does not grow properly, and then, probably the mother shaved off what there was because of disease – '

I felt abruptly sick. I hope it was mainly hunger.

'Her head is – '

'There are the marks. I think it's healing now. She needs good food, vitamins. . . . Don't expect too much. At her age, my daughter was almost as ugly.' He gave a little, taut laugh and patted my arm. 'Are you ready?' He opened the door and held it for me, his eyes gleaming like wet stones in the darkness.

I turned numbly to go in, then stopped again.

'The name! What name shall I give her?'

He thought for a moment. 'Better not to try to talk to her tonight at all. She won't understand you in any case. If she is still awake, simply smile at her, pet her if she'll let you. . . . Wait for her to come to you, like the poor little animal she is . . .'

Inside the door were a series of low, interconnecting rooms, like white-walled caverns, lit very badly or not at all – the only light in the first room came flickering through arched shadows from a room at the far end of the house. We passed through two small, dark, stone chambers to reach the light. There was little furniture – low couches which were simply raised sections of the floor, a few rugs and cushions, a lowering wardrobe incongruously flanking a deeply-recessed window. In the last room, it was clear, most of the living was done. Here there was a big table, some chairs, a stove, wall-hangings, a clutter of objects which had been acquired cheaply in the market . . . but there was nothing ugly or crude. The colours were the colours of earth, stones, animals' coats and blood. There was a surprisingly large number of books lying in piles on the floor. The light came from two bright paraffin lamps standing on the deep whitewashed window-ledges.

I took in these alien impressions out of the tails of my eyes, as Aladdin might have noticed the walls of his cave unconsciously while all his attention was focused on the treasure lying on the floor. Hanna was sitting on one of the raised couches, wearing a grubby flannel nightgown from the neck of which her thin throat rose like a stalk to support her tangled rust-coloured head. She was reading a big, tattered picture book. Lying some distance away on the stone floor, regarding us with huge red-rimmed eyes, was the child – my child. She was the most pathetic sight I've ever seen. She lay there like a little brown dog with her muddy hands flat in front of her, supporting her head, and the rest of her knobbly carcase curled up against the cold of the stone. Her skin was so dark – both naturally and from dirt – that she looked almost black. Her face had a glazed featurelessness – even the eyes were without expression. Her head was covered with patches of dark fuzz alternating with scabs which had been treated with some dark-blue disinfectant, so that it looked like some bizarre global map. She was shivering and abject; one felt she would surely scuttle away on her belly like a little lizard if she had enough strength left to move.

While I stood staring back into those blank black eyes, Kofi went to kiss Hanna. He asked her a question or two in Arabic and then propelled her gently off into one of the other rooms – to bed on one of the stone couches, presumably. Then he went to the other child. He lifted her up in his arms and took her to the couch where Hanna had been sitting. There were blankets and rugs there, and he began undressing her.

'I told Hanna to put her to bed,' he said, 'but she said she wouldn't let her come near.'

He spoke softly. The child gazed up at him, lying quite passively while he removed her clothes.

'Shall I help you?' I asked.

'You can try. She is very nervous. Don't persist if she seems frightened.'

I came forward slowly, as if approaching a young wild horse. Her head snapped round as I came near, and her eyes widened.

Instinctively I put my hand out towards her, as if for her to smell. It was extraordinary how it worked. I think she actually did smell it. Anyway she fixed her attention on it and I gradually came closer and replaced Kofi beside her.

'Shouldn't she be washed?' I asked when all the poor rags had been removed and the thin, tautly-curled, grimy little body lay exposed. She smelled of stale urine and, oddly, of fish. Her belly palpitated like an exposed membrane in the oval made by her jutting rib-cage and her pelvis. 'Look how thin she is! Oh Kofi!'

'She is by no means starving, if that's what you think. She walked with me this morning three kilometres.'

'Why didn't you carry her?'

'She kicked and fought until I put her down. She is strong enough.'

He brought a tin basin of luke-warm water which he had been heating on a primus stove in one corner. There was a rag of towelling in it, and a piece of coarse soap. Very gently I tried to wipe the child's body. She immediately gasped, rolled up like a hedgehog, and turned on her face, so that her serrated spine and concave flanks were all I could see of her. Her buttocks were inflamed like a baby's. I washed them with one hand and stroked her back soothingly with the other. She trembled violently and dug her fingers and toes into the blanket. I washed as much of her as I could get at, and then Kofi said: 'That's enough now. She's not used to it, and it's cold in here. Wrap her up and leave her alone for a little. I'm getting her something to eat, and you too. I don't know which of you needs it more.'

Chapter 11

That was two days ago. In the meantime I have been wrestling with the suggestion that Kofi made the next morning, when I came to get better acquainted with the little girl, whom I have decided to call Ella.

I had hardly slept at all, and only a great mug of black coffee in the grey damp early morning cleared my head sufficiently so I could stumble through the empty streets to Kofi's house. Only when I got there did I realize it was far too early to burst in upon him. I wandered about in a fever of impatience; the rain began to fall again in sheets and I took shelter in a tunnel-like archway. I could see the minaret of the big mosque from there, and soon the muezzin came out on the circular balcony, a small, oddly heroic figure, and gave his call to the wet empty morning like some lonely bird crying for company. The minor-key notes burst from his throat like a series of underwater bubbles and streamed through the rain almost visibly, splashing open on closed wooden doors and bruised yellow walls and the eardrums of faithful and unbelieving alike.

I glanced at my watch and came out from shelter to walk slowly through the narrow lanes, past dwellings mysterious in their age and squalor, which were already beginning to discharge their occupants as if the muezzin's call had triggered some ejecting mechanism inside.

Would the child accept me?

How would I keep her?

She was raddled, ugly, scarred with the marks of filth and poverty and neglect. Had I the courage to be proud of her and treat her as my own daughter?

And she was an Arab.

At last it was late enough, and I found the archway with the three deep steps and knocked on Kofi's door. Hanna came and let me in without surprise. 'She's still asleep,' she said as we walked through the dank cellar-like rooms. 'Will she be your little girl?'

'I don't know yet.'

'She's ugly.'

'She can't help it. She'll look better when her hair grows.'

She turned her face, full of enlightenment. 'Oh! Will it grow?'

We went into the main room. Kofi was sitting on the edge of his couch in a very old robe of some indeterminate material so worn that you couldn't distinguish the weave in it any more. His ruff of black hair stood out round the back of his head like a monk's tonsure. He was scratching it sleepily and groping round for his glasses. Hanna found them for him. The little girl was sound asleep, curled up on the ground beside him on a rush mat, her body tangled in two grey blankets so that most of her was hidden. One bare foot stuck out and kicked every now and then, like that of a dog having hunting dreams.

'She wouldn't sleep on the bed,' said Kofi. 'Daughter, put the water on.'

'We haven't any left.'

'Then go and get some. There's plenty outside,' he said dryly, looking at the dank light drifting sluggishly through the recesses in those thick walls. The windows were at waist height at street level, and heavily barred. The room was cave-like even by day.

When she'd gone, taking a pail, Kofi patted the stone couch beside him. 'Gerda, you are tired this morning I can see, but still we must talk before the little one wakes up. I have been thinking. I can lend you some money, but it is not much – ' He ignored my interruptions and went on – 'and it cannot be regular. Also you wouldn't be comfortable I know. Therefore we must find a solution for you and this one, because for a long time she will need above everything a feeling that you are near her – only so will she learn that you are hers and that you love her.'

Can I ever love her?

'But I shall have to work.'

'Exactly. Now, I have been thinking. How can a woman work for her living and yet be sure her child is cared for? How can she be near her child even while she works?'

'How?'

'It isn't how, Gerda. It's *where*.'

'The kibbutz.'

'Yes.'

I got up abruptly and started to walk about. I needed a cigarette, but, incredibly, I had forgotten to bring any. The child's foot kicked, rustling on the matting like a snake, and was still again. I sat down on the opposite couch and stared at the mural on the big wall behind Kofi. It showed four attenuated dancing figures. It was clearly derivative – I had seen something very like it on wood-mosaic on the wall of the kibbutz dining-room. There was something touching about the obviousness of the debt, as if Kofi had been trying to pay a compliment.

'But would they have me?'

'I think so. They are always hungry for new hands.'

'A woman with a child – and no husband?'

'You are young and strong. You have a useful profession. You are Anglo-Saxon.'

'What has that to do with it?'

'It's generally thought that these make the best material. Of course it's not admitted. But it is felt.'

Suddenly I couldn't wait any longer to see the girl again. Was she as pitiful a poor little creature as she had looked by lamplight? I crouched on the floor near her and cautiously lifted the blanket from her head. She lay curled up like an unborn baby, only the one leg escaping from the tight protective circle of back, arms, legs; her patched scalp was drawn in between her forearms. She seemed to be wearing a man's flannel shirt, through which her shoulder-bones showed like vestigial wings.

'If I won't take her, what will happen to her?'

After a pause he said, 'I'll have to keep her. But it will be terrible both for her and for me. I don't know how I shall manage.'

'Couldn't you take her back to her grandmother?'

'No.'

I crouched there, staring down at her, trying to know if I could feel anything for her but pity.

'Did she speak last night?'

'No. But when you left, she cried.'

I looked up at him swiftly. He could have been lying.

'She was tired and bewildered.'

'Certainly. But she took food from your hand.'

'She's so – pathetic, Kofi. Perhaps she's retarded. We don't know anything about her.'

He looked at me for a moment, and then stood up, tightening the robe around his squat, strong body. I could hear Hanna coming back with the full pail. Kofi lit the primus stove on the floor in the corner.

'When you gave birth to your son,' he said quietly, 'you knew nothing about him, either.'

'At least I knew his parentage!'

He gave a sudden gusty sigh.

'Do you want a child, or don't you? Because Gerda, I truthfully think this may be the only one you will get while you remain unmarried.'

We didn't say any more for the moment. I felt suddenly exhausted, and sat with my back against the stone side of the couch staring numbly at the little girl while Hanna and Kofi between them made a breakfast of sorts. When it was ready, Hanna brought it to me – thick black coffee and a rather dry *pita* with some white cheese in a saucer. Then she and Kofi sat down, also on the floor, on the other side of the sleeping figure, and we ate and drank silently, as if by common consent all patiently watching her.

At last she stirred. Kofi immediately said, 'Talk. Talk quietly. If she hears voices she will not be frightened when she sees us sitting around her.' With that he began to talk in Arabic to Hanna, in a calm, level voice. Ella moved her head back and opened her eyes. They stared into mine. I smiled and offered her a piece of the bread. She rolled abruptly on to her face, her back hunched as before, like a supplicant.

'Take no notice,' said Kofi. 'Leave the food where she can smell it.'

I put the bread and some cheese up near her hand. I wanted to fondle her; my hand went out but Kofi shook his head. He went on talking, his voice gurgling in his throat like water in a pipe. Sometimes Hanna answered, but she, like me, was watching the child with all her attention.

After a short time, the folded arm shielding the face moved – lifted – returned to earth on the other side of the food, and drew it in to shelter.

'Put the blanket back over her head,' Kofi said. 'She wants to eat in peace.'

I draped the blanket back over her. She looked like a grey armadillo. Little movements at one end indicated that the food was being demolished. I moved until I was sitting on the couch, further away from her, and Kofi's voice went on. He was now evidently telling a story, for Hanna was gazing at him with breathless interest. After a time, the edge of the blanket was slowly lifted and a little hand came groping out. The fingers felt about stealthily; I slipped some more bread into them and the hand disappeared in a flash.

'Is it a game?' asked Hanna.

'No,' said Kofi. 'It's not a game.'

Finally the grey hump began to move slowly across the floor. Hanna couldn't restrain herself at this, and laughed delightedly. The hump stopped moving.

'Now she wants to play, perhaps,' said Kofi. 'Go on, try to play with her. But softly, softly. Don't startle her.'

Hanna went down on hands and knees beside the hump. She touched it with her hands. Immediately it shrank, stiffened. Hanna lifted a corner of the blanket and said 'Kuku' and dropped it again. She did this two or three times. The hump stayed stiff and small.

'She doesn't want to play, Daddy.'

'No. So leave her alone. It's time for you to go to school.'

'Will she be here when I get back?'

'Probably.'

'I'll read her a story.'

'Good. Now go. Shalom. Learn well.'

Kofi and I now sat alone on either side of the grey, motionless hump that was Ella.

We sat there waiting until lunchtime. We talked. I told Kofi how Jake died. He said: 'You were both to blame.'

'But I more than he.'

He didn't contradict, but frowned and said, 'I don't understand why he should tell you the boy could swim if he couldn't.'

I sighed. 'Alec had wanted a son so badly. And I'd wanted a daughter.' My eyes strayed towards the grey woollen hillock. 'I kept on about it being a girl, and even after he was born I was – disappointed. I didn't mean to, but perhaps unconsciously I tried to keep Jake too close to me, too . . . it's hard to explain – I didn't exactly spoil him – but I used to call him pretty, and – dress him in rather fancy shirts. . . . Alec hated it. We had our first rows about it. He said I'd make a sissy out of him.'

'What is that?'

'There's no word for it in Hebrew. It means a mother's boy.'

Kofi turned his mouth down and shook his head. Such a concept was wholly foreign to him.

'Anyway. . . . To counteract this, Alec was always trying to push him into being very manly. He started teaching him to swim when he was seven months old. He put him up on a horse when he was less than a year. Once when he was two he took him in a terrifying ride at a fair – one of those things like a double-headed rocket that goes whirling up and spins round at the same time. Jake was sick and screaming by the time the ride was half over, and by the time that ghastly thing stopped he'd turned grey and he couldn't speak. . . . I can't even remember the row we had about that, it was so ugly I've forgotten it. Alec's argument usually was that Jake liked all these things, that he was a real little tough-guy and enjoyed all the rough and tumble. . . . I could see he didn't always, but Alec made such a thing of it – and Jake adored him – he was so big and handsome – Jake began to say he didn't want to be with me because only sissies hung around their mothers – that was when I started to lose my temper with him sometimes and even hit him for little things – male things like dirtying the floor or breaking something or fighting. He was five years old, Kofi. He was five years old, and I was hitting him because I was jealous.'

Kofi let me cry and then said, 'Enough now. She may be listening.'

I stopped abruptly and looked guiltily at the blanket. Sure enough two little bright eyes were regarding me from under its edge. I sniffed and held out my hand to her.

'Come out, Ella,' I said to her. 'Come on.'

The blanket came down like a blind.

I lay down by her on the floor, my face level with hers. I lifted a corner of the blanket. It was like coaxing a mouse from its hole. 'Ella,' I said. 'Hi. Come on.' I whistled softly. She turned her face for a second and then hid it again. Again I whistled and again she looked. This time I ventured to put my hand on her cheek and stroke it gently. She hid her face again, but more slowly.

'Enough of this,' I said.

I stood up and lifted the grey bundle in my arms. It stiffened instantly. I sat down with her in my lap. It was like holding a block of wood. There was a bowl of wrapped sweets beside me; I stripped one and offered it to her. Her eyes were screwed tight and she ignored it.

'It will not be easy,' said Kofi, watching the disappointment on my face. 'Patience is the least you will need.'

I felt foolish with her lying on my knee like that, so unresponsive. 'Should I put her down?'

'You shouldn't have picked her up.'

'But this can go on all day!'

'And all tomorrow, and all the day after. And then one day she will climb on your knee of her own accord. She needs you more than you need her.'

'How do you know so much?'

'I read much about children when I had to be mother and father to my daughter.'

'But what, then? Shall I take her home with me?'

'No. Let her stay here. My little one will help her more than we can. Be here as much as you can – but you must also go to the kibbutz and see if they will take you. That is, if you think that is the right thing to do.'

And there it rests.

I go round early every morning and spend most of the day there. Today Kofi has a job and has left me alone with her. She sits this moment in a far corner hooded by her blanket. She has begun to play a very little, if you can call it that – as she sits silently, she traces the outline of the cracks in the cement floor with one finger, and once she trapped a spider in her hand and played with that for some minutes before she lost interest. She watches me when she thinks I'm not looking. . . . I am forcing myself to leave her alone, except to smile at her, but at meal-times I do try to lure her a little, and at lunchtime today I succeeded in getting her to come to the table. True, she came only long enough to snatch her sausage and orange before rushing back to her place on the floor, but I noticed with joy that for that brief sortie she left her blanket behind.

I have not been to the kibbutz. I can't make up my mind to it, even though I know there is no other solution. Somehow I can't see myself there, in one of those little boxes. . . . But as Kofi points out, I must begin to think of the child, first and foremost, and not any longer of myself. And the children there are so beautiful, so healthy and happy. Perhaps even if I were rich, I couldn't offer her such a good life . . .

Another reason I don't go is because I'm afraid they'll refuse to take me. Also, Kofi says I must lie about her, pretend she is a Moroccan Jewish orphan that I have adopted, and I don't know how well I can carry that off. Suppose they check? Kofi says they won't, they will merely ask a great many questions, and then. . . . He warns me there will be a gap perhaps of weeks while they talk about it and decide whether to take us or not.

And if they don't take me – what? It is a dead end.

Just look at her . . . a proper little Arab, with those black eyes peering over the frayed edge of the blanket which is draped round her face. . . . She has sores, some healed, some still raw, all over her body. She must have good food, fruit, treatment – injections, perhaps, I don't know. How can I afford it alone? Even if I got the best job in the world, what would I do with her? I must go to the kibbutz. I'll go tomorrow.

Part Two: The Kibbutz

Chapter 1

For over five weeks I haven't written. Not because there hasn't been time – there was plenty of it, aching days of it, at the beginning, but I somehow couldn't get down to it because I was so on edge, waiting for the kibbutz to make up its mind. And then, when they decided at last to take us, there really *was* no time; I had a million things to do – to get rid of the room in Acco, to sort out my things, to shop for Ella. ... I spent my entire quarter's allowance, plus a little borrowed from Kofi, on basic equipment for myself and Ella so that we wouldn't arrive at the kibbutz like beggars, with nothing but what they saw fit to give us.

I see I'm already slightly on the defensive about my position here. *That* must be nipped in the bud. The chief trouble at the moment is that I haven't begun to work yet, because Ella is still at home with me, and even after only a week I'm acutely conscious that I'm like a sick bee in a very active hive – I rather have the feeling that, if they suddenly all turned with one accord and stung me dispassionately to death for the crime of uselessness, it would be no more than my just deserts! Not that they've shown the least signs of doing so, so far. In fact, they've been very good on the whole, except that ... well, I'm new, I'm strange, I'm husbandless, and I've brought a problem-child into the kibbutz where apparently, despite the beauties of their educational system, they have problems enough with their own.

However, I'm going too fast. This journal (with eight notebooks filled I think I can dignify it with that Boswellian name!) is no longer so necessary therapeutically, but I'm going to try to keep it now as a record of Ella's progress. In that connection I can now write that after four weeks with Kofi and Hanna, and ten days with me, the change in her is nothing short of remarkable. To begin with, thank God, she talks – not very much, and not very loudly, but enough to prove that she can and that she is not seriously backward, if indeed at all. She has begun to pick up Hebrew from me, just odd words so far, but enough to give us some sense of communicating. But the day Kofi promised me, when she will climb in my lap unbidden, has not yet come. I long for it immoderately, but I know now that it can't be hurried; the two attempts I've made so far to cuddle and kiss her have ended disastrously – she obviously thought I was attacking her. I wonder if her own mother may have been too busy, or too ill, or just not the type to demonstrate affection.

One word she says constantly, awake and asleep – 'Faud.' It's her brother's name. She says it in no particular context, but periodically when she's playing and seems quite at ease she will suddenly jump up and begin searching the room, under the bed, behind curtains, in the tiny shower-room, calling him piteously: 'Faud? Faud?' I dread these moments for they always end in her crawling away into a corner, dragging her blanket, sobbing exhaustedly. Then no amount of coaxing will bring her back until she is hungry.

Food has a miraculous effect on her. God knows the kibbutz food is not very exciting, but to her every meal is a banquet. She has stopped wolfing everything as if it were going to be snatched away from her, and now she plays with it for some time first, picking it up, turning it, looking at it from all angles like a small baby, tasting her fingers, and often dropping it and taking it in her mouth direct from the table. At first I tried to stop her doing this because it was so messy, but the psychologist who visits the kibbutz and who has been advising me, told me to let her do what she wants. 'Whenever she behaves in a babyish way,' this woman said, 'even to wetting herself and sucking her thumb, don't try to stop her. She has regressed because of the shock, and she has to pass through this infantile stage again before she can adjust to her real age-level. Have you tried letting her suck a bottle of milk?'

This was all bewildering and a bit distasteful to me, but I tried giving her a baby's bottle of the same sweet thickened milk mixture that they give in the baby-house here, just before she went to sleep at night. The effect was extraordinary. Instantly she rolled on her back, holding the bottle up, and began sucking. Her nails were white, her face screwed up with concentration. After a while she visibly relaxed; her grip on the bottle slackened, the sucking became less frantic, her eyes half-opened and an expression of peace spread over her face. She fell asleep with the bottle clasped to her chest.

The kibbutz nurse has checked her thoroughly and tutted over her, in fact she tuts every day when she comes to see her. This woman, whose name is Dahlia, came originally from Germany, and her war-experiences (she wears a number on her arm) have made her familiar with conditions resulting from deprivation. But several times she has exploded with rage against the child's parents, who of course she thinks were Moroccan Jews: 'That's the sort that's flooding the country, primitives from the tenth century! As if we hadn't enough troubles without absorbing ignorant cave-dwellers!' I wonder if she means it. ... Between them she and the visiting doctor have given me a fantastic assortment of ointments, coloured liquids, pills and tonics to apply to Ella or get her to swallow; neither operation is easy; while she lets me wash her now, dress and undress her and take her to the lavatory, if I have to do anything which hurts her even a little she pulls away with surprising strength and crawls with great speed and agility into the most inaccessible corner under the bed. I can't help feeling that physical fights with her at this stage, even in some necessary cause such as giving her her medicine or disinfecting her sores, will hamper our relations. Because of this I let Dahlia do most of it, and oddly, Ella doesn't object nearly so strongly to that. The psychologist says this is a good sign, that she is beginning to associate me with comfort and pleasure, and that that's why she objects so violently to anything unpleasant from me.

She is still in quarantine and is not allowed to mix with the other children, who of course have seen her and are all mad with curiosity about her. I am very worried indeed about what will happen when she begins the transition into the life of the children's house where she will live with the others of her age. Her hairlessness, her dark skin, her inability to talk properly, not to speak of her psychological problems; will all leave her open to God knows what teasing and tormenting. I've had long talks with the girl who will be her house-mother. She seems a very nice kid, but she's only about twenty-three and this is her first 'group'. She's clearly as worried as I am as to how she'll fit Ella in. Everyone is agreed it will have to be done very slowly and carefully, and in any case, not yet, not until she has got used to me as her special person. An extra complication to my private worry is that she will not have got over missing her brother by the time she is sleeping with the others. . . . Faud is such an unmistakably Arab name. (Would the kibbutz kick me out if they knew the truth? Perhaps not for the mere fact that she is an Arab, but I feel it would ruin everything if they knew I'd deceived them.)

Re-reading these pages, it's clear that my whole life is centred on Ella, almost to the exclusion of myself and my surroundings. But my own life here has to be built up, if only because hers will depend on it. So now I will conscientiously write about myself. Perhaps it'll help to bring the violent change in my circumstances into some sort of perspective: at the moment I feel like someone being whirled round in one of those centrifugal machines, where only concentration on a single static object (Ella) stops the feeling that one will fly apart at any moment.

The kibbutz, after due discussion on various levels including a vote at the weekly general meeting, decided to give me and Ella a six months' trial initially, extendable to a year if things were going even reasonably well. After that I have to decide whether I want to live here permanently, as a member, and the kibbutz has to decide whether they want me.

They have given me a one-roomed flat with a minute kitchen (just a sink with some cupboards really), a porch, and a shower room with lavatory. I can't complain, though I am suffering acutely from claustrophobia which I didn't even know I had until now. . . . I suppose because I've always had plenty of elbow-room all my life; I even find myself guiltily missing my vast cold empty room in Acco, with its miles-up ceiling and view over the roof-tops. . . . Beyond the porch is a lawn – quite a large one – with a hedge round it, and a fir tree. At the back one has a view of another house, and on either side there are similar rooms to mine (four altogether in this building). My neighbours are, respectively, a young couple (from the Argentine, I think – their Hebrew is almost non-existent) with a baby whom they bring home every afternoon and play with on the lawn – very good for Ella, who has already shown interest in it; an old man who is one of the parents of a member, living out his old age in rather hard-working peace near his family: and Raya and Dan, who will shortly be moving out into their new 'veterans' house' which I helped to paint.

Raya has been extraordinarily good, and so has Dan if it comes to that. I really think Raya was overjoyed at my sudden arrival. If it hadn't been for them, in fact, I don't see how I would have managed, because, having accepted me formally and assigned me the room, the kibbutz as a whole seemed rather to withdraw when it came to the crunch and leave me to do my settling-in as best I could. And it was no simple matter. The room was reasonably clean, and there were basic furnishings, but that was all – among the things that I had to do on that first unbelievable day, when I arrived by taxi with all my things strapped to the roof and overflowing from the boot were: find cleaning materials and scrub the place out properly; re-hang my own curtains in place of theirs; find someone to replace a non-functioning tap; find a table-lamp to replace the central one which would have disturbed Ella at night: scamper round finding an endless series of small essentials which I and everyone else had overlooked, such as a broom, a bowl to bath Ella in, some cutlery, clothes-hangers, a hammer ... and so on, and so on.

All this, apart from the basic, and back-breaking, business of unpacking and finding places for all my bits and pieces. For once I was glad I don't own much any more; as it was, there were moments when it seemed quite impossible that I would ever get straight. The furnishings – a couch-bed, a small table, an armchair, a bookcase, and a wardrobe – had to be completely rearranged to accommodate my trunk. And the rain poured down outside, so that somehow everything got damp and covered with mud. .... Oh well. As I say, if Raya, and later Dan, and later still their son Amir, hadn't come in and lent a hand with the practical details, I think I'd have rung the taxi up to come and take me away again.

While all this was going on, Ella sat silently in a little chair I had bought for her, draped in her precious blanket, being no overt trouble whatever – which was very disconcerting. 'Is she all right?' Raya kept whispering. 'I never knew a child be so good!' And later: 'Poor thing! She's like a little bald mouse.' She was obviously itching to cajole her but I had asked her not to pay direct attention to her – strangers coming at her suddenly can reduce her to a state bordering on terror. Dubi got maddeningly underfoot and Raya tolerated his whining and interference to a point where I wondered if perhaps he was invisible to her.

Raya is at once a blessing and a curse as a neighbour. She really *is* the prototype of a Canadian small-town housewife. Having helped enormously and earned my undying gratitude, she now takes it for granted that we are intimate 'buddies'; she wants me to consider her room as an extension of mine, and she certainly returns the compliment. She is in and out of here like a blue-tailed fly all day. I find myself ungraciously thanking heaven she works all morning, for after she comes home there is no peace from her. She is forever popping in with little kind offerings – cups of 'cawfee' (which she pronounces with an exaggerated drawl in imitation, I think, of some long-ago radio comedian), dishes of cookies, fruit from the kitchen where she works, and other odds and ends, most of which are undeniably very useful and welcome. .... Her favourite excuse for coming is that she's found a new toy for Ella. These things rather embarrass me, and in any case we very seldom find one that Ella responds to.

On the whole there are just two things that she plays with – one is her blanket, and the other an old child's boot she found under the hedge. This disgusting sodden object is her chief delight; she slides it about the floor like a boat, or puts her hand in it and makes it walk, or simply lies on her back (in her babyish moods) and turns it this way and that over her head. Once I saw her sucking the aged, earth-blackened lace that still adheres to it.

The psychologist saw her cradling the ghastly thing in her arms and positively beamed. 'First the blanket, now the boot,' she said gaily. 'Soon her love will spread out to something with more risk attached – to something alive. . . . What about a cat, or a dog?' 'But I want her to love *me*!' 'She will. But don't forget what happened the last time she loved anything resembling you. She woke up and found it cold and dead in bed with her.'

It's odd . . . at nights I go to bed early, partly because I don't want to disturb Ella with the light, and partly because, having been up with her since about 5 a.m., I'm good and ready for bed by nine. But it's not always easy to sleep. . . . I lie listening to the peaceful night-sounds of the kibbutz, the rain on the roof, the scrunch of rubber boots on the wet gravel path beyond the hedge, the voices, Raya's radio next door – and Ella's breathing. And I wonder. . . . Of course I don't know *yet* the full extent of what I've undertaken, but what fills me with anxiety is trying to analyse my own feelings towards her. I am obsessed with the need to make her well, to see her fat and laughing, to hear her chattering away to other children. I watch her by the hour, trying to imagine her with a head of curly hair, with an expression of happiness on her face. And I want her to turn to me. I want that desperately, that, even more than her health, is why I am really doing all this.

But do I love her? Do *I* love *her*? Or do I just want her to love me?

Chapter 2

I've been here a month now. I've settled into the room as well as I can, and the claustrophobia has gone. Every day Ella comes a little farther out of her shell. It is invisible but perceptible, like the movement of a clock's hands or the growth of a baby. One watches constantly and anxiously; nothing seems to be happening, and then suddenly one notices something which has been going on for a long time. For instance, she moves about much more now, venturing to the bathroom by herself, examining things on the way, and playing more freely inside the room.

But recently a new and disturbing thing has happened.

A few days ago she wandered out on to the porch, I thought on her way to the bathroom, but when I looked through the screen door I saw her standing in the opening, gazing out on to the lawn. Of course she has played outside the house often, but always with me. As I watched, she stepped tentatively over the threshold and cautiously walked over to the fir-tree. I prayed that Dubi would not appear and start teasing her, but all was quiet. She sat under the tree and began to fill her boot with pine-needles. When it was full, she emptied it and filled it again. Suddenly she dropped it and began to beat her hands on the ground like an excited baby. She had thought of something she wanted, and, jumping up, she came running back.

'Mayim! Mayim!' she shouted in a high, commanding little voice.

I was quick to take the hint. I filled her bath-bowl with water and took it out to her. It was a fine day for once; the ground was very wet, but I thought it better not to bother just then, though I am perpetually frightened lest in her vulnerable state she catch cold or something worse. The sun was shining strongly down through the branches of the tree and glinting on the bowl of water. Ella began struggling out of her clothes. Obviously she associates water with nakedness because of her daily baths, a process she has always seemed more to endure than enjoy. I tried to help her but she shook me off and finally shed the last garment. She looked at the water for a little, and touched it with her dark brown hands. Then she picked up the boot and carefully emptied the pine-needles into the bowl. Then she held the boot on the surface, making a boat of it. When she let it go, it sank out of sight beneath the floating needles.

She looked at the water for a minute and then – suddenly – she opened her mouth and let out a piercing scream. My heart almost stopped. I ran to her. When I touched her she flung herself backwards on the ground, arched her back in a spasm and then began drumming her feet on the ground, screaming all the time in short, piercing bursts. I was terrified. I thought she was having a fit. I tried to lift her but she fought me like a wildcat. I took the boot out of the water and tried to show it to her, but she was beyond seeing it. I put it in her hands and she flung it away, threw herself on her face and wept and raged. I stood helplessly. Never had she behaved anything like this, and I had no notion what to do. Eventually I ran into the room and brought out her blanket. Using force on her for the first time, I rolled her up in it and then released her, letting her lie there on the wet ground, her little stick-arms with their knotted fists protruding from the grey roll, pounding the ground.

I stood away from her, watching in a panic of uncertainty. I prayed someone would come along to help me (to do what?) but no one came. She kept up the screams for what seemed like an eternity, but at long last they began to lose strength and eventually died away into shuddering sobs. When I crept back to her, she had fallen asleep and I was able to carry her to bed. I found the bottle which she had almost stopped using, filled it with milk and left it beside her. Then I sat and waited.

When she woke up she grabbed the bottle, sucked it for a while, and then sat up and started playing as if nothing had happened.

I could hardly wait for the psychologist's visit.

'But that's wonderful,' she said, unpredictable as ever. 'It means that all the fear and anger that's been locked inside her until now is beginning to burst out. The best thing that could happen.'

'Is she likely to do it again?'

'Oh yes! Probably many times. She'll probably also attack you.'

'Me?' I said, aghast. 'Why me?'

'Look,' she said patiently. 'She loved her mother, like any child. Her mother left her, and not only left her but gave her a horrible fright as well. Now along you come and offer yourself as a substitute for her mother. Before she accepts you, she's got to vent her anger on you for the pain her mother caused her.'

As Judy's Len would say, 'It figures.' But for all that, I dread the next outburst. I won't be so frightened next time, since I know now what it is, but the actual violence of it seemed to touch off a corresponding violence in me . . . I felt physically ill while it was going on. I can't exactly pin down my feelings, or even remember them very clearly, but what I felt for her then – through my alarm – was certainly not love.

It's not all roses in this place, by any means. To start with, I miss Kofi and Hanna more than I would have thought possible. There are some 150 adults living around me, and except for Dan there's not one so far I feel I could ever be really close to. Of course I suppose it's a bit early to judge, but I can't say they're exactly putting themselves out to be friendly. If one tries to develop a conversation they nearly always seem to be in a hurry, or have nothing much to say. . . . I have a strong feeling I *must* try to be sociable and make friends, for Ella's sake later, but somehow it's very difficult.

Raya, as I said before, is really too friendly, almost sticky somehow, though I feel ashamed of not liking her better after all she's done for me. But Dan is very nice. I don't see much of him, but whenever we meet he stops and chats to me in his quiet, contained way. Once or twice Raya has sent him along to do running repairs or to put up a shelf or something for me; on the most recent occasion, he brought with him one of his little iron sculptures. It was one I had admired in their room, a male figure bent back as if he had been shot while running. He shyly asked if I would like to 'have it around' for a while. 'Don't let me force it on you if you don't like it,' he said. 'An amateur artist feels always embarrassed at giving away his work.'

'But I'm crazy about it! May I really keep it?'

'Sure,' he said, the Americanism coming oddly in his accented voice.

He is very masculine – not in an aggressive way, so that one is conscious of some oblique menace (I feel that so often around men, even with Kofi sometimes when his eyes are on me in that controlled-hungry fashion) but in a comforting, natural way; I 'sense' him with some inner awareness, some conditioned response like the response to a lighted window or a plate of soup or a warm coat ... or perhaps some kind of defensive weapon. ... This feeling is difficult to describe because it goes so deep, it's an indefinable and rather primitive thing that women feel for men apart from sex, a feeling of oneself as the weaker of the two and safer and happier because of it. (Come to think of it, that was what I must have been missing with my early affairs. The young men I made love to were *all* weaker than I was. Was Alec? Not at first. Afterwards, grief, deprivation, hopelessness, guilt perhaps, all combined to reduce him, and I believe he shrank inwardly until he became even 'smaller' than I was. Perhaps that was why I couldn't want him any more.)

Of course Raya is trying hard to pair me off. I have been thrown together, usually over the tea-table and in the deflating presence of their children, with *five* wildly unsuitable single men so far. I won't enumerate them, for they are all impossible – I think most kibbutz bachelors must be pretty well un-marriageable by definition – as Raya put it, with great sim-plicity: 'You've *got* to be married to live here without going nuts.' For myself, I don't know what I want. I am mortally afraid of the bed side of marriage, and yet ... if there was a chance. ... What woman truly wants to face her middle age alone? Maybe I can find some nice warm-hearted, cold-blooded fellow who'll bring his own camp-bed ...

Come off it, Gerda. Your blood's been stirring a little recently – admit it. When Dan –

I was interrupted by Ella throwing another of her fantastic tantrums. The first one was nothing compared to this. She'd been playing quietly on the floor near my feet, and I'd felt her fiddling around with my shoe, only I hadn't really been paying much attention. She must have tried to get it off, and failed, because suddenly she burst into shrieks of rage. It really was *pure* rage this time, I could see it. She actually began banging her head against the tiled floor, and when I lifted her up to stop her she kicked me squarely in the stomach. Her strength when she's crossed is astonishing. She hurt me quite badly, so that for a moment – it's dreadful to have to own to this – I wanted to slap her, as much for the ear-splitting noise she was making as for the pain. Anyway, I put her down in her cot, where she got on to hands and knees and began bashing her head against the bars in a fearful rhythm, screaming with every blow. It was terrible to watch her. She stared at me out of eyes red with fury, banging and banging as if every bang was directed at me. I came nearer; her screams mounted in pitch and volume, warning me off.

Raya came running in, and together we stood and watched her as one watches an animal which has gone mad in its cage.

'Go out,' she said after a moment. 'She's doing it on purpose. Leave her alone and she'll soon stop.'

This not only seemed like sense, but accorded thoroughly with my own wishes. We went out on to the porch.

'Close the door.'

From beyond it, I heard the screams and bangs going on. Raya suggested I come in to her place and try to get right out of earshot, but somehow I felt I must stay where I could hear her. It didn't help either of us, but it was desertion to leave her altogether and sit somewhere having 'cawfee' while she was suffering.

I persuaded Raya to go, and I sat out on the porch. Spring is well advanced; things have grown green under the floods. There is a hill beyond the kibbutz, where whitish rocks grow out of a swirl of white and blue and yellow wild flowers. I tried to concentrate on the sight of it, so beautiful and gay, and think how pleasant it would be to go walking on that hillside. . . . *Oh Ella! Stop, for God's sake stop it!* It was driving me mad. How could she go on like that? I felt as if she were torturing me.

It stopped only when she had worn herself out, and me too. The old father from the house next door shook his head at me from his deckchair. He didn't speak, but it was clear what he thought: that I shouldn't have left her to scream, that I should have done something to comfort her somehow. But what? What does she need? I felt shaken to my very core, all my nerves were jangling as if someone had put a metal pail over my head and banged it with a broomstick. Dear God, I hope she doesn't keep this up! I don't know how long I could stand it.

She's doing it every day now. Life is pure hell. I watch her with something akin to terror, and she, seemingly all unconscious of my tension, plays her own self-absorbed games, eats her food in an increasingly disgusting way (I am sure she deliberately throws things on the floor or upsets her drinks just to see my reaction), talks and obeys me only when she feels like it, and then, without warning, she will explode. The walls vibrate with her shrieks, strangers passing by come running to see what I'm doing to her. I don't even know what sets her off, half the time.

It's hard to describe some of the things she does. Every morning her clothes and her bed are in a state of filth. If I don't watch her, and clean her up quickly each time, she positively wallows in it, smearing herself, her clothes, the walls. . . . It is utterly sickening.

The awful thought is constantly with me now – perhaps she is deranged? The psychologist isn't due for another week. In the meantime, far from getting closer to Ella or feeling more sure of my love for her, I am scarcely able to endure her. If she were 'having accidents', or crying from unhappiness, that would be entirely different, I could feel sorry for her; but this – this dirtiness and viciousness are hateful. She seems to be inviting me to be angry with her, even to hit her, and I have been very close to it sometimes.

I've written to Kofi to come as soon as he can – I must see him and talk to him. I am beginning to resent him in my thoughts, to feel that he's landed me in this hell and that he must, somehow, get me out of it or at least help me to get through it. But through it to what? Dahlia says Ella will get over this, but she can't tell me how long it will take. And in the meantime – I may as well admit it to myself – I'm beginning to detest her. I wish I'd never seen her, never taken her on. It is like being shut up all day with a vicious, dirty, half-mad little animal, with whom one has no communication, no ties of fondness, nothing except an inescapable responsibility.

Chapter 3

Kofi has been. He was no help at all. He saw my desperation; he listened to what has been happening; but instead of being sympathetic, he told me quite sharply that it was only what he had warned me to expect and that it seemed to him as if I were doing the very worst thing possible – to wit, 'taking my love away' from Ella. (The maddening thing was, the psychologist hinted much the same thing the day before, telling me I must 'love her now more than ever', not fuss over the 'messy habits' as she called them, suggesting, God save us! that I *sing* cheerfully and smile at the child while I clean up after her so as to 'show her it didn't matter'. . . .) Kofi sat there, looking big and awkward in the small, crowded room, drinking some coffee I had managed to make amid the chaos – for before he arrived, Ella had begun to pull the room apart, grabbing, dragging down, tearing, chewing and breaking anything she *could* reach – and talking in quiet, measured tones about patience and kindness and love . . . and all the while that wretched child sat in her chair as good as gold, gazing at him with a sweet smile, and at the end, damned if she didn't go over to him and start putting toys on his knee and talking to him. . . . The most shocking pang of jealousy and anger went through me when she did this. I recognized it, fortunately, and was able to deal with it, but the awful thing was Kofi noticed my expression and said:

'You should be glad of the hurt that is going through you at this moment. It shows that you do love her, and don't hate her as you fear.'

That perspicacious bastard! I watched him cycle off with a mixture of relief, anger and misery. It is horrible to be so well-understood. But as always, his words stuck. Can there be love under all this hateful battling? Is the psychologist right, is she doing all this to test me?

I've determined to try to control my feelings, to try to be calmer, more rational about it.

*

There's been a breakthrough. I *think*.

She's out of quarantine now and I can let her out alone to wander about and begin to make her way with the other children. Twice I've taken her round to the children's house where she'll live.

The first time I took her to the *gan*, as they call it here (it means kindergarten), we played together, she and I, just beyond the fence. The five children soon came running to inspect, and freely comment on, the newcomer. They heaped me with questions: Whose was I? Whose was she? Why was she so 'black'? Why was she so ugly? Why didn't she talk? And of course, inevitably, where was her hair? (At first they referred to her in the masculine!) Ella sat quietly through all this, watching them with her blank black stare which could be observant or could be merely withdrawn, I am never sure which. Two of the children wanted to play with her, but at their approach she got up, tugged at me, and clearly wanted to go home – so we did.

Today we went a second time. I left her sitting near the fence in the grass, playing with some toy she'd found, and went off a little way to see what she'd do. The 'gang' came and hung over the fence, asking her questions which she ignored. At last one of the boys, annoyed by her unresponsiveness, began to shout at her: 'Tip-shon-et! Tip-shon-et! (silly thing!)' The others took it up. When she still paid no attention, he picked up a ball and threw it at her from point-blank range. It hit her squarely on the ear. In a flash, she was on her feet. She flung herself half over the fence trying to grab him, but he danced away, laughing tormentingly. Then she turned and began to run towards me. She was shaking her head as if a bee had stung her. She came pelting straight for me and I really thought she would run into my arms – I had even opened them to receive her and I held my breath, feeling an almost unbearable longing to hold her close to my body. .... But before she reached me, she stopped, flung herself down and began to scream.

The children stopped laughing and stood stock-still in a row at the fence, gazing in awe and interest at the spectacle. The sound triggered off my usual reaction – anger and frustration – but this time I forced it down. Instead of leaving her to it, I went and sat by her in the grass. As always she kicked and screamed harder as she felt me beside her, but I ignored it. Some impulse made me push aside the memory of the many times she had tried to hit or bite me in these fits, and I took her under the arms and dragged her into my lap. She stiffened and fought, but somehow, I felt, without conviction. I held her with one arm and stroked the back of her scabby little head. She dug her fingernails into my thigh but when I didn't let go I suddenly got the impression that she was trying to burrow into me. I held her more tightly, and began talking to her softly. The screaming stopped at once, the sobbing soon after. In five minutes she stood up her back to the fence, and said clearly in Hebrew: 'Habayita' – 'Home'. I took her hand and we walked home together. She let me wash her face and I gave her something nice to eat. She sat in her chair and ate it quite cleanly. My heart lightened. A turning point!

But *ten minutes* later I went out for a few minutes to bring our lunch from the kitchen and when I came back she had deposited a nice little present for me right in the middle of the bed and was sitting primly beside it, her eyes bright with expectancy.

'I did kaki,' she announced. This was, ironically, the first complete Hebrew sentence she has spoken.

I felt nauseated. I could so easily have whacked her! Then I thought grimly. *Sing, Gerda. Sing.* And that reminded me of one of Len's – Judy's husband's – feeble semi-rude jokes, about a man who married an opera singer and on the morning after the wedding shouted at her: 'Sing! For God's sake – sing!' I could suddenly see Len's fat, good-humoured face, bursting out laughing at his own tag-line (how meaningless, how ridiculous are the things that make it possible to go on!) and I burst out laughing myself. Well, she *did* look funny, sitting there on the bed with her pants round her ankles and her hands sedately folded ...

'You little devil,' I said, and then made a mock-fierce face. 'You know quite well where that should happen, and it's not on the bed. Right?'

She nodded.

'So next time, in the bathroom and *not* on the bed or anywhere else. Okay?'

She stared at me and then got up and walked into the corner where she sat down. Cleaning up, I began to sing conscientiously but it sounded so forced that after a while I started laughing again. She turned her head swiftly.

'I'm not angry this time,' I said. 'Because it's the last time, isn't it?'

And she nodded.

Did she understand? After six weeks of Hebrew, she probably did – enough, anyway. She has been angelic all evening, running up to me with toys, eating her food nicely (tomorrow I've promised to take her to eat in the big dining-room, an idea that seemed to appeal to her) and towards her bed-time, when I ventured to sit down on the floor beside her she suddenly reached her hand out – without looking at me – and clutched at my leg with all the strength in her fingers. The pinch hurt, the same as any pinch, but I suddenly knew it would be all right to put my arm round her and give her a kiss. I did it. She didn't respond or look up from her game, but nor did she pull away.

... I have sat for twenty minutes – the length of two cigarettes – since writing the last sentence, looking through the darkness at the edge of the pool of lamplight I'm writing by at her tough little paw sticking through the bars of her cot. I am trying to define in words my feelings about today, but it's no use – they are not in focus yet. I feel there's something terrible about only beginning to love a child when it begins to love you. The adult should be able to love without return, just for the good of the child. ... But love is not attracted by need. Love is as honest, as unpretendable an emotion as hate – it comes when it comes, one can neither force it nor deflect it nor even decide oneself on whom to 'bestow' it. And more and more I think that to some extent it's *always* a two-way current; if nothing is coming in, the outflow will also soon run dry. Today, somewhere, somehow, Ella turned on the current. Now the hand which has always been a clenched fist in sleep, lies open and soft, and there are no unhappy little rustlings and mutterings from under the blanket; that goddamn boot is still clasped to her chest, but what the hell, Rome wasn't built in a day.

Chapter 4

The time has come to start giving Ella up.

Raya has forbidden me, in her 'now I'm gonna scold you' tone, to use that expression or even think of it in that way. 'You're *not* giving her up,' she said sternly. 'She'll be yours just as much when she's living in the gan as she is now – more in fact, because all the dirty work, all the training and chores and tellings-off and all that, will be done by somebody else. All you'll have to do is love her and have fun with her.'

I must try to see it like that. I must try.

She has begun to take her afternoon nap with the other children. We – their housemother and I – managed this tactfully by showing her a nice little bed and telling her it was hers whenever she wanted it. The other children cooperated by referring to it as 'Ella's bed' and no one else was allowed to go near it. At first Ella was puzzled. 'My bed's at home,' she said. But gradually the idea of having two beds began to appeal to her. Out walking with me she would suddenly get the urge to go and check up on her bed, to see if it was still there, and empty. And one day we 'happened' to be there around lunchtime. Rifka, the housemother, suggested Ella might like to have a bite with the others. Afterwards it followed naturally that they all lay down to take their rest together. .... It was fun for her; afterwards she actually chattered – one can nearly call it that – about the experience.

And I? I, who should have been delighted by how well and smoothly the first step had been taken, was delighted far more, if not exclusively, by the way she took my hand when I came to get her and by the small sigh of satisfaction she gave as we came into our own small untidy room which she still calls 'home'.

We now go together every morning for breakfast in the big dining-room. I feel strangely embarrassed to go in there alone, so often Dan or Raya meets us and accompanies us in. (It's not that people stare and whisper; it's just that I feel they would like to.) Dan comes from the metal-shop in his working clothes, covered with oil and rust. There even seems to be a metallic smell about him, perhaps from the welding. He unfailingly apologizes for his appearance, but it's quite pleasant to sit near him and have him to talk to. He is such a quiet fellow; it's a wonder he doesn't go crazy with Raya, who is a compulsive talker and eater. The table-manners here, incidentally, are pretty awful on the whole. Does this stem from a time when good eating habits were regarded as 'bourgeois'? If so, Dan remained bourgeois to the last, eating always as if he were handling silver and crystal in a sombre restaurant in pre-war Vienna. Raya gobbles and chatters all at once, in a jumble of words and bites and the clatter of forks and spoons on teeth and plate. Poor Raya … I shouldn't feel sorry for her since she is evidently 'happy' in the psychiatrist's sense of being 'adjusted', but there is something pathetic about her … why? – when she has 'three lovely children and that *handsome* husband' (I hear my mother's voice, rhapsodizing over the ideal situation for a woman to be in). But nobody talks as much, or eats as much as she does who is not lacking *some*thing.

The *Maskir* of the kibbutz, whose job is – roughly defined – to see that everybody's happy, last night paid me his second call since I arrived. The wind had been blowing from the east all day with breath-stopping dryness; we were glad to sit outside, for the room was stifling. The maskir's name is Michael; he's a very small, lively man with a slight paunch which his strutting walk carries before him like the proud beginnings of pregnancy.

'Well,' he began, rubbing his hands and adopting what I can only call a cheerful bedside manner, 'and how are we getting on?'

'Okay,' I said.

'How's the daughter? I hear she's on the point of moving.'

'Yes. Another week or two should do it, Rifka says.'

'Well don't look so glum about it! That's what you came for, isn't it?'

'To hand her over to Rifka? No, it isn't, actually.'

'Now now, that's not the way to look at it!'

'I know. I can't help it.'

'She'll be terribly happy – you wait and see. You won't know her in another six months.'

'That's what I'm afraid of.'

'Now now, you know what I meant.'

'Yes. Sorry.'

'She's already looking a different child.'

Eagerly I asked: 'Is she? In what way?' – for I long to hear she is looking better; I simply can't tell.

'Well, she's put on weight to start with – everyone's noticed it. And her hair's started to grow, hasn't it?'

'I had thought so – I wasn't sure.'

'Are they giving her vitamins?'

'Yes, among other things. I – ' I stopped. I felt I had been a bit ungracious about what the kibbutz was doing. 'I hope to start working quite soon,' I said at last, in what was not really a non-sequitur.

'Yes, well, no hurry. What about you? Are you settling in all right?'

'I'm not sure.' He waited for me to go on, but somehow I couldn't explain.

'Made any friends?'

'Only Raya and Dan.'

'Oh – yes. Good fellow, Dan.' I noticed he didn't mention Raya. 'You'll find it'll be easier to feel part of the place when you're working. Now, on that subject . . . has anyone been to see you?'

'No.'

'I thought Dahlia might've said something. She's bursting with impatience. So is our second-string nurse. You'll find you'll have plenty to do with all the middle-aged aches and pains around here, not to mention training our ladies-in-pod how to give birth with a smile . . .'

'I don't mind what I do so long as I'm earning my keep and Ella's,' I said again.

'Oh, I wouldn't worry about that,' he said comfortably.

'I do worry about it. Apart from just living here, all the medicines and the psychologist's visits –'

'Look, er – Gerda. Could I try to explain something? The kibbutz has accepted you on this trial basis. That's not because they want to do you any favours. It's because we want new members, and especially of a certain calibre. Everyone hopes you'll settle down here, and that the little girl will grow up happily, and that perhaps you'll ... well, marry, or ... anyway, that's for the future. For the moment, just remember that you're not here on sufferance but because the *chaverim* decided they wanted you. We all knew the child needed treatment, and that was taken into account. All that's expected of you is that you work the normal hours, without killing yourself, and try to be happy. You don't have to feel you owe us anything beyond that.'

'Thank you,' I said, feeling ashamed. The fact is I *have* been feeling a certain resentment against the kibbutz lately, which they haven't deserved – partly because I felt under an obligation, and partly because – I don't know – I've sensed a sort of wary atmosphere, as if everyone were waiting for me to prove myself before they made any lavish welcoming gestures. Also – just lately – I've begun to have an inkling of what it's going to mean when Ella moves out and I am left alone in this room. It is quite absurd, and incredible, how I miss her during the few hours at noon when she is at the gan. I can see it's doing her all the good in the world, but at the same time I just can't imagine what it will mean to give up bathing her, putting her to bed, being woken by her in the morning ...

I've begun working three hours a day in what they call the *communa*. This is the place where clothes are ironed and mended and given out. Michael suggested it as a way of getting to know people, 'getting absorbed'. It is a good place to begin kibbutz life, for here, in a sense, is the crux of a woman's existence here – a place whose very name bespeaks the communal system, where the good aspects and the bad are combined.

One of the great things about kibbutz life is *not* having to think about preparing meals or doing laundry. I've been enjoying this boon for nearly two months. Now I see the other side of it, for in this long, wooden room women work eight hours a day at nothing but sorting, damping, ironing, mending, folding and piling clothes for other people. To my eyes it is a sort of protracted death-sentence, but, amazingly, ninety per cent of them don't seem to find it too unbearable. True, it is quiet and restful (the pregnant women come to work here during the last months, and also the nursing mothers); a stove warms us on chilly days, a radio plays pop music; the flow of gossip is unceasing; and there is a green view from the windows in front of the ironing-tables. It's even true that one catches a certain rhythm quite soon. Today I ironed twenty-one flannel shirts in my three-hour stint, and undoubtedly the first five were the hardest; after that my hands did the work by themselves and my mind was free to wander. But one would surely have to be blessed with an unlimited source of inner reserves to keep sane for very long (or else to have nothing much going on in one's head at all, which, judging by the level of the conversation I heard around me, seems to be the prevailing condition.)

I live for the moment when I can switch off the iron, and, after going home to wash and change, hurry along the shaded paths to the gan to collect Ella. Every day now she runs up to me, burbling about what she has been doing. Rifka always makes her look as nice as possible, dressing her in the same baggy blue Dutch-boy trousers as the others, plus a gay checked shirt and one of the little pointed 'idiot hats' pulled well down to keep her head warm. She is still so thin that the trousers always have to be hitched up several times during the short walk home, but surely her face is filling out now and there is no doubt that her skin is clearing rapidly – the scabs on her head have all come away, and the reddish-black fuzz is beginning to spread, hiding the marks and giving her an enchanting piccaninny look. I am beginning to think she is far from ugly, and now that she is talking and we can communicate more freely, I can see that she is not only quite intelligent but also very much of a person.

The other day there was a crisis. Some woman I don't know came into the *communa* to get her laundry, and said as she passed behind me:

'Your daughter's having a battle-royal with some of the boys – I could hear her screaming all the way here.'

She spoke as if it were nothing beyond a mildly amusing part of the scenery, but I dropped everything and ran. I, too, could hear the yells from afar. When I got there, I found Ella clinging to a post as she once clung to her cot, kicking out fiercely and screeching while two of the boys made darting sorties into range and threw handfuls of sand and small stones at her. As soon as they saw me coming, they turned and bolted like rabbits into the house.

I knelt by Ella, embracing her and the post together.

'What goes on?'

'They hit me! They hit me!'

'Did you hit them back?'

'I couldn't!'

'All right. It's all over.' I stood up and took her hand, unhitching her from the post. 'Come and let's find Rifka,' I said a trifle grimly.

'She's not here.'

'Then who is?'

She shook her head.

We went into the house. It consists of a kitchen-dining-room, bathroom, and two bed-play-rooms. Apart from the other children, who were innocently towing carts around the bed-legs, there was no one there.

'Why were you hitting her?' I asked Meir and Avner, wanting to murder both of them. (I didn't think it was possible to hate four-year-old children, but I hated both those little boys for at least ten minutes.) They made no reply, so I asked again, louder.

'We didn't,' they answered gaily.

'I saw you.'

'We didn't hit her,' said Meir. 'We only threw sand.'

'And stones,' I said, feeling the rage rising in me again like a bottle filling up.

No answer. They continued playing as if I were not there.

'*And stones!*' I said, giving Meir a shake.

He pulled away, annoyed. 'Only little ones.'

'But why?'

'She made me angry.'

'How?'

'She's silly. She's peepee. She's kaki. And you're kaki too,' he added calmly.

The whole thing seemed to be getting out of hand.

'Where's Rifka?'

'She went.'

'Where?'

'Out.'

Controlling the conviction that I was in retreat, I took Ella's hand again and started to leave. I met Rifka coming up the steps.

'Where have you been?' I asked. She must have seen from my face that I was gunning for her, but she didn't seem anxious.

'To bring their lunch,' she said. The saucepans were piled on a wheeled device at the foot of the steps.

'You leave them alone every day to bring the food?'

'Only for a few minutes.'

'And in that few minutes, the boys attacked Ella and threw stones at her.'

'Ah! Poor! Did they hurt it then, the rascals?' She bent to Ella. I wanted to jerk her away, but I had to stand and watch while Ella submitted to her hug. She shook her head.

Rifka straightened up. 'They always go for anyone new, at first,' she said placidly.

'You seem very calm about it!'

'There's no point getting excited. They have to work their way through it. As long as she stands up for herself – which she certainly does – they'll soon get tired of teasing her and begin to accept her.'

'But they threw *stones* at her, Rifka!'

'Did they throw stones at you, sweetness?'

Ella nodded solemnly.

'Which stones? Show Rifka.'

Ella went down the steps, selected a pebble and brought it back for inspection. It really did look rather small and harmless, all by itself like that.

Rifka held it up to the light, frowning heavily for my benefit. 'They're very naughty boys,' she said, chiefly to Ella. 'Aren't they?' She nodded, her eyes wide. 'What shall we do with them? Shall we give their ice-cream to the pussy-cat? Or shall we give *them* to the pussy-cat for his lunch?'

A slow, broad grin spread over Ella's face. 'Give them to the pussy-cat!' she crowed.

'Come on, we'll go in and tell them.' Rifka took her hand and led her towards the house. Ella was dancing up and down; she had forgotten me, the fight, the whole thing. Rifka turned at the door.

'Try not to worry,' she said lightly. 'These things are inevitable. She can take care of herself, believe me! She raised an egg on Yossi yesterday throwing a potty at him.'

As brother Len would say: 'Wind out of sails. Go back to Square One.' Maddening. But, no doubt, all part of some larger design which I shall only get the hang of when I can look back on it.

Chapter 5

Something fantastic has happened, something utterly un-planned-for which has thrown a spanner in the whole carefully thought-out works. Faud has turned up.

Faud, till now, has just been a name that I wished Ella would stop using. I have never actually thought of him as a six-year-old Arab child who, until ten weeks ago, Ella-Fatma had seen every day of her life. But now I am forced to recognize that he is real, and not only real but very determined and a very much bigger danger in the flesh than his name alone could ever have been.

What happened was this. Ella having begun to sleep in the gan, I was sleeping there too on a camp-bed (the usual thing in these cases) to make her feel secure for the first week or so. I had just bedded down at about 9 o'clock when someone came along and announced that there was a visitor waiting for me in my room. I was afraid to leave in case Ella woke up, so I sent a message to whoever it was to come to me there.

It was Kofi, of course. He looked quite distraught. I've really never seen him so upset. He was wearing his *kefia* on his head, Arab-fashion, which is unusual for him, and his face was white in the dim light they leave on at night in the children's dining-room.

We sat down together at the children's table on two of their pint-sized chairs – we must have looked like giants in toy-town. Kofi was wringing his hands and I had a paralysing moment of fear that he had come to take Ella away. If I had had any doubts left about what I felt for her, that moment's terror would have scotched them.

Kofi's first bald announcement that Ella's brother had run away from his uncle's and turned up somehow at Kofi's house seemed at first like a morsel of farce by comparison with what

I'd feared. But his face and the raw anxiety in his voice brought me up short.

'But what happened? Why did he run away?'

Kofi tossed his head about as if he could hardly breathe.

'It's awful! Awful, Gerda! His uncle beat him. He says his grandmother used to beat him too, but that that was different. He expects me to do something about it – take him in myself, or take him back to the old woman. What can I do, Gerda? What can I do?'

'Well, Kofi. . . . I honestly don't know. If he's willing to go back – '

'How many times must I tell you? He can't go back.'

'Perhaps you could take him to the authorities?' He stared at me, his mouth open. 'There are bound to be organizations who could take care of him – '

'Impossible,' he said shortly.

'But why?'

'He's an Arab.'

'So what? There must be Arab societies for – '

He shook his head sharply twice. I was silent. Idiotically, I still hadn't grasped what he had really come about. I felt sorry for his predicament, but didn't see what I could do about it.

'Maybe you could go along and talk to the uncle,' I suggested at last. 'Bully him a bit – threaten to call the police . . .'

This time Kofi laughed outright, a harsh, shrill laugh so loud I gestured him to be quiet. 'I will not do that and he knows it,' he said.

That was the first time, oddly enough, that it's ever occurred to me that Kofi's 'mystery', whatever it is, could be something on the wrong side of the law. 'Kofi. . . . Won't you tell me the truth?' I asked him.

'No. It's not your business and I don't intend that it should be,' he said shortly. 'As to what you suggest – I've been to see the uncle already. I've just come from there. He says . . .'

He stopped, gazing at me through the thin light. He pushed the *kefia* back from his forehead and his bald head gleamed. Suddenly he took my hand.

'Gerda, if I tell you what he said – then you won't do what I

137

want – what I've come to ask you. Be kind to me. Don't ask for truth; don't even trust me, I don't deserve it. Just do this for me without stopping to think. Oh, what is it I'm doing to my friend? But what can I do otherwise? Gerda, help me, please help me!'

He was on the verge of tears. The sight unnerved me completely. This man had been my anchor to life for months and months, his inner calm had kept me steady or dragged me back from unstable brinks so often ... now *he* was on some fatal edge of desperation. I felt quicksands shifting under me.

'What do you want me to do?'

'Take him. Take him.'

I was speechless for a moment.

'*Me?* Kofi, how can I?'

'Explain to them. Say he is her brother, that his relatives were cruel to him. Say she is pining for him. Say you must have him. Say anything that will move them. Gerda! You won't have to look after him! The kibbutz will take hold of him and heal him as it's healing the little girl – '

'Heal? Is he ill?'

'Gerda – such children are – always ill.'

'You mean he's delinquent.'

He hung his head. 'The uncle says so. But who is he to judge? The man is a brute. He says – oh I had better tell you – he says the boy's a thief and a liar, that he is vicious. Vicious! You should see his back! You should see the pigsty where he's been living! And it was I who took him there! If only I *could* go to the police! If only I could go!'

He really was weeping now, the tears slipping down the ridges of his hard, aquiline face – my own throat ached as I wiped his face with the flat of my hand. 'Don't, Kofi. I can't bear it.'

'My dear Gerda. My dear friend. Forgive this. But ten weeks of it – through me – it is too much – ' He put his great shoulders and head down on the low children's table.

'How can you blame yourself? You were only trying to help.'

'One cannot explain that to a child who has suffered. One cannot explain it to God.'

138

I was silent. I was somehow amazed, and touched. I'd never guessed he was religious. I wondered if he were Moslem or Christian.

After a while he pulled himself together and stood up, wiping his eyes and blowing his nose ashamedly.

'Will you try for me, Gerda? Yes or no. I can't plead with you, I have no right.'

I couldn't look at him. 'It's got to be no, Kofi. I can't. I simply can't take on a – You don't understand what it's been like with Ella. And this would be worse.' He was silent. I looked up at him at last. He was standing with his head bent as if waiting for an axe to fall on his neck. The sight of him like that woke something in me; there was pity and tenderness and an agonizing kind of sensuality in the feeling, as if I wanted to give myself to him, as freely and completely as possible, as compensation for refusing him help in this crisis. My body became flooded with lusty heat very suddenly, as it hadn't for years; the sensation was so unexpected – the mere physical manifestation was something I had 'given up for dead' – that ironically I wanted to weep for joy and relief, even though my heart was wrung.

I stood up unable to resist the abrupt charge of this multi-faceted emotion, and put my arms round him.

'Kofi – forgive me – ' I began.

He mumbled. 'Forgive you?' without raising his head, as if the words had no meaning.

It was in my mind in that moment to invite him back to my room, and there to let this renewed sexuality take charge of us both. But at that moment I heard the footsteps of the night-watchman making his rounds, stamping up the steps of the children's house. Instinctively we moved apart, and a few minutes later, he left with a muttered goodbye.

This last night. All day today, of course, I've been able to think of nothing else. I feel like the worst kind of heel for my refusal, but what could I do? To begin with, I simply don't know how I could have approached the kibbutz to take on *another* difficult child. The children live so close to each other, that if there is a rotten one among them they are inevitably all influenced, and who can be certain in advance which influence will be the stronger? Besides, Kofi is quite wrong in thinking that the kibbutz 'takes over' the children and that none of the burden would be on *my* back. I think of Ella now as mine, the kibbutzniks refer to her as my daughter and she calls me 'Ima'. But it was a hard fight, and the difficulties are not over yet. Am I now to jeopardize all that I've gained with Ella by re-introducing into her life the brother she adored and is only just ceasing to pine for? And if he came here, he would be mine, too – not just for the moment, but *for the rest of my life*. I confess I didn't, until just recently, begin to think even of my relationship with Ella in that light. A child to me was an *immediate* need, I didn't really consider the burden of responsibility stretching *from now on* until I die. I still haven't quite faced it or come to terms with it. Anyway, to take on a disturbed three-year-old is one thing. A commitment to a delinquent six-year-old is quite another.

No, it was madness of Kofi even to ask me. It's true he has done a great deal for me and I owe him a debt, but nothing that calls for a lifetime's payment.

Nevertheless, the need to discuss it with somebody (to justify myself?) is so strong that I've decided to try and have a talk with Dan. He's the only possible person; but it must be with him alone, and not with Raya, or it will be all over the kibbutz inside half a day. I must be careful what I tell even to him, though I have a feeling I could trust him with most of it. Only what concerns Kofi and his secret trips I must keep quiet. I have a strong feeling now that whatever it is he does could get him into very serious trouble if it ever got to the authorities.

I talked to Dan last night.

I first found out that Raya had some kind of a rehearsal (she's very active in all sorts of things like choirs and drama-circles) and then, having made sure Ella was sound asleep with her boot within easy reach and that the night-watch knew where to find me, I knocked on Dan's door – they're already in the new house – and asked if he could spare me a few minutes. A few minutes! Poor devil, I was still at it two hours later. . . .

After living so long alone, and keeping my own counsel, it was extraordinary how badly I needed to talk. Perhaps there's something in the enforced gregariousness here that infects everyone who lives here! One is no longer an island ... everyone is interdependent, and even secrets are communal! Let's see, what *did* I tell him? Well, a bit of necessary background so he could understand – much more than I'd intended, in fact I was quite stricken when I heard it all coming out; but his silence, wreathed in pipe-smoke, was so magnetic it just drew the words out of me. My marriage (briefly), Jake's death (I wish I hadn't now, there's something sickening about a guilty woman parading her guilt as if asking people to deny it); something of the two years' fruitless marriage-therapy in Haifa, then the long empty struggle just to keep going, in Acco. Hanna – and the moment when I knew I could try again – that in fact I couldn't go on without trying again.

At that point the prevaricating had to start. I didn't want to bring Kofi into it at all, it seemed too risky; so I said that I'd seen the two children on a trip to one of the New Towns in the south, where a lot of new immigrants from North Africa were sent to settle. They'd been pointed out to me by a welfare worker who knew their circumstances and knew I wanted a child, and he had suggested that the grandmother (I kept her in) might be happy enough to let me have them. This was all more or less what I'd told the kibbutz in the first place; but now I was introducing the brother into the story for the first time. I said I'd only felt able to take the girl, and that the boy had stayed with his grandmother; but that now the grandmother, too, had died, and the boy had nowhere to go. I suddenly found myself embroidering it lavishly here by saying that the welfare worker was putting pressure on me – the girl was only with me 'on trial' so to speak, and if things didn't go well they could always take her away again; now they wanted me to take the boy too, and I was afraid. .... God forgive me, what a tissue of lies! But somehow it all came out so pat I almost convinced myself of the truth of it – due to Kofi's advice, I have been trying to *think* of Ella as a Jewish Moroccan orphan so as to maintain the fiction through thick and thin for her sake; but I was not aware that somehow I had become such a *detailed* liar that I could make up such a story! Dan, of course, hadn't the slightest doubt that it was all true. But what intrigues me now, writing twenty-four hours later, is the way I instinctively made out such a strong case for my taking the boy. It was almost as if I were trying to talk myself into it, deluding myself with this tear-jerking fabrication. ... I actually got myself quite worked up by the end, at the prospect of some cold-eyed government official coming stamping along to tear Ella away from me. ... I was almost waiting for Dan to say, 'You'd better take him if the alternative is losing Ella ...'

What he actually did say was, 'Have you seen him?'

'No,' I said, adding quickly, to bolster my lie: 'Except that once.'

'What impression did he make on you then?'

Caught. 'I didn't really pay much attention to him. I wasn't looking for anything as old as that, and in any case I wanted a girl.'

'Six isn't so very old.' He knocked out his pipe and sat looking at me steadily. 'Other things being equal, would you have liked another?'

'I don't know.'

'Because if so ... after all, they are brother and sister. Doesn't she miss him?'

'She did at first.'

'It might be a wonderful thing for her, to have him near her again.'

'Not if he's a thief and liar.'

He frowned. 'The welfare officer told you that?'

Caught, caught, caught! 'He did sort of hint that he had some pretty trying habits.'

'Could be just symptoms of insecurity, unhappiness ... almost certainly are.'

This was getting serious. He was beginning to sound as if the thing were not only a possibility, but desirable from all points of view.

'But what about the kibbutz? It never occurred to me for a moment that they might consider ...'

142

'Well, you know ... the kibbutz regards it as part of its duty to ... you've heard of Youth Aliya?' I nodded. 'Well, these two children, Ella and – what's his name, by the way?'

That was the worst moment of all. I nearly turned my brain inside out trying to think of a bible-name beginning with F. Why it had to begin with F I don't know. Anyway, either there aren't any or I've never heard of them, because after what seemed like an endless pause I suddenly said:

'Peretz.'

'Unusual name for an Oriental child.'

'Yes, isn't it? I thought so too.' I laughed self-consciously. (Maybe I'm not a natural-born liar, after all – I was hot and cold all over from the shock of that one. Where did 'Peretz' pop from? God knows.)

'Well, anyway ... children like these two, they're the sort that Youth Aliya deals with. And at a certain stage, the kibbutz takes groups of Youth Aliya children. We've reared two groups like that. Of course not every child is what you might call a success. Some drop out, some few we have to send away ... and some, good ones at that, leave in the end, but that doesn't count as failure because whatever happens after they leave here at least they've got a sound basis for their lives. If you ask me, it's one of the best justifications for existence the kibbutz has. ... Anyway ... if the kibbutz is prepared to take on a group of forty-odd deprived, maladjusted, wild – you should just see the way they reach us – you'd think nothing could ever be done with them – and they're all about twelve or older, well-set in their ways. "Trying habits" hardly describes most of them! A three-year-old and a six-year-old really can't seem insoluble problems after that.' He was filling his pipe again, not looking at me. 'If you want him – I'm saying *if*, because a lot of the responsibility, for love and so on, will be yours – a good argument you could put to the kibbutz would be that this very child might turn up at some kibbutz or other, years from now, when he's far worse and more difficult in every way, whereas if we took him on now ... everyone will be saved a lot of trouble ... and the boy a lot of misery. ...'

He spoke in a low, slow voice larded with thoughtful pauses.

I seemed to stop breathing in some of them. I was watching his face and finding it more and more attractive, brown and full of kind lines under the strange white hair. I was shocked to find I had stopped thinking about Faud, or why I had gone there. Now I wonder whether I really went about Faud in the first place. . . . My God! I do hope the female beast in me isn't going to rouse itself from its slumber with too much violence! There was a moment there when my hand started to move towards him by itself, the way it used to reach for the urchins in the market.

When I forced my mind roughly back to the subject at hand, it was to realize that all my reasons for refusing Kofi were being snatched away from me; or rather, not snatched but quietly, subtly removed. All but one. Did *I* want him? How on earth could I answer? Well, I could answer 'no' and finish with it, but somehow now I knew there was a possibility of my having him, my certainty was destroyed. To have a son again – a ready-made, sturdy little six-year-old – now, of course, I can't get the thought of it out of my head, and the desire to see him at least is growing to a point where I *know* I shan't be able to resist it.

Chapter 6

I've seen him. Dear loving God! What is the matter with me? I must be out of my mind! What sort of a bloody fool does a crazy thing like that and hopes to get away with it? I've seen him – I went, deliberately, of my own free will, *knowing* (oh yes, I must have known) the risk I was running, *needlessly*. ... The folly of it! The stupidity! I cannot blame Kofi or anyone else for this one, I walked into it and I bought it, and now I'm landed.

I've just re-read the last part of what I wrote before I went. It nearly made me throw up. 'A sturdy little son' indeed – Christ! Well, I've got my sturdy little son, in one fell swoop I've doubled my family, quadrupled my responsibilities, compounded my lies and the complications of my once simple life to a point where I feel I can hardly stand up under them. And why? Idle, idle, idiot curiosity. That's all it was. I simply wanted to see him. Could I *really* have kidded myself it was going to stop there?

He was playing in the alley outside Kofi's house. I knew at once who it was – he is like a better-developed male version of Ella. But here was no pathetic little hairless specimen, cowering under blankets and hiding its face. Here was a tough, independent, wiry little street-child; Ella's eyes in that surly face stared back at me boldly as I stopped in front of him.

'Are you Faud?'

'No.'

'Yes, you are.'

'I won't come! You go to hell!'

Thus our first conversation. His Hebrew was in its infancy, but he had learned the swearwords first. His mouth sneered defiantly; I remembered putting out my hand for Ella to 'smell' and thought that if I did the same thing now, I'd get it bitten. I don't like him, I thought. I don't want him. He's hard and he's nasty. I tried to feel relief, and wondered why I couldn't. The reason, I was soon to realize, was because I was already committed.

It can happen like that with a woman and child, just as with a man and woman. I didn't like him; I don't like him now. I'm afraid of him as a matter of fact. But I love him. Suddenly, as it should have happened with Ella and didn't, it happened between him and me.

There was nobody at home in the house, so I sat on the deep steps into the yard, with my back to the street, and waited. Faud had run off, but after a while I knew he was back. I could sense him watching me from around some corner. After a while I said over my shoulder, 'Faud, come here.'

'Go to hell.'

'I haven't come to take you away.'

'You're old and you'll die soon.'

'I want to talk to you.'

'I'll piss on you.'

I said, 'I know Fatma.'

There was a silence and then he appeared at my side, standing on the top step. His face had changed. He asked me something in Arabic. My incomprehension infuriated him and he began to clutch at my clothing, shaking me and shouting his question again and again.

'Softly, softly! Speak Hebrew,' I said, unloosing his grubby hands and holding them.

'Where is she?'

'In the kibbutz with me.'

'I want to go there!'

'We'll see.'

'Now! Now!'

'Faud, take it easy. I'm waiting for Kofi.'

He looked blank and I realized he didn't know him by that name. 'The master,' I said, using the all-embracing Hebrew word for boss, landlord, husband. . . . I pointed to the house. He at once began pulling me to my feet. 'He's there! He's there!' he

146

shouted, and tried to drag me along the alley in the direction of the market.

'We'll wait here,' I said.

We waited. Faud sat on the cobbles and stared at me fixedly. He has a crop of stiff, curly black hair; his skin is dark brown; his body is thin but very strongly-made. He already has several of his grown-up teeth, which make his mouth the most extravagant feature of his face. He has the beginning of a powerful, narrow jaw and a high-bridged semitic nose. While he sat there he picked it with a long, thin finger and watched me as a hawk watches a snake, uncertain whether it will attack or try to escape, and well-prepared to stop it either way.

At last Kofi turned the corner. He had aged in the two weeks since I saw him. His face was pale and he had lost weight – his clothes, shabbier-looking than ever, seemed to hang on him, or perhaps it was the loose, stooped carriage of his tired body. He carried his yellow shopping-bag of groceries as if it were full of rocks, and he stumbled twice on the jutting cobbles as he approached. His head was bent so that he didn't even see me until he nearly fell over me.

When the boy saw him in the archway he flew at him, shouting at him in a high-pitched, excited voice. Kofi put a hand on him and looked unbelievingly at me. There was a glow of naked hope in his face that I had to turn my eyes away from. He wasn't listening to Faud, but waiting for me to speak.

At last he interrupted the boy to say, 'You've changed your mind ...' In Hebrew, only the inflection tells the difference between a sentence and a question, and his was ambiguous. It was the inflection of a bursting hope.

'I – no. I only came to – '

'But you've told him! You told him about his sister! Why would you do that if you weren't meaning to – '

Taken aback by the obviousness of this, now I thought of it, I said: 'I just came to visit you. I didn't mean to – '

'I don't believe you, Gerda! Look at him! You couldn't be so cruel!'

The boy was jumping round us, forming a moving circle of noise.

'Well, we'll see – perhaps he could visit her –'

'Gerda, Gerda! You can't do that!'

'I can't even think with all this row going on!' I shouted at last, driven to exasperation by the boy's harsh cawing cries and my own confusion.

'Let's go inside.'

We went in. I could still have withdrawn at that point, but every moment that passed was making it more and more impossible. The boy was frantic with excitement. Kofi, also driven beyond patience, suddenly turned on him and told him to stay outside and keep quiet. He obeyed at once, possibly from surprise since I don't suppose Kofi has ever used that tone with him before. We went through into the big room and I sat down on one of the couches. Kofi sat opposite me, his big head hanging.

'Gerda. ... If you have not come to tell me you will take him, you shouldn't have come. The sight of you gave me such hope – I feel sick after it.'

'Has it been so bad?'

'You don't know. I've been so worried. I am not working. ... I missed a job because I had to stay at home with him. He threatened to go to the police because he was afraid I would take him back to his uncle. He's seen that I fear that, and now of course he will use the same threat to make me take him to see – Ella. I pretended not to know where she was. My only prayer was that you would change your mind somehow because otherwise I don't know what will come of all this.'

I didn't know what to say. 'How's Hanna?'

'That is almost the worst – they hate each other. She is mad with jealousy and they fight like wild animals – he is as strong as a young ape – he hurts her. I dare not leave them alone together. My house is a battle-ground. And Hanna is no longer Hanna ...'

'You call her by that name now!'

'It's a thing that happened – you did it, and she wanted it also from me. Things were good before this one came. He is so unhappy he – one cannot manage with him.'

'And you want to give him to me!'

He looked up at me – piteously, beseechingly. 'Gerda, believe me, it would be different in the kibbutz! He would have his sister and he would have you! And an atmosphere of – Gerda – there's still time for him – but let him stay here for a few years, months even, and he will be ruined for all his life. And what will he do to my daughter? Already in two weeks she is changed. He gives her no peace – '

'And does he lie? Does he steal?'

His head dropped low again. 'When I must go to the market or to see someone, he – I must lock him out of my house. I spend my days watching him. How can I go out to work? I have almost no money left.'

'Perhaps I can lend – '

'Gerda! Don't do that! Don't offer money. It's not money I need. You can do only one thing for me. Only one thing! Please! Take him!'

A shadow fell on the gloomy room. Faud was crouched by the window in the street outside, his hands round the bars, peering in. We both looked through at him, then back at each other.

'You saw how he was when I came back,' said Kofi quietly. 'That is the first time I have ever seen him behave like a normal boy. "I'm going to see Fatma!" he kept shouting – '

'All right!' I said suddenly. 'He wants to go. You want him to go. And what happens if I take him? He's only six – '

'He is nearer seven, I think. He is very independent for his age and very intelligent – '

'Kofi, I'm not *buying* him! Is he "intelligent" enough to remember all that he will have to remember? That his name isn't Faud, that her name isn't Fatma, that he's a Jewish boy from Kiryat Gat whose parents came from Morocco? You realize what will happen if the kibbutz finds out the truth?'

'You may believe this or not,' he said slowly. 'When he first came here I told him that he must pretend to come from – a certain place – where he does not come from. That he must not tell anyone about his uncle or his grandmother or his sister. That he must pretend *I* am his relative. He has done all this; I know it because I have listened to him talking to children in the street when he didn't know I was there. There are,' he said with a flicker of a smile, 'some advantages to being a liar. Lies become more real than truth, and easier to stick to.'

The boy's shadow lay across us like a prophecy. I felt his eyes on me; they seemed to burn like the eyes of a witch affixing a curse.

I went to see Michael that evening. I repeated my lying tale, but with great conviction this time because I am possessed by that boy and I have to have him. My room is wholly, unspeakably empty – crowded with the absence of Ella – and I have to fill it again with this sharply de-sentimentalized creation of mine called Peretz. Michael threw up his hands and clutched his hair with them.

'My dear girl! You know I'm for you, I want you here, but I won't say it was easy to get you in with just the little girl. There's an Opposition even in a kibbutz, you know!'

'Have I "enemies" already?'

'You have opponents. It's nothing personal. All the old arguments. We've got our own troubles without importing any. A single woman always means trouble. Etcetera, etcetera.'

'But that was before I came.'

'Yes, well, even since.' He coughed. 'Things haven't exactly been plain sailing with Ella in the children's house you know. You don't hear everything that happens.'

I felt suddenly furious. 'And why don't I? I want to hear everything? She's mine, isn't she? I want to know all about her!'

'Oh, the housemothers don't tell the parents every little thing – it's accepted procedure; they act as filters, letting through only what's pleasing or what's necessary. Otherwise the mothers would drive them mad.'

'Oh yes, I'm sure the mothers are a great nuisance! Well, we'll see who'll go mad if I find out important things have been happening with Ella, or to her, that I haven't been let in on!'

'Look, don't get worked up. Take it from me, this system works. It may have flaws like any other, but in the long run the children generally turn out pretty well. We've raised three and I won't say there haven't been heart-aches, but on the whole we're pretty satisfied.'

'Yes. Now, about the boy – '

'Well, *I* can't tell you to go ahead and bring him. I'll have to bring it to the central committee first, and then to the General Meeting – '

'Michael, it's very urgent! He can't stay where he is. Couldn't I – isn't there some way I could have him here as my guest until you make up your minds?'

He looked at me very straight. 'And what about work?' I had no answer. 'You wouldn't be able to work while he was here, would you? And if he were accepted, you'd have to take a long time – maybe months – to settle him in, like you did with Ella.'

It was true. The awful thing is that the kibbutz made so little fuss, and brought so little pressure to bear on me to start work or rush the process of acclimatizing Ella, that I suppose I'd simply been taking it for granted that they would do the same again. But how could they? And why should they anyway, if it came to that?

What could I say? 'I'm ashamed to ask it. I'll work myself into the ground afterwards to make up for it. Only try for me, Michael! Please try! I want him so badly.' My voice sounded to me just like Kofi's had when he was humbly pleading with me.

Michael put his hands across his small paunch and regarded me with a mixture of sympathy and doubt.

'You're sure you really want to stay here? I mean, you sometimes give the impression that you're not – you know, not 100 *per cent* in favour of communal education.'

There was a difficult silence.

'Does one have to be – 100 per cent in favour?' I asked at last. 'Won't, say, 85 per cent do?'

'Rather depends on the – er, the *vigour* of the other 15 per cent. You know, whether it expresses itself more violently, proportionately, than the – perhaps rather passive – 85 per cent. If you understand me.'

'You mean like just now, about the housemother's not telling – '

'Exactly. That was part of the 15 per cent, but a – er – casual observer might have thought from the excitement it caused that it accounted for a higher percentage.'

'All this isn't a joke, is it?'

'Not really. Because you see, a member can get away with all sorts of criticism and grumbling and temperaments, she might even get things changed, but a stranger – if you'll excuse me – who's only just arrived, who starts making a lot of fuss, well, the attitude towards her is likely to be, if she doesn't like our way of doing things, you know, why doesn't she go somewhere else?'

'Yes. I see.'

'You don't mind my mentioning it, do you?'

'Have I been doing this a lot?'

'Well . . . I've talked to a few people . . . you know how things get about . . . especially in the *communa*. Some of the women there seem to have got the impression that you're not very satisfied – '

'I've scarcely opened my mouth in there!'

'And Rifka feels you – well, that you rather take her for granted. A bit like a hired girl, you know? You come in and take Ella whenever you feel like it, without warning her; sometimes you simply take her off out of the yard and Rifka doesn't know where she's gone. And she's really doing her best to fit Ella in, you know. It's not an easy thing, when a group's been together since they were born, to – '

'But Michael, I swear I don't – '

'No, well, there are always two sides to these things. That's just her *feeling*. It's very natural if you resent her a bit. After all, she is *with* Ella more than you are – '

Suddenly the old, helpless tearfulness came over me; it was true – I did resent Rifka since Ella began spending most of her time there. I felt shut out – Ella had begun to talk about her a lot. 'Rifka says' and 'Rifka does' and 'Rifka's pretty' and 'Rifka's sweet'. . . . I had almost stopped saying 'Shalom' to her myself, I suddenly realized. How stupid to pretend to myself, to think she wouldn't notice! How damned ungrateful, just because *I* wanted to do the rehabilitating myself! I lowered my eyes and hoped Michael wouldn't notice that idiot tears had come into them.

'Thank you for telling me. I'll try to be more – friendly.'

'I'm glad you take it like that. Ah, here's Gila! Stay and have coffee with us.'

'No, thank you, I must get home.' I stood up, managing to smile at Michael's wife who had just come in. At the door I stopped. It was as if that taut, angry little figure stood in my way and said *But you haven't settled about me yet.* I turned.

'About the boy.'

'Oh yes. Well, I'll bring it up at the meeting tomorrow evening.'

And now it's 'tomorrow evening' and I'm writing all this while this vital meeting is in progress. Before my life-and-death question can be raised there will be many other things to discuss – the building of a new children's house, the setting up of a committee to inquire into possible industries, the question of whether to start a new 'branch' of tomatoes, the buying of a new tractor, a student group arriving next month for the summer season. ... All so much more important. Knowing how they talk, they probably won't even get around to me. And meanwhile every day that passes is like a piece nibbled off Kofi and Hanna by Faud, who in his turn is being slowly corroded by having no fixed place, no fixed person. And I – I am – how can one say it? 'in love' is the only phrase which expresses it, but that is ludicrously the wrong one. He belongs with me, and he knows it and I know it, and no amount of logic or rationalizing will change it.

If the kibbutz won't accept him, I will leave with Ella. We'll manage somehow. ... It's eleven o'clock. I'm going to Michael's to see if the meeting's over yet.

Chapter 7

Peretz is asleep at long last, and I have a moment, a rare and precious moment to myself before, I, too, fall asleep from sheer exhaustion. Today is my fortieth birthday; I feel a hundred and five.

Ella was nothing – an angel, an invisible child – compared to this one. Useless to upbraid myself with phrases like 'You should have realized' and 'You knew it all the time'. I did – and yet I didn't; to foresee a thing in theory is drastically different from tolerating and coping with it in reality.

Yet somehow, although he is twenty times more difficult, more taxing, more infuriating, although I am driven to distraction by him for twelve hours out of every twenty-four, I have only once so far (in the three weeks I've had him) become as *submerged* emotionally as I was during that terrible time with Ella. Perhaps my experiences with her have helped me, although the problems were so different, to keep a sense of proportion with him. Or perhaps – and this is a hard thing to face – that sudden, irrational 'in-loveness' which took possession of me the first time I saw him, has helped to make everything bearable, just as one can endure every sort of behaviour from a man one is in love with, even if none too easily.

(In this connection – and in definite parenthesis – I have decided to stop hiding from myself the fact that I have taken a mild header for Dan. It is not important and it will not last; nor is it doing anyone the least harm. Even I am too occupied to suffer any great torments over it. But it is there, and I prefer to bring it out in the open with myself. As a matter of fact I think it's very good for me. It is therapeutic to know that I *can* feel this – really, I must admit, rather high-school-girlish – ga-ga feeling still. It's lucky it has no outlet, or I should probably make a complete fool of myself – it's that kind of 'thing', rather romantic, fluttery and juvenile. It's like having one's capacity for love resuscitated and having to begin with it all over again from a state of immaturity. Never mind. *It* may be immature, but *I* am not, and I can keep an eye on it and see that it doesn't get out of hand.)

The kibbutz accepted 'Peretz' on trial, on condition that I did my best to speed rather than delay his absorption by his 'group', and that I 'cooperated in every way' with his housemother and teacher. So much for the general view of the way I've behaved about Ella, but so overwhelmed was I with gratitude that they accepted him at all that I agreed to everything and couldn't even feel offended at the implied rebuke. As a start I talked things over with his housemother, who happens to be Michael's wife Gila. She is quite a different kettle of fish from Rifka – a woman of my own age, with ten years' experience; yet even she, tottering away after spending an afternoon in my room discreetly 'observing', whispered: 'I'm shaking in my shoes. We've never had anything like this before.'

He has some bottomless source of energy which doesn't dry up until any three other children would have dropped in their tracks. And the uses he puts it to make it impossible to take one's eyes off him. At first I wanted him to understand that I considered him trustworthy. Being locked out of his own home, it seemed to me, could do nothing but harm, and likewise being followed about, obviously to see that he didn't misbehave, must also madden him at a time when he was warily getting his bearings. I decided just to be around for him when he needed me, and to make my surveillance and disciplining as subtle and unrestrictive as possible.

This worthy resolve lasted a little less than four days. Since then I have scarcely dared let him out of my sight, though he occasionally still manages to escape; and as for restrictions, several people have grimly suggested that I might even try chaining him up to a tree – on a very short chain, or he might destroy the tree.

Despite my most strenuous efforts, he has contrived so far to commit an extraordinary number and variety of crimes, from the affrighting of the entire flock of sheep – with a subsequent sizeable milk-loss and two prematurely-dropped lambs – to the destruction of a member's garden. This contained a valuable and cherished cactus-plant ten feet high for whose bi-annual nocturnal blooms its proud owner erected special lighting-effects. Peretz carefully hacked this down at the roots with a blunt knife and then ran to me with a martyred expression saying he'd got spikes in his hands from picking sabra-fruits.

A rash of petty thefts has occurred. He is not fussy what he takes; like a magpie, all is grist to his mill: garden tools, bathing caps, children's slippers, teapots, toys, pails, potted house-plants; once he brought home a brassiere he'd found on some-one's drying-frame, and another time he robbed a hapless dog of its collar and bowl. Of course I was almost blasé during the poor psychiatrist's routine text-book explanation for all this – need for security, love-substitutes, etc. etc. etc. I just wish she'd tell it all to the victims, though I must say an astonishing number have been extremely understanding about it. And at least people know where to apply when they find their porches stripped. So far – thank God – he hasn't ventured into any of the rooms: that seems to be his criterion of fair game – anything which is not behind a door. He may be a thief, but at least he's not a burglar!

But the worst thing he does, and I include the time he blacked out the entire kibbutz by cutting a vital wire from the gener-ator-hut, is to get involved in the most ruthless and bloody fights with the other children. Like Ella, he knows no fear of his contemporaries, but unlike her he is a match for all of them in strength, toughness and underhand battle-tactics. And he always starts it. They don't even have to annoy him – in fact none of them would have dared to after the first couple of fights he had (he actually knocked an eight-year-old out cold the third day he was here by hitting him over the head with a broom-handle). He will be walking quite demurely along a path past a children's house, and suddenly he will turn aside to fall on some luckless boy and begin silently beating hell out of him. The kids here constantly fight among themselves, but nothing on this level – this is street-fighting, with no holds barred and no quarter asked or given. Shrieks rend the air; adults come running; the two are pulled apart; I am the butt of bitter looks from the rescuer, and I haul the villain away to catechise him privately: 'Why did you do that?' 'I felt like it.' 'But he hadn't done anything to you!' 'I hate him, he's a pig.' 'You don't even know him!' 'If he starts with me tomorrow, he'll get it on his head. I'll kill him, I'll break down his house. I'll cut his peepee off. *I'll cut his mother up! I'll cut his father up!*' At this point the whole thing becomes so sad I can't say any more, except to dry his sudden furious tears and say 'Try not to hate them, it doesn't help. Come home and have some food' – food having the same magic properties for him as for Ella, though she has become quite world-weary about it after so long of having enough.

But it's his attitude towards Ella that is the only truly baffling thing. After nearly going mad with excitement at the prospect of seeing each other again, when they met – the day I brought him here for the first time – they simply stood, far apart, gazing at each other, like two strange dogs, and since then he has hardly spoken a word to her. He understands that they both have new names and mustn't use the old – even she understands this, though she slips occasionally. I thought perhaps this business of them being 'different people' might be a barrier between them which obviously time would have broken down; but it can't be that. When Ella comes home for tea in the afternoon and finds him in the room, there is an atmosphere from both of them that one can only compare to animals of alien species shut up in the same cage. Once and only once she tried to hug him, but he pushed her off quite roughly, and when I went to pick her up and told him off, he went out, slamming the door violently, and didn't come back until nightfall (that was the day he cut the cactus down). The next day, *she* didn't come home at tea-time, and when I went to the gan to fetch her Rifka said she was refusing to go. I brought her none the less, but arrived back to find *he'd* flown the coop again. When he finally came back, I asked him straight out:

'Don't you like your sister any more?'

'No.'

'But why?'

'I don't know.'

Is it that she looks different, with her new fleece and her added layer of healthy fat? Is it that he resents sharing me with her? Or is it, as the psychologist suggests, that the actual sight of each other reminds them both of a life and people they would rather forget?

In Ella's case, I believe the cause of her antagonism is simple jealousy. Until Peretz came, I was hers alone; now she knows that I belong to him, too. The climax came quite early on, when I still had hopes that the rift, whatever it was, would heal quickly. They had been playing in separate corners of the room, ignoring each other. If Ella approached me Peretz would begin throwing things violently at the wall; if I went near Peretz, Ella would rush at me and try to pull me away. However, it was the first time he had consented to stay at home at tea-time, the first time they had been together in my room for more than a minute, and I was full of hope. At seven o'clock I got ready to take Ella back to the children's house, something she hasn't objected to since she first began to sleep there – she's far too happy there now to mind being taken back. But now she suddenly balked at the door, and pointed at Peretz, still playing with his tractor on the floor.

'Why isn't *he* coming?'

'He doesn't go to bed yet because he's older,' I hedged.

She thought about this, her black eyes staring into mine. At last she asked the question I had been dreading, though the intelligence it showed would otherwise have given me acute pleasure.

'How many beds has he got?'

'Just one, like you.'

'I've got two.'

'No ... You just have one now, the one at the gan.'

She looked round the room. She had been with us when we transferred her cot permanently to the children's house, but now suddenly she behaved as if I had whisked it away surreptitiously.

'It was here, my bed was here!' she cried, pointing to the

place where it had stood, now occupied by Peretz's camp-bed. She flung herself on this face down and clung to the wooden edges. 'This is my bed! This is my bed!'

Peretz stood up slowly and started to move towards her. I caught him by the back of the shirt, but he pulled away and in a flashing second he was on her. He had her off that bed and on the floor before I could reach them. Then, struggling in my arms, he shrieked at her: 'Don't you touch my bed, you pig, you dirty pig!' I hadn't realized how much Arabic I had picked up, living in Acco all those months; I understood that perfectly.

She stood up and came at him like a mad thing, pulling and tearing. I had to drag him away and shut him in the bathroom. He pounded the door and shrieked: 'Don't you let her on my bed! I'll tell the police! I'll cut you up!'

Ella was clinging to me like a spider-monkey, arms and legs wrapping me round, weeping violently. I picked her up and tried to calm her through the racket. 'It's my bed, it's my bed! You gave him my bed!' she kept sobbing. She beat my shoulder with one hand and clung round my neck with the other. Through the door came the sound of more sobbing, mingled with the filthiest, most heartrending abuse.

It was at this moment, suddenly, that I really came to grips with what all this means to me. The hard, protective, scaly shell broke and fell away, leaving me all mucous-membrane, exposed, defenceless, quivering. I nearly cried out at the pain those two children were inflicting – every sob and every word from both of them was like a blade sliding into that pink palpitating mass that was myself without the shell. I looked ahead into the future and I wanted to die right then, it was like looking forward to endless torture. Must I now accept again that when you love a child you feel its sufferings, even the senseless, unnecessary ones, in the flesh of your own heart and body? Yes, I remembered acutely, it is so, it was so with Jake and it will be so with these. Was this what I had wanted? Was this anguish what I had so hungrily believed I couldn't live without?

I somehow pressed down the raw fear in my brain and carried Ella back to her gan, talking to her all the way, telling her that soon Peretz too would be living with the other children,

159

that she had slept with me when she first came and so must he, that I loved her, loved her, loved her. . . . She wept quietly into my neck. I put her into Rifka's arms, unable to look into her red, wet face. 'I'll come back when you're in bed and kiss you goodnight,' I said.

'Go away!' she shouted suddenly. 'I don't want you!'

I went home through the twilight, cringing with hurt.

All was quiet in the shower-room. I unlocked the door. Peretz was sitting on the lid of the lavatory. As soon as the door was open he made a lightning dive, but I caught him and held tight. It was only then I noticed the broken glass on the floor – he had managed to smash the mirror and the shelf above the sink, plus a bottle of bleach. His foot was bleeding. Wordlessly I hiked him through into the room and sat him on the floor. Not for the first time, I felt acutely the lack of communications between adults and children, compounded for us by his limited knowledge of Hebrew.

'Now you listen,' I said, and stopped. I was bursting with things to say but I felt none of them would reach him.

'What do you think I'm going to do now?' I asked him.

'Hit me.'

'No. I'm going to wash your foot and your face and hands and then we're going to supper in the dining-room. After that you're going to bed early and I don't want to hear any more from you till morning.'

He let me wash him and sat watching me covertly while I swept up the glass. Then I combed his hair with a trembling hand but a calm face and we walked side by side through the fading light to the dining-room. He ate almost nothing, just sat staring at his plate. I made a sandwich for him and we walked back again.

'Now,' I said. 'You get undressed and into bed. I'm going to say goodnight to your sister. Then I'm coming back here, and I expect to find you in bed.'

His voice stopped me at the door.

'Send her back.'

'What?'

'Send her back to grandmother.'

160

I stood staring at him.

'We don't want her,' he said coaxingly. 'What do we want her for? She's only a girl.'

'But I want her.'

'Why? You've got me now.' He sounded very persuasive and reasonable.

'I want you both.'

He looked at me, hope draining from his face.

At the gan, Ella turned her face to the wall and wouldn't look at me or speak to me. 'Jealous,' whispered Rifka. 'It's quite natural. She'll get over it. Don't get hurt by it, that's the thing. If they see they can hurt you, *oy-v'voy* to you! They'll punish you like little tyrants.'

When I got home again, Peretz had vanished. I went out, torch in hand, to look for him, and found him at last, a desperate hour later, throwing stones at the hens in the children's farm – their unseasonable uproar had brought me to them. One of them lay still, its head a bloody pulp. Several more were squawking with pain and dragging bruised wings or feet.

He made no effort to escape, just kept throwing stones from his pile till the last moment, harder and more viciously with each running step I took towards him. Can I now write in one sentence that his cruelty so appalled me that the sight pushed me beyond control – and that when I caught hold of him I slapped him until my arm was tired? I'm well and guiltily aware of the paradox. I held him by the arm and smacked his bare legs again and again. It was clearly what he had wanted, for it gave him the excuse to fight back at me; I got the worst of it, for he scratched, bit and punched, but I was so wild with fury that I didn't feel the stings until later. I don't think he felt my slaps either. We stopped suddenly, by some sort of mutual impulse, and stared at each other through the semi-darkness, our breath coming fast like boxers breaking out of a clinch.

'I hate you,' he said at last.

So far had I degraded myself by losing my temper that I had to catch myself on the point of saying 'I hate you too, you little savage!' It was the hate which is the reverse side of love, but it was hate all right.

Anyway, thank God I didn't say it. I took his wrist and more or less dragged him home, sick and shaking with shame and fury. I locked the door from the inside and hid the key. When I turned round, to my utter astonishment I saw that he had climbed into *my* bed.

'What are you doing there?' I asked him.

'I want to sleep here.'

'Sorry, nothing doing. You've got your own bed.'

'I want to sleep in yours.'

'All right then, I'll sleep in yours.'

He looked baffled. I sat down on his bed and began to take my shoes off. He instantly left my bed, ran over and got into his own. I went to mine without another word.

Chapter 8

This ridiculous business with Dan is beginning to cut across my absorption with the children. The trouble is, it's begun to 'develop' – I mean in the sense that I begin to think he is also interested in me.

It's again the height of summer. How incredible it seems that I began these diaries less than a year ago – looking at the early pages now I blush and squirm; my only respite is imagining they were written by someone else, which is relatively easy since I don't often recognize my present 'self' in those outpourings of self-pity and grovelling misery. Life has utterly changed, not only its course but its flavour, even its very nature. Can I call myself happy now? Not exactly, I am too full of anxieties, there are too many petty annoyances, hours of boredom interlarded with hours of fulfilment and tension ... and then there is the complication of Dan.

At first it seemed simple. I had been man-starved, and sex-starved, and here on my doorstep was an attractive male with what Judy used to call 'all the makin's' – from the essential crudities of physical appeal to the subtler charms of a quiet manner, kindness, a feeling of containment and control. . . . As I told myself at the beginning, it was natural that I should 'want' him in the most obvious and uncomplicated way. But, as I remember from my early days, one can 'want' a certain man and be well aware of wanting him, without having the least intention of doing anything about it. After all, he is married, and to a woman who, however irritating I frequently find her, has been very kind to me, and done more than anyone else here to help me through my kibbutz teething-time. So far as I can see, she and Dan are happy together. Apart from that, there could hardly be any question of an affair in any place as confined as a kibbutz (though I understand it can be managed!) I am not yet any too popular (I still have occasional outbursts and the children are still causing endless problems) – all that is really needed to kill stone dead any chance I have of a reasonable social life here is for me to start something with a married founder member.

All this reasoning, of course, is so obvious that I didn't even think about it, until I began to realize that there is something doing on the other end of the wire. Love is a two-way current ... and certain 'charges' are unmistakably coming through.

For instance, there was the Night of the Battle; that was the first indication of something more than friendly sympathy from him. To lead up to this climactic Black Friday I should say that getting Peretz moved into his children's house was not the straightforward matter it was with Ella, when really only I suffered. To begin with, when he got the idea that the arrangement whereby he slept in my room with me was not a permanent one, he made it very clear that he had no intention of ever moving out; nor would he consent to spend even the few 'bridging' hours a day with his group.

Deadlock. To make matters worse, I had promised Ella that Peretz would soon be living somewhere else, on the same footing as herself, and as the weeks went by and he was still here she grew more and more wretched: she regressed right back to the bottle-stage, began wetting herself, refused to eat ... whenever she saw me she either clung to me tearfully or pretended not to see me at all. All this time I was becoming more and more embarrassed by the fact that I was doing nothing to earn my keep; but it was no good worrying about that – Peretz still needed constant watching.

Finally I began to think that I was actually, subconsciously, favouring Peretz over Ella by letting him stay on with me despite the effect it was having on her. I had conference after conference with all sorts of people – the overworked psychologist, of course; Rifka and Gila; and a very nice woman who is the kibbutz expert on educational problems ('education' in the kibbutz sense begins at birth). The general consensus seemed to be that Peretz was stronger, constitutionally and emotionally, than Ella, and that in fact once the move was brought about he would probably adjust to it quite quickly, whatever ructions there might be in the beginning. Thus I was advised to take a firm line, and action-stations were called.

None too soon. The very night before I'd decided to tell him, I was awakend by the most hideous shrieking and threshing sounds. The shock was terrific; I thought two large dogs were fighting to the death in my room. I groped for the light, and saw the two of them, Peretz and Ella, locked in combat on the floor, rolling over and back, clawing, pummelling, pulling, biting. . . . Oddly, Peretz was losing at that stage, since Ella had had the advantage of surprise. She had come creeping into the room (which for once I had forgotten to lock) and fallen on the sleeping Peretz with fell intent, quite ready to kill him apparently. . . . I dragged them apart, but both were so aroused to fury and bloodshed by this time I couldn't have held them apart for long alone. Thank God, Dan happened to be on nightwatch. He had noticed, on his rounds, that Ella's bed was empty, and had come straight along to see if she had come to me. He burst in and collared Peretz.

We stood at opposite sides of the room, each holding a child. The children struggled in our arms and glared silently at each other. I could feel Ella's misery, the desperation in every twisting muscle. . . . In that moment I felt sure I had been shamefully wrong to bring Peretz; my oft-repeated bleat 'I should have known!' rang in my head. My own selfish wish had dictated what I'd done – and here was the result. I looked at Dan beseechingly, for I had not the remotest idea what I should do next, torn as I was by two desperate and apparently conflicting needs.

'Take her back to her bed,' he said to me in English.

'In this state? I can't!'

'You must. If you let her stay now, you'll never get her back at all.'

'And him?'

'I'll have a talk to him while you're gone.'

As I was going out of the door, he said softly, 'Don't be angry with her. She couldn't help it.'

'I know.'

I walked back to the gan through the quiet darkness, carrying Ella now limp and trembling, closely in my arms. An owl swooped overhead, showing its white underparts, and a silver moth dropped through the lamplight like a falling star. The pepper-trees moved their fronds in whispers near my shoulders, brushing Ella's new, shining fuzz. I talked to her crooningly, meaningless soft syllables to soothe her. At the gan I sat down with her in my lap and gave her a drink of milk.

'You go to sleep now, and no more bad dreams. All right?'

Her head sagged against me; her eyes were closing.

'Was I a bad girl?' she asked. 'Was that why you sent me away?'

How children hurt! For a minute the pain was so sharp I looked down into her little brown face and saw Jake.

'You're a very good girl and I love you. I didn't send you away. You sleep here because all the kibbutz children sleep in their gans.'

'But not *him*.'

'He will soon.'

'You said that before, but he's still there,' she mumbled pathetically.

'Very soon now he'll live in a gan just like you.'

She fell asleep before I could even get her into her cot. I spoke to the woman night-watch over the intercom connected to the baby-house, and asked her to come and look at her from time to time.

Then I went home. Dan was standing in the shadow of the porch, his hands in his pockets, his pipe sending a quiet curl of smoke out into the moonlight.

'Nu?' I whispered through the placid chirp of the crickets.

'Fast asleep.'

'Did you talk to him?'

'Yes. But he was probably too sleepy to understand.'

'What did you say?'

'I told him he's a big boy now, and that if Ron and Dubi sleep away from their parents, didn't he think he could?'

'And?'

'Oh, no answer ... dropped off to sleep like a stone falling down a well.'

Suddenly I was so unhappy I felt my throat stiffen with tears. Now I would have to 'banish' this beloved demon – to a houseful of children he hates and has given reason to hate him; he has no relationship with his sister any more, and now wouldn't he think I'd betrayed him too? I leant against the wall and covered my face.

Dan watched me shaking with silent weeping and finally said, 'Tell me. Why did you really start with these children – with all this? You don't seem to have looked ahead at all before you began.'

This reproach only made me more miserable. I began to sob out muffled half-sentences – 'It wasn't real to me – really – just a sort of outlet for the emotions, something to – dream about – until I saw Ella. She was so ... you couldn't imagine any child who – *needed* more – more care, more love – and I wanted her for that, to be needed, to be – depended on. With him it was different. ... I loved him from the beginning – when I first saw him I had to have him. And by that time, Ella was – part of me, so *he* had to be added. And now – they're oil and water – and he's a menace – and here I am, alone in this place, living on charity no matter what anyone says, getting through to them one after the other and then having to part with them – and when it's done I shall be alone completely in this – foreign life. I can't, Dan, I can't! I've bitten off too much and it's choking me ...'

And suchlike self-pitying maunderings. One would really have thought me in the last stage of maudlin drunkenness, and Dan just stood there listening to all this and undoubtedly thinking me utterly contemptible, but it seems there is something about a helpless stupid woman which brings out the protector and the comforter in men of his sort, because suddenly I felt his arm around me. Of course in my low and weakened state I couldn't have asked for anything more desirable. I clutched him in the darkness and hung on like a drowner, both arms wrapped round his waist and my head on his shoulder ... he seemed to like it ... he kissed me, the idiot ... what a pair of fools! My blood runs hot when I remember it, but at the same time I can't help feeling a little contemptuous. And this is something very new for me, this double-image of a man both desired and despised for desiring me. He should have pushed me off to bed and told me to behave myself instead of encouraging me. ... Fantastic! I'm forty years of age and I still expect men to protect me from my own lack of sense and self-control!

We stood there embracing in the shadow of the porch ... my body flared up like molten glass so that I hardly knew what I was doing, yet my brain ticked coldly on, waiting for *him* to call a halt to it – and at the same time triumphantly registering that the frozen carcase was thawing, had thawed, was still filled with hot beating blood. I stopped first in the end, pulling away, legs trembling with the need to give way and let me sink down under him, yet mind filled with impatience and anger that *I* had had to take command.

I lay awake for an hour, muddled, wretched, frightened, my body screaming for satisfaction as it hasn't for God knows how many long years. How easy it is to use that alone as a justification for everything! I remember all the emotional sequences of my 'maidenhood' – I want him – I may never want again like this – one mustn't waste chances ... the body has its own reasoning and rationalizing equipment – and the mind keeps functioning separately, but feebly, crackling out the truth in the background like an old radio with weakening batteries, drowned by the blare of the sensual trumpets. At least I am *writing* the truth ... but every night since then I have waited for him to come, furious, relieved and half-mad that he never does.

Chapter 9

The difficulty with writing only for oneself is to avoid the self-pity that goes on in one's head and forces itself into the writing-hand to be expressed; it would be easy to disguise it if one knew that someone were reading over one's shoulder. It is like being brave when people are watching, and failing to be brave alone. I can't be brave any more, I must say it – this is the lowest, the most miserable and wretched, that I have been at any time during the past few years. Incredible as that seems, it is true.

Where to begin? Peretz has been swallowed – that is the only way to say what I feel – by Gila and his 'group', may they all rot. ... Oh God forgive me, why can't I feel the gratitude they deserve – 'absorbed' is the word they use here, and when I hear it I see images of a giant sponge sucking Peretz in through one of its wet gaping holes, or a fissure in the earth, closing over his head forever. ... It is all wrong, and I know it, for me to feel this way – they have done everything to help him, and if they have not been able to help *me* it's because I haven't helped myself to bear it, to adjust to it. ... He was so sweet those last few days, after the fight ... it was as if he knew at last that we were partners, believers in one another ... the tension broke, I unlocked the door, he ran where he liked, and came back grinning, his hands empty of 'love-substitutes', to take me to see some wonder he had found. ... It was so miraculous and perfect a sudden relationship that I did not see what had caused it, I looked for no cause, I only leapt like a happy suicide into the destroying pleasure of it. Now I see that it was all so that I shouldn't send him away. And I – I was deluded into thinking everything would be all right now, that the tide had turned as it did with Ella, and that he had recovered a normal balance and would adjust 'sensibly' to the move.

I spoke of it to him once or twice during those short, staggeringly happy days, but he said nothing, he ignored me as if I hadn't spoken, or turned his newly opened face to me to pour out some story of confidence. ... I let myself think he had understood and accepted it ... the others – those all-wise, all experienced Others – told me the time was right, that he had 'focused' on me and that it would be quite 'safe' to move him over. I agreed to it ...

I took him there one hot morning. His bed was waiting, and there was a bed there for me as well. The children, on their best behaviour, primed by a smiling Gila, clustered round to make him welcome. In his new out-goingness he reacted well at first, playing and laughing with them. ... Gila took them all up to the pool, and I, for the first time, went too.

This had all been planned like a military operation, so I was not taken short in the matter of a bathing-suit – the communa had supplied me with one. While I changed in the women's changing-room I could hear Peretz' high-pitched laughter from the other, and one boy asking 'Can your mother swim?' and he saying carelessly, 'Of course – *and* dive – *and* pick up things from the bottom.' Fear shrank my skin for a moment, but then I thought: 'What am I afraid of? I *can* do all those things. Swimming is like riding a bicycle ... you never forget ...' I looked at myself in the mirror; I have put on weight, but children don't notice those things and I was still less bulging than most.

I stood by the edge of the pool; I trembled ludicrously, as if the shining surface hid monsters. I really did have a momentary illusion that there were thick weeds at the bottom waiting to entangle me. I don't think I would ever have made it, except that Peretz and his cronies suddenly appeared on the opposite edge and stood there, waiting. I met Peretz' eye. He grimaced involuntarily as if to say 'Come *on*!' I caught my breath high in my nose and dived.

The acquamarine water of the pool received me beatifically as I broke its surface with my hands – it ran over me like cold fire, enclosing my feet last and burbling tenderly in my ears. It seemed a hundred thousand years since I had last enjoyed this delight of delights; my body went a little mad. I found myself plunging and surfacing like a porpoise, twisting and turning. . . . I had no cap and I could feel the air from my lungs streaming up past my eyes and forehead and racing through my hair – a child's fingers and palms, patting, tugging . . .

Through refracting eyelashes I could see 'the group' jumping and shouting on the edge. 'He's proud of me,' I dared to think. I am crying now as I write this . . .

Afterwards we all walked back down the hill together, the children full of excited energy, squabbling over the tricycles. Peretz kept running to me about this and that – 'I swam three strokes – I can turn upside down under the water – did you see me jump in? Can I have a tricycle?' I said yes, his tricycle was coming to the gan next week with the lorry. I stressed the words 'to the gan' but I couldn't tell whether he had taken them in or not. My heart began to hammer as we approached the gan. Could it be that all would go smoothly? Gila winked at me reassuringly as they all rushed up the steps. Lunch was laid out ready: 'Can I eat here?' 'Yes – this is your plate.' He stopped for a moment. 'But how did you know?' 'I guessed.'

He sat down to eat. He was quieter now. He kept glancing up at me, quick little looks under his black brows as if to make sure I had not disappeared. Once when I stood up experimentally he dropped everything and stood up too. A look passed between us which I didn't want to understand. I sat again and so did he.

After lunch he came to me and pulled my arm. 'Let's go home now.'

'Wouldn't you like to stay here and take your rest with the others?'

'No.'

'Well, look, Peretz. The thing is, I'm going in to Acco this afternoon – '

'I want to come!'

'Not this time.'

'But I want to!'

'No, darling. I'm sorry. I have to do some business. You stay here with the others.'

He took hold of me with both hands and began to take deep, whistling breaths.

'You're not going to come back!'

I managed to laugh. 'You're crazy. Of course I am! I'll be here to get you at tea-time. I'll bring you some ice-cream from town – '

He gripped my clothes and took a step nearer to me. He laid his head hard against the side of my leg. The whistling breaths went on. The room was very quiet; all the other children were watching. I looked desperately at Gila.

'Peretz – you just come through here and see the canaries – '

A sudden sharp movement, as he threw both arms round my thighs, was the only answer.

I shook my head at her – 'I can't do it – ' But she shook hers back – 'You must.' She came to him and detached him from me gently. 'Peretz, Mummy won't go to Acco today if you don't want her to. She'll stay here with you.'

'I want to go home.'

'No, I wouldn't do that. We don't go home at this time. We go home at four o'clock.'

'I want to go now!'

She was crouching level with him, holding his shoulders. She shook her head at him. 'Not now, Peretz. Later.'

He looked up at me. His eyes were bursting to shed tears; his jaw muscles stuck out with the effort of holding them. 'And tonight?'

'Tonight you'll sleep here, and Mummy will sleep here with you.'

'Always? Will she sleep here always?'

'As long as you want her to.'

But he knew. This was what he had dreaded, the moment when he would 'lose' me as Ella had 'lost' me. I saw in his eyes as he stared up at me that he saw it as raw treachery. 'I haven't taken anything,' he said clearly. 'Not for a whole month.'

Those words dug the pit of misery I have slid into since that moment. I tried to take him in my arms to reassure him, but he simply turned and walked away. He walked into one of the bedrooms and slammed the door.

'He'll be okay,' said Gila. 'Go on, don't worry. It has to be like that at first.'

... That was the beginning, and that was ten days ago. He has not been back here once, since then.

Every tea-time I wait for him. When he doesn't come I go to fetch him; but either he has disappeared, or he shuts himself up in the bathroom when he sees me coming.

Gila has done everything she can, including leading him back here – but when he sees what she's doing, he pulls away and runs. When she tries to talk to him he shouts at her – she hasn't told me this, but I heard him once through the window when I came to get him – 'She's not my mother! My mother's dead! I won't go there! My mother's dead!'

It takes every morsel of self-control I have to play with Ella and behave to her, during those three endless, lonely, anxious hours, as if I were happy. She is blooming back into health, everything about her improving by giant strides – her looks, her speech, her capacity for love. ... I am glad of it, of course, yet all I can think of is that, in fetching her, I must walk past *his* house and risk his seeing me hand-in-hand with his rival ... even though I stop, every day, and call him, and make her call him (in a whisper after the dutiful call: 'But he won't come, will he?') it tortures me because it tortures him –

Or does it? A more terrible thought is that he really doesn't care any more. What if he doesn't come because he doesn't want to? What if he's not punishing me, but has simply stopped loving me? Yesterday I didn't go looking for him. A sort of futile anger seized me. If he wanted to come, he'd come. Why should I diminish and humiliate myself by running after him? I gave Ella all my attention and my affection that day, I took her to the pool and played with her concentratedly, even though I received something like an electric shock when I saw that Gila had brought Peretz up with Ron. We ignored each other, and I pretended not to see Gila's signals. Afterwards she talked to me:

'You shouldn't have ignored him like that.'

'He ignores me.'

'But he's only a child.'

'Am I supposed to go on chasing him forever?'

'Yes, if necessary.'

'Well I won't! If he doesn't want me, let him do without me.'

She looked at me stonily. 'You talk as if he were a grown man who was slighting you,' she said coldly.

I was too unhappy to care what she thought.

I am working all day in the commune. Why won't they let me start in the clinic? Something to do with proving I can do 'ordinary' work, with putting myself on an equal footing with the other women before I become a 'specialist'. Anyway it is unbelievably awful. Unspeakably hot, unspeakably tiresome, unspeakably monotonous ... a voice in me keeps repeating angrily, hour after hour, 'I am fit for something better than this.' I work as hard as I can, furiously hard; I try to do the dreary job better than any of them. But anger, the anger of total boredom, burns my brain and I can scarcely bring a civil word out of my mouth.

At night ... oh, the nights are by far the worst! This little room is a nun's cell, full of finger-pointing reminders of my single, single, single state. ... What is the sense of it all? I came here because only here could I have the children, yet no sooner had I won them than I found I hadn't got them any more. What is three hours a day – even if Peretz came when he should? What does one do in those three hours – that matters? Rifka does everything for Ella that matters to her – washes her, dresses her, feeds her, scolds her, comforts her, teaches her – Rifka is her mother, not me. I am the nice lady she visits for tea. Jesus. Jesus. What did I do it for? I want to go away from here but I can't any more, ever, I am caught and trapped and I am getting *nothing* for myself, nothing but days of boredom and nights of furious loneliness, with three hours of enforced 'happiness' with Ella sandwiched in between ...

Dan is avoiding me. Wise fellow. But let him so much as walk past this house one dark night and my long, sticky starving tongue will flicker out and – splat! I shall draw him in and close my mouth round him and eat him alive. I will use him to kill this agony of uselessness and to punish . . . to punish whom . . . I don't know . . . something must happen. Dan must happen to me — he must fill up one empty space in me at least or this paper-thin burnt-out fabric of myself, that still glows hot when the wind of lust or frustration or anger blows on it, will collapse in fragments and scatter into nothingness before the next tiny problem-wind that blows.

Chapter 10

One looks back on these desperate crises and wonders if one will ever learn to accept them calmly in the certainty that time will solve them, in its own slow, imperceptible inevitable fashion.

It's winter again, and nothing has happened, yet everything has changed – slowly, subtly, moulded by time's quiet pressure.

For children, even more than for grown-ups, time is the solvent – especially here, where every circumstance of every day seems to insist on their health and happiness. No child can resist happiness for long when it is on constant offer.

Peretz is as different now as Ella was after her first weeks in the gan. He has, in Gila's triumphant phrase, 'found his place'. His battles are now normal give-and-take ones; he has emerged as the natural leader of his group, and it would seem that having plumbed the depths of infant iniquity, he now takes a moderate and rational view of wickedness. He is like a reformed rake, a cosmopolitan among innocent rustics, deciding for them what mischief is worthwhile and within bounds and what is likely to be dangerous or beyond the pale. Gila takes him into her confidence, she says, almost as one adult with another ... (or, perhaps, like a prison governor with a 'trusty'? But no, that's in my old pattern of thinking. My resentment is nearly all gone.) He is a tough, healthy, more or less normal seven-year-old. . . . Which is – surely? – what I wanted?

He comes home for tea, most days. His attitude to me is still tinged with caution; one can't compare it to those few golden days before he was 'absorbed'. But that was time out of life; one can't expect anything so perfect to persist.

Between Peretz and Ella exists a state of slowly thawing

truce. As each becomes more stable in his own little gan-world, their antagonism towards each other seems less and less possible to persist in. When it came time for Peretz to have a birthday, I arranged his party at home and all his gang came, bringing presents – home-made cards, pinned to bunches of roses, half a bar of chocolate, a box of balloons, some chewing-gum with a two-dimensional 'television' picture, a plastic whistle, a some-what dog-eared picture-book. ... The table was laid on the lawn with bowls of pop-corn and salt-sticks, sum-sum crackers and sweets from the kitchen, big iced chocolate cake, chunks of water-melon. ... Ella arrived in the middle of the excite-ment. She gazed at it all from the edge of the lawn, the milling children, the food, with Peretz in the heart of it, Peretz the King. ... I went over to her. 'It's Peretz' birthday,' I said. 'Would you like to give him a present?' She looked up at me. I put the parcel in her hand. 'What is it?' 'It's a mouth-organ.' 'I want to see.' I unwrapped it and she took it in her hands. 'It's for him?' 'Yes.' 'He didn't give me for my birthday.' I didn't remind her that she hadn't let him come near her party. 'He will, next year, if you give him this now.' She put the mouth-organ to her lips, frowning. Evidently next year was a long way off.

She made up her mind to do it, and squaring her shoulders, she walked to him boldly through the crowd. He watched her come, his eyes narrow. When she reached him she shoved the parcel into his hand and said, 'Mazal tov it's a mouth thing you blow, I want some cake,' all in one breath. It seemed he was affected but couldn't give in all at once. 'We haven't cut the cake yet,' he said. 'A sweet then.' 'All right.' She became absorbed at the table, while he tore the paper off the mouth-organ. He blew a blast on it and she grinned. It was an armistice.

And I? Well. Nothing in the event is ever wholly what one expected or wanted. Now I can look back on this year fairly dispassionately and recognize that I had my usual irrational 'great expectations' – an intimate relationship with the children, a sense of identity through them, a 'meaningful life' (whatever I thought that meant) within the kibbutz; and, no doubt, if I were completely honest, and dug down deep enough, I would unearth a secret, now sensibly buried, girlish hope of finding a husband here as well. No less!

The facts of my life are baldly these: No man. Dan had sense, or caution, enough not to come within range of my furiously flickering tongue, and this has now been rolled up neatly again and tucked into my jaws. About Kofi I don't know what to write. ... I haven't seen or heard of him for months. ... I simply cannot understand it, and it has hurt me beyond all reason, to a point where my purely feminine disappointment-relief about Dan scarcely ruffled the surface by comparison. Twice at the beginning of his silence I wrote notes to him, but he didn't reply ... my hurt began like a tiny wound, festering at his silence. Now it has nearly healed, though it's left a pretty ugly scar, because I rather suspect – now that it's too damned late, of course – that I really did love that fellow and those are the sort of sunken opportunities one never really forgives one-self for not keeping afloat. I am grateful for what I have – security, a sense that I'm earning my living honestly and with-out undue strain; my children, who are as much mine as I ever had any right to expect; the sight of them happy and well and growing, to lay over the thought of what they were, what they would have been now, if I hadn't come here. ... Come to that, what would *I* be now? An alcoholic wreck, I should think, if I hadn't found some non-courageous way of putting myself out of my misery.

I have 'settled down' to the life of a candidate kibbutznik, and am working my socks off to make up for the months when they kept me. I function as an adjunct to the two 'nurses' (both with considerably less training than I), making the rounds, and running a daily clinic for slipped discs, rheumatics, strained muscles, fibrositis, rehabilitation for mended bones, and just plain aches and pains, plus a once-weekly class for the pregnant women in natural childbirth. The doctor comes twice a week from a neighbouring kibbutz. He's not very good, it seems to me; nor does he need to be, since anything beyond the simplest ailments are sent to a specialist in the local national health clinic; but he's been lavish with his praise of me which hasn't hurt my position here, since the nurses hang on his words and have not been slow to pass on his approval of me. It's not a hard life at all (though massaging muscle-bound backs on a hot day is quite exhausting) – my rusty techniques have returned to me surprisingly quickly and I have that feeling of security that comes from knowing I can do what I'm supposed to do; but it was never 'my' sort of work and I find it very boring.

Nor, unfortunately, does it use up all my 'hours'. The remainder I spend as what is known as a 'cork', fitting in here and there as I'm needed. A couple of hours laying tables or washing dishes, folding or ironing clothes, or even spraying weeds in the gardens with a noxious oil. .... Nothing to grumble at, just dull, dull, dull.

Why can't gratitude invest boring work with some kind of spark, or at least make one hate it less? Well, it doesn't; that's all. Perhaps it's right that it doesn't. Perhaps the boredom is part of the payment, like a penance; perhaps you wouldn't feel you were paying your way if the work interested you.

But the daily eight hours is, in any case, not all. Through Raya (I suppose) the powers-that-be have discovered that I have these tiny talents for painting, acting and so on, and various 'cultural committees' (it doesn't sound so bad in Hebrew) have fallen on me from a height to persuade me to participate in some extra-mural activities. How could I refuse? I owed too much. So now I am busy three or four evenings a week. I teach English to a class of adults. I am acting in an emasculated version of 'Death of a Salesman' – of all things – with the drama-circle; and recently I helped decorate the dining-hall for Hannuka and wrote a sketch for a wedding. In other words, I am sinking without trace into the life of this community.

All very good, and much better for me than rotting and brooding alone in my room. Or so I tell myself, repeatedly.

I have become friends (to a limited degree) with Michael and Gila. It was they who told me the full story behind my acceptance, which I had taken all too much for granted. .... It was a battle-royal, I now discover. Raya fought for me like a mother tigress for her young. Oh, how glad I am, really glad, that nothing came of the Dan business! I didn't realize how she lobbied and campaigned for me, how much propaganda spade-work she has been putting in on my behalf, ever since I got here! Since Michael told me all this, I have made a renewed and determined effort to be friendly with her, but being in the same room with Dan still produces an uncomfortable effect com-pounded of an uneasy conscience and what my brother-in-law crudely but accurately calls 'hot pants' ... when I look at his mouth I remember the white dive of the owl reflected in the hot swoop in the loins ... we turn away our eyes and let Raya's warm senseless chatter flow over us, and I excuse myself early though I meant to stay all evening ...

Speaking of my brother-in-law, I recently received a most astonishing and unexpected letter from him. Except for the in-evitable moments when one of his colourful phrases presented itself to my pen I've seldom thought of him, and Judy I have, or had, put right to the back of my mind lest her smug and evasive and humiliating reply to my s.o.s. should stick in my soul and turn gangrenous. ... But his letter has mysteriously renewed the link between my half-forgotten 'young days' in Toronto, and the present, so far removed ...

Dear Old Shoe [his habitual name for me] –

I sure as hell wish I had your skill with verbiage because this letter would take a Thoreau or a – well, one of those heavy corre-spondents, anyhow, to do properly. Still, seeing as how I ain't no goddam Thoreau, you'll just have to read between the lines, only not too much. ... Hell again, here goes. ... As you know, Jude and I are happy as little peas in a pod together, and we don't go poking our noses into every little phone-call or letter that the other one gets, which is why I didn't get to hear one bloody thing about your letter until the other day when – don't read between the lines on this one, it just happened – I came across it in J's desk and kind of read it. Of course I skated straight into the kitchen where she was standing thigh-deep in kids whipping up a soufflé and asked her when it came and what we'd done about it. She looked kind of embarrassed, as (God forgive me for being a disloyal husband for once in my life) so she should, and, well, Shoe, the long and effing short of it is I find out we-that's-to-say-she did not do one single solitary thing about that letter that can have helped in the slightest degree. What I had to say to my Little Woman on the subject I will not go into here, but what I do want to say to you is that if it's not too darned *late*, the whole business being already God knows how old and nobody having heard a word from you since, as long as Jude and I and the kids are managing to live on the right side of the tracks there'll always be enough for a family emergency. Jesus, I'm saying this like I had a mouthful of hot pastrami and in fact that's pretty well how it feels because I'm still boiling mad about the whole business, too mad to think how to put this tactfully. You know I always thought you were a pretty good kind of sister-in-law and when I think what may have been happening to you in the last year frankly I just don't know where to put myself and I haven't said a civil word to my wife for two days. .... Please write back post-haste and save our marriage by telling us you are allright-no-thanks-to-us, and/or that you would like a cut off the old advertising cake which *believe me* will be no skin off any little frozen arses at this end. I know you'll feel kind of queer about it because of Jude but I still bring the pay-roll home around here and have some say in what happens to it.

All the best, Shoe, and I'm sorry we let you down –

Len.

I felt ashamed – chiefly because I had forgotten Len, forgotten his unfailing good will, good nature, generosity; ashamed that I had mentally tarred him with the Judy brush and cast him out of my thoughts except as a sort of plump cheery joke-face that popped sometimes unbidden into my head. I wrote at once – to him, to his office – saying not to worry, I was okay, had adopted two kids, was living in a kibbutz learning to be a laundress. .... I made a pretty funny letter of it describing Peretz' early depredations and my efforts to 'fit in' in the lightest and most comic vein I could muster, in order to put his mind at rest and Judy's damned complacency right down her throat to choke her. I said I didn't need a thing, thanks a million, and when were they coming over for a visit? (God, am I crazy? What if they cruise in here one day with six kids in tow? That's all the kibbutz needs from me! But that's one thing about relatives with large families, they don't tend to land on you because they can't get around much.) I was unspeakably relieved that I was able to write that independent sort of letter, and not a Dear-Len-I'm-just-dandy-but-if-you-could-spare-a-dime type ... another small thing to be grateful to the kibbutz for. ... I *wish* I could feel I belonged here – I suppose it's bound to take a long time.

Chapter 11

... So the months go by ...

Haven't written in here for an age ... reason is simple – very little to write about except trivia. Doesn't seem worth the effort of describing what goes on from day to day ... it's an almost unvarying routine: up at 6, work till 11.30, lunch, after popping in to see the children (not encouraged since some mothers simply can't and it's not considered quite fair, but since the kids are the be-all and end-all of my existence, the only thing that qualifies it all with some kind of stimulation and meaning, I simply feel to hell with it, and I go) – another few hours' work, home, shower, tidy the room, try to muster something interesting for tea (the only meal I have with them) and then it's time. The next two or three hours are wonderful. The kids and I are a family now. It all took endless time, but it's happened, finally, as they – the all-wise They – promised me it would. We are easy and natural and loving with each other; the rows between the children are occasional and normal; I am no longer afraid to scold sometimes or disagree or refuse permission – in other words, to be a parent – for fear of reprisals which I can't bear. Peretz has taken to referring to me as 'Ima', though not to my face ... my fear of them giving themselves away is fading as their own memories of the past fade. I love them ...

Then they go back, and I am left to face the evening.

I never thought I should long, literally long with a sort of angry violence, for a television! Since I left Canada I have never regretted that particular lack in my life until recently. Now the evenings are truly hard, and a people's opiate is just what this cog among the masses would sell her soul for. Oh, to sit before the idiot's window and lose my awareness of my 'singularity' for the long hours between supper and bed-time! I read, of course I read – I read till my eyes ache and the print bounces like little black rubber balls all over the pages; but how many books are there that absorb one that completely? It's like painting over cracks. I love the kids; they absorb the overspill of my feelings, but I can't somehow manage to tip the brimming container and pour the whole love-contents out over them. It fills me to bursting and I am aware of the constant pressure. Children are not partners, they can't relieve one of the need to love woman-to-man. That is one of the main (obvious!) things I didn't know.

It is physically beautiful here. The seasons change and delightful festivals come and go, enchanting the children and me, too, through them. I repeat endlessly to myself the patent truth that nothing could be better for them than to live in these surroundings; Peretz is already very absorbed in 'the land', helping in the children's farm, wandering about the big cowshed and chicken-run, pleading to be allowed to ride the horses, scrambling on to tractors; he has shown a surprising awareness of growth cycles and is beginning to learn quite a lot about birds and animals. Fine, great, wonderful. . . . I don't want them to be little urbanites, whining for artificial distractions. . . . But . . .! I suppose the trouble is that I *am* an urbanite, that like all city-bred people I may crave, while enclosed by asphalt and concrete, for country air and a return to Mother Earth, but when I actually find myself knee-deep in soil and the wholesome smells of the farmyard I am nearly distracted with boredom.

Boredom. There it is, it's out. I am bored, bored with nature, bored with my same little room, so small I can't even re-arrange the furniture, even bored with my 'clinics' with their endless succession of aching backs and bulging stomachs – and most of all – God forgive me, but I can't help it! – I am bored with the people I see every day. Is there some fundamental thing wrong with me that I haven't made one real, close friend? I 'like' everyone, in the tamest sense of that rather colourless word, and love no one. I am well aware that the most reasonable distraction on these long spring evenings would be to visit or to be visited, and sometimes I do, when my thirst for human companionship of any sort becomes too strong to resist; but it always leaves me unsatisfied because – through my own fault, through my own withholding of myself which I can't help – there is none of the intimacy which can alone bridge the gap between people. Not with anyone. I thought once I could have it with Dan, but the bridge there would have had to be a physical one first, and without that we remain very much two separate people.

Is it better to face up to the fact that under one's quite thick surface layer of 'contentment' one is deeply and fundamentally unhappy? Or is it better to concentrate on the calm crust at the top and not break it to look at the unsightly and uncomfortable primitive bog underneath? Like the Canadian muskeg. ... I find myself thinking of Canada more and more lately .. not exactly with hunger but with nostalgia ... those 'wasted years' between school and my marriage to Alec have taken on the strangest glow in my thoughts. They were so full of stimulants! Every day, new things, new faces, new reasons to jump when the phone rang or the mail came.... I had friends then, perhaps I wouldn't care for them now or have anything in common with them, but then one had at least the illusion of intimacy in the hen-parties and endless phone-calls and even in the cocktail parties which I affected to detest. I can laugh at what I'm going to write – that I would give five years of my life (this life) to have one to go to tonight, a smart one worth having one's hair done for, perhaps worth buying a new dress. ... I think of dull olive satin and nylons and a lace-topped slip laid out on my bed, which had a coverlet now amusingly bizarre in memory, brought back from a short crazy trip to Mexico which meant months of retrenchment but now shines like a nugget in my mind for its very prodigality and frivolity. ... God, my sentences, like my thoughts, are racing out of control! Yet now I wear nothing but cottons and wools, provided by the *communa* – very simple, very suitable, hand-made to my own design, material chosen by me, but no reason for satins or taffetas or velvets, no place for jewellery even if I had any left.... I have even stopped wearing make-up.... I have a sense of defeat about it, because I swore to myself I never would; yet when I saw it embarrassed Peretz and when I found that

I sweated it off during work-hours anyway, somehow ... it went.

Am I becoming 'like them'?

Such questions disgrace me. 'They' are my superiors in everything but my unbreakably conceited thoughts. Yet I feel myself secretly unable to bring myself to terms with the fact. I occupy my mind during long hours of 'manipulation' by inventing justifications for my need to think myself different – and better. The 'tiny talents'? Crap. They are nothing. They were never anything except a forged passport to self-respect. Here, they are a useful subsidiary way of paying my debt, no more. Am I more intelligent? It's true that there is very little intellectual curiosity here, for the simple reason that as they all basically think alike on matters of politics, religion and nationalism, and as for the last twenty years they have shared a common life, the stimulants for discussion and argument and intellectual development are nearly all fiddlingly small and transient – matters of principle (but within a closed framework), but chiefly day-to-day minor dissentions, 'internecine strife' ... hence the emphasis in conversation on practicalities and personalities, abstract ideas having long ago been put aside as settled. Yet my actual intelligence, my brain-power, is trifling compared to many of them – Dan for instance, who, in the rather odd words of Raya, 'Could have been anything he'd wanted'. (And he chose to be a metal-worker in a kibbutz? Why? But of course I know the answer really.)

No, there lies no confirmation. I cannot even hug to my secret self the conviction that I have 'lived' more, seen more, felt or done more and thus gained superiority. Half the people here were born and educated (some very well indeed) in Europe, and as for experiences, nobody who has not lived through a war, through hunger, fear, refugee-hood, 'the camps', through post-war renaissance, idealism, illegal immigration, another war, up-building, privations, more terrors, more victories – nobody, in a word, who has not rebuilt a broken life and pioneered a nation, can compare himself in experience or 'depth of character' with someone who has, even if that person now seems, in his outlook and conversation, inexplicably lacking in any of the special qualities that are supposed to follow 'successful' suffering.

So I rub and manipulate and call out 'up, round, out, down', and brood on my last remaining little, little superiority, and that I am ashamed ever to mention, it's so trivial, so petty! But it's all I have left to justify the cocky little chipmunk character which keeps me sane by poking up its head from the woodpile of my muddled brain and chirping: 'Don't lettum getcha down, kid – you're the queen.' And what is it? Simply this: I appear to be more entertaining.

Not more witty, not, I hasten to add, more charming or brilliant. By virtue, perhaps, of my being different, by that alone, I have a certain attraction. When they are bored with each other, they come to me for a quick laugh, because I can make almost anything into a good story, usually against myself. When visitors come, they bring them to me. 'Gerda's unique!' they cry, as the latest rage of radio comedians. 'You must meet Gerda!' What they mean is that Gerda's room is off-beat with its oddly Arab flavour, that Gerda is good for coffee, or even a meal, and a couple of hours' bright often irreverent talk of a type that visitors to a kibbutz don't expect. They say as much when they leave. 'Never expected to meet anyone like you in a kibbutz!' – as they wave and smile and back down the path. Michael, or whoever is the host, grins at me and that grin pats me on the head and I know that I've delivered the desired goods once more.

Why do I resent it somehow – why do I resent playing the very small part they ask of me, the only part I'm fitted for? The clever, gifted ones work in Tel Aviv or abroad for 'the Party', campaign, make speeches, collect contributions, or simply stay at home and hold the kibbutz together by giving up all their spare time to 'communal, social and educational activities'. And I? I decorate the place. I ease the aches caused by overwork by day and frisk about makeshift stages by night and have the nerve to resent it when, very occasionally, my all-too-burdensome spare time is borrowed to make campus conversation with some plump old man and his wife from Manhattan or London or Rio. So what if they're a dead bore? They're good-hearted and furthermore they're rich, and if they see that we're not too off-puttingly isolationist and doctrinaire and left-wing, they may fork out a bit which we need.

And what, then, is the most frightening thing of all? Well, there it is in that last sentence. It is the moment when one begins to think 'we' instead of 'I'. It is the knowledge that that moment is the necessary beginning of adjustment, of future happiness. It is the knowledge that one has chosen a way of getting what one wants, buying it if you like, which involves paying that particular price for happiness. Thinking 'we' instead of 'I'.

I guess if I were a nicer woman, or even just a stronger one, I'd have been able to make my happiness some other way. Being as I am, the eternal malcontent, I'll just have to settle for this and stop whining over the submersion of my little ego which, if I were only honest enough to evaluate it rightly, I should be only too glad to get rid of.

Chapter 12

Something's happening – something terrible is going to happen. I must write about it, yet I'm so frightened I can hardly think what I'm doing. I hold the book steady with one hand but the other, holding the pen, shakes so that the writing can't be read. ... It was all too easy, I wasn't grateful enough. ... No, that's absurd, nobody watches and adds up and decides what one deserves, there is no sense to it all except what we make ourselves. I've done my best – haven't I? – to make sense of my life this last year, I've tried, I have damn well tried, but there's nobody bookkeeping so it's all going to be taken away from me and I'm going to be chucked on the rubbish-heap again with my hands empty ...

I'm alone in my room but there are people all round and if they hear the sounds I'm trying to stifle they'll be in here and I'll blurt it all out, everything, because I'm alone and women alone go mad and don't give a damn any longer who they hurt, including themselves ... what would I care if Kofi went to prison, let him rot there for my part so I can keep the children – bloody, bloody liar and cheat that he is, how could he do this to me after I loved him and trusted him, these dirty *expedient* Arabs, they've got no idea of honesty or truth and I should have known that, they're only interested in themselves and even that in the lowest, most primitive way – why I didn't kill him when he dared to come and tell me – I was too stunned, that was it, it wasn't only because of the children that I was stunned into helplessness, it was because of what *he*'d done, I couldn't believe he'd do that. No, that's not it either – I could believe the part about the smuggling, I think I knew it all the time really, but I couldn't believe he'd give me the children along with lies about where they came from, knowing, damn his soul, *knowing*

189

there was always the chance that this would happen and I'd lose them –

But I won't lose them. I won't give them to him! When he comes for them tonight I'll go back on what I said (could I have said it? Could I have agreed? I was insane, crazy from the shock of it, I'd have said anything to get rid of him) – I'll hide them – he shan't take them! I'll get Dan – no. I can't get help. The kibbutz couldn't help me over this. There's nobody in the world who can help me to keep them. And it's wicked and wrong because they're mine, mine, and I've earned them – how can he take them back now? Back to what? To the refugee camp in Lebanon that he took them from? He says he'll give them sleeping pills and hide them in the bottom of the fishing-boat (Hanna talked about a trip in a fishing-boat – could he have taken her once on one of his illegal, dangerous 'journeys'?) and his smuggling friend will help him row them round the point at Rosh Hanikra and they'll come in at the little hidden bay where they always land, up the coast from the border . . . and someone will meet them there, some relative, and the children will be carried – still trustfully asleep – in a donkey-cart, perhaps, buried in maize-leaves, to the camp where they came from. How often at the beginning did he repeat to me that he couldn't, no, no matter what happened, he couldn't take them back? But he hadn't thought then of his own hide being in danger, that someone might betray him because of a piece of typical Arab feuding or rivalry or jealousy, drop a hint to the police that two children had been smuggled across to relatives on this side, two illegal Lebanese immigrants. . . . Suddenly the impossible has become possible, essential, imperative – the inquiries are being made, clues followed up, neighbours questioned . . . it may only be a matter of days, hours, before they're traced . . . and when the police come, the children must be gone, or if not I may be arrested too. 'But they won't do anything to you, Gerda, because you can say you didn't know – but don't mention me, Gerda, I beg you, don't talk about me, deny it if they ask you, say there never were any children, say anything . . . because you know what it will mean . . . who will look after my Hanna, Gerda? Don't think about me, *I* don't, I think only of her and

what will become of her if I am taken away . . .' Liar, Kofi!
You lie! You are shivering in your worthless dishonest skin!
Easy to say now that you only began to smuggle for her sake, to
make a little extra for her education, and to see your refugee
relatives sometimes, that you never, never smuggled drugs or
arms, only transistors and other things to sell. . . . I don't believe
you. . . . I don't believe any single word you say any more, you
lying, lying, treacherous bastard.

And my children. What when they wake in the morning?
What when they find themselves back with their grandmother,
some filthy Arab crone living in a corrugated iron hut with a
dirt floor and no – nothing? They lie tonight in clean beds, their
bellies full and their minds at peace, and if I do what Kofi wants
this is the last time they will lie like that. How will I live
through tomorrow, and tomorrow night, wondering how *they*
are living through it? The grandmother has had a message, she
is expecting them, she has found a younger woman to help her
look after them – but what's the difference? Some sluttish creature, doing the primitive minimum to keep them alive so that
they can grow up fit to work. . . . I can't do it. Nobody has the
right to ask me. They're not chattels to be shuttled back and
forth between countries and between lives. They're mine.

I'll go to the police. I'll tell them everything. I don't give a
damn what happens to Kofi. Why should I? The police will see
that it wasn't my fault. They'll let me keep the children, they'll
see at once that they are better off here . .

But they're not really mine. I have no papers for them. Why
didn't I think of that before? Perhaps they wouldn't let me keep
them. Perhaps they'd say they had to be handed back to the
Lebanese anyway, otherwise Israel could be accused of kid-
napping them. Then I'd lose them just the same and I'd have
betrayed Kofi for nothing.

Oh God, what can I do? I might go to prison myself. Why
didn't I ask myself in the first place where Kofi had got them,
why he was so insistent that they couldn't be returned? Why
didn't I add up all the clues I had to his secret journeys? They
could only have given one answer. But even so, can I be blamed
for not guessing that he would be such a reckless idiot as to

bring over two orphaned children – even though as it turns out their dead mother was his half-sister – how could he have been mad enough to smuggle them in to hand them over to their uncle, their only other relative, who was his own brother, and whose reactions he should have foreseen? He says *now* that he had me at the back of his mind all along, that knowing how slight were my chances of finding a child here, when he saw these he needed little persuading by the grandmother to bring them because he was thinking, not of the crude, brutal brother, but of me, especially as a possible refuge for the little girl. Thus he appeals for my gratitude! He did it all, ran this insane personal risk, for the children's sake – and for mine! And in recognition of *this,* I must not give them up, help him to take them back, 'not hate him too much' for putting me in this unspeakable trap . . .

And if I obey him? If for his sake and mine and because there is no way out, I obey him? How shall we endure afterwards, any of us, and what shall I say when the police come, what shall I say in the morning to the kibbutzniks? 'At half past two last night I carried the children one at a time to the wood that divides the end of the kibbutz from the road, carefully avoiding the nightwatchman who was eating at the time, and handed them over to an Arab whom I know, who put them in the back of a borrowed van and drove them away. . . . And now we have to pretend there never were any children . . .'

I used to think Kofi quite clever, but his brain has ceased to function over this whole business. I cannot deny there were ever any children. They have been living here with me for over a year. There is only one possibility – I must leave tonight myself. I must pack my things and go with Kofi when he comes with the van. . . . I must disappear somewhere, Tel Aviv is the obvious place, or Jaffa, somewhere big and anonymous. . . . God, this is madness. How can I break my life like this? This morning I gave a clinic and massaged the backs of three men and joked with them and looked forward to the moment when Ella would paddle up the hill to see me on her way to the cowshed with her gan . . . eight hours ago the three of us sat round this table and had tea . . . and Peretz brought me a picture he'd painted. Was that false, and is this true? They cannot both be true, that happy hour and this desperate one . . . not in the same world . . .

It's nearly time . . .

Perhaps I bought this moment when I accepted unquestioningly the miracle of those two children. I am an adult and I should have outgrown fairy-tales and magic; I should have known there is no such thing as a child without birth-pains or without papers. Every child comes from something, comes *with* something. These two fell into my arms with no past and now they are being taken away again, there is no one to complain to, no one to weep to. . . . I must do it somehow . . . but my poor little ones . . . my poor little ones . . .

I didn't take them. I couldn't.

It's three a.m. and I've just come from seeing Kofi on the other side of the wood. I got there easily without being seen. He was waiting in the deep shadows; I could see the van parked a little way down the road, its lights off. When he heard me coming he ran forward through the narrow pine-trunks to help me, and when he saw my arms were empty he stopped dead, wringing his hands with that peculiarly feminine gesture of his. . . . 'Where are they? Why haven't you brought them?' 'You must wait another night.' 'Gerda, I can't, I can't! Everything's arranged for tonight! The boat, my friend's waiting . . . they're waiting on the other side, tomorrow may be too late . . .' 'That's just too bad, you'll have to chance it. You're not having them tonight.' It is not the heart but the stomach which turns to lead at such moments, I had a great weight in my belly but my mind was clear. Nothing, no tears, no pleas, could have moved me. He clutched me beseechingly, his huge hands closing on my shoulders, vibrating like an engine. I shook him off coldly. 'It's no use, Kofi. I've decided. It's for your sake as well.' 'What do you mean?' 'If they go tonight I must go too; I wouldn't be able to explain to the people here what had happened. If the three of us disappear in the night, the kibbutz will have inquiries made, the children will be traced back to you . . . the mere fact that they've gone doesn't mean they were never here, and the police will get you just the same.'

He stood silent in the darkness, his kefiya a faint white smudge. I thought I could hear a faint squeaking sound as he ground his teeth. I saw that he understood, was in fact wondering why he hadn't seen all this clearly before. 'Give me twenty-four hours,' I said. 'Tomorrow I'll go to the kibbutzniks and tell them some story to explain the fact that I'm leaving with the children. I may even tell them the truth, or part of it. . . . I don't know, in the end, which of us two is the bigger liar, though your lies have done more damage. . . . If the kibbutz will help us, even by not making any fuss or drawing attention to my going, it will increase the chances of your getting away with this heartless, cruel madness you've done.' He lowered his head like an ox and I pitied him for a moment, and detested myself, because whatever sort of madness it was, it was neither heartless nor cruel but the opposite. Incredible that at that very moment, filled as I was to the brim with anguish and fury, I should have felt a strange voluptuous quiver, and directed towards him, the source of my misery . . .

'So what will you do?' he asked at last in a low, submissive voice, as if handing his fate over to me without any further struggle.

'As I say, I'll leave here tomorrow. Tomorrow evening would be best. I have nowhere to go so you'll have to take the children directly from me . . . we must arrange somewhere quiet to meet . . .' How could I have talked about them like that, so clinically, so coldly, as if they meant nothing to me, as if I'd already turned my back on them both? Yet now as I sit here, shivering with cold and reaction, my whole mind is flooded with wretchedness . . . and still my children sleep untroubled and I am clutching mentally at the knowledge that I have gained another day for them, for myself, another few hours for us to be together, though they will be terrible hours and I half-wish I had got it over tonight so that the true suffering could begin . . . as it is I feel as if I were keeping alive something that is dying, clinging to it with all my strength because every minute of its life is precious. . . . Can it be that I have some furtive baseless hope that I will not have to do it in the end, that something will save us? A few hours gained . . . it is nothing . . . by tomorrow they will be in that boat, I will have lost them as surely as if I had sent them tonight ...

I must go and see them. I must see them and touch them ...'

I have been – first to Peretz, then to Ella. There is no sharper poignancy than the sight of one's children sleeping. It is the most powerful activator in the world, that helpless innocence, that trust, that sweetness. I stood staring down at Ella, at her little brown paws, one bare foot, the gentle peaceful movement of the chest, the motionless lashes, and I knew it then, I can't give them up, not as he wants, not without a struggle. I don't know what I can do, but I shall do something. I shall do something.

Part Three: Jaffa

Chapter 1

I am terrified, elated, triumphant and full of a crazy, unreasonable joy. I have run away – successfully run away! – from the kibbutz, from Kofi, from everything. I am a fugitive! And so excited that my mind seems to be bursting after these long long months of self-control and conformity. I want to crow with childish glee, 'I've done it, I've done it, to hell with all of you!' No, but I must sober up (though I'm only drunk with success and freedom) and write it all down calmly, if only in order to repossess my awareness of the dangers that still exist. Oh, but I feel wonderful! As I have not felt for years and years.

First, then, my immediate surroundings – my hide-out, my refuge! It is a little, a dear little flat in the squalid heart of Jaffa; well, no, not in the heart, but somewhere near the toes, for it is a stone's throw from the shore. An acre of cobbled square, with a well in the middle, a low wall, and a long slope of scrub-covered sand is all that divides us from the sea. But that is outside, and though I can see it through my windows, narrow as a fortress's, I have no desire to venture out of the tight, safe, womb-like confines of these three little rooms, boxes, the biggest no larger than my room at the kibbutz, the smallest (where the kids now lie asleep) little more than a large cupboard, just fitting the two campbeds – there is no room for Ella to fall out! She is so thrilled to be sleeping in a 'grown-up' bed. . . . They have both been so good, and I love them so much, and I am a little mad with relief and joy that I didn't give them up –

But wait. A little at a time. I must go back to the beginning and enjoy myself, writing of this personal, unscrupulous, operational triumph, my escape with them . . .

The same night I met Kofi in the wood, as I sat over the table forcing my frozen mind to come up with some solution, I

199

suddenly remembered something – a tiny fact, irrelevant perhaps, and yet I couldn't dismiss it; how could there be room in my thoughts, at that moment, for anything not strictly relevant? At times like that, when one's mind blunders along the borders of desperation, one trusts one's instincts as the religious trust inspiration, simply because there is no other help.

The sly little fact was that Raya was away from home. Where she had gone I can't remember, but she was not at home. And instantly, with no other spur than that apparently random thought, I suddenly began to act.

God knows whether I knew clearly, then, what I was about, but I found myself going to the bathroom, combing my hair, putting on perfume (the only truly feminine aid left to me). . . . I found myself undressing, quietly, calmly, and putting on a nightgown which I had almost forgotten I owned. . . . Looking back, I am appalled at my own deliberate intent, the unswerving way I went about it. Yet despite all the vicissitudes of feeling I have passed through about it since, I can't help laughing now almost with rapture as I think of it. I was going to seduce Dan. Deliberately, recklessly, for my own purpose. . . . I felt my blood stirring with the sheer calculated wickedness of it. . . . I flitted along the paths and up Dan's steps like a shadow, and, still without a qualm, let myself into his house.

Shall I write the details, quite shamelessly? Shall I face the fact that despite my agony of mind, my misery, despite the fact that I was doing it not even from honest lust but to get poor Dan so entangled that he would arrange things for me, help me more whole-heartedly and be my ally – to bewitch him, in fact. . . . Despite all these bloodless motives, when the moment came and I found myself gathered into his warm bed, I did not feel at all like a tart, as I deserved, detached and self-detesting, but full of genuine amorous heat and enjoying myself like a woman in love?

Yet it was so. I have deserved some pleasure in my life which I have not had, and felt cheated; here, perhaps, was the reverse – a reward for guilt. Surely I can't still be looking for a sense of balance and justice in this crazy world. . . . But I remember the feeling of surprise, of hesitancy. . . . 'I don't deserve this . . .'

Oh well. There is no explaining the reactions of the flesh! I got my joy and so did he, and good luck to him at least, dear Dan ...

First I told him as much as I dared of the truth, crying the first tears of that hideous night, and he held me tenderly and asked how he could help.... I told him I wanted to run away, to hide with the children, but that I didn't know where to go or how, or what to tell the kibbutz, and our bodies were drawing closer. ... Gone my deliberate cold seduction technique; the body has its own will, and mine was for him. His arms closed on me like a protective door and I heard him whisper with a trace of sadness and reproach, 'But you know I'd always help you ...' And for a second I thought 'He knows,' and perhaps he did, but it was too late for him then. He tumbled me into his bed, the sheets were still warm and rumpled, and stripped me in the trembling warm cave, and everything else fled and vanished, even the children, for which I should be ashamed but I'm not. ... In that bursting instant when two years' celibacy ended I even thought the word 'love' in big blinding capitals, but in the sinking quiet aftermath I knew it was nothing like love and that I would leave him that day without pain; but now I look back and am glad that, in that most primitive essential way, I paid him a fair price for all that he did for me afterwards. And the payment was no less, from his point of view, surely, for the fact that I revelled in it myself.

I crept away just before dawn and lay on my own chilly bed wide awake until morning. Then I dressed and drank coffee calmly (feeling my body my own again, returned to me more complete than before I gave it, as always when it's been good) and met Dan as arranged in the office. His face was white and pinched (exhaustion or guilt? Whichever, I pitied him). He had called together a few of the more active members of the Central Committee and had already told them the story. It was mostly the truth. ... The children's origins were laid before them now ... oddly, they accepted that so easily that I bitterly regretted not having been honest with them from the first. ... Then, the new information that they were Lebanese, and my 'tip-off' that the authorities were on to something – 'Naturally,' said Dan, 'they would be more concerned about how the children got across, and who brought them, than in the children themselves. But still, if they find them they won't let her keep them – they couldn't. They'd be handed over to the Mixed Armistice people who'd find some bloody bureaucratic way of coping with the problem ... they'd probably end up back in the refugee camp ...' Several people wanted to know how they *had* got across, but I said it was much better if none of us knew the answer to that, then no one would have to tell any more lies (they all exchanged looks at this and I felt very ashamed).

Dan explained that I and the kids would have to disappear. He suggested that we go initially to the flat in Tel Aviv which the kibbutz keeps for when members go to town on business, but there was a sudden wave of opposition to this plan. 'It's all very well,' said one man. 'Don't think I don't sympathize, but this could be serious. It's one thing to help her do a flit, I'm even prepared to pretend I don't know where she's gone, but to put her in Movement premises, our official guest so to speak ... this could involve the whole Movement in a scandal ...'

The others agreed. Dan looked at me, and I fixed him with my eyes and I saw the memories of the night sweep through his mind; he closed his eyes for a moment. 'Well then,' he said calmly, 'the least we can do is to give her transport and send some man with her to help her find a flat quickly – today – in some crowded, anonymous district where it'll be hard to trace her.'

There followed a rather glum silence. Clearly many of them resented me for putting them on such a tricky ethical spot and didn't know how to react. But Dan kept talking and gradually won them over. . . . 'I'll go myself. I'll drive them to T–A in the Sussita – we can pile enough stuff in the back so that she can manage for a few days even if we can't find a furnished place. Someone can go down again later and take her anything she needs. . . . Damn it!' he interrupted himself suddenly. 'Why are you all so quiet? She's lived with us for eighteen months, she may not be exactly one of us but she hasn't broken any rules and she's worked hard – when you think of the useless dead-weights we've helped with clothes and furniture and money and

202

a place to live when they decided to leave and that reminds me, Gerda, you'll need money. We'll let you have some. All right?' He glared round at the small circle of unresponsive faces. 'What's the matter?' he asked again challengingly.

'She didn't have to lie to us,' muttered one.

'Didn't she? I wonder if she'd have been let in if we'd known from the start that those kids were Arabs.'

There was a silence, and then one man, one of my long-term patients, suddenly grinned. 'Well, I owe her something, anyway,' he said. 'I was walking around bent like a hairpin until she came.' This raised a laugh and suddenly their faces were more friendly. The meeting ended with general agreement to Dan's plan and, perhaps more important, agreement that my whereabouts should be kept a complete secret. The story if the authorities came to inquire was to be that I had just upped and left one day, no one knew where.

Afterwards Dan and I were left alone, and I thanked him. He looked at me steadily. 'Perhaps you think I'm doing all this because of what happened last night,' he said. He began to say something else, then changed his mind and stood up. 'Come on, there's a lot to do,' he said shortly.

I followed him, feeling more and more uncomfortable. The elation and triumph of the early morning had vanished, and now I felt suddenly rather cheap. If I had made myself more popular, been less insular, less determinedly an outsider, those people would have needed no persuasion to help me. And why should I have felt that I had to create, in that peculiarly crude manner, a sense of responsibility and debt in Dan before he would give me his support? No doubt because I have no belief in my own power to make people like and sympathize with me. I had settled my purely material debt to the kibbutz by my work and in other ways, but I had not succeeded in winning them to me, and I felt this now for the first time – that I had not been likeable. Kofi is the only one who's ever liked me, I thought suddenly, painfully aware of the irony.

Perhaps it was because of this that I made such a tremendous effort – belated, useless no doubt because of that – to leave a pleasant impression with the two housemothers, Rifka and Gila.

I took time while Dan was loading the van to talk to each of them and tell them the story, begging them to try to understand and to forgive me if I had ever seemed ungrateful or difficult. . . . Their reaction was astonishing. . . . They both melted completely, all reserve was dropped at once and Rifka, the hardheaded Sabra, actually threw her arms round me and kissed my cheek, saying 'I knew all the time you were like this underneath. . . . It must have been awful for you alone. We've so loved having Ella, I never minded the trouble, at least I don't mind now I know for certain you appreciated it – ' Gila took my hand and said, 'Michael and I have always hoped you'd settle and stay – this is a real blow, a personal blow for us both. . . . I hope to God you'll be all right, all of you: I'll miss the demon-child but I'll miss you, too. . . .' I could have wept with the sudden conviction that it could all have been so different, so much warmer and better, if I had only tried earlier to meet them half-way on a friendship level. Looking at Gila I saw – too late of course – the makings of a close and intimate friend, if I had only just once taken her into my confidence.

Gathering up the children was harrowing, and only bearable because I kept the alternative in the forefront of my mind through their tears and protests. It was Peretz, oddly enough, who minded most being parted from his group. Ella was more interested in the journey, and her sense of importance as the others watched her clothes being packed. But Peretz went very quiet after the initial outburst and kept his face turned towards his gan even as he was being led away, tearing himself free at the last moment to run back to Gila and hug her blindly.

The rest of the day was pretty fair hell; first a three-hour drive, and then the flat-hunt. It wasn't any too easy to find a suitable, or even a semi-suitable place to stay. Dan walked his feet off, down alleys too narrow for the van, up twisting flights of stairs in crumbling buildings; I would stay near the van with the children, who were of course increasingly restless and fretful as they grew more tired and bored, and wait for Dan to appear at some upper window, each time shaking his head and giving the thumbs-down. . . . 'Out of the question,' he'd say gloomily on his return. 'Filthy,' or 'Far too small', or 'no lavatory'. This last was the chief difficulty. I was in no position to be fussy, but I really felt I couldn't manage without plumbing and running water, and an incredible number of buildings in Jaffa have neither.

At tea-time we were still nowhere. We drove down to the shore and Dan stood us a much-needed meal at a little café near the old docks. Jaffa is strongly Arab-flavoured like Acre, but there are large areas in it where the crumbling ancient squalor is being renovated by a certain Government department with an eye on tourism. Areas of ruins have been cleaned up, opened out, and the obstructions removed so that the beautiful old moorish façades, with their graceful pointed archways and engraved stone friezes, are able to stand out clearly. Along the shore, parks and gardens are replacing a jumble of slums and heaps of fallen masonry. Sitting near one of these newly-reborn sites I said to Dan, 'How marvellous if one didn't have to live in a slum, if one could find a flat somewhere here.'

'They're all newly converted,' he said, 'mainly for artists. They're trying to make a colony here, to attract visitors – there'll be galleries and nightclubs and all that – and studios.' I sighed. 'Very expensive, no doubt?' 'I expect so. Which reminds me ...' 'No, don't ask. I haven't thought yet. I shall have to find a job manipulating backs, or perhaps put up a sign and set up in business at home ...' 'I'd be careful of that! There's no knowing what interpretation a lascivious-minded Arab might put on a sign saying "Aches and pains eased while you wait". ...' I laughed. It was my first laugh for some time and I put my hand out to him in gratitude. His own laugh stopped and he moved his wrist away uneasily. There was a very uncomfortable moment wherein I suddenly sensed the burden of guilt I'd imposed on him with my ruthlessness.

After the meal we got ready to set off again. Having seen the lovely open spaces and pretty frontages, so full of character and charm, it was doubly hard to turn back to the greasy cobbled alleys and strings of shabby washing. As we were crossing the renovated square, with its old well in the centre, I said, 'Let's just ask around here. There's nothing to lose.' Dan shrugged. 'I'll wait here.' On impulse I knocked on a door at random. It was open, and I had a view of a low whitewashed passage, leading through to a small open court bordered with potted greenery and partly roofed with a vine. It was like looking down a short tunnel into a miniature paradise. Ella instinctively set off down it, and I had to hike her back, though I sympathized deeply.

I called out, and a man's voice answered. I entered cautiously. The voice came from the courtyard itself, in which I found a tall, elderly man with a beard, painting a rather sinister abstract consisting of heavy black beams like a burnt-out ship.

'I'm looking for a place to live,' I said.

'Can't help you.'

'You don't know of any rooms going begging in this area?'

'How many for?'

'Myself and two children.'

He looked round at me and encompassed me with a glance. 'Aren't many children around here,' he said.

'What? This whole town's swarming with them.'

'I meant, in this area. Mostly single people, artists, live in these houses.'

'There's no rule about it is there?'

'No – just happens that way.' He went on with his work, laying on the rusty black paint with a pallet-knife. The kids stared at him fascinated. Ella was open-mouthed. 'What's that on his face?' she kept asking. She'd probably never seen a beard before.

'Well – I'm sorry to have disturbed you,' I said at last, moving with indescribable reluctance towards the passage again.

'Are you any sort of artist?'

'Not really, except in an amateur way. I'm a sort of physiotherapist.'

He stopped painting and turned round. His craggy face suddenly showed a gleam of extraordinary interest.

'Do you treat polio cases – spines and hips?' he asked sharply.

'Yes of course.'

'Wait a minute.'

He put down his pallet on a small stained table and hurried through a door, wiping his hands on his shorts. After a moment he came back with a woman of about forty, who also looked as if she might be an artist – she was very dark, with black hair cut off straight at the shoulders and in a fringe above heavy eyebrows; her face was scored with deep lines, adding strength to it, and she wore no make-up. She was dressed in very faded levis and an orange pancho with points back and front; her feet were thrust into cotton mules.

'This is my wife,' said the man. We shook hands; I was not surprised to see the tattoo number on the underside of her darkly-haired, rather sinewy arm. She spoke, like her husband, with a strong Romanian accent. 'This lady is looking for rooms,' said the artist. 'She's a physiotherapist. These are her children.'

The woman looked at me closely. Her eyes, startlingly, were light blue. She exchanged a glance of understanding with her husband.

'I see,' she said. 'Well ... we have some rooms here. We didn't intend to rent them ... but perhaps we might come to some agreement. ... Sit down, please.'

I sat on a low stone bench beside the thick twisted stem of the vine. It was pleasant and cool there; the walls round the court were all of a flaking white, shadowed with green; there were several pictures hanging there, and some stone statues, making a sort of open-air gallery. The woman asked the children if they wanted a drink, and when she returned with it she brought some toys with her for them to play with.

'You have children?' I asked.

'We have a child,' said the man. 'A daughter. She's fifteen now.' He looked at his wife and added quietly, 'She's very lame.'

'Polio?'

'There was an epidemic here some years ago. We were lucky – many died. She was badly affected and must go now in an iron.'

I waited a moment. Then the wife said, 'I think what my

husband has in his mind is. .... We need someone to treat our daughter, special, private treatment, perhaps every day. We are not rich. .... We might perhaps arrange something, regarding the rooms, if – '

It was too wonderful. I felt the healing quiet all round me, the beauty; I envisaged peaceful white rooms, a private haven ... the artist and his wife were looking at me with that awful child-like expectancy, that one sees in doctors' offices or at seances, the look that waits for a miracle.

I sighed heavily. The temptation was almost more than flesh and blood could stand, but one can't play around with people's feelings to that extent.

'First, I have to tell you that I'm not fully qualified,' I said. Their faces fell. Qualification, with some people, is all. 'Not that it would make that much difference. If your daughter had the disease when she was a young child, nobody in the world could offer you a cure for her lameness. The best I could do would be to give her massage and exercises every day and hope that the stiffness would ease a little and that she might become slightly stronger, slightly less lame.' I stressed the word 'slightly', forcing myself to make the picture as black as possible so that they wouldn't take me in with false hopes.

The two of them sat there with the moving vine-shadows playing on their middle-aged pain-worn faces. No doubt I shall hear their story eventually; I imagine it will be harrowing. I think they are both 'good' people in the strict sense of the word, the kind that suffering is supposed to ennoble. What hideous nonsense all that cant is! This morning I looked out of my window into the court and saw Suzy – the wife – hanging up washing with the bright sun full on her face, obliterating the lines, and I saw her for a second as she would have been had she not passed through that hell in her girlhood – the hardness gone, the whole face softened and smoothed . . .

But then, I could see that she is a tough, hard-headed woman, accustomed probably to dealing with all the mundane matters of their family life (for her husband is certainly not the practical type in any respect); I saw that she was bitterly disappointed that the miracle was not forthcoming, though less so than her husband, for she probably had never allowed herself to believe in it for more than a second. I saw her asking herself whether such a slender promise was worth three rooms and the nuisance of two young children in her home. She saw me reading her eyes, and she lowered them to her thin tobacco-stained hands.

At last she looked up again and said, 'I'm prepared to let you have the rooms at a reduced rent if you will treat the daughter every day.'

'Of course I'll treat her,' I said, 'but what do you call a "reduced rent"? I ask because I'm really going to be very hard up until I can find work.'

They looked at each other and had a short, silent conversation. I watched enviously, wondering how long you have to be together before achieving that degree of communication. Finally the wife named a sum which seemed at once eminently reasonable and much more than I could afford.

'I have enough to cover the first month's rent,' I said. 'What if we try it out for that time and then I see how I'm fixed?'

They both stood up and the wife said, 'Come and see the rooms. Have you any furniture?' I said I had a little. Leaving the children in the courtyard, she led me through another door and into this tiny apartment. The walls were rough-plastered and whitewashed; the ceilings low, the windows arched, the floors tiled in red. It was dusty, but otherwise clean. The only furniture was a low couch, some chairs, a card-table, and a rickety clothes-closet with some shelves in it. It even had its own little lavatory.

'You'll have to share our shower,' she said as I looked round, my heart suddenly light.

'You mean, you'll have to share it with us,' I said. 'We'll try not to be in your way.'

'Don't worry,' she said, and added, 'I quite like young children, I don't find them tiresome.' She spoke in a tone I've found typical of her, a cool, almost cautious reserve often at odds with warm words.

I turned to her suddenly, wanting to thank her, and she smiled, the first time she had done so, showing small, rather stained teeth. I put my hand out on impulse and she shook it, looking a little surprised. 'Are you English?' 'No, Canadian.' 'I thought only the English shook hands all the time.' I laughed. 'There are moments when what you really want is to kiss someone so you shake hands instead.' 'Why should you wish to kiss me?' 'From thankfulness, from relief.' 'I see.'

We left the flat again and, back in the courtyard, we introduced ourselves properly. The artist's name is Zev and his wife's, as I said, the unsuitably cosy Suzy. They have the apartment on a long lease and a small rent because Zev is quite a well-known artist (Suzy is a sculptress in her own right too) and the Tourist Board is interested in such couples settling in this district. They explained that sub-letting is not officially allowed, and asked me to 'try to look like a visiting friend'. I was on the point of telling them that they must keep quiet about me for my sake as well as theirs, but I was suddenly afraid. People like that, very often, have a built-in fear of 'the authorities' and I wanted to establish myself with them before introducing the alarming factor of my fugitive status ... not very straight of me, perhaps, when they have been so kind, but the words just wouldn't come.

Belatedly I remembered Dan, but hurrying out I found him asleep with his head and arms resting on the steering-wheel. I put my hand on his shoulder and he came awake suddenly, giving me a rather wild stare which dissolved through an abrupt, almost instinctive tenderness to matter-of-fact control. He seemed to veil his eyes as I looked into them, and I realized he was preparing himself to part from me and that this would hurt him more than I had foreseen. One gets accustomed to the idea of the woman being the one to suffer through brief relationships – it gave me an unworthy little pang of satisfaction to see that this time I would be the one who 'got clean away'. But I instantly regretted the unkindness, which was more than half vanity, and wished that I could share his pain half-and-half ... why is nothing ever half-and-half with love or even the suburbs of love? The suffering and the pleasure, too, are always unequal.

When I told him my good news he was genuinely delighted

for me, but after he had heard the details he relapsed into doubt.

'Of course it seems marvellous on the face of it,' he said, 'but I don't know ... This isn't the "crowded, anonymous" district we thought of, where you could just disappear without trace. ... Are you sure you won't automatically attract attention in an area like this – living with artists? They're such a conspicuous lot – '

'Possibly. ... On the other hand, I might stand out more, cause more talk, in a poorer district – after all, I can't very well go about in shmatters and pretend to be some old Arab's widow ...'

'There's something in that,' he said, but he still seemed worried.

He helped me unload the van and carry the stuff in; Zev came out and lent a hand. It struck me that they must have thought it odd, my having my furniture on my back so to speak, but they said nothing. The children dashed about excitedly, and at one point I had to spring very sharply across to the well in the centre of the open square to drag Ella back from climbing on to it.

'Are we going to live here?'

'Yes.'

'For always?'

'Nothing's for always,' I said without stopping to think. I spoke lightly, but Peretz stopped dead and stared at me. I hugged him quickly. 'Except me,' I added. He kept staring at me through those coal-black eyes. 'What's the matter?' I asked, irritated by my own stupidity.

'Are we never going back to the kibbutz then?' he asked.

'Some day perhaps, for a visit.'

'I thought we lived there.'

'We did, and now we live here, and perhaps afterwards we'll live somewhere else. It's nice to live in different places, don't you think?'

'No,' he replied at once.

It was dusk by the time we were settled in and Dan and I stood on the far side of the van, dumbstruck by the necessity of saying good-bye. I must admit I felt very little at that moment except acute embarrassment and a desire for it to be over, but I let him kiss me and had no great difficulty in returning it warmly. Or so I thought ... but he let me go at once and said flatly, 'I thought so.'

'What?' I asked, miserable and uncomfortable at the thought that I might have let him feel my hurry to part from him.

For a moment he didn't answer, and then he said quietly, his arms at his sides, 'There was no need for you to do it that way. I'd have helped you anyway.'

I decided in an instant that denials and protests were useless and rather insulting. 'But aren't you glad?' I asked.

'Glad?'

'That we – that it happened at last. It had to, didn't you feel that?'

He said nothing for a moment and then said, 'I don't care for short, meaningless affairs. They don't justify the burden they put on one's conscience.'

I couldn't help smiling. 'Oh! You mean, a longer, more important one would be less guilt-making?'

'I mean only that – with a one-night relationship one not only betrays one's marriage, one insults it as well.'

'Insults it?'

'One's marriage should – arm one against falling into such traps,' he said in an unexpectedly bitter voice. I felt very sorry for him and genuinely guilty again myself, yet I couldn't control a secret amusement at his rather pedantic, 'impersonal' way of putting it – all the 'ones', never a 'my'. Yet I understood his situation suddenly and realized that my instinct about him and Raya had been right – they weren't suited, presumably not physically either. I could have put my arms round him then with wholehearted tenderness, but he was nobody's fool and would have seen at once that I was pitying him and been deeply offended.

'Dan, would you believe me if I said I wasn't just using you? That I had – love-thoughts when we were together?'

'But for how long after we ceased to be together?' I had no reply. He put his hand on my shoulder and looked down at me. It was quite dark now, and only a distant street-lamp cast a little light on his face. We could hear the waves beating the sea-wall in the stillness of the quiet square. 'Never mind, Gerda. You have so many problems. I don't blame you really. I only wish – ' He hesitated a moment, as if weighing up his words, asking himself if I deserved to hear them. 'I only wish I had the right to stay and look after you,' he finished softly at last.

I put my face against the shoulder of his shirt. 'You're good,' I said, and for once in my life I felt really humble, for he'd given me more than I had any right to, a sweetness to keep when I should have had a smack in the face for my callousness. And suddenly the callousness was gone. It thawed and fell off like defrosted chunks of ice, just as another area of my defences had fallen away ages ago with the children. I felt my heart become vulnerable again, all hardness left it; and thinking back now, I feel that was a more important moment in my – what's the word, rehabilitation? – than the sunburst I experienced in Dan's bed. And the strangest thing is – that this renewed feeling of being once again capable of love has veered away from its cause, that is Dan, and returned to another, and, damn his eyes, totally unworthy object, to whit that accursed Kofi ... it's not love, it's the knowledge that love was there, just outside my rusted iron gates, pushing and straining to be let in, during those lonely terribly months in Acco and afterwards. ... The pain of knowing this has been tormenting me for days; the after-heat of love has enveloped me now the gates are down, and it shows up his betrayal in an even crueller light ... yet at the same time it makes it possible to at least try to understand – poor, frightened Kofi! What did he feel, what did he do when he returned for the children the following night and waited among the pine-trees until dawn drove him away? But we have disappeared as effectively as if he had really carried out his plan to ship the children back across the border. ... He is not in danger now unless we are found. And please God we won't be.

Chapter 2

My happiness here has been so powerful that I'm afraid of it. I'm torn between the superstitious fear that if the gods see how I'm revelling in my satisfaction they'll take it away from me, and the equally irrational feeling that they will do so if I don't appear to be appreciating it! Better to revel and (Len again) 'dunk my donut in the whisky while I got it'.

Everything is falling into place with almost uncanny luck. No sooner had I arrived here (it's about three weeks already) and begun treating 'the daughter' than other work began to fall into my lap like manna from heaven. First a friend of Zev's who suffers from rheumatism came to me. What he really needs is heat-treatment and of course I haven't got a lamp, but if things go on like this I shall soon be able to get one. Next, first one, then two more, and finally no fewer than *five* pregnant young ladies found their way to me so that now I have a weekly 'class' in psychoprophylactics – a word I've taken care to use freely since they are too madly impressed by it to notice that I have only very recently mastered the techniques myself (a girl in the kibbutz brought me a book about it from which I revised the rather outdated methods I was taught twenty years ago). 'The daughter', whose name is Ziva, a most attractive child with whom I get on extremely well, is so loud in my praises that two of her friends from the local school, who suffered less serious attacks in the same epidemic, have persuaded their parents to send them to me too. I feel a fraud, since, poor little devils, there is little I can do except patiently massage the shrunken muscles and give them exercises, but Ziva swears she feels better and that the treatments relax her and strengthen her legs. Suzy says she can already see a difference in Ziva's walk. Unfortunately there is no actual improvement, and couldn't

214

possibly be in the time, but if it pleases them to think there is I suppose nobody's harmed by it.

My two have settled in fairly well, though Peretz worries me ... he has become insecure again, going off by himself to play (I guess) in the streets after school and not coming home until late, then being rude and sulky if I check him about it. I am in the dog-house again, it seems. ... Ella crows and says, 'He's bad. Isn't he bad?' She likes it still when he's 'bad' and gets into trouble, and snuggles up to me smugly, as if her relative 'goodness' gave her a special and exclusive claim to me again. I have to be cross with her too, sometimes, before he sees this and she gloats and makes him worse. When he is feeling particularly contrary he has a trick of lapsing into Arabic, which he is picking up again from the street-children. Ella has entirely forgotten her Arabic and can't understand what he says to her (just as well, I fear) and of course it infuriates her, so that she has no alternative but to start teasing him. Although Zev and Suzy have both assured me that the thick old walls make our wing of the house practically sound-proof and that in any case they 'like the sound of children about the place' I can't help getting anxious about the amount of noise these quarrels cause. ... I have the fugitive's uneasy instinctive need for quiet as a means to concealment – I am constantly 'shushing' the children – which we all hate. But really that is a small price to pay for this incredible situation.

This is the first time I have really borne the brunt of looking after the children. ... I remember ruefully my misplaced resentment against the kibbutz for abrogating to themselves the duties (dare I be quite honest and call them tiresome?) that I now do. I can only thank God for school hours when they are off my hands. I've been spoilt, that's the trouble. ... It's not so much the chores, it's *coping* with the children when they're at home – keeping them reasonably quiet, settling fights, entertaining them. ... I have been ashamed recently of the relief mixed in with my feelings of worry when Peretz doesn't show up straight after school. Ella is so much easier to be with when she's here with me alone. At the same time his absences hurt me in a way that is even more shaming, since I recognize in the hurt something of what Gila stigmatized as man-woman rather than woman-child — I am wounded in my female vanity that he doesn't want to hurry home to me, or that he turns his back on me, sulking, punishing me for taking him away from his happy kibbutz world. I am grateful to Gila for being so frank in showing me the truth behind this feeling; knowing it, recognizing it as dangerous, I can scotch it as it appears, or at least keep it under control.

But perhaps one of the best things about my present situation is that I am developing a friendship with Suzy, a real woman-friendship which I have lacked for years. At first I found her rather forbidding, with her carved black looks and her reserved manner and her rather harsh, gravelly voice. But even then I sensed something in her that I could respond to, something ... kin to me, a common root somewhere. Since our histories couldn't be more dissimilar it's impossible to say what that could be, but as the weeks have passed I've noticed that we both grab, or even make, opportunities to speak to each other, to seek each other out, each short meeting bringing us closer together. Zev spends the mornings painting in the courtyard while Suzy cleans the house and prepares food. (She is a wonderful cook in the Romanian manner of making much of the cheapest foods — she told me that, at the beginning of the war before they were 'caught', her mother was reduced to making cakes of potatoes and pig-lard and saccharine.) Then in the afternoons she takes over the yard for her sculpting. She works chiefly in wood and stone; I hear her from my room, her chisel making a series of musical chinks. One window in my flat overlooks the yard, and sometimes I go and watch her at work; she keeps to one corner, where the overhang of the roof gives her shade; her levis white with stone-dust or wood-chips, she moves slowly round the crude revolving stand which has ceased to revolve, her eyes riveted to the point of her chisel, as it grates in little sharp movements against the block. Her hair is tied back with a bright bandana which covers every strand, so that her profile stands out clearly, the extreme bulge of the chin and round forehead almost out to a level with her small sharp nose, the brows knotted in concentration, the naked lips, rather blistered-looking and always closed round a cigarette, pursed in an expression of permanent speculation, as if what was emerging from the block under her tools was as much a surprise to her as anyone. She often goes barefoot, leaving her mules neatly on the edge of the shadow so that if she has to cross the burning cobbles in the centre of the yard she can slip them on. I've noticed her feet are very ugly, the toes somehow misshapen – perhaps that's why she never wears sandals, and takes off her mules (intolerably hot in this weather) only when no one is about.

Once she glanced up while lighting a fresh cigarette and noticed me watching her. For a moment her frown deepened, but then she beckoned me. By the time I'd come out she had replaced the mules and was standing back from her work, her weight on one leg, the other hip thrust out like a young girl under the loose hem of the pancho.

We stood looking at the lump of stone – a virtual six-weeks-foetus of a statue, showing only the vaguest outlines of two people clasped together – embracing, struggling? One couldn't possibly tell – Suzy smoking and scowling, I gazing almost reverently as the amateur, the appreciator, always gazes at the processes of the professional mystery. I felt comment would be an impertinence, and Suzy (I've noticed) never asks for criticism even of a finished work ('It only confuses me, since no two people ever see a statue with the same eyes'). So we stared, and at last she said, 'Coffee?' and I said, 'Let me get it from my place.' 'No, take from us. By me, there's always coffee on the stove.' 'That's a Canadian custom.' 'Romanian too.' 'Let me bring it.' 'Good. Use big mugs and be free with sugar in mine.'

Thus most of our conversations – terse, but somehow easy, underpinned by some subtle accord. We sat on the stone bench to drink, the sunlight glaring down just beyond us, giving us the feeling of shelter from some bombardment; Suzy was remote, studying her statue, one slippered foot resting on the other thigh. I felt relaxed and comfortable in her company, for she has a built-in strength which is perhaps why the children are always quiet and un-tense when she is nearby – it is that she gives one a sense of security in her presence, an enviable thing, but presumably one which has to be bought and paid for in some currency of suffering unknown to the likes of me. I wondered if she were at all curious about me, as I was about her, if there were enough of the woman left in that whittled-down, concentrated personality to make her share the common hunger of human interest stories. I wondered what she and Zev talked about in bed. . . .

As if to answer my thoughts, she turned to me suddenly and smiled, the black thick eyebrows separating and showing me a wide expanse between the blue eyes. 'Will you be able to stay on here?' she asked.

'I very much hope so. It depends on how the money comes in.'

'Can't your husband help you at all?' And then, quickly – 'Excuse me, of course I shouldn't ask that, but you see we want that you will stay if possible.'

'That's all right. I haven't a husband.'

'Oh. . . . But the one who brought you here?'

'He's just a friend. He's someone else's husband, as a matter of fact.' I had the grace to blush. Dan has been back once to make sure I was all right, and to tell me nobody had been asking for me. The meeting was very formal; the children were there, but it would have been formal anyway – I could feel the tension between us like a wall, his determination to show nothing, to betray nothing more of himself to me.

Suzy asked no more but I felt that it was now my turn to volunteer some information about myself. I had felt from the start that it was neither fair nor honest not to tell them something about the situation, though of course I had to wait until I was sure I could trust them.

'The children aren't mine,' I said. She looked at me quickly, but without surprise. 'They're adopted.'

'Ziva also.'

'Really! I didn't know that. But she looks like you.'

'And your little boy has your mouth. It is so, often.'

I was absurdly touched and pleased to hear her say that Peretz looked like me. I had never thought of such a thing.

'But didn't you notice how dark they are?' I asked her, feeling my way.

'Yes . . . one cannot help noticing things.'

I was delighted with her. She was a real 'girl' after all, not nearly so stern and aloof as she looked. I laughed aloud and she looked up again, surprised. 'Why do you laugh?'

'I like you.'

She looked more surprised than ever, and didn't say anything. It was clear she was unused to anything so unsubtle as my declaration. But I felt it pleased her all the same, though perhaps she disapproved a little.

'If I make dinner one night instead of my usual sandwich, will you and Zev and Ziva come?' I asked on impulse.

She pursed her lips rather primly. 'It's kind of you – '

'But. But what? You like to keep to yourselves and you don't want to get involved with me – is that it?'

'No,' she said, 'no, by no means. I – Forgive me, we know so few people here. We've become rather insular. In Jerusalem, where we lived before, it was different . . . there we had a whole circle of artists and other friends . . .'

'It must have been hard to leave there.'

'Yes.'

'Why did you?'

She glanced at me again through the cigarette smoke, a narrow, measuring look. She shrugged very slightly.

'It is a small battleground – artistic Jerusalem. Small and fierce. Zev is not a fierce man. I am fierce, but not enough for us both.'

'But will it be any different here? Surely every art-colony has its own endemic rat-race.'

She shrugged again, and smoked in silence for a few minutes. The shadow moved a little farther away from our feet, and bees droned amid the big yellow flowers of the gourd-vine that had been trained up one of the pillars. The coffee was wonderfully fragrant and good – it had a touch of *hale* in it, in the Arab style, which reminded me of Kofi. How studiously I have been avoiding him in my thoughts during these weeks! – as if thoughts of him might give him a clue to my whereabouts, might draw him to me somehow. But the aroma, the taste of the *hale* made an immediate, almost instinctive connection which was irresistible and not even unpleasant, since it was associated with the early days of our friendship.

'Zev is a good artist and in some ways he is brave,' she said slowly, breaking into thoughts which had left her behind for a moment. 'I would not have lived through the War . . . and in the Siege (she meant of Jerusalem) he was never afraid, never even depressed, even when there was no water, when we were starving, expecting the Arabs to break through every moment. . . . But when it comes to fighting for himself, for his work, he cannot do it. He doesn't think it matters enough to be angry for. And that makes *me* angry – even with him. Luckily I am only a coward in war-time. For the work of my husband, I fear no one and can fight like a tiger.'

'Yet you left Jerusalem.'

'Yes. I fought too hard and made myself hated. And Zev could not bear to see me so angry so often. So we came here to start again, and we both made promises. I promised not to fight so hard and he promised to fight harder. So far there has been little reason for either of us to fight because there are so few customers and the artists are still scattered, fighting their little battles for sales in their own corners. We are not against each other here. We are for keeping alive, artistically, and that takes all our time.'

They came to dinner. It was a Friday and I remembered to put candles on the table, feeling awkward about it because who thinks of that these days? I haven't lit candles for years. But the children's enchantment as I explained the custom rather sheepishly made me remember my own childhood, where Friday candles were as automatic as daylight at noon, and I wondered if I am cheating them with my indifference to the old traditions. I borrowed enough glasses and dishes from Suzy and arranged fruit in a big wooden dish that I found, work-eaten but still with its chisel-marks clear on it, in the bottom of a cupboard. I have settled in more or less by now, my few bits and pieces arranged. . . . I look round at them now, tracing those which date back to Canada (not many) to Haifa (a few added) to Acco (a copper

220

dish, some stones, a piece of driftwood) through the kibbutz, where I added nothing except Dan's statue and some polished Jacaranda pods. Yet somehow the effect in those small white obliging rooms is pleasing. Suzy looked round and touched an arrangement of stones and pods in a dish; near it, some bleached, bizarrely-spiked dry thistles stand stuck in a lump of clay. I have no pictures; the only wall decoration is a piece of batik that was given to me a hundred years ago by Judy's eldest daughter, who made it at an evening class. Dan's statue stands by itself on the deep window ledge. This drew Suzy next; she stood back from it, staring through the spirals of smoke.

'A male sculptor,' she said at last. 'They tell us women that we are too literary, that our pieces must always tell a story. Yet look at that . . . it might be a scene from a film, where the hero has just been shot in the back.'

Ziva said gently, 'Not right, mother. It is just a study in arrested movement. I think it is very abstract and not at all literary.'

Suzy's face broke into a smile, the heavy eyebrows parting suddenly, the blue gaze expanding to fix itself on Ziva's face, as open as a kiss, all concealment abandoned.

Dinner was a success. 'We so seldom eat anything but my food,' said Suzy, 'and alas! I know only three dishes.' '*Four*, mother, not counting the omelette.' 'Then it's five. We must count the omelette since it is my best thing.' And Zev, quiet, a calm but somehow wavering presence, his attention flickering like the candle-flames as if he kept going away somewhere, tucking into his food in smiling silence, watching his women with a gentle, wandering gaze.

How pleasant it was. Afterwards Ziva went off to bed, and we sat a long time over coffee and the small bottle of cheap brandy I had splurged on, my first 'drink' for longer than I can remember. . . . I had a slight stab of superstitious reluctance before tasting mine, like a cured alcoholic, but after the first mouthful I wasn't assailed by an uncontrollable urge to swig the whole lot down in one and grab for the rest of the bottle . . . it merely filled me with a mild glow of extra well-being. . . . I found myself talking a lot, making them laugh. . . . Suzy's laugh is a bird's caw, with a note of self-surprise in it, Zev's is a strange sort of crackle, like dry paper being crumpled . . .

When we were all good and mellow, I began to talk about myself. It was quite uncalculated. . . . I felt an overpowering need to share something with them. I hadn't meant to unburden myself to the degree I did, but by midnight they knew most of it. There were long pauses during which I tried to decide that I had said enough and to control my snow-balling urge to get it all out; my guests sat wreathed in smoke, watching me quietly, waiting, the candle flames flinging soft shadows as they flapped in their spreading low pools of wax. . . . In the end I even told them about Kofi, though without naming him. There was a very long silence after I'd finished.

'I should have told you before,' I said lamely at last.

Suzy slowly shook her head. 'No,' she said. 'No. Even yesterday, perhaps, would have been too early.' I still don't quite understand this cryptic remark. Perhaps she meant that every day our relationship deepened a little more until tonight she and Zev were prepared to accept what they would have been doubtful about any sooner. 'Children without papers,' she said softly, as if speaking to herself – but she was speaking to Zev; 'refugee children.' They exchanged a look and he put his foot in brief accord against the side of her bare leg.

Chapter 3

Dan has been again. He's just left, throwing the Sussita hurriedly into gear and veering away round the well with a painful screech of tyres. ... He's obviously terribly nervous and upset.

And why am *I* suddenly so calm? I feel armoured and secure in this place as if in a stockade. But it's ridiculous. I am no more safe here than I would be in an open field. Suzy and Zev can do nothing to help me. Why should I feel that they can?

My impulse is to run through the court and into Suzy's kitchen, with its pots of geraniums and its strangely out-of-place paintings, and pour everything out to her ... but this is childish. I must think it out first, the implications. It may mean very little. ... After all, we expected it, or something like it, although the business of Raya is an unlooked-for complication ...

Dan arrived an hour ago without warning. He had just found time to change his shirt before setting off, but his trousers were grease-stained and he hadn't cleaned his hands and nails properly ... they jumped on his knees as he sat in my living-room, his eyes moving about restively, avoiding my face ...

'Where are the children?' he asked first, his tone abrupt, almost sharp.'

'At school.'

'Do you go and fetch them from there?'

'No – they know their own way.'

'You should fetch them.'

I began to be afraid. 'What's happened?'

'Several things ... the Police have been back.'

'Back? Have they been before?'

'Of course, three weeks ago they came – I wrote to you.'

'I never got your letter! You shouldn't write to me, anyway – should you?'

'I couldn't get down. There was no other way. These damned posts ... can't rely on them. ...' He was fumbling for a cigarette. I hadn't one to give him and I needed one myself. I've been trying to give them up recently to save money.

'Well?'

'Well, it was no more than we'd looked for. They came, they asked about you ... we told as much of the truth as we could ... said you'd been with us for a year, told us the kids were Moroccan, then one day you'd said you'd decided to leave and taken yourself off .. they made a lot of inquiries. The person they spent most time with – oddly enough – was Raya.'

'Raya? Why Raya?'

'I can only suppose because she's a fellow Canadian. Perhaps they thought she'd be your most likely confidante.'

A silence followed. I felt the greatest possible unease suddenly. Raya was so silly, and at the same time so. ... But surely Dan would have been careful to tell her as little as possible, her of all people. Or would he?

I felt I must ask. 'What does she know?'

'From me, nothing.'

'What does that mean?'

'It means that the whole kibbutz talked of nothing else for two weeks after you left. I'm the only one who knows your address but several others – on the committee – know the story, the general plan. How safe is such a secret in a kibbutz? Might someone tell his wife, might she not tell her best friend? Who can be certain?'

Now my flesh began to creep with real fear. 'And Raya?'

'Raya. ... Raya has been behaving – unnaturally recently.'

'Towards you?'

'Yes. She nags me incessantly. Why did I help you? What do I know? Why won't I tell her? She won't let it alone.'

Our eyes met. His were still rimmed with guilt.

'She couldn't know – about that. Nobody does.'

'Some wives – don't have to be told things.' He dropped his eyes. 'Sometimes it's not possible – to behave exactly the same as before.'

'Dan! Christ! But if she guessed *that* –'

'She would be a danger to you. Yes.'

I stood up. There was nowhere to go to. I sat down again, my nerves jumping. 'I must have a cigarette –'

'Come on. We'll go out. Buy some.'

'Good.' Anything was better than staying in that room. I thought we might walk to the school, I thought I might catch a glimpse of the children, perhaps take them out early and bring them back here and lock them in . . . my fortress! Idiot that I am.

Outside it was very hot, but we walked briskly as if we had to keep ourselves warm. The kiosk was a short distance beyond the calm pristine square in the warren of narrow alleys. We bought packets of twenty each, and matches, and lit up in silence, drawing in gulps of smoke.

'Fancy me forgetting my pipe,' he said, his voice unsteady.

'Dan . . .'

'What?'

'I've given you a bad time.'

There was a pause as he looked down at the cobbles. His match had just joined a pattern of papers and water-melon seeds and peanut shells. There was a tremendous noise all round us, the noise of market, and the strong hot smells buffeted us. Dan said, 'It's been very difficult for me.'

'I'm so sorry.' I meant it.

'*One night,*' he said bitterly.

'Dan, I'm sorry!'

'So am I!'

We walked slowly, aimlessly through the streets. They were the same streets through which the children found their way home each afternoon. I looked now, and saw danger in every face, every grimy unshaven figure hanging about round the kiosks and shop-doorways seemed a potential menace. After all, Kofi was not alone.

'But you said the police had been back again,' I remembered suddenly.

'Yes. Early this morning. We thought it had all died down – we hoped. Then they came back. The same men.'

'So it's a case to them now.'

'Yes. The same men – the same questions. How could you have just left like that? Did the kibbutz give you money? Surely someone must know where you were? They tackled Raya again. I managed to get a word with her first. She and I – had a row last night. A bad row. She had dropped hints. . . . I told her – I only had a few minutes before the men came – I told her that whatever she knew, *whatever* she knew, she should think only of the children – your children. And she looked at me as she looked at me last night during our row and said, "Am I to think of the children? All right, I'll think of them. I'll ask myself if a woman like that has a right to children, if they wouldn't be better off with someone else . . ." '

My legs stopped moving; I felt my body lose its strength. I had to clutch his arm. After a moment I was able to ask: 'And – did she?'

'I don't know. They spoke to her alone. She wouldn't tell me what they'd said. But they left immediately afterwards. And I left to come here.'

There was a long silence. We were walking through a narrow alley with tiny shops on either side, their wares spilling on to the pavement, mostly clothes so old one could scarcely tell their original colour. . . . Every now and then one saw a little copper-shop, like a grimy jewel-box among shabby wardrobes, with bowls of broken Hebron beads catching the thin rays of sunlight filtering between the awnings. I love this place and often wander about in there, fending off the accosting shop-keepers who persist in thinking me a rich tourist in disguise, just as they used to in Acco. . . . Now the heaps of cloth and strings of phoney clay antiquities spun past the tails of my eyes in a blur. I was conscious, in the background of my perceptions, of Dan's bitterness and regret, and so it was an immense surprise – enough to make me jump – when I suddenly felt his hand close round mine.

I looked up at him. His face was a study of confusion. He gripped my hand so hard that it hurt – as if deliberately. Then he muttered something and I said stupidly 'What?' and he repeated, 'I love you.' His voice was full of anger and bewilderment. I said his name – not knowing what else to say, not knowing even what I felt – but he said irritably, 'Don't say "Dan" in that stupid way, like a line in a play. Let's turn back, these flies are maddening me.'

We walked back hand in hand. I felt the pressure building up between us like a head of steam as we crossed the square. Apprehension took hold of me. Dan began to hurry like a hungry child who can smell dinner cooking, pulling me along by the wrist, his eyes fixed on the door of the house.

Indoors it was cool and dim. My front door closed behind us and instantly Dan grabbed me. He kissed me all over my face and neck and felt me – it was not like caressing, but as if he was making sure I was all there – with his hands. I stood immobile, letting him; if my mind had not been so occupied with my sudden new fears, I might have tried to stop him, but as it was I half-welcomed this physical assault which promised a few minutes' relief; and besides, *morally* I didn't know how to say no to him. He backed me to the couch and pushed me down on it – it had caught me low on the legs and I really fell, quite gracelessly, with him falling heavily on top; it was anything but romantic and well-managed, in fact I thought at the time how ludicrous it must have looked. Then there was a tremendous fumbling and wrestling with his clothes (my straight shift was more accommodating); by this time I was only thinking how the whole business could be dealt with as smoothly, as uncomically as possible – sex is really quite ridiculous if one doesn't manage it with some care and dignity, and Dan wasn't concerning himself with that, he was going after it like a sex-starved soldier in a foreign whore-house. This was so out of character that I was puzzled – until I remembered that he was angry with me, that this was probably his way of punishing me, to 'use' me like this in the crudest possible way, as I had 'used' him. On that thought I felt something like an inner shrug and a smile; I helped him, feeling suddenly that I had an indecent

227

amount of power over him which I must use kindly. It was even pleasant in the event, because when it came to it Dan is too civilized a man to bungle something like that, even when he was trying to. Afterwards he sat on the edge of the couch, his head in one hand, the other hand holding mine like a miserable child, but he said 'I'm sorry, Gerda,' in such an adult voice that I knew he had understood his own motives much more clearly and painfully than I.

'Don't be. I'm glad, it was lovely,' I said, childish too in my embarrassment.

'You don't know what I've felt. I can't shake you off. Now – fool that I am – it will be harder than ever.'

I made coffee and we sat together talking. Oddly enough we were closer now than ever before; Dan's anger was used up and he was once again the quiet, controlled person I had once thought could be my friend.

'My advice to you,' he said, 'is to keep moving until this all dies down. It's not safe to stay in one place. Must you send the children to school at all? Can't you give them lessons at home? It would be much better if you didn't let them out of your sight.'

'Why? What exactly do you think could happen?'

'Your Arab friend is probably in a very tight spot by now. If I were him, I'd try to get across the border, taking the kids with me.'

'But why taking the kids? If he goes across himself, he's safe, isn't he?'

'You said he had a daughter.'

'Hanna.' My memories of her came sharply into focus. In some recess of my mind, since the time I had her with me, I always thought of her as partly mine.

'He might not want to take her to Lebanon. It's not much of a life there for a girl brought up in a peasant village.'

'If you're suggesting he'd leave her behind, I assure you he wouldn't. She's the only thing in his life he gives a damn about.'

Dan thought for a bit. 'In that case,' he said, 'he'd either take her with him, or he'd try to take the kids across and come back. To do that he'd have to find them first.'

I didn't answer. Despite all the evidence, despite his own words, I *still* can't believe that Kofi would actually take the kids away from me. It just doesn't make sense. When I think about it, my mind sheers off, I find myself thinking incredulously, 'But it's Kofi! *Kofi!*' Can fear so alter a person's whole nature that he could do anything so cruel, even to save himself? As if in answer, Dan reminded me: 'Don't forget, there are more in it than him alone. He may be under very heavy pressure to get rid of the evidence.' I suddenly had a clear mental recollection of a face – a long, dark face with a moustache and oblong eyes, high gleaming cheekbones ... at once I remembered. The face of the man I had seen, so long ago, sitting with Kofi at the café on the wharf in Acco. Kofi might have scruples – had them, I was still certain – but that man would have none – none at all. To protect himself, he might even. ... But that is too dreadful to think of.

'I feel so safe here,' I said. 'I don't want to move on.'

'It's a nice place,' said Dan non-committally. 'What are the people like?'

'Wonderful.'

'How much do they know?'

After a slight hesitation, I admitted that they knew nearly everything.

'Was that wise?'

'I think so. I think they'd help me if the need arose.'

'How?'

I shrugged. 'Hide the children, perhaps – say I wasn't here – ' It all sounded so improbable. 'Surely the whole business will die down soon.'

'I don't know so much. Smuggling across the border is serious. Smuggling *people* is something they can't just allow to peter out unsolved.'

'If only I could get them out of the country myself!'

'I'm afraid that's hopeless.'

All sorts of wild ideas went through my mind – bribing someone at the Canadian Embassy to put them on my passport, sneaking them out somehow – all quite crazy and useless. I am stuck here indefinitely, doomed to hide and feel afraid – and perhaps to keep on the move as Dan says, to keep running like a criminal, trying all the time to protect them from the knowledge of my fear. . . .

I wish I hadn't remembered that face.

Chapter 4

Days pass – long, hot, slow, oozing in a thick solid brown stream like molasses from a big ladle. Sometimes my mind goes wandering off into the strangest places ... this rather literary simile about time has lodged in my imagination somehow, and I keep thinking of it as a potful of shapeless brown stuff that some mindless hand scoops out meaninglessly and pours back, scoops out and pours back, slowly, on and on, the same substance used over and over again repeatedly ... certainly the days have this sameness, even though each one brings new conversations, new doings, new people (patients. ... I have quite a little practice now). But the thick sticky blackness is darkly over all of it. It is, I suppose, fear, the fear that colours everything, makes everything tacky to the touch, prevents one really feeling anything cleanly through it.

I have not, cannot, decide to move away from here. Can I possibly have struck roots so quickly? If so, it is in the people, not in the place – all my roots go down into people, perhaps that's why I never became rooted in the kibbutz, there was nobody there that I loved. I belong in this house and to leave it would be an effort more wrenching than I have strength for now. ... But I take precautions. I walk the children to school every day and fetch them home. Sometimes I wonder if this does not draw attention to them more than letting them go alone, but at least I know where they are. ... Peretz hates it. ... He makes me leave them at the last corner, and even so scowls horribly if any of his class-mates see me. I have tried to explain to him, as well as I could, and at the time I thought he understood.

'There are some people who think you ought to go back to your grandmother's.' I didn't want to frighten him, and yet I had to warn him of the danger. 'They might try to take you.'

'But I won't go!'

'Well, you might not be able to help it. That's why I don't let you go out alone any more.'

'But we always went to school alone before.'

'It's only now that there's any danger.'

'But who wants to take us? We're yours now.'

I hugged him against my side, and for once he didn't pull away. 'Some people. I don't know them myself. I can't tell you what they look like. Just don't go with anyone, don't talk to anyone in the streets. And don't let Ella talk to anyone either. Do you promise?'

He didn't answer, just stared down at the red tiled floor.

'But can't I ever go out and play alone in the market any more?'

I knew he had a street-gang there – I had seen the furtive little figures flitting round corners, behind booths, making signals as we passed through the brilliant light-and-shade of the morning alleys . . . His prestige was suffering sadly. I had a sudden fear that, to explain my humiliating presence, he might now use the dramatic information I had given him. . . . 'And you mustn't tell anyone what I've just told you. Peretz, are you listening? If you don't want to be caught and sent back – ' I hated to use such alarming language, but I had to impress it on him – 'you must do as I tell you for the time being.'

He left me and walked slowly to the window. He stared out of it like a prisoner through his grille. 'Will it be like this always?'

'No! One day everything will be normal again.'

He was silent for a long while and then he said, in a cold little grown-up voice, 'It was much better in the kibbutz. Much better.'

'I'm sorry, Peretz. That's how it is sometimes.'

He turned to me. 'But you like it here, don't you?'

It was like an accusation. 'Yes. But I didn't leave the kibbutz because I wanted to come here.'

'Then why?'

'Because of what I told you. It was too dangerous to stay

there. Now nobody knows where we are, and that's better.'

His straight black stare wavered after a moment, and slipped to my knees. Suddenly he ran over to me and I held him tight for the brief instant he gave me before pulling away and saying roughly, 'I want to play in the square.'

'All right,' I said unwilling. 'Stay where I can see you.'

He didn't, of course, and I couldn't be looking out of the window every minute, but he came when I went out and called him. I can't keep them cooped up here all day. . . .

Meanwhile I draw closer and closer to Zev's family. Ziva one day brought some schoolbooks with her when she came for her treatment, setting them on the table as if by chance, and afterwards shyly asking me if I happened to know the opposite in English for 'excited'.

' "Calm" I should think,' I said.

She frowned, her eyebrows drawing together in an exact replica of her mother's mannerism. 'It can't be. We've never had that word.' 'Well, try it, and see.' 'Can you spell it for me?' I spelt it and she wrote it carefully in a copybook with triple lines, exactly like the ones in which I write all this. . . . She had fine, careful handwriting.

The next day she returned, elated. ' "Calm" was right!' she said. 'I was the only one who got it! The others all put "bored" or left it out.' She stood on one leg, the good one, lanky as a water-bird with her thin limbs and long straight hair, her bony face and large bright eyes. 'I hate English', she said suddenly.

'Oh, why? It's a lovely language.'

'Too difficult.'

'Maybe I could help you,' I said without thinking.

Her face flashed on like a bulb. 'Oh, would you?' I felt a wry sinking sensation. Trapped!

But I didn't mind really. I have this overpowering urge to play a part in their lives, to be a member of this household. Nothing delights me more than when Suzy pops across the court to borrow something, or when I see her crouched down, her heels rising out of the battered mules, holding Ella between her knees and talking to her earnestly as if to a business-partner. . . . This gives me the feeling that the children, too, are accepted, are being absorbed into this safe, strong, impregnable little world of the white house built round a vine-roofed square.

My utter conviction that this place is a safe haven, physically as well as emotionally, needs examining, for it is the basis of my ignoring Dan's excellent advice to keep on the move. Again, it is not the locale, it is not the building, sturdy and protective as it is, it is the people. It is Suzy and 'Zev. ... People who have survived so much, and not only physically survived but with their spirits preserved, their desire to go on creating, love and generosity unblunted, even their gaiety intact and still fit for use. ... I have learned a lot about them since I began seeing more of Ziva. She knows their history, more than one would have expected them to tell such a youngster, but the kids here take the camps as facts of life, as a child at home might accept without question that his now-comfortable parents were once poor and jobless, or that they suffered hunger and privations in the great prairie droughts. Suzy was in Ravensbrück with her mother, who looked young enough so that their relationship was not suspected and they were left together. ... It is easy now for me to participate in these horrors, not float guiltily on the surface wondering why I cannot feel in my own body the foulness. ... Now all I need to do is imagine Ella, a few years older, old enough to be of interest to the soldiers, stripped naked and paraded past some cold-eyed bespectacled clerk in a muffler, making life-and-death marks on sheets of paper with a fountain-pen leaking from the cold. ... Their shoes were never returned to them, Ziva said. They tied strips of cloth round their feet, anything they could find, with dead leaves and even earth inside to protect them from the frost. But it didn't help Suzy. 'Have you noticed that she doesn't wear sandals?' Ziva asked quietly. 'Parts of her toes are gone. She got gangrene and would have died only her mother stole a knife from the kitchen and ... and ... and afterwards she couldn't stand remembering what she'd had to do and she killed herself with the same knife.'

How do you tell a child a thing like that? Why do you tell it, why do you not find some softer explanation for the poor pillaged feet? For a minute I almost hated Suzy for the look in

Ziva's eyes as she told this. But then I remembered the Eichmann trial, and what had been said at the time: 'That our children may know, and not forget.'

And there is more. Ziva is not their own child. She's the daughter of a cousin who died of asthma brought on by her camp experiences. And why have Zev and Suzy no children of their own, after twenty years of marriage? For the same reason that many camp-bred women have no children, because of what was done to her there for the sake of 'convenience' and which arrested the vital life-flow for ever.

Zev's story I still don't know. Either Ziva doesn't know it, or she isn't telling. Somehow I think the latter, for her eyes swing away at the mention of him in the same breath as the war. She adores him, and yet – there is something there she's ashamed of. I can guess at it. . . . I had thought he was about fifty, but he is much less, not older than me. He was only a young boy when war broke out. He would not be the only one the Germans forced to help them. . . . I heard a woman in the kibbutz communa say once, her voice, above the homely whir of darning-machines, more bitter than any I've ever heard, 'None of us who got through it have clean hands.' Not true, of course, but something that *she* did to survive obviously still haunts her, and it could be that Zev too bought his continued existence in some way which he cannot now bear to think of. Poor Zev! If it is so, I pity him, I love him more than ever . . . since this idea occurred to me, I have seen more in those heavy, brooding abtracts with their poised black beams criss-crossed menacingly over red backgrounds, than I did before.

What a relief it is to write of other people! When I look back over this thickening pile of notebooks, glancing through them as I sometimes do, catching here and there a genuine whiff of what I felt when I was writing this page or that, I notice my lack of outward-looking. I could dub the whole lot 'Diary of an Ingrowing Toenail' or just 'Introspections'. Yet I am not a natural introvert, I have merely been utterly selfish, utterly egotistical. . . . So many lost chances, so many pieces of wanton stupidity. . . . Such a pity. Surely I am better now? Surely I am changing, improving? ... I want to, for the children's sake.

I've never been a person who gets premonitions, but quite suddenly, three days ago, I was gripped (it literally felt like something taking a grasping physical hold on me) by a nightmare conviction that a net is closing round me. My peace of mind, such a strong, tangible thing until then, my sense of safety, was demolished and blown away in a matter of hours as this terrible feeling became stronger and stronger.

It was not totally causeless. Someone is watching us. I didn't discover this suddenly, but came to realize it slowly over a period of days. One sees the same faces every morning and evening as one passes through the same narrow streets – the faces of shopkeepers, of passers-by who live in the area, of children – one scarcely notices how they are building themselves into one's eye, becoming familiar until one would be surprised if a different face confronted one from behind a certain counter or leaning indolently out of a particular window. It was a long time before I knew with certainty (the certainty did come suddenly) that one man who, in the mornings, is always leaning against a wall just inside the first alley leading from the square is the same one who sits at a café just across the road from the school near where I wait for the children to take them home. The thing that finally made the connection was that one day I saw him in a new place – leaning against the sea-wall diametrically opposite our front door, just across from the well. As I came out to call Peretz home from playing I saw the man turning his back abruptly. He was alone there and he stood out, and I suddenly knew that he didn't belong there, that he didn't belong in the other places where I always saw him; I realized that he was never doing anything, just waiting and watching.

I stood frozen, staring at his back, the fear, the premonition, beginning to get its grip on me. He was short, rather stocky and strong-looking, insignificantly dressed in well-pressed shabby clothes and a nondescript hat. He didn't belong, he didn't belong at all. He was dark skinned and he had a small, well-tended moustache, but I didn't think he was an Arab. If he was not an Arab, and if my fear was right, that meant he was a policeman.

I have stopped letting Peretz go out to play in the square since that day. It makes life hell at home, but I've told him about the man and this interested him enough to make him accept the situation with slightly better grace. I then broke down and told Suzy my fears. They were real and awful for the first time since I moved here – even Dan's alarming information didn't frighten me properly, not for long, but that man did. Only the sight of that long narrow face in the crowded market – the face of Kofi's confederate – could have terrified me more. And now I keep looking for it, peering into shadows – I know it's neurotic, but I keep thinking I see him, it is a common type of face here, half the young Arab men look something like that, though not with the same hollows under the high egg-shaped cheekbones, not the same odd eyes, like shallow rectangles. . . . How extraordinary that I remember him so clearly after seeing him only that once!

Suzy. . . . Suzy was wonderful. She stopped me from feeling so frightened just by the way she said, 'Just remember, you're not alone any more.' I was so grateful to her. . . . Though what can they do for me? Even if there were anything, I have no business to ask it.

Ella is playing near me as I write this. She is nearly five now. Some of her puppy-fat has gone, for I don't give them as many cakes and sweets as they got in the kibbutz. Is she pretty? I can't tell any more. Her hair is lovely, bright coppery black, full of little tight curls, enough of it now to make a 'kuku' (you can't call it a pony-tail, it is more like a bottle-brush) at the back with an elastic band. She is not specially intelligent, as Peretz is, but she has the most adorable nature, warm, gentle, affectionate, full of sudden sly sparks of humour. She sees a joke far quicker than Peretz, in fact her redress against him when he annoys her is to make fun of him, which maddens him, as this is a type of in-fighting that he cannot understand or answer. She and I tease each other by the hour and it draws us closer and closer together.

The chores of looking after them have become routine now.

and much of it is even fun. Peretz gets homework from school, and it always amuses and touches me to see how he settles down, as just now, at first with heavy sighs and a great show of reluctance, and then in a few minutes has become absorbed to such a degree that nothing can disturb him. His teacher talked to me recently. . . . She said, cautiously, that he seems to have a rather better-than-average brain and should do well at his studies 'if he can learn to pay attention and behave himself'. I asked in what way he fails to behave himself, and she pressed her lips together and said that his ingenuity in finding ways to misbehave might be taken as a pointer to his intelligence, but that it was a pity it could not find more constructive outlets. I rather liked her . . . one is lucky to find that rather old-fashioned, wry, dry type in a school like that, vast, old, the classrooms crammed with desks, a bell like a fire alarm going off every forty minutes, loud enough to make you jump out of your skin. . . . But it is a school and he is learning there, he is even enjoying the process though he would never admit it, almost as much as Ella enjoys her 'gan' where they do clay-modelling and finger-painting . . .

Four pages, the pencil running on and on like a mad thing, afraid to stop for fear of something running behind which will pounce and tear. . . . I am writing like a witch-doctor chanting spells, to keep away the evil spirits. Strange . . . now I don't even feel safe when both of them are indoors with me as they are now. What a change for one little man in an old straw hat to be able to make.

Today as we walked through the crowded market to school, somebody – some brushing, passing shadow – pushed a note into my hand. It happened so quickly that I couldn't locate the person who'd done it. I grabbed the kids' hands and rushed them forward, as fast as possible, till we emerged in the open street beyond the maze of alleys, where the school, squat, black and comfortable, stood waiting to engulf them. I kissed them good-bye and pushed them off, then watched them till they were safely through the door before opening the note.

It was from Kofi. It was written on the cheapest lined paper, stained with sweaty finger-prints, the creases black and fluffy as if it had lain for some time in the depths of a dirty pocket. I clutched it so hard when I saw the writing that the central crease came apart and I had to hold the two halves together to read it. My hands were actually shaking. It was written in Hebrew and there was no greeting. It simply began.

'You were right, and I was mad. I am glad from my heart that you took them and in case you worried (why should you but in case) nothing has happened to me yet, but it is going to if I don't get away. The police know where you are and are watching you to make sure, to see if you are in touch with me, with us. Try and take the children and go somewhere else or they will take them away. I am leaving. Tonight. I am taking H. and going the way you know. I won't see you again. I ask your forgiveness. You were my only true friend I will always think of you with my heart.' He signed it with a clumsy Latin K. and then scribbled on the bottom, 'burn at once'.

Oddly enough, it was difficult to destroy it. It was difficult to think or act at all. Everything I had ever felt for him, the whole confused medley of love, dependence, gratitude, hatred, descended again, all of them together, and I felt numbed and crushed. I held the torn paper in my hand, staring at its faint scrawled message of love and warning and the words that mattered most of all were 'I won't see you again'.

I have not destroyed it yet. I will, but not yet. I sit here staring at it, touching it, re-reading it again and again, trying to think what to do and thinking only of Kofi, fled across the border (how long ago? How long did the folded paper lie in that alien pocket?) – gone with Hanna to God knows what – and how will he live over there? As a perpetual fugitive, without past, without papers? Dear God, how awful it all is! How needlessly, pointlessly cruel! Why must our already over-complex personal situations be complicated still more by a hopeless international one? If the Lebanon were not an enemy country, nobody here would bother to this extent about two stray orphans ...

The thought of Kofi is a permanent inflammation of the heart, more than I can rationally explain. But it is Hanna's fate that troubles me most sharply. I have been thinking about her such a lot recently. I haven't seen her for nearly two years. She must be getting on for ten now. I wonder if her mother thinks of her half as much as I do . . .

What am I doing, drivelling on about these people who have gone out of my life for ever? I can do nothing about them, and my immediate problems are so overwhelmingly grave that I should have no thoughts to spare for anyone else's. I keep getting up from the table and going to the narrow, fortress-like window that overlooks the square . . . the place by the sea-wall is empty, the passers-by are few and slow-moving in the heat, like creatures oppressed by the weight of an ocean. The children are at school. . . . It's not time to fetch them yet, but I can't sit here idly any longer. I'll go and wait in that café, and if I see that bloody cop I'll go straight up to him and. . . . Fool. You'll do nothing of the sort. . . . You'll grab those two kids and hike them home as fast as their legs will carry them, and you'll start packing. . . . Why haven't I been packing all this time? I have sat here like someone 'high' on dope – I feel paralysed. It's fear. . . . There's someone at the door –

I've finished everything. I've ruined everything! Now there's no room for hesitations or doubt. I've got to get out and at once.

It was him – the policeman. He took off his hat as I opened the door. There was another man with him. They asked if I was – who I am, and I, dumbstruck, stared at them, bearing for the first time the full weight of foreboding and dread. They asked again, the same flat, toneless question, and at last I said something, some affirmative word or sound, and they – it must just have been one of them, but it seemed as if they spoke together in a roaring chorus like water in the ears of a drowner – broke into a torrent of legal jargon from which I understood what I had known before they opened their mouths, that they had come to take the children.

Instead of being calm, instead of showing myself to be mature and civil and controlled, I felt sense shake loose of its moorings inside my head and leaning both hands against the door-jambs I lurched suddenly towards them and began to scream. I screamed at them to go away, to leave me alone, but I used language that I scarcely would have believed I could let out of my mouth, the language of a trapped whore.... They glanced at each other in the midst of it and my hate was intensified so that when they turned their silent, impassive faces towards me again I spat at one of them.... Oh, dear Christ! What a moment to go mad! Now I have no chance, no chance at all ...

They went away when I had spent myself, but first one of them quietly said that they would be getting a court order to allow them to take the children. 'By force?' I said, my voice low at last, but from exhaustion, not control. 'We hope that won't be necessary,' said the man who had watched me, and they walked away.

Chapter 5

Suzy has gone. I made her go at last. She only went when I had promised her faithfully that as soon as the door closed I would begin to write. She believes that will keep me from despair, and perhaps it will. I know she is standing outside the door, listening for the safe sounds – the scrape of a chair, the striking of a match. I have given her those, and now I am writing, pressing hard with the pen as if she could hear the reassuring scratch through the door. But from where she stands now, exhausted, anxious, there must be an alarming and ambiguous silence. . . . Not that I threatened anything. . . . I would have done once, but somehow not any more. Even through this nightmare few days of emotional expenditure, I have been left something, perhaps it's no more than gratitude to Suzy, but it must be more than that or I couldn't have forced her to leave when I so needed her to stay. But it wasn't fair to keep her sitting here any longer, stifling in my private grief. Besides, I have to face it alone eventually. The quicker the better.

I remember when Jake died there was a moment – right near the beginning – when I thought to myself: 'If only it were five years from now! If only the worst of bearing it were over!' I wanted to feel normal again, to be released from the oppression of grief and guilt, to recover my happiness. And even though I should have learned that all the years of life don't finally heal something like that, I have the same feeling now. My wounds are wide open, fresh, raw and bloody – the pain is like a constant scream and no turnings or twistings free me from it for a moment – I long for sleep with a kind of futile anger, I long for utter drunkenness, even for death – in other words, oblivion. And all the time my mind is jumping forward – two years, ten years – (knowing I won't die, that this has to be got through) when I may hope to emerge slowly. . . . Oh, but I shall be old by then! What's the use of emerging into a time when one is in any case too old for anything but backward-looking? What hope have I, what small, distant hope, to keep me from despair at this moment?

I see I'm writing rationally, even to some extent objectively. There's hope for me in that, surely. . . . There is a lot of the male in me. . . . So Alec always used to say. 'You don't submerge in your feelings, as most women do.' I *am* submerged and yet – a part keeps aloof, a part can keep writing lucidly, a cold observer. . . . How strange. The first man I ever slept with, bright, callow, with 'winning ways,' was a local reporter, and I asked him once in disgust how he could remain uninvolved enough to write coldly and pointedly about other people's tragedies. He didn't know. . . . 'One has to, it's one's job.' Is it 'one's job' to keep an objective watch over oneself in one's own moments of agony? Is that a form of self-preservation? If so, why do I feel that I shouldn't be able to sit here, writing about it, any more than that shallow boy should have been able to watch poor people dragged out of train-wrecks and interview them before the soot and blood had been cleaned off their frightened faces, going home afterwards filled with satisfaction because of the 'story' he'd obtained?

This is a form of escape surely less degrading than the usual ones. . . . Not that I have not taken my quota of relief in tears tonight, and drink, and outpourings on to a patient, willing, untiring friend. . . . But one must take one's relief where one can. It seems I *can* write it. I can ease myself like that, at least until the hypnotic flow of the pen stops and I have to close with myself again.

. . . I packed. I had everything ready. It was nearly time to get the children from school. On the way out, I met Suzy in the courtyard. She was working on a piece of stone, chipping, chipping, the white pieces flying away from her like disturbed moths. . . . I told her I must leave, I told her about the note. I showed it to her. She asked me where I was going and I said I didn't know, to a small hotel in Tel Aviv first perhaps, then I had thought of moving to another town, Beersheba or. . . . She interrupted with sudden ferocity to say that the whole thing was fantastic. '*Fantastic!*' She suddenly struck her chisel against the stone with great violence and made a long, unwanted scratch which caused her to swear. 'You can't keep running away like that,' she said. 'Your friend has gone. He's out of it. Why don't you go to the authorities yourself, why don't you try and sort it out openly? Skulking about in shabby hotels . . . scuttling from town to town. . . . *This* is your home, Gerda, *here*. If you don't straighten things out, for better or worse. . . . Gerda, it's only a little country. You can't keep hidden here for ever, you are too conspicuous. You'll put yourself through hell, and in the end they'll catch up with you anyway. Believe me, they will. They must.'

Something like that, she said. It was suddenly, obviously, hopelessly true, every word. . . . I had known it myself really. It was not mere inertia that had kept me from 'moving on' before, it was a sense of futility. But the policemen's visit had panicked me. . . . I stared at Suzy and at last I nodded. 'Openly,' she repeated. 'Let everything be open. You have nothing to be ashamed of.'

I had no time to pack before I left. It was late as it was. I ran through the alleys to the school, still mortally frightened but somehow relieved that I had made a decision, however dangerous. I stood on the usual corner near the café and waited until I heard the piercing bell ringing like an alarm to dismiss the school. The children came pouring out like a flood-wave through a desert wadi, a screaming tide. I waited. . . . The tide thinned to a trickle, then stopped. The door stayed open for a few minutes after the last one had come out. Then someone came and closed it. I heard the slam, the finality of it, clearly from my distant watching-place.

I waited. I was no longer hoping they would come. I was waiting for strength to move, for the panic to recede a little and give me some freedom to breathe and act. At last I was able to walk across to the school, knock on the door and ask the person who came what I wanted to know.

It took some time to find out – the relevant teachers were not to be found. But one of them, miraculously, was on the telephone. When my anxiety was noticed, I was given the number and allowed to call her from the principal's office. It all took longer than any other action of my life, it seemèd. Every ring of the phone at the other end took years to be followed by the next. But at last she answered. .... It was Peretz' teacher, the one I had spoken to before.

Yes, he had been absent for the last half of the morning, from the time they went out for the main break. She had thought nothing of it. .... I couldn't say anything to her. I just put down the phone.

I left the school without a word, without looking at anyone. I blundered back here, my eyes fixed on the way ahead. I came in through the door and found Suzy in the courtyard waiting for me. Her face had changed. It was obvious that something had happened, and when she saw that I was alone, she became a shade paler, a shade stiffer in her bearing. She looked as if someone were standing behind her holding a gun.

'A man has been here looking for you,' she said.

'They've taken the children,' I said, and then we each repeated what we had said as if neither of us had quite understood.

She nodded, twice, quick little mechanical nods like a doll. We stood staring at each other. Then Zev came out and said, as if he'd been there all the time, had heard all my confidences to Suzy and knew everything, 'But they're our people. There's nothing to fear. He came to tell you, to explain. Of course there'll be formalities, but don't worry. They're our own authorities here, they'll do the right thing.'

Suzy looked at him. Then she looked back at me and now her head shook, in the same clockwork way as she had nodded before. The depths of my understanding with her were clear to me then for the first time, for I could read that one movement just as if she had spoken. It said: he's wrong, don't hope, they are not infallible and anyway they can't help themselves, there are laws. .... The head-shake was the exact antithesis of what she had said before about being open. It was as if she had suddenly seen the fallacy of her own arguments.

We sat silently waiting. I don't know what my thoughts were;

245

only my feet seemed to have any feeling in them, they were tingling, the rest of my body and brain were numb. Suzy brought coffee but none of us drank. Suddenly Suzy said, 'We must pretend the children are ours.'

Zev looked at her. 'Are you mad?'

'We can say they are ours. We can swear it.'

'But they'll know it's not true.'

She pressed her hands together, like a child beseeching: 'But we could try! We could swear it.'

'And their documents?'

'We can invent something – a fire –'

Zev put his arm round her. She sagged against him and began to cry silently. I watched them both in amazement. Neither of them looked at me. It might have been solely theirs, their private problem. Feeling began to return to me as if this incredible portion of love, unlooked-for, quite undeserved, had been injected into me like warm blood into a corpse.

At last the knock came. I rose before the others and ran down the short passage to the door. Two men stood outside with the square behind them, silent, empty.

It's hard to recover the conversation now; I can only remember the outcome, not the details. But it would have been useless to lie or to argue, I remember knowing that. I think they were even kind, if immeasurably cruel actions can be performed kindly. Or no, perhaps it was not kindness, only reluctance on their part which gave me the feeling that they would be kind if they could.

The two children, they said, had been 'taken into custody'. They had taken them straight from the school to 'save unpleasantness'. They apologized. ... Someone had come round here to explain to me, but must have missed me. They hoped I had not been unnecessarily upset.

The children were quite safe, and were being well looked after 'meanwhile'. Whether I could see them or not depended on the matron of the 'home' – they called it 'institution' – where they had been taken. I could always ask, but. ... The matter was not really in the hands of the police any longer. The children were foreign nationals and would have to be handed to 'the proper authorities'.

I said everything I could think of to say, trying desperately to keep my head and not to lose control of myself. We stood there in that narrow doorway for an eternity, but all the time I knew it was hopeless and panic was attacking me like some great bird swooping from overhead, sheering off, swooping again.

They gave me a card with the address scribbled on the back. Then they turned and I watched them walking silently to their car. They didn't talk to each other. I stood in the doorway, seeing them grow smaller, and felt that those two strangers were walking off with my life. (I remembered suddenly the same, identical feeling as I watched Jake's coffin being carried carefully down the stairs and out through the front door. One of the wreaths slipped off and was left lying on the mat just inside the door – such a little wreath, specially made to lie on a small casket.)

But suddenly there was more.

At the car door, one man stopped, spoke to the other, glanced back at me, and after some hesitation, returned. I watched him dully as he approached. He stood some short way away and said, 'Do you know a man called Ibrahim El-Wasif?'

No, I said.

He asked if I were sure. I said I had never heard the name. And then he said, 'He is a house-painter from Acco. I think you do know him.' And he showed me a picture.

I stared at it. I had no strength left to think. Kofi's face was almost unrecognizable in the picture. It had aged; the eyes were closed; he looked, in fact, as if he were dead. It was, I saw then, a photograph taken at a downward angle on to a pillow.

I looked up at the man. He was putting the picture away.

'He wants to see you,' he said. 'He has been asking for you.' I couldn't speak. The man, seeing I had nothing to say, shrugged slightly and began to leave. I reached after him and held his arm. 'Where?' 'He is in hospital under police supervision. He was shot trying to cross the border. . . . If you want to see him, I think you had better hurry.'

It was a dreadful decision to have to make. Every instinct

drew me towards the children, sitting forlorn and probably terrified in some barren institutional room. And meanwhile, in the Rambam Hospital in Haifa, more than two hours' journey away, Kofi lay dying.

There was no choice really. I asked Suzy to see the children. It was more, much more than she could be expected to understand; I saw in her stern, scored face that she didn't; but it was my decision and she said nothing beyond agreeing to go and to take the clothes and candies and favourite toys that I packed for her. The look that passed between us as I gave her the shabby suitcase would have shrivelled my heart if it had not already been frozen to numbness by the task of folding Peretz' clean underwear and hunting for Ella's beloved doll. My imagination, however, was not numb; it was impossible not to know, not to feel, what the children would feel when I didn't come. But Kofi was dying.

(Was I already tearing myself away from them? Was I preparing my inner ground? No. . . . I hadn't faced it yet, I hadn't given them up; somehow I hadn't even thought the separation might be permanent. I'd thought of it a thousand times before, but not that day, not in the context of reality.)

It's good to have a lot to do at such moments; I remember that so well from Jake. When they all go, after the funeral, and you're putting the crumb-filled plates together and stacking cups on the tray, and the house is quiet, that's the time you wonder how and why to put one foot in front of another. I dressed and made up my face, which was looking so desperately ugly that even a dying man might have been distressed by it; I took a taxi to the *sheroot* station, and found a place in one of the communal taxis to Haifa. Then I sat in it for two hours, I sat and watched the sea and listened to the blaring radio and felt a damp patch growing on my back and on my thigh where it was pressed against that of a fat woman sitting next to me; my hair was blown into a stiff tangle by the constant pressure of the sandy wind and I kept brushing a strand from my mouth. But what did I think of? I can't remember . . . my thoughts were tangled like my hair, flapping and stinging in my mind, getting caught, pulling free. . . . I felt the children, behind me, dragging at me as if attached by wires. . . . I didn't cry. I felt, as I felt with Jake, that tears were for the innocent.

At the hospital at last, I showed the card that the man had given me and told my name. At first it seemed they would not let me in. Now that I was there, now that I could smell the disinfectant and knew Kofi was somewhere near, waiting to die, a great rage seized me, the first real anger I had felt all day, and I had to grip the edges of the desk to prevent myself shrieking into the faces that blocked my way to him. I said the police had told me to come. The woman went away again, with a sound of exasperation, but when she returned she brought with her a man – a doctor perhaps – who simply said 'Follow me', and led me past the barriers and up the old-fashioned stone stairs, along curving corridors lined with the overflow beds, up more stairs, the dark green paint sliding past my eyes – and now I was fighting to realize it, fighting to be ready, but there was no time left, I had wasted all that in the taxi; because here was the door and it opened; screens were moved aside a little to let me through; and I was faced with a white metal bed, a white cover with two coarse, clean hands resting on it, and above them Kofi's face sunk in the pillow.

His eyes were open and he turned them towards me immediately. Even having just seen the photo, showing him so old and ill, so utterly changed, I might not have known him. Only the eyes themselves, the lustrous damson eyes, resting on me with an expression of naked love and relief, were wholly recognizable and the same as before. The tears came then, to both of us, because I couldn't hide my pain and he saw it and was sorry for me. I think it was the clean, clean hands, resting so submissively on the white sheet, over a bulk that spoke of a short, thin body and not the stout sturdy figure I had so often leaned on in my despairs, that shook me most deeply. The emaciated yellow face I had expected, but not the hands, so antiseptic, so unused and scrubbed ready for death.

A chair was brought and I sat up close to the bed and took one of those hands and held it. . . . It was cold, and I knew from that that he would die soon, because the room was furnace-hot. Some words came into my head – 'And so upward, and upward, and all as cold as any stone.' The tears kept rolling down my face. Kofi shook his head at me slightly, and I shook mine – 'Don't cry' – 'I can't stop myself.' Nothing beyond that silent exchange at first; he was very weak. I wondered for the first time where the bullet had gone into him, and, also for the first time, felt a futile feeble anger against the necessary, scared young soldier in the border-patrol who had challenged, and fired in the air, and challenged again the figure creeping through the dark (why had he not gone by boat?) and finally, in desperation, shot straight at it, seen it stagger and pitch forward. . . ; And the little girl at his side, what did she . . .?

Hanna! How was it possible, how was it conceivable that until that instant I had not thought once of Hanna? I leaned forward and spoke her name, a harsh, demanding question.

He opened his dry lips, closed them, swallowed with pain, opened them again and said in a voice I barely knew – 'All right.' I stayed poised over him, waiting – there was more, I could see. 'It was for that I – partly for that. . . . I – wanted – I asked for you.' He made a faint motion with his head, and looking round I saw a glass of water on the table. I put my hand under his head, feeling the chill dampness of his neck, and helped him to drink. He lay back again and stirred his hand fumblingly on the cover until it found mine again. His voice came more strongly now. 'Gerda . . .' He rested for a moment on my name, closing his eyes and smiling faintly. 'Gerda . . .' He seemed to be drifting away, so I said 'I'm here.' 'Yes,' he said, quite clearly this time. 'Listen. It's all right. I've told them everything, about you, how you knew nothing. . . . They'll ask you questions, but they believed me, they wrote down what I said and I signed it. Just tell them the truth, that I did everything, that I lied to you. . . . Listen,' he said again. 'She is with the police. I have given her to you. That's in the paper I signed. Do you hear me, my friend? I have given her to you.'

Dumbstruck, I could only stare at him. His eyes opened again and fixed themselves on me. For a second – a split second only – I nearly laughed. Was it possible? Did he really expect me to go through it all again, this incredible, extraordinary man, did he believe my strength was bottomless?

'No,' I said, but perhaps no sound came out.

'She is yours,' he went on, much more strongly now. 'I've told them. This time it is all in order. I have all her papers. She is mine to give, this one, and I've told them. They will give her to you. She is yours now. Gerda.' His eyes closed.

I sat, unable to move or speak. The unanswerable, the inescapable death-bed injunction! The Lord taketh, and the Lord giveth. . . . Lord God Kofi!

I mustered my forces and suddenly found myself very angry, too angry to remember that I loved him, that he was dying; remembering only what I had suffered because of him and what I still had to suffer. Realizing that my children were gone, swallowed in the maw of an untouchable legality, and that I would never recover them . . . that it was all his doing – his – his! And I leant forward and cried out at him:

'No! Kofi! I won't take her! You can't do this again. She has a mother. Let her go to her mother. I don't want to be a mother any more – I'm empty – I don't want her and I won't have her – so don't die in peace, thinking I'm going to take her – '

His eyes had opened slowly at the beginning and were resting on me, but there was a curious passivity in them which suddenly halted me. His expression had not changed from the quiet one with which he had spoken my name, and I saw with a sense of despair – intolerably mixed with exasperation at that moment – that it would never change again.

He had gone. The bastard – the unpardonable, buck-passing bastard – leaving me facing the unfaceable. I clenched my teeth and dropped my face hard against the unbreathing ribs, sobbing furiously over and over again: 'Out from under! Out from under!' – still clutching his hand, until they came in to lay out his body.

Chapter 6

The children were put in a home, run by a charitable women's organization. The matron even had an accent which gave me an illusion, the first time I spoke to her, that I had stumbled across a compatriot who would be certain to help me. But the woman was immovable. She sat at her desk with a face of stone and ashes, and out of it drawled nasal-vowelled English saying no, no, no to everything I asked, to everything I demanded. Suzy had been allowed to see them, yet I was not to be allowed! That was the bitter, the incredible thing. She invented a thin, a transparent excuse – that Suzy had arrived at a moment when she, the matron, was absent, and some inexperienced underling had fetched the children without knowing it was against the institution's rules. But it is not against their rules, I know that because I have seen other women go there who would only be visiting their children. . . . I was determined, this time, to keep calm, because I knew – God, I knew too painfully well – why she would not let me in: because she had had a report of my behaviour from the police and had drawn her own, unassailable conclusions about the nature of my character and how bad it would be for the children to see me. I tried to convince her that it would not be bad for them, that I was responsible, that I would be self-controlled; but it was hopeless, like trying to convince the authorities in a mad-house that you are sane and are there by mistake. Her eyes never changed, her thin grey face remained as impassive as a statue. Her thinly crimsoned mouth opened and closed, saying sentences which all meant 'no'.

I went away and walked for hours, talking to myself, or rather to the matron, afraid to let myself think beyond that charitable loathsome figure to the children who sat or ate or played somewhere behind her, protected by her from the impact of my desperation. Ella would not cry all the time, just at night probably; the rest of the time if happiness and companionship were offered her she would be lured into contentment. But Peretz would know that I have betrayed him again, this time I will never get a chance to change his mind. He will grow up remembering me as his betrayer. . . . Why couldn't I find the words to persuade that woman that I *have* to see them? Even afterwards I could not think of them, and so when I went back, the next day and the next, our duologues followed the same pattern, me beseeching, she refusing, with the inevitability of some stale drama played out daily in hell, with only one ending possible. It always began with the same opening sentences, a ritual we both followed with increasing weariness: 'How are they?' 'They are settling down as well as one could expect.' And they always ended the same way, too – with me in tears, backing away from the desk so that she could see the hatred in my eyes that I hoped without hope would shrivel and demolish her as my poor ineffectual implorings had again failed to do.

I went to a lawyer – Zev's and Suzy's. I begged him to help me. He said he could apply to the high court for a writ of Habeas Corpus which would restrain the authorities from handing the children back to the Lebanese until after I had been given a hearing. 'But I have to warn you,' he said, 'that you will not succeed. You have no chance whatever.' I asked why, why had I no chance? Would the children's welfare not be a consideration? Or their inclinations? 'A country,' he said slowly, 'owns its own citizens. The Lebanese own these children – they have a right to demand them and to get them back. That is what I expect they have done.' 'And what will happen to them?' 'They will be taken by the U.N. and handed over to the Social Welfare people on the other side. They will look after them.' He saw my face, which felt as cold as wet clay, and suddenly with a gesture of unexpected compassion he touched my arm. 'It is a civilized country,' he said. 'They will care for them lovingly, I am sure.' 'Lovingly? In a refugee camp? In an institution?' 'Perhaps they will find homes for them.' 'The Arabs don't adopt children. They have enough of their own.' He looked at his desk and removed his hand from my arm. 'An institution,' he said at last, 'is not the worst place in the world to be brought up. I was raised in one myself.' There was no answer to this; the lie, if it was a lie, was for me, and I couldn't bring myself to discount it.

I asked one final question. If I insisted on a case in the high court, would I see the children again? He said no. Then there was no way in which I could ever see them again? He did not answer.

I sent Suzy back. She came back with the holdall emptied of the desperate substitutes I had sent, but with her eyes empty too. They had not let her see them.

Yesterday I went again, prepared to go through it once more, arming myself with hope even though the matron had left word that I am not to be admitted even to her – it has been, recently, some other woman, of humbler importance, who has said the no's. But this time the matron met me in the doorway. She was not smiling of course, that would not have been charitable, but there was something in her eyes – relief, I won't call it triumph – because she knew that this would be the last time.

'I'm sorry,' she said before I could begin, as I had always begun. 'You need not come back any more. They've gone.' She watched me with her little sharp welfare eyes which only see into the depths of the hopeless. 'Please,' she said, so gently that my hatred knew no bounds. 'you mustn't upset yourself. They went quite willingly. They will surely be better off among their own people.'

You dirty do-gooding Yankee bitch, I hope one day you'll roast on a fire as slow as mine. It would comfort me, just a little bit, to see your spirit charring to blackness at my side and smell your psychic flesh splitting and cindering as I can now smell my own.

I think only hatred can keep me alive now. Will I one day be grateful to that woman for giving me a target?

Chapter 7

I refused you, Kofi. You heard me, didn't you? In the last half-minute of your life, I know you heard me. I'm not betraying you because there was never even a tacit promise, not even the one that may be offered to the dying to comfort them (and then can shut the giver in an eternal trap) ... If I could find the strength to refuse you in that moment, do you really think your nagging ghost of three months will persuade me to change my mind?

And if you can't, then certainly the police can't. Different faces under different hats, but limbs of the same body as those others with their smooth kind unfightable law-backed efficiency who took away what was mine. (What creates ownership of a child? No law does it. Love and cleaning up their messes and drying their eyes and noses and breaking into their secret worlds. ... How can a government claim ownership of a child? I will never understand it, I will never forgive it. And how, can somebody tell me, do you go on living with the unforgivable? I have asked Suzy outright and she said: You concentrate on what's left. And what is left to me? Shut up, Kofi! Go back to hell and leave me in mine. I will not have her.)

Three months. I work hard, I smoke too much. ... I don't drink. I wish I could ... the taste of the stuff makes me sick, as it did when I was pregnant. I don't understand it. ... Suzy says it's psychological, that I've grown up and realized, sub-consciously, that 'the cheap escape-route' is no good. ... Suzy has saved me, up till now. Each day is an exhausting struggle, but she has made the struggle seem inevitable, even worthwhile. How? By making me feel that I am worth saving, I as a person, even without the children she says my life is justified. Ziva really does seem to be a little better – perhaps that's why she thinks so – anyway I don't ask myself too many questions. It seems important and not just necessary to keep living, and that is something. Something? It's all, it's everything. That, and the family, and Kofi's wretched ghost, nagging, nagging . . . and the police visits, less frequent now. It is an incredible irony that they have put her in the very same home where the children were. . . . 'At least go and see her, let her feel she has somebody . . .' Do they take me for an idiot? I sometimes imagine that bloody woman, her crimson lips abruptly smeared in smiles, now standing aside and welcoming me in. . . . To hell with her.

There is still room, it seems, for the unexpected. Tonight I was sitting with Ziva, who is quiet and who for that reason is bearable to me as other children are not, when I heard a taxi stop and then someone at the front door. Suzy came tapping, and said there was someone to see me. I said if it was the police again I wasn't going to see them. 'It's not the police,' she said. 'He says he's a relative.'

I went out slowly, unable to imagine that she had not somehow misunderstood. . . . Yet there, unbelievably, his great bulk blocking the doorway, was Len. He wore one of his smoothly tailored suits, a knitted tie (it seems a hundred years since I saw a man wearing a tie) – even a tie-pin with a hint, a discreet hint, of flash about it. In the semi-darkness his snow-white shirt with the button-down collar shone like a harbour beacon, and brought Toronto suddenly and stunningly back to me.

As I came near and stopped, too surprised to say or do anything, I found myself being hugged to that white shirt, I felt the tie-pin press a smooth indent into my chin – I'd forgotten how enormous he was. I smelt the too-clean smell of his shaving lotion, hair oil, toilet water, talc, and remembered ludicrously how fussy he was about using one 'range' of 'toiletries for men' – discreet tins and jars and bottles in shades of ochre, I even remembered the brand name, Tabac, it had that French-cum-masculine ring that would take the sting out of the use of such preparations for a man like my brother-in-law. Oddly, the scent was now so poignant that I had to pull away quickly to keep from crying – not tears of true emotion, but instinctive, purely physical ones, onion-tears invoked by the perfume . . .

'Shoe,' he kept saying. 'Shoe. . . . I've found you' – and giving me little quick hugs against his comfortable paunch. 'Jeez, Shoe, it's good to see you, honey . . .' He got out a spotless handkerchief and I suddenly saw he was crying himself, quite openly – he wiped his whole face and blew his nose thickly. 'Sorry,' he said. 'Been all over the world since last night – hardly any sleep on the ol' plane, thinking and – then of course today was a plain cut of hell, went to your kibbutz, asked everyone. . . . I went nearly nuts by the end of two hours, I thought they were bugging me on purpose, I still don't know what the hell went on there, but finally I got hold of some guy who let your address be dragged out of him. . . . What gives, you in hiding here, or what?'

'Not any more.'

'Hey, let's go inside, okay, Shoe? My feet're killing me, and I got to get a proper look at you . . .' There was something about him I didn't understand. . . . He was still crying, still wiping away his tears and blowing his nose in great blasts. . . . Surely the sight of me couldn't have had such an effect? I took him through into my room, whose hideous emptiness I feel with a renewed impact every time I walk through the door, and it was not less now because of this unexpected visitor – glad as I was to see him.

We sat down facing each other and for a few moments we both just stared. Len hadn't changed much, put on a bit of weight which made his smooth round face smoother and even gave the illusion of decreasing age, he'd lost a little hair. . . . When he saw me glance at his head he ran a shaky, large hand over its well-oiled surface and said, 'Yeah, well there's still enough there to camouflage the bald spot', and we tried to laugh and failed. Then he began to cry again and I felt alarmed for the first time.

'What is it, Len? What are you doing here? What's happened?'

'You got to forgive me bawling, Shoe,' he said. 'You may not believe this, but I haven't bawled since I was 12 years old until lately. . . . I guess I got a lot of tears piled up in there, 'cause I just can't seem to stop.'

'Would you like a drink?'

'I bought a bottle on the plane – here, let's both have some.' He took a flat half-bottle of whisky out of his hip pocket like a cowboy and passed it over to me. I went into the kitchen and arranged drinks, remembering he liked his just with ice and a squeeze of lemon, and while I was running the tap over the back of the ice-tray I suddenly put it into the sink and went back into the room. Len was leaning forward, holding his face in his hands, his shoulders shaking. When he sensed me standing there, he half turned, blew his nose once more and said, 'I'll stop soon, Jesus I sure hope so . . .' And I said, 'It's Judy, isn't it?' And he was quite still and quiet for a moment, a huge hunched blue figure, and then he nodded.

I said nothing then, but went slowly back to the sink and fumbled about with the ice. My mind was quite clear, even though my finger-tips seemed numb and clumsy. Was she dead? Of course she must be. Anything less would not have freed him to come here. Judy dead . . . pretty, shrewd, feminine, practical, fecund Judy. My sister Judy. I waited to feel like crying, to feel anything, except dread of returning to the other room, but I couldn't. Eventually there was nothing to do but carry in the two drinks and sit down opposite Len again to face this new awfulness, his emotion and my frightening lack of it.

He took his drink and drank most of it. Then he looked up at me under his thick eyebrows. His eyes were red-rimmed; he looked, I noticed, not for the first time, very like a moose, the huge Roman nose, the large, sad eyes . . . he looked so truly pathetic in his big, helpless grief that I suddenly felt the tears start, but they had nothing to do with Judy and they hurt me because of that. I went and sat beside him on the bed and he put his great arm round me; our heads rested together like a romantic young couple. I felt deeply uncomfortable, miserable only with misery.

At last I said, 'How did it happen?'

He straightened a little, as if he'd been waiting for me to give him the chance to talk about it, blew his nose yet again and said,

'Well, Shoe, it was the damnedest thing. You know she was always 100 per cent fit, but with the last kid, Danny, the doc said that should be it, 'cause he found a little heart-murmur – he said it was nothing to worry about – only no more babies. Okay by us, we had our quota. But you know – a thing like that – you can't help worrying, and I used to make her take it easy, called up every day to see she took her nap, got in extra help, the older kids were just great the way they helped out too. . . . She had regular check-ups, the doc said it wasn't getting any worse, but you know, Shoe, if it had been *that*, well, somehow . . . We'd've been a bit more – not prepared, no one's ever that, but less – stunned. . . . Only what? It was something else, not the heart at all, it was that god-damned leukemia if you want to know what it was, the damnedest thing you ever knew. . . . She was talking about it only a couple of months back, some kid in Chuckie's class died of it and Jude said she was sure it was on the increase, you never heard of it twenty years ago, and she believed it was to do with fall-out from A-bomb testing. . . . I kidded her up about it – I kidded hell out of her . . . and then Jesus Christ if she didn't get it herself! It took hold of her like a god-damned prairie fire, just ate her up, and in under a month she was gone.

We sat silently, our heads together. I breathed in that strong, hygienic smell and tried to think of Judy but I could only think of Kofi, his poor shrunken face with the wide-open eyes fixed on me confidently . . . I wondered if Len had actually watched Judy die, watched her eyes go out like lights; you had to believe in the soul at that moment because you could actually see the body losing something, becoming empty. It wasn't just a stopping, it was something missing which had been there a moment before, something much more tangible than just an abstract concept called life. I wondered if I could say anything of this to Len, but Len's religion, I suddenly remembered, was strong and formal, though he kept it quiet in the background of his life, and presumably he had his own sources of comfort which would make my small, empirical discovery seem like theological baby-talk.

There were still a lot of unanswered questions, but somehow

I sensed his weariness and that, having found me and unburdened himself of his black news, he wanted nothing now but the escape of a long, deep sleep. I went into what had been the children's room for the first time since I lost them, and made up Peretz' bed for myself (it would have collapsed under Len). While I was doing it I wondered how I should get through the night in that room, which still smelt faintly of child-flesh and was full of small reminders. But when I got back to the other room, Len, wearier or more drunk than I had realized, was already stretched out on my couch asleep; I loosened his tie and took off his shoes, covered him with a rug and left him there, with the half-empty flask within easy reach.

And now, to occupy the frightful lonely hours until sleep frees me, I am writing this. . . . As I think about it, I understand less and less. . . . To make this long journey, leaving the kids somewhere, just to tell me what he could have told me in a telegram, doesn't make sense . . . there must be something behind it which he hasn't told me yet. I suppose I shall find out tomorrow. Meanwhile I try and try to think of Judy and grieve for her, but all I can feel is pity for that poor giant out there who would have got down on his knees and kissed her insteps every morning if she had wanted it. . . . Her friends used to call him her Nubian Slave. And the kids . . . the youngest can't be two years old yet. . . . I've even forgotten how many of them there are . . .

*

Len has been here three days now, and at last he has come out with it. It is hard to believe, and yet it makes such perfect sense that I'm surprised I didn't guess at once. Only Len could possibly. . . . And yet there is so much one doesn't know about people. No, I could never have guessed.

Things have gone along quietly enough since that first evening; we seemed to soothe each other and keep each other company, and he only cried occasionally, when something unbearably poignant struck him. He hasn't been drinking much, either. During the days I have taken him out and traipsed him round the local sights, all too silly and pointless and yet, incredibly, necessary to both of us and a life-saver in that it used up time and occupied our minds. . . . One bad moment came when he suddenly remembered (oddly, for the first time, after two whole days) that I had written about having two children, and abruptly, in the middle of his lunch, put down his knife and fork and said: 'But where are your kids?' and I had to tell him. His appalled stare, mouth slightly open, eyes glassy with a mixture of pity and anger, helped me somehow to get the words out. 'But they can't do that!' he cried. 'They can't do that!' He flung his chair back and began stamping up and down the tiny room. 'There's got to be something we can do!' I told him there was nothing to be done. He stopped walking and stared at me. 'My God,' he said quietly, 'and here I've been . . . hell, no wonder you couldn't cry about Jude. Guess you got no sorrow left after what you've been through.' So he had noticed my shameful absence of tears. I felt ashamed, and yet somehow his words consoled me; they seemed to be true. I am almost drained of feeling. Even entering the children's room now produces no more than an inner hardening, as if a metal door were closing against attack.

This came up after he had been telling me about his own family. He had left the two youngest with his mother, who is old now but still 'a tough old number, God bless her', while the others were more or less looking after each other at home. 'Marney's married now,' he told me, 'but she's come back to look after things. They're wonderful kids, Shoe – the greatest. You know?' It was then he remembered, and asked about mine.

But it wasn't until this evening that he broached the subject I had been waiting for. I'd given him openings, seeing that it was hard for him, but he hadn't seemed able to take them. However, it was clear that it wasn't going to be possible for him to stay away from home much longer, that in fact he would have to speak up soon or miss the bus altogether. I could feel it coming all the evening. He talked on and on about his children, in a strained, compulsive voice that reminded me oddly of Alec. (Alec was only mentioned once. It seems he is about to marry again. . . . Len told me this carefully and with great tact, sounding out every inch of ground before treading on it, but in fact he needn't have bothered. I felt as if I were hearing of the doings of some distant acquaintance. If anything, I was glad at the news, but the truth was I scarcely felt a ripple of any emotion.)

I knew he was pushing himself closer and closer, and wanted to help him, but failing to see his direction I wasn't able to. At last he stopped talking rather abruptly and sat looking down into his evening glass of whisky, which he turned round and round in his large fingers.

'I don't know what you must think of me for – for forgetting about your kids,' he said at last. 'It's the simple truth, Shoe. I forgot about 'em. Since Alec came back alone, I guess I've just always thought of you as – you know – alone too, more or less, and your letter just didn't – impinge, somehow, on that image I had of you. I expected to find you alone, and in fact – everything depended on that – yet now I can't think why I was so sure you would be – why shouldn't you have found someone, I mean, apart from the kids? I guess I took a lot for granted.'

I waited, curious, more than curious, bewildered. The glass in his hand turned and turned, slowly.

'I guess you know what I want to ask you,' he said at last, without looking up.

'I don't, Len, and that's the truth.'

'Ah hell. I hoped. . . . But I guess it's not all that obvious. Look, Shoe. I'm in the crap now, but for real. I've got a family to raise, three of 'em are still in school, one's only a baby. The older two'll be okay, and if Marney'd still been at home we might have managed, but she's got her own home now, and a baby coming, and Louis's in college. . . . I can't depend on Mama, it wouldn't be fair, she's an old lady already. I could get a living-in help, but that's not what I. . . It's not right for any of us. So what I thought was. . . . I wondered if you would be ready to come back with me and help out.' He looked at me quickly, saw my expression, and dropped his head again. 'Ah hell,' he said again, miserably, 'I've bitched it up. Why can't I ever say things so they come out right?'

There was a long silence during which I tried to find *some* words, any at all, but in the end he had to begin again.

'Well, since I've fouled everything up anyhow, I may as well finish. Maybe you're thinking I'm just schlepping you back as unpaid nursemaid, that I'm offering you a future as a drudge to someone else's child. . . . Shoe . . . it's not like that. Lookit, I'm a one-woman man and she's dead, but that doesn't mean I can't ever marry again or that I wouldn't have *something*, something less, maybe, something a whole lot different but still something, to offer you if – in a year or so maybe, you felt like. . . . What I mean is, I can't say much or feel much at the moment but I need you *now* and it wouldn't be fair to you to let you think I wasn't ever going to – ' He took a drink, desperately. 'I wanted to be straight with you, Gerda,' he said, using my name for the first time. 'The kids need a mother, not a nurse, and listen, I know myself, one day I'll need a wife. If the – if you could think about it – I'm not a bad guy – and there's a family waiting for you, ready-made, six of 'em, the best kids you ever saw.' He looked straight at me suddenly. 'Hell, I don't have to be ashamed of what I'm offering. It's all I've got.'

I said the first thing that came into my head after a long moment of shocked surprise. 'But you can't marry me! You can't marry your – your dead wife's sister! It's forbidden.' I had nearly said 'incestuous'.

He looked at me in surprise. 'Not among us,' he said. For a minute I didn't know what he meant. Then it struck me that by 'us' he meant 'us Jews'. 'I guess you're like Jude,' he said slowly. 'She hardly knew a thing about stuff like that. Didn't you know that when a man dies, his widow has to marry his brother, if he's got one?' 'Yes, but this isn't!' 'It's the same thing. I mean, I wouldn't hold you to it or anything, but looking at it in one way, we *should* marry.'

After a long pause I said stupidly. 'But I don't see it like that.'

His face worked like a small boy's. 'Lookit, if I'm repulsive to you, you know what I mean – that's something else – just, just say so, and I'll – '

'Len, it's not a question of – I've never even thought – '

'No. Well, hell, of course you haven't, nor've I, that wouldn't have been ...' He rubbed his vast hand over his vast scalp, now gleaming through the thin oily strands of hair, and one of them fell sideways across his ear, and in that second I thought, 'I couldn't' – even before I'd thought about it properly or even asked myself if I could or not. Thus the answer came before the question and the matter of the children didn't come into it.

I think the rest of the evening was the most hideously embarrassing of either of our lives. Len felt he had 'boobed' and I felt completely befuddled and kept trying to think about it rationally. After all, for someone in my situation it was a fair proposition – security, a family, a 'good' husband eventually ... since, I have thought of how many women would jump at it, the women who write to marriage bureaux and insert advertisements in lonely hearts columns. ... I am neither different nor better than they are, so why should the whole thing strike me as being so impossible? Because Len is too big, too shiny, too slangy, too – Canadian? Too Jewish? Because he is going bald, because he oils his hair with 'Tabac' brilliantine, because his tie-pin catches the light, because his hands are too soft and clean, because he could never, even in his most libidinous dreams, rape anyone? Because he is not Kofi? At the end of two dreadful hours of conscientiously 'speaking of other things', he suddenly opened his wallet and brought out a thick packet of snapshots, which he handed over to me without a word and then sat in utter silence while I looked through them – reluctantly. ... He sat there like the sort of applicant for a job who needs it so desperately that he knows before he starts that his references will not be satisfactory, that he will be sent away with a polite promise of the kind which is made to be broken.

The snaps showed the children. ... Typical little Canucks, all from the same mould, the Judy-mould, not the Len-mould, except one egg-shaped little boy with glasses who looked enough like a moose-calf to make me want to smile. ... The rest were latter-day versions of what I remembered, the bangs, the posed smiles, the toboggans, the knee-socks, all arranged in warm family groups, glowing in Kodacolour – one could just imagine Len rushing about like a sheep-dog, herding them together, telling this one that her brace wouldn't show even in a *big* smile, getting mad at one of the boys for pulling a face, making the littlest take up a cute pose on someone else's lap. . . . His pride in them, naïve, touching, fathomless, shone out from every one of those neat colour, prints; I could feel it, as if I felt his need, his silent pleading, reaching out now across the brief space that separated the couch where he sat from my chair – an inarticulate high note that sang like an electric wire between us, please, please, please.

I handed them back at last, when I had screwed up my courage to meet his eyes, and gave the polite, made-to-be broken promise: 'Len, they're wonderful. I'll think about it.' He let hope leap like a naked figure into his face; I turned sick against myself. I forced myself to say, 'You know I haven't much to give. And what you ask would take a lot of – all the things I haven't got any more.'

The hope stayed right where it was, vulnerable, and he held it out to me shamelessly. 'We need you, Shoe. I guess I feel human now for the first time since Jude went. You've done that for me just saying – you'll think about it. Kids – give back as much as they take. What you say you haven't got, maybe you'll get from them.'

Poor Len. Oh, poor Len! You slept so peacefully last night, and this morning the whisky level was not down by even half an inch. But my dear, there is nothing to think about. You and Marney and your mother will have to manage until – inevitably – you find somebody . . . somebody with something left.

Chapter 8

Len went home, his coloured snaps bulging in his wallet, his eyes red from disappointment and pleading. He didn't let me off scot-free, of course. That was too much to expect, even from someone basically so kind. . . . Even the question 'Well, so what *are* you going to do?' spoken with a certain edge, can get under the skin when one's future is a frightening blank beginning at one's very feet. 'If you need money, you only got to ask – ' He even tried to press a wad of dollars on me as he left me in the airport lounge . . . silly to be so offended; thank God I didn't show it.

And I came back here, and went on with my so-called life for an indefinite period of weeks, and wondered periodically if I hadn't been a fool. But Suzy laughed when I told her – that curious sudden harsh laugh like a raven's cry – and said, 'That one? Don't think about it any more, he's not for you.' Some perversity made me find this contemptuous dismissal annoying. 'Loneliness is a great compeller, Suzy.' 'Then why doesn't it compel you to go and see the – ' But I don't listen when she presumes to speak of Hanna, and even regret for brief moments that I ever told her.

The police paid a last visit. They brought me a final statement to sign, a statement utterly incriminating to Kofi, so much so that my hand burned as I wrote my name on it, though it was all true and can do no harm now. Afterwards they spoke again of Hanna.

'Do you know what it is,' said the man, this same detective or whatever he is who has conducted the whole investigation, 'to be the only child in such a place who is never visited, who has no one?' 'Rubbish. Of course she is not the only such child there.' He looked uncomfortable, as if one had caught him out in a piece of almost feminine sentimentality. 'I've seen her,' he went on doggedly. 'She is a little *mensch*. Full of character, full of guts.' 'I know her,' I said flatly. 'But she is very unhappy. She is quite fierce with grief. It is a very sad thing to see a really fine child being eaten away by misery as if you had put her in a lime-pit.' I stared at him, astonished that he, a Jew with the brands of the camps on his arm, would use such an image. But his eyes were fixed on me and I knew he had done it deliberately to move me and I turned away my head in disgust.

'If instead of pestering me,' I said coldly, 'you would concentrate on finding her mother – '

'Oh,' he said, shifting in his seat and taking a paper out of his shabby brief-case. 'Thank you for reminding me. We have traced her.'

I looked up quickly, my whole mind suddenly sharpened to a fine point of hope; I knew in that moment what a hideous unmanageable burden the undeserved guilt of Hanna has been to me.

But it wasn't to be lifted. The detective glanced at the paper in his hand and then looked up at me, saw the hope in my eyes and shook his head at me gently. 'No use,' he said. 'She has left the country. A year ago. She has gone back to France.'

'But can't you contact her?'

'She left no address. Even we cannot be expected to locate a needle in a haystack.' He smiled again ruefully. 'I'm afraid, Mrs Shaffer, that the little girl, whether you like to accept it or not, is your sole responsibility.'

'But she has other relatives – on her father's side. Surely?'

He slowly replaced the first paper with another. 'Well,' he said. 'She has an uncle. He lives in a small village in Galilee. He has a large family and a new young wife. . . . I have not myself met him, but from what I understand he is not perhaps the most suitable – '

I remembered the marks on Peretz' back, and said, 'No,' more loudly than I had meant.

He echoed my 'no' in a gentler tone, shook his head again and put his papers away. 'In the ordinary way,' he said, 'there would be good hopes of having such a bright, attractive child adopted.

But you see, there is her mixed blood. It's very odd. The waiting-list for adopting a child is so long' – he held up his hands – 'yet there is scarcely a family on it who would not turn quite pale at the thought of a little Arab blood in the family. It's very odd.'

I said nothing. I was amazed to realize how much I had been depending, deep in my thoughts, on that mythical bitch who had fled to France. I had now a new target for hate, but none of the pressure inside me eased. Recently I have begun to have agonizing headaches, and I felt one beginning now, nothing sharp or stabbing, just a hard, hot, throbbing ache as if my whole brain were inflamed and in need of lancing.

It will get easier in time. I can't spend all the rest of my life in this anguished state of missing my own children and suffering the urgent summons of another who is not mine. . . It's too hard. My head is bursting. I'm glad of it. The pain is so beauti-fully physical and one cannot think through it.

I have stopped everything – work, everything. Drink tastes good again. My door is locked and I do not go out or let anyone in. They come knocking, Suzy and Ziva, and sometimes Zev too, but I don't let them in. It's quiet here, and very dirty now; I've covered up the windows with bits of cloth and cardboard so it's dark as well and there is just the endlessness of myself and my cigarette smoke and my beating infected head-blood and sleep, as much sleep as possible.

It is like at the very beginning, except that there is no more Kofi. Suzy is Kofi now, but I don't let her in. I wait till she is asleep to open my door and creep out like a fugitive for drink and cigarettes . . . the night-streets are squalid with the day's refuse and I always hurry and keep my eyes on the ground. Once someone bumped into me, I felt the pressure on my arm, and I struck out with all my strength and heard him yelp. . . . I liked it. I liked the violence of it. Sometimes when they're all asleep I talk to myself in my room. I have conversations with the matron and with the detective and with Hanna's mother and very often with Kofi. I can be as angry as I like, I can hit out at them; once I threw a heavy vase at Kofi's face, my arm ached afterwards for half an hour. The pieces are still on the floor. . . .

Once I struck the wall with my fist, and quite often I smack my own face again and again until I am exhausted. Then the tears will come, simple pain-tears, and after the tears I can sleep.

... And now I begin to talk only to Hanna. I talk to her all day and all the waking hours of the night. In my self-imposed dark it is hard to tell one from another, but sometimes I grow so weary of the gloom that I lift a corner of the covering from the window and look out at the square ... it seems to be summer again. Children play out there, the noises they make come in through the coverings. I look long and often at the well and imagine those echoing wetbricked dark depths. ... Once Peretz dropped a stone through a knot-hole in the nailed-down cover and told me he counted six slowly before he heard the splash. Bodies fall at the same rate as stones. One, two, three, four, five, six. But there are easier ways, and why, oh why, don't I take one of them? Because I have to talk to Hanna first, I have to explain, and she won't answer, she won't believe me, she doesn't listen. ... She won't understand. When I have made her understand, then I will do it. Then I will get out from under.

Suzy's found a new ploy. She stands outside the door and recites what purport to be news bulletins.

Dimly I hear unfamiliar place-names repeated with increasingly urgent inflections. Today, for instance, there was something about the U.N. withdrawing their peace-keeping force from the Egyptian border. I suppose it all means something important – if it's true. Suzy could be making it up as a way of getting me to ask a question, or open the door, or respond in any way at all. But I don't care, that's what she doesn't yet understand. I don't give even the smallest of bloody damns.

A war, she says. There'll be another war. Her voice – that stern, steady voice, as solid as packed gravel – shakes nowadays. Suzy-the-brave who 'is only a coward in wartime' is frightened. ... Of course she is. She has a child to be afraid for. She is the weak one now and I am strong and impervious inside the armour of total indifference ...

A shell from the sea. ... A swift, sure emissary from one of the little grey warships which Suzy tells me are speeding at this moment through the Black Sea. ... Actually I am not as indifferent as I thought. I believe I rather *like* the idea of being alive in this welter of drunken pain one second, and the next – nowhere, not one bit of flesh hanging to the next. Nothing left to feel with! Yes, I like it. I like it. Come on, you nice little Soviet sailors, hurry on down. ... Jaffa sits in its bright bath of May sunlight, white as a bride, waiting for violence, expecting it, quivering with a sort of ecstasy at the prospect of it. If not a swift barrage of shells across the blue shining sea, then what about a missile from the stark secret depths of the desert? Zev said long ago that they've got rocket bases hidden away down there. Those long, slim, phallic creatures of man, silently aimed at us, needing only the lightest gesture to send them ploughing into our vitals ...

I love writing like this! I adore the teeth-clenching violence of my thoughts. I take ferocious pleasure in thinking of myself ripped and smashed. I look forward now to Suzy's Cassandra-calls. Today she brought her little radio with her and turned up the volume so I could hear the news. She must have guessed that I doubted the truth of her warnings. Things sound good and bad. When I went out tonight for my bottles, I could feel the tension in the streets. The Arab traders are restless and jumpy, the Jews meet one's eye with a sort of sardonic grimness, the look that says, 'It's coming at last!' and all but adds, 'Thank God.' The square by day is beginning to be noisy with lorries full of soldiers ...

Zev has been called up. At his age! Suzy and Ziva are alone. Ziva, that calm, contained child, suddenly grew hysterical. I heard her, laughing and crying and screaming today across the courtyard: 'They'll capture us and put us into – ' Then Suzy smacked her face and she stopped and afterwards I could hear Suzy talking to her in a low, strong, loving voice. ... It must be hard for her without Zev.

Today Suzy brought me a letter. She pushed it under the door, after relaying the latest figures of troop concentrations on the Sinai border. I was less drunk than usual at that hour, because now I have 'the crisis' to think about I feel quite stimulated inwardly and don't need so much brandy. Or at least, I didn't. But this letter. . . . I stared at it for a long time before going to pick it up. I wanted to care little enough to be able just to leave it lying there but in the end my idiot curiosity got the better of me.

It was written on headed paper and signed with a sloping American signature, 'M. J. Susskind', masculine yet unmistakably belonging to that hated woman at the Home. She wrote that they were trying to arrange for the children to be evacuated. (Where the hell does one 'evacuate' children to, in a country this size?) 'It's not safe for them in the city. . . . We are trying to farm some of them out to individual families who will take care of them until the current crisis is over' (when they and we will probably all be dead, so there will be nothing further to worry about). 'I understand you have rejected responsibility for Hanna, but I would urge you to think the matter over again in the light of the present situation. We do our best to keep the children from becoming alarmed, but with the more sensitive of them this is not an easy matter. . . .'

The more sensitive ones. Yes, well, the half-and-halfs are always more sensitive, especially when the two halves are on the point of going to war.

I hear Ziva's voice now. She's laughing. Her laugh is not hysterical any more – a little shrill, perhaps, but under control, a child's laugh. Suzy has done the trick. The shell or bomb that killed me would kill them too, I suppose. Or what if Suzy came back from the shops one day and found . . .

No.

What shall I do now, quickly, before anything begins to stir inside me? I know. I'll write a letter to Hanna. That's it! No need to go and see her. I'll draft it in this notebook and copy it out afterwards. I'll explain it all to her.

Dear Hanna,

I've decided to write to you and explain why I haven't come, and am not coming. You and I are in separate corners of hell and you're entitled to know why I don't come and hike you out of yours, since it must seem to you that I could if I wanted to. . . . [Already I can't send it. Never mind. Keep writing. . . .]

It isn't that I don't love you. It's that I don't love you enough. As a matter of fact I've never loved anyone quite enough. I've had three children now, not counting you who were my child for three days, and I know now that I didn't have it in me to love any of them properly. I had a husband and I didn't love him properly, any more than your mother loved your father. Both she and I left our men when things got too hard. My body stopped loving before I did and perhaps it didn't really start with the body. I think back now, oftener than you'd believe, and think how I despised your mother for deserting so good a man as your father, not to mention you, and I sneer at myself, because I was no better. I left my husband, and then, when life gave me another chance at happiness with a far stronger, more interesting, deeper person, I was too scared – or merely too snobbish – to let him touch me. . . . Or was it the fear of failure? That's a kind of poison. It seeps through the system and weakens every part of it, including the capacity for joy and for self-giving. It even destroys the ability to trust. I remember the days when I thought Kofi had abandoned *me*, when I wrote to him from the kibbutz and he didn't answer. I might have known there would be a good – I mean a generous, protective, loving – reason. Having given me my children, on the wrong side of the legal blanket, he relinquished contact with me because he knew that his activities could have endangered me, through him. I don't blame him for anything, any more. Not the border-crossings, not the smuggling, not the lies. I've come to love him in retrospect more completely (and more hungrily) than ever I managed to do when he was alive. I love him now rather as you must have done: uncritically, almost desperately. Too late, of course. Too late too late – oh Hanna. . . . Didn't we have enough in common before, you and I, without the addition of this pathetic longing for just one more sight of him, one more chance to make him some kind of feminine amends?

There were four young men, years ago. I wasn't too fastidious or too afraid to let *them* touch me – perhaps because I was in no danger from them. I went to bed with them and duly received from each that white-blossoming roman-candle that can mean the world or it can mean sweet fanny adams. It wouldn't hurt to remember these four men now, if I could add to myself that I loved even one of them as men should be loved, but the point is that I didn't. I never really loved any of them. Perhaps they didn't deserve to be loved, in which case I should have left them alone in the first place; but Kofi was not like them. Nor was Alec, if it comes to that, and nor was Dan. They all cared for me, yet I couldn't love them. Not properly. Or at least, not at the proper time. Something stops me loving wholly. I don't know what it is. Is it a natural limitation for which I'm not to blame, or is it a withholding of what I could give if I only knew how?

*

Suzy came while I was writing all this rubbish. She said, 'Gerda, Hussein's been to Cairo. He and Nasser are suddenly turned into friends and allies. They kissed like brothers at the airport. War's inevitable now. The British and Americans are not going to help us, we are on our own. I have rung up the Canadian Embassy and the girl there said two words: Clear out. That's their advice to all their nationals. There's nothing to keep you here, Gerda, it's not your fight. Go quickly before it's too late.'

I didn't answer her, but for a new and peculiar reason. I felt furiously angry with her.

Dear Hanna,

I am no worse, you see, than the greatest nation on earth. I simply don't want to get involved any more. And in my case my natural reluctance to get hurt is justified by the fact that I have nothing to offer. No big guns and tanks, no reserves, no defences even. Of course I'm aware that my attitude to you is indefensible. Suzy has said so, the policeman said so; Kofi's ghost whispers it without cease ...

Darling, are you frightened? Do you break down and cry as Ziva did? That frozen-faced bitch in the front office would not know how to comfort you, if you did. ... You know, I would be very frightened myself if I had anything left inside me capable of a feeling as profound as fear. This country is so small. It's so very small and vulnerable. It's also very brave. ... I see courage in the faces around me when I go out at night; I peer through my shutters into the square and watch the faces of the soldiers in the lorries. They are forcing me to feel something; they force me to think of you, who are also small, vulnerable and brave. I am always thinking of you. But I can't come, Hanna. I can't come.

I do feel something. But it isn't love. It mustn't be. Let it be fear. Fear destroys more quickly and harms no-one else. The news is very bad. Even the French have done the dirty on us – for the sake of their oil supplies, I suppose; or maybe it's just that senile old idiot de Gaulle changing faces for the fun of it. Bastards. . . . Christ, I mustn't start caring. Once I start getting filled up with patriotism the floodgates will open to every kind of emotion; it will all begin again. . . . No. Even the past is a better place to live in.

Dear Hanna,

How is Mrs Susskind? You know, that lady who comes round every now and then to your dormitory or playroom or wherever you spend your time, to pat your head and say 'Your father's friend hasn't come yet, I'm afraid'. . . . Perhaps you'll give her a message from me. Tell her she's lucky that I can't love properly. If I could, I would have found the words to move her bodily out of my way on the very first of those many mornings I confronted her; or if not, I would have smashed her and got past her and broken down doors until I found them – real love gives one strength for anything. Yet what did I do? I went every day and sometimes I even felt I didn't want to go; I went to a lawyer and let him talk me out of making a big case of it because I was afraid, afraid of my own anger, afraid for myself in all sorts of ways, and so I let those two children be taken to where there was nothing more to fight for, or hope for.

And afterwards? Oh, I grieved, I cried – that was the least I could do. But do you know what went on in the depths of me? I have a sort of idea there was relief there, too. Perhaps there was even relief when Jake died, perhaps that was why I let him drown, perhaps the guilt was so acute because, deep down, I didn't really want him. Children demand so much! I used to feel so sick when I had been angry with him; sometimes I felt as if he were draining me; I would look at him and see the enormity of his needs from me and feel overwhelmed. In any case I didn't want him enough to save him, and I didn't save the other two, either. Did I only go through the motions, as I did with Jake? They've gone now – and I grieve. . . . But sometimes it doesn't seem real, Hanna. I'll tell you something. Sometimes I lie in bed in the mornings early and I have a hangover from the drinking I did the night before, and I hear myself thinking, 'It's good not to have to get up, isn't it? There's no way you can go wrong with them today. It's better this way.' Better *without them*. How is it possible to think that? And all the rest of the day spent thinking of you and thinking of them, all of you in 'homes' which are not homes, because of me, does not cancel out that second of idle loveless self-indulgence at 6 a.m.

And that's what tells me I'm no good for you, Hanna. But that's not the only reason I don't come. That's only the good reason, the one that protects you. The other reason is for me. I'm afraid. Even if I didn't love the others enough, I did love them, in my own shallow insufficient way, and then I lost them, all of them, and that contemptible moment in the mornings can't be compared to the long hours of the day and night when I miss my babies, there are no adequate words for that. I can't face that again. You – you know, now, what it is to miss someone and to have that loneliness compounded by the aching permanent certainty that you will never see them again. But it doesn't help. It's all over; we have to concentrate on what's left. Which in my case is very little, and in yours ...

In yours, till now, it has been (I know this is true) only your hope that every new day will somehow bring me. I wish I could stop you hoping. I can feel it. Your hope reaches me, I feel it as a pain in my head, I know when you are thinking of me and saying to yourself, 'Today Gerda will come for me.' One day the headaches will begin to grow less and I'll know that it means that your one poor fragile hope is dying and perhaps your spirit is breaking at the same time ...

What nonsense, as if a child's resilient spirit could break so easily! Oh, if she could only hear me now, arguing with myself! She'd soon see, with that beautiful common sense that made her such a person at seven as most people are not at thirty, that she was better off among people who are consistent, who do the right thing by her because it's their job, and whose feelings are simple and unwavering and not broken up into fragments by anger and selfishness and failure and laziness, and by deeper, more complex things that I don't myself understand. At least she can know where she is with them and they'll never disappoint her, if only because she places no special hopes in them ...

Why can't I stop this nonsense? As long as I keep writing these unsendable letters, it can only mean that I'm still fighting against Kofi, that I haven't finally decided. ... And I have decided. It's just that I *cannot* stop thinking about her. I might have stopped – I thought I was stopping, two weeks ago before the crisis began it was getting easier not to think about her, to still the argument going on with Kofi. But now I find she fits in

275

uncannily with what's going on out there: the trucks rumbling past half the night, going south; Zev, forty-three, carrying his shadow of unexpiated past guilts, off somewhere in the hills dishing out ammunition; the radios far and near blaring and murmuring away in unison every hour on the hour, '*Hinneh ha hadashot* ...' And now I have begun to want to hear these newscasts, to be curious, to be involved. God damn it, I've begun to care, not to want to die. And if I don't want to die, it must mean I want to live; and *that* might mean that I still have something left to offer Hanna.

Is something – my poor, failed something, thrice tried and found wanting – better than what she has now?

Chapter 9

I am very quiet inside. The turmoil and muddle and inner quarrelling have completely subsided. It feels like the morning after a long storm at sea, such mornings as I woke to here sometimes in the spring, when I opened my shutters and looked out on the square and the ocean and the city all calm and sparkling; now, as then, I am breathing in deep, slow, even breaths, and there is a clear view all round.

Suzy came to the door at about nine o'clock this morning and said rather sedately through the jamb, 'I don't know if you are interested or even still alive, but you had better know that the war has begun.' I had the door open before she could turn to go away. She stepped back, astonished . . . and her face registered the change in mine, after so long, before she could control it. 'Ah!' she said a moment later, when she'd recovered from her surprise. 'So you are still with us? Good. So do you now care to hear the news?'

I cared. I cared very much. My exile was ended, and I felt glad, as the dead would be glad, had they had to live on in their stiff chilled corpses, to feel warm blood begin to pump miraculously through the limbs again. It would hurt, no doubt – a sort of monstrously extended pins and needles, through all their flesh and spirit – but health is the natural condition of all of us who are even remotely normal, and so is happiness; we have to be dragged away from it, and, given the slightest opportunity, we snap back towards it again as soon as possible. I've held myself away from life and wholeness because I thought I ought to want to die, but I don't, and if that's a kind of treason to the children then I must bear it along with the other guilts – that's all.

We listened to Dayan's speech while Suzy arranged the

blackout in my rooms and Ziva and I pasted blast-strips in Union Jack patterns over the windows. I was crazy about the bit about not wanting any British or American boys to die for Israel. What marvellous stroke of one-upmanship! I always sort of thought that the dear old Sixth Fleet would fire a broadside or two in our support if the worst ever came to the worst, but now they're obviously not going to and I don't care. Let the French abandon us and the British keep their skirts and noses clean; we'll do our own dying. The three of us looked at one another at the end of the speech; we felt lonely and scared and fine. Even Ziva had got her colour back, and she stared at us with wild, excited eyes. 'Our soldiers will defend us,' she said in her funny, quaint little voice. By Christ, I hope she's right . . . all that's certain right now is that the poor kids are getting killed by the score at this very moment. Ziva and Suzy are sitting in a stuffy shelter and I'm sitting here writing in the stillness that lies in wait for the all-clear like a held breath, and at the same time, such a very short way away, lives are going out like lights in the midst of noise and fire and smoke like the old vision of hell. If Jake had lived. . . . Well, he wouldn't have been nearly old enough. And we wouldn't have been here. I would have been in the house in Montreal with Alec; I would never have felt a quarter of the things I've felt; I would be a totally different person. Better, I suppose, but somehow smaller. . . . I'm scared, sitting here alone, but it's a healthy sort of fear. The desire for annihilation has deserted me just when it might have been damned appropriate! There go more planes . . . ours, I presume. Ours. . . . Funny, it's a word, or at least a concept, I never used about Canada. So now I'm a member of a country again. . . . Very good, provided there remains a country to belong to. . . . One needs a country to be loyal to, or at least I do, as some people need a religion.

Strange about one's death-thoughts. I still have them now, but the kind of death I might die in these circumstances seems so extraordinarily meaningful suddenly that I'm ashamed to think of the wasteful wanton squalid self-indulgent way I was regarding death a week ago. To die in a war which is about something one believes in, appears to me now almost as reasonable and pointed as continuing to live. But I don't think I will die, somehow. I don't think any of us will. 'Our soldiers will protect us . . .'

But who will protect Hanna?

I have tried everything to put my heart at rest about her. Everything except going to see her to explain. Why haven't I done that? Obviously because I know quite well that as soon as I see her I shall not find a word to say. She will not have to plead, or throw me one imploring glance from those grape-green eyes. I shall simply pick her up and carry her home.

I have sat here for a long time, smoking and thinking. The light has gone, and so has the all-clear. One can still hear faint sounds in the far distance which could be firing or explosions, or it could be just the throbbing in my head. Hanna's hope is still awake. Peretz never really believed in me, but Hanna did, and still does. Her hope will renew itself every morning; every night she will make new excuses for me and go to sleep expecting me to come next day. And that will go on for a long time, unless, in the next unforeseeable days or weeks or months, she dies with that hope unfulfilled.

It's dawn. The second day of our war, and the last day of my private one, has begun. All the doubts and fears went away in the night. I have lived through many hours of frightful awareness of young men getting killed, of sharing in advance the hells of grief awaiting a lot of women who are now sleeping, who can keep their hope a little longer until the telegrams begin to come. I've lived through a night of vivid imaginings of all the horrors that could happen to us here, too – to the whole Jews and the half-and-halfs alike. And then, just now, putting out the last cigarette from the last packet with a hand that shook from the pressure of my thoughts, it was as if my imagination suddenly said: 'Right, that's all. Now I'm going off-duty. Wake me when it's over.' And my fear has left me – all my fears.

Okay, Kofi. You and the war have won. I'll make up the little bed with clean sheets and wash the floor and open the windows wide to let the fresh air in; I'll throw away the empties and the stubs; I'll make myself look as pretty as possible, and then I'll go out into the ominously peaceful morning sunlight and get a taxi and go and fetch her. I can't see a yard ahead in time, I have no confidence in myself and the desert is a charnel-house this morning. I have no right at all to be so happy and to feel that everything is beginning.

FOR THE BEST IN PAPERBACKS, LOOK FOR THE

In every corner of the world, on every subject under the sun, Penguin represents quality and variety – the very best in publishing today.

For complete information about books available from Penguin – including Pelicans, Puffins, Peregrines and Penguin Classics – and how to order them, write to us at the appropriate address below. Please note that for copyright reasons the selection of books varies from country to country.

In the United Kingdom: Please write to *Dept E.P., Penguin Books Ltd, Harmondsworth, Middlesex, UB7 0DA*

If you have any difficulty in obtaining a title, please send your order with the correct money, plus ten per cent for postage and packaging, to *PO Box No 11, West Drayton, Middlesex*

In the United States: Please write to *Dept BA, Penguin, 299 Murray Hill Parkway, East Rutherford, New Jersey 07073*

In Canada: Please write to *Penguin Books Canada Ltd, 2801 John Street, Markham, Ontario L3R 1B4*

In Australia: Please write to the *Marketing Department, Penguin Books Australia Ltd, P.O. Box 257, Ringwood, Victoria 3134*

In New Zealand: Please write to the *Marketing Department, Penguin Books (NZ) Ltd, Private Bag, Takapuna, Auckland 9*

In India: Please write to *Penguin Overseas Ltd, 706 Eros Apartments, 56 Nehru Place, New Delhi, 110019*

In Holland: Please write to *Penguin Books Nederland B.V., Postbus 195, NL–1380 AD Weesp, Netherlands*

In Germany: Please write to *Penguin Books Ltd, Friedrichstrasse 10–12, D–6000 Frankfurt Main 1, Federal Republic of Germany*

In Spain: Please write to *Longman Penguin España, Calle San Nicolas 15, E–28013 Madrid, Spain*

In France: Please write to *Penguin Books Ltd, 39 Rue de Montmorency, F-75003, Paris, France*

In Japan: Please write to *Longman Penguin Japan Co Ltd, Yamaguchi Building, 2–12–9 Kanda Jimbocho, Chiyoda-Ku, Tokyo 101, Japan*

FOR THE BEST IN PAPERBACKS, LOOK FOR THE

A CHOICE OF PENGUIN FICTION

Maia Richard Adams

The heroic romance of love and war in an ancient empire from one of our greatest storytellers. 'Enormous and powerful' – *Financial Times*

The Warning Bell Lynne Reid Banks

A wonderfully involving, truthful novel about the choices a woman must make in her life – and the price she must pay for ignoring the counsel of her own heart. 'Lynne Reid Banks knows how to get to her reader: this novel grips like Super Glue' – *Observer*

Doctor Slaughter Paul Theroux

Provocative and menacing – a brilliant dissection of lust, ambition and betrayal in 'civilized' London. 'Witty, chilly, exuberant, graphic' – *The Times Literary Supplement*

Wise Virgin A. N. Wilson

Giles Fox's work on the Pottle manuscript, a little-known thirteenth-century tract on virginity, leads him to some innovative research on the subject that takes even his breath away. 'A most elegant and chilling comedy' – *Observer* Books of the Year

Gone to Soldiers Marge Piercy

Until now, the passions, brutality and devastation of the Second World War have only been written about by men. Here for the first time, one of America's major writers brings a woman's depth and intensity to the panorama of world war. 'A victory' – *Newsweek*

Trade Wind M. M. Kaye

An enthralling blend of history, adventure and romance from the author of the bestselling *The Far Pavilions*

A CHOICE OF PENGUIN FICTION

The Power and the Glory   Graham Greene

During an anti-clerical purge in one of the southern states of Mexico, the last priest is hunted like a hare. Too humble for martyrdom, too human for heroism, he is nevertheless impelled towards his squalid Calvary. 'There is no better story-teller in English today' – V. S. Pritchett

The Enigma of Arrival   V. S. Naipaul

'For sheer abundance of talent, there can hardly be a writer alive who surpasses V. S. Naipaul. Whatever we may want in a novelist is to be found in his books . . .' – Irving Howe in *The New York Times Book Review*. 'Naipaul is always brilliant' – Anthony Burgess in the *Observer*

Earthly Powers   Anthony Burgess

Anthony Burgess's magnificent masterpiece, an enthralling, epic narrative spanning six decades and spotlighting some of the most vivid events and characters of our times. 'Enormous imagination and vitality . . . a huge book in every way' – Bernard Levin in the *Sunday Times*

The Penitent   Isaac Bashevis Singer

From the Nobel Prize-winning author comes a powerful story of a man who has material wealth but feels spiritually impoverished. 'Singer . . . restates with dignity the spiritual aspirations and the cultural complexities of a lifetime, and it must be said that in doing so he gives the Evil One no quarter and precious little advantage' – Anita Brookner in the *Sunday Times*

Paradise Postponed   John Mortimer

'Hats off to John Mortimer. He's done it again' – *Spectator*. A rumbustious, hilarious novel from the creator of Rumpole, *Paradise Postponed* examines British life since the war to discover why Paradise has always been postponed.

The Balkan Trilogy and Levant Trilogy   Olivia Manning

'The finest fictional record of the war produced by a British writer. Her gallery of personages is huge, her scene painting superb, her pathos controlled, her humour quiet and civilized' – *Sunday Times*

FOR THE BEST IN PAPERBACKS, LOOK FOR THE

A CHOICE OF PENGUIN FICTION

Maia Richard Adams

The heroic romance of love and war in an ancient empire from one of our greatest storytellers. 'Enormous and powerful' – *Financial Times*

The Warning Bell Lynne Reid Banks

A wonderfully involving, truthful novel about the choices a woman must make in her life – and the price she must pay for ignoring the counsel of her own heart. 'Lynne Reid Banks knows how to get to her reader: this novel grips like Super Glue' – *Observer*

Doctor Slaughter Paul Theroux

Provocative and menacing – a brilliant dissection of lust, ambition and betrayal in 'civilized' London. 'Witty, chilly, exuberant, graphic' – *The Times Literary Supplement*. Now filmed as *Half Moon Street*.

Wise Virgin A. N. Wilson

Giles Fox's work on the Pottle manuscript, a little-known thirteenth-century tract on virginity, leads him to some innovative research on the subject that takes even his breath away. 'A most elegant and chilling comedy' – *Observer* Books of the Year

Last Resorts Clare Boylan

Harriet loved Joe Fisher for his ordinariness – for his ordinary suits and hats, his ordinary money and his ordinary mind, even for his ordinary wife. 'An unmitigated delight' – *Time Out*

Trade Wind M. M. Kaye

An enthralling blend of history, adventure and romance from the author of the bestselling *The Far Pavilions*

FOR THE BEST IN PAPERBACKS, LOOK FOR THE

A CHOICE OF PENGUIN FICTION

Stanley and the Women Kingsley Amis

Just when Stanley Duke thinks it safe to sink into middle age, his son goes insane – and Stanley finds himself beset on all sides by women, each of whom seems to have an intimate acquaintance with madness. 'Very good, very powerful . . . beautifully written' – Anthony Burgess in the *Observer*

The Girls of Slender Means Muriel Spark

A world and a war are winding up with a bang, and in what is left of London all the nice people are poor – and about to discover how different the new world will be. 'Britain's finest post-war novelist' – *The Times*

Him with His Foot in His Mouth Saul Bellow

A collection of first-class short stories. 'If there is a better living writer of fiction, I'd very much like to know who he or she is' – *The Times*

Mother's Helper Maureen Freely

A superbly biting and breathtakingly fluent attack on certain libertarian views, blending laughter, delight, rage and amazement, this is a novel you won't forget. 'A winner' – *The Times Literary Supplement*

Decline and Fall Evelyn Waugh

A comic yet curiously touching account of an innocent plunged into the sham, brittle world of high society. Evelyn Waugh's first novel brought him immediate public acclaim and is still a classic of its kind.

Stars and Bars William Boyd

Well-dressed, quite handsome, unfailingly polite and charming, who would guess that Henderson Dores, the innocent Englishman abroad in wicked America, has a guilty secret? 'Without doubt his best book so far . . . made me laugh out loud' – *The Times*

FOR THE BEST IN PAPERBACKS, LOOK FOR THE

A CHOICE OF PENGUIN FICTION

The Ghost Writer Philip Roth

Philip Roth's celebrated novel about a young writer who meets and falls in love with Anne Frank in New England – or so he thinks. 'Brilliant, witty and extremely elegant' – *Guardian*

Small World David Lodge

Shortlisted for the 1984 Booker Prize, *Small World* brings back Philip Swallow and Maurice Zapp for a jet-propelled journey into hilarity. 'The most brilliant and also the funniest novel that he has written' – *London Review of Books*

Treasures of Time Penelope Lively

Beautifully written, acutely observed, and filled with Penelope Lively's sharp but compassionate wit, *Treasures of Time* explores the relationship between the lives we live and the lives we think we live.

Absolute Beginners Colin MacInnes

The first 'teenage' novel, the classic of youth and disenchantment, *Absolute Beginners* is part of MacInnes's famous London trilogy – and now a brilliant film. 'MacInnes caught it first – and best' – *Harpers and Queen*

July's People Nadine Gordimer

Set in South Africa, this novel gives us an unforgettable look at the terrifying, tacit understanding and misunderstandings between blacks and whites. 'This is the best novel that Miss Gordimer has ever written' – Alan Paton in the *Saturday Review*

The Ice Age Margaret Drabble

'A continuously readable, continuously surprising book . . . here is a novelist who is not only popular and successful but formidably growing towards real stature' – *Observer*

'How lucky we are to have Lynne Reid Banks!' – *Daily Telegraph*

Casualties

A brilliant look at the cold war of modern marriage and at a world still claiming its victims. 'The plot grips; the prose is fast-moving and elegant; above all, the characters are wincingly winningly human' – *Daily Telegraph*

The L-Shaped Room

Unmarried and pregnant, Jane Graham is cast out of her suburban home. Lighting dejectedly on a bug-ridden room in a squalid house in Fulham, she gradually comes to find a new and positive faith in life.

The Backward Shadow

After the birth of her son, Jane exchanges the L-shaped room for a remote country cottage. She is joined by Dottie, and together they embark upon an enterprise that is to change both their lives.

Two is Lonely

Now living with her son in the country, Jane is a long way from the L-shaped room . . . 'A tender and delightful final volume . . . Lynne Reid Banks has that rare gift of evoking a scene or a situation in little more than a line' – *The Times*

An End to Running

Seeking refuge from the domination of his sister and from his own Jewishness, Aaron Franks turns to Martha, his secretary. Together they travel to Israel and a kibbutz – Martha with strong misgivings, Aaron full of anticipation.

Defy the Wilderness

After fourteen years of self-imposed absence, writer Ann Randall returns to her beloved Israel. In Jerusalem, she attempts to interview veterans of the first Arab-Israeli war. 'A powerful and professional novel' – *The Times Literary Supplement*